Set All Afire

Set All Afire

A Novel about
Saint Francis Xavier

by
Louis de Wohl

IGNATIUS PRESS   SAN FRANCISCO

First edition published by
J. B. Lippincott Company
Philadelphia and New York

Biblical quotations from the translation by Ronald Knox
© Sheed & Ward, Inc., New York, 1944 and 1950

Cover design by Roxanne Mei Lum
Cover art by Christopher J. Pelicano

ISBN 978-0-89870-351-1
Library of Congress catalogue number 90-85368
Printed in the United States of America

Book One

No ONE EVER disputed that the Street-of-the-dogs in Paris was well named. The students of Montaigu College said it was called after the students of the College of Sainte Barbe. The students of Sainte Barbe said the same thing about those of Montaigu. The worthy citizens of Paris said it was called after the students of both colleges. Real dogs were few. It was the one street on which they could not find much worth eating. When they found anything, it was sure to be something the students of Sainte Barbe had thrown away. Those of Montaigu did not throw away anything—they ate it themselves. Montaigu was one of the poorest, Sainte Barbe—relatively speaking—one of the richest and most progressive of the colleges.

On dry, sunny days the Street-of-the-dogs was dirty.

On rainy days it was almost impassable.

The dark-haired young man at the window of a small room in Sainte Barbe chuckled. "Eh, Pierre," he said, "ever seen a donkey going to college?"

Pierre Favre, twenty-two, with the face of dreamer, went on writing, but he smiled. He did not know that his smile won over everyone who saw it. "If it weren't against charity, I'd say I've seen many", he answered.

"Ass", said the young man at the window. "I mean a real donkey. Four feet. Tail. Come and have a look."

Obediently, Favre rose, quill in hand, and joined his friend at the window.

"There's a beggar with the donkey", he said.

"What a fool he must be, to try and get anything there, of all places."

"Oh, I don't know", mused Favre. "His donkey is laden with books. Perhaps he wants to sell them."

"What a chance! Poor old man."

"Do you know, Francis," said Favre, "I found out that we always call a man old when he is about sixteen years older than we are ourselves. That man is in his mid-thirties."

"I don't believe it. He's getting bald, isn't he? I wish he'd turn round so that I can see his face. Ah, he's finished talking to the doorkeeper. No sale."

"He's limping."

Francis turned away from the window. "Shame", he said angrily.

"Well, yes, they might have given the poor man something. . . . "

"It isn't that, Pierre. The man's a Basque."

"Well?"

"The face and hands of a man of good family. He has no business being a beggar. Absurd. Wish I knew his name. I'd write a letter to his relatives."

"Would you now?" Little Pierre Favre beamed. "You'd probably never finish it. I don't think you've written one in the two years that we've been sharing the same room."

"You're quite wrong. I write every time I need money, three times a year."

"But your famous letter to the King is still on your desk, I believe—and you started that months ago."

"You're better with the quill than I am, my good Pierre. And it's a very difficult letter. By the Virgin, Pierre, you have no idea how difficult! My family wants me to become a canon in Pamplona. But the chapter will never elect me, unless I present my patent of nobility."

"Well, you are a nobleman, aren't you?"

"I am but anybody calls himself a nobleman these days. . . . "

"I don't." Pierre smiled. "The only thing I ever lorded it over was a flock of sheep in Savoy. It's a good thing, looking after sheep, Francis. Gentle creatures. And it gives you time to think. I used to weep, longing for an education,

6

then. Now that I am getting it, I feel I should never have left my sheep."

"You'll be a good priest, one of these days", said Francis. "And you'll have a lot of two-legged sheep then. Not so sure that you'll find them so gentle, though. I also have had some experience with sheep, you know. Helped my father and brothers round up a flock of the brutes when their owners tried to smuggle them across our estate without paying toll."

"But I thought it was the privilege of the King . . . "

"That's just it, don't you see? Exactly fifty years ago my father was granted by royal patent, for himself and his heirs, the civil jurisdiction of Ydocin in the valley of Ybargoiti, with all the homicides, demi-homicides, sixantenas, calonyas and civil rights—together with the right to create mayors, judges, bailiffs and other officials."

"Phew", said Pierre, overawed. "What on earth is a demi-homicide and a calonya?"

"They're fines", Francis said nonchalantly. "Paid by the families of murderers, libelers and the like. Anyway—I chased sheep, and you looked after sheep."

"But if your father had such a patent, what are you worried about?"

"Oh that—that's nothing. The chapter of Pamplona wouldn't accept a man just for having that kind of thing. You've got to be a hidalgo, Pierre, a man with four noble grandparents. So I am, too. But it has to be confirmed by His Majesty."

"It's simpler to be a simple man", said Pierre Favre. "But if this is so important to you, why don't you finish the letter?"

"I told you, it isn't so easy. Besides—quite between you and me, I don't know whether I want to be a member of the chapter. There are other plans—life may be more enjoyable elsewhere. I don't know yet. There is lots of time. . . . "

"For playing handball." Pierre Favre smiled again.

"There's nothing wrong with that", was the quick answer. "And I'm good at it. I'll win the university match this year,

7

just as I won the last. I'll get down to old Picaro's speeches in time for the examination, never fear."

"Picaro's speeches?"

"Yes, yes—the speech against Catalina and against Averroës. . . ."

Pierre Favre shook with laughter. "You mean Cicero", he spluttered. "And it's Catilina, not Catalina. And Verres, not Averroës."

"All right, all right, you know I can never remember names."

"You do remember the most difficult ones of the lot. Ydocin and what was it? Ybargoiti and . . . "

"That's different. Those are Basque names. Real names. I don't really care whether Picaro wrote a speech against Averroës or against Verres. Now, if you'll forgive me, I must run. There's a contest on the meadow of Pré-aux-clercs. . . . "

"Handball again?"

"No, wrestling and fencing. These Frenchmen think they know all about it and I must go and take them down a peg or two. Miguel! Where is that fellow?"

"You called, master?" The valet had the deep-set eyes and high cheekbones of the Basque mountains.

"My horse, Miguel. We're off for the afternoon."

*   *   *

The limping man with his book-laden donkey was a beggar. But he had not tried to beg from the doorkeeper of Montaigu College. He asked for his name to be inscribed on the college roll as a student and the doorkeeper thought for a while that he was a little touched in the head. A student, aged thirty-seven and looking a good five or six years older, too. Not enough money to pay for board either. He told him the address of the poorhouse, where he could live for nothing and the strange man expressed his gratitude with the grave courtesy of a grandee. Only when the doorkeeper told him that the rule of the poorhouse forbade leave before dawn and after dusk, the pale face of the stranger showed

8

bitter disappointment, as that meant the loss of two lectures a day.

But nothing could be done about that.

Pursing his lips, the doorkeeper read the name the beggar had written down. Iñigo de Loyola. A Spaniard. Nothing good ever came from Spain.

*　　*　　*

The family council in the castle of Xavier was as grim as its stone walls. Even birds would not stay at the castle which was bereft of all green and almost prehistoric in its primitiveness.

Since the death of her husband, thirteen years before, and the misguided Navarrese insurrection, seven years ago, in which her older sons had taken part and had had to pay heavily for it, Doña María d'Azpilcueta had waned, not to a shadow exactly, but to a thin, bony, austere lady, forbidding and funereal in appearance.

Spanish vengeance had shorn the castle of Xavier of its towers and outer walls. The drawbridge was dismantled, the moat filled up. Only the living quarters were left to the mother of two rebel sons. And very little money.

"A valet", said Doña María grimly. "A horse."

"After all, Mother," murmured Juan Xavier, "it is not easy to live anything like the life of a nobleman without those two commodities."

"If you wish to pay for your youngest brother's extravagances, you're very welcome to it", snapped Doña María.

"That man Miguel Landivar is a student himself, I believe", said Miguel Xavier. "Is it possible that nobles and their valets are sitting on the same bench in those new-fangled colleges?"

"Everything is possible in France", said Juan Xavier bitterly. The King of France had deserted the cause of Navarra when things went wrong.

"A valet and a horse", said Doña María. "What next? It was a mistake to send the boy to Paris. He will never pass the examinations. I shall have him recalled. He is twenty-two. He hasn't got your looks, Juan, but he's still handsome

9

enough to find a respectable girl with enough dowry to satisfy his needs—I hope. It is ridiculous that you're still unmarried, Juan."

"Girls", said Juan, "are out for money nowadays, Mother. And we are not exactly in favor with the King."

An old servant entered and whispered to Doña María. He was as lean and bony as his mistress, and so excited that his lips were trembling.

"Pull yourself together, Mateo", said Doña María sharply. "*Who* is it?"

The old man whispered again.

"What?" exclaimed Doña María, her eyes wide with astonishment. But she regained her composure quickly. "Show Her Reverence in at once, you fool." The old man slunk out and she turned to her sons: "Her Reverence the Abbess has come to see me."

Dumbfounded, the two young men rose to their feet.

The lady in question was their sister—Doña María's eldest daughter—but six years ago she had entered the Convent of the Poor Clares at Gandía and was now its Abbess.

At that time there was nothing unusual about the visit of the Abbess of an enclosed Order to the house of her parents. But Magdalena was different. Since the day on which she took her solemn vows she had never again been seen in the world and when her relatives came to visit her, they had to talk to her through the iron grille which protected the enclosure.

Doña María, too, rose, when the tall, thin nun entered, and she bowed to one who was no longer her daughter, but a chosen servant of God, as did her sons.

The Abbess returned the bow. The "kiss of courtesy" was omitted. There could be no intimacy, not even the symbol of it.

"Will Your Reverence take my chair?" asked Doña María.

The Abbess declined politely, but accepted another, lower, chair opposite. She sat on the edge of the seat and Juan Xavier, a shrewd observer, saw that all her weight was still on her feet and calves. She would remain in the same posture, if somebody drew the chair from under her. She had accepted a seat out of courtesy, but she did not wish to relax. She looks like a ghost, he thought uneasily.

His mother saw the deep furrows at the corners of Magdalena's mouth, the purple rings around her eyes, speaking of fasts and vigils. She is overdoing it, she thought. She won't live long. Stirred to the heart, she wanted to tell her so, to warn her, to beg her to look after herself. But she knew this would be overstepping the mark. "We are most grateful for Your Reverence's visit", she murmured.

"It is because of Francis", said the Abbess.

"Francis?" Doña María gasped. "We were just speaking of him!"

The nun nodded, smiling. "Of course you were", she said. "I was troubled about it."

The two brothers exchanged uneasy glances.

"We are troubled about him, too", said Doña María. "He does not seem to take his studies at all seriously. We have heard that he has engaged a valet and bought a horse, that he is wasting his time on all kinds of athletic pursuits—he does not seem to have any clear-cut aim at all."

To her utter surprise, Magdalena smiled again. It was a warm, joyful smile that illumined the thin, waxen face.

"Dear Francis", she said.

"Your Reverence seems to take a very lenient attitude", said her mother dourly.

"There is not much that is bad in Francis", said Magdalena. "And so much that is good that God cannot fail to make use of it to the full."

"It will have to be in Navarra, then", said Doña María. "I am about to recall him."

"Now I know why I have come here", said the nun quietly.

"You said you were troubled about him, too. . . . "

Magdalena shook her head. "Not about him. About you."

"I fail to understand Your Reverence", said Doña María severely.

"I knew in my heart that you were about to put obstacles in his way", said the Abbess gently.

"I cannot possibly afford to pay for the kind of life he wishes to lead", cried Doña María. "God knows I am plagued enough as it is, with difficulties of all kinds."

"He knows it and sees every sacrifice you make, Mother", said the nun cheerfully. "You are not asked to let Francis live a life of luxury. But do not recall him, I beg of you."

"But . . . but . . . the valet! The horse! I can't . . . "

"He will dispense with such things in due course," said Magdalena. "He himself will be a valet of God and a horse of God, and he will do much for God's glory. But for that he must be equipped and therefore he must stay where he is now."

There was deep silence.

"As it is Your Reverence's wish", said Doña María stiffly, "I will not recall him."

"It is God's wish", said the nun. Her smile was radiant. She rose, bowed to her mother, bowed to her brothers and walked out without a further word, swift and light, more like a merry young girl than an abbess.

Doña María dismissed her sons with a curt gesture.

They obeyed silently. Outside, Miguel made a beeline for the cellar door. "I need some wine", he said gruffly.

"And so do I", cried Juan. "And a hunk of meat. Wait for me, I'm coming with you. I feel quite weak."

* * *

As usual, Pierre Favre awoke at the harsh clanging of the college bell at four o'clock in the morning, and as usual Don Francis Xavier did not.

Pierre was glad that the night was over, at least for him. Outside it was still pitch black and he could hear the rain drumming at the window.

His nights had been uneasy lately, and he knew why and yet did not wish to admit it to himself. He was troubled and the reason and source of his troubles was sleeping on the palliasse opposite, breathing heavily from somewhat puffed-up lips. Francis had been out again. That meant his valet Miguel Landivar had been able to borrow some money somewhere. The fellow was a past master in the art of borrowing money for his master, and somehow it always served for *that* kind of purpose. It was strange such a strong character, a man to whom rank and nobility meant so much, could allow his valet to influence him. But perhaps it was not so much Landivar's influence, but Professor García's. It was an open secret that García took some of his students with him on his nightly carousals. The doorkeeper, his palm well greased, kept quiet, but the students themselves boasted about their adventures.

Was that kind of life really so enjoyable? And if so — was he not a fool, not to share it?

At the age of twelve little Pierre Favre had taken the vow of perpetual chastity, all by himself, in a tiny mountain chapel. Was it really necessary to keep it, that vow of a child who knew nothing of the world?

Nothing of the world — but much of God — more, perhaps, than he knew now, after all his studies.

He lit a candle. "Francis — wake up."

Francis sat up with a jerk. "Take her away", he said angrily. "I don't want to see her again."

"What are you talking about? The bell has gone. . . . "

"The bell?" Francis yawned. "Another day, eh? The last one is still marching up and down my poor head." He jumped to his feet and stretched himself. "You're lucky, Pierre — you had some sleep. García has shown us a new haunt. They're all the same, really. I think I shall give it up. Today is Tuesday, isn't it? The high jump match on the Île-aux-vaches — and me with barely two hours' sleep. Damn that fellow García. You'll see, I'll lose the match."

He began to wash, water splashing right and left.

"Did you — did you have good company?" asked Pierre. And he thought: Why must I ask him that — why do I want to hear the story he has to tell? Because it gives me some kind of horrible joy to hear him mention things I must not think of. The very question is the first step. . . .

"García may call it good company", said Francis brusquely. "He has nothing to lose."

"What do you mean?" (Why go on asking? Why?)

"He's wearing overlong sleeves lately, haven't you observed that? I've seen what he's hiding. He's got the French pox, Pierre. It's damned ugly. And I saw a fresh ulcer on one of the women." He shook himself violently. "Just as well I . . . I drank too much from sheer disgust. Pierre, if I don't win that match today, I'll never go out with García again."

"I hope you lose", said Pierre fervently.

Francis stopped rubbing himself with his towel, stared and laughed. "We can't all be little saints like you, Pierre."

"Saints . . . " said Pierre Favre. To Francis' utter dismay he began to cry.

* * *

It was a bad day right through. Francis won the high jump contest, but only because his best competitor, a long-legged Englishman, did not turn up. His own jumping was far below his best form. And when he came back for the afternoon lectures, Pierre whispered to him, "They've put two more fellows into our room."

"Two! It was just right for the two of us—four is too many. Are we supposed to sleep on top of each other? What madness is this?"

But just then the teacher marched in and they fell silent.

As soon as the lecture was over, Francis tackled his friend again. "Who is it anyway?" he asked. "Anybody we know? Spaniards?"

"Spaniards, yes."

"A very small ray of sunshine. But who?"

"One is Juan de Peña. . . . "

"It could have been worse. Decent family. And the other?"

Pierre blinked. "I'm told . . . it's the one who came over from Montaigu."

"I don't know about anybody coming over from Montaigu. Who is it? Don't you know his name?"

"No. But I've seen him. And so have you—a few months ago, no, I think it must be a year now. Do you remember the beggar with his donkey?"

"You don't mean it's that one! What is Sainte Barbe coming to? That tattered old scarecrow? Santísima madre, this is too much. I refuse to have him in my room."

"You know very well that you can't do that", said Pierre Favre. "And he's quite a nice little man, really."

*   *   *

The nice little man was introduced to Francis Xavier in the evening of the same day by none less than Diego de Gouvea himself, the Principal of the college.

"Iñigo de Loyola", said Gouvea, "is a fellow countryman of yours. He needs some coaching—particularly about the philosophy of Aristotle. I trust you can render him that service easily in your spare time." He walked out, before Francis could answer. It was just as well.

Francis looked at the pale, balding little man with ill-concealed disdain.

"I am sorry to cause you this trouble, Don Francisco", said Iñigo de Loyola gently. "I shall try hard to please you."

But Francis was too angry to be receptive to the older man's grave courtesy. "The Principal has made a poor choice", he said. "I'm the world's worst teacher. He should have given you into the care of a good scholar, like Pierre Favre here. I'm sure he'll do much better than I. You'll try, Pierre, won't you? Now, if you will excuse me . . . " He walked out, chuckling.

"You must not mind him, Don Iñigo", said Pierre Favre goodnaturedly. "He is a little abrupt sometimes, but he has a good heart. If you will permit me, I think I shall be able to comply with your wishes."

"You are most kind", said the older man humbly. "I am entirely at your disposal."

Later, when Francis found Pierre alone, he apologized in his own way. "Sorry, Pierre, but I just couldn't face it—and

15

you did say he was quite a nice, little man. So I thought better you than I. Me—I don't like him. There's something unhealthy about him."

"He's absolutely voracious for knowledge", said Pierre. "Did you see his eyes?"

"What's the matter with his eyes?"

"They are beautiful. He is very humble and very gentle. Considering that he could almost be my father—or yours. . . . "

"Thanks", said Francis aghast. Resentfully he added: "He ought to be very grateful to me. I've got him a new donkey."

*   *   *

"Is Don Iñigo in?" asked the student Bobadilla.

"Yes", said Francis. "He came back an hour ago."

"Oh, excellent. What a wonderful day it is!"

"Why?" asked Francis. But the student Bobadilla did not hear it; he was mounting the stairs, three at a time.

Miguel Landivar came along, with his elegant, feline gait. "Master . . . "

"What is it?"

"Professor García says he is going out again tonight."

"Nothing to do with me", said Francis sullenly.

"I'm sorry I couldn't get the money this time", said Landivar. "But the Professor says it doesn't matter and he regards himself as the host."

"Is Don Iñigo de Loyola in?" asked the student Salmerón eagerly.

"Yes", said Francis. The student Salmerón smiled broadly and went up the stairs.

"I don't want to go out with García", said Francis wearily. "I need my sleep."

"But, master, Professor García says . . . "

"Yes, Don Iñigo is in", said Francis, before the student Laynez could open his mouth.

Laynez grinned cheerfully. "At long last I have found out what *you* have been studying, Don Francis. Thought-reading is a great art. Good morning."

16

"That man is a Jew", said Landivar disdainfully.

"I think he has some Jewish blood", Francis nodded. "And he's the most intelligent of the crowd. I can't understand, why . . . "

"Professor García says . . . "

"Will you stop harping on García? I told you I don't want to go and that's final. How am I to pass that damned examination, if I go on like this? I've got to do some work."

"Professor García says there is no doubt about my master passing his examination. There is talk about a professorship at the college of Dormans-Beauvais. . . . "

Francis looked up. "You're invaluable for that sort of information, Miguel", he said. "Your ears should be as large as those of an elephant. Still, a little work can do no harm."

"Like poor Señor Favre", said Landivar, showing his very white teeth. "Always work, work, work. He is a glutton for work, that one, like all the disciples of the holy beggar."

Francis frowned. "Disciples! You're very near blasphemy, you old scoundrel."

"God forbid", said Landivar, still grinning, "that it should be blasphemy to speak the simple truth. They all sit around the holy beggar, sucking in every word he says. They go to confession and communion twice a month with him. . . . "

"It isn't healthy, that sort of thing", said Francis, shaking his head.

"It is a little suspicious, if my master asks me", ventured Landivar.

"You mean they want to show off?"

"I mean that my large ears have heard certain tales about the holy beggar. He's been in trouble with the Inquisition."

"Good Lord! You mean . . . "

"Twice — some say three times. He's been in jail for heresy, in Salamanca."

"What? They condemned him to jail? He was guilty, then?"

Landivar shrugged his shoulders. "I'm no theologian — I wouldn't know", he said. There was a note of embarrassment in his voice that did not escape Francis.

"Come on, Miguel—was he guilty or was he not?"

"If he'd been really guilty, I mean, gravely guilty, maybe he wouldn't be here", admitted Miguel. "But his teaching was suspect enough."

"Anything is possible with that impossible man", Francis grunted.

"There is more", muttered Landivar. "He is hiding something in his knapsack—a book he has written."

Francis burst into laughter. "A book—he!—why, his Latin is ludicrous. It's getting better now, I'll admit, but you should have heard him when he arrived. Even Pierre Favre shook his head over it. And he goes and writes a book."

"And he shows it to no one", said Landivar.

"What do you think it is, then?" Francis' curiosity was roused. "A treatise about magic?"

"I don't know", said Landivar ominously.

"Pierre Favre wouldn't fall in with that sort of thing", said Francis, frowning. "Nonsense, Miguel. The man's a crank, a quack, anything you like, but that's all. Why, he talks religion all the time, as if he got paid for it."

"Those", said Landivar darkly, "are the worst."

*　　*　　*

"It's a pretty serious matter", said Professor García, tugging nervously at his long sleeves. "I felt it to be my duty to give you all the information I possess."

Don Diego de Gouvea played with his gilded quill. "Loyola *is* a strange man", he admitted. "I can't make him out at all. Why? Why does he gather those young idiots around himself? Why these pious formalities, these endless debates—as if they had no opportunity for debates in class. What is he up to?"

"Exactly", said García. "And if I may go a little further: why does he demand that they submit to all kinds of ascetic exercises, to dress without ornament, practically like beggars, most unfitting for their status in life and for the role and rank we are trying to equip them for? Our students are not beggar monks. We have boys from the best families here and ours is the responsibility for their upbringing. All this talk about imitating Christ—I heard the student Laynez say so in so many words—are we going to look on whilst this elderly good-for-nothing tries to model our students after his own misguided example?"

Don Diego de Gouvea frowned heavily. "Thank you for informing me about all this", he said. "I will think it over. After all, his circle is small. Laynez, Nicholas Bobadilla, Salmerón, Favre and that young Rodríguez, I believe."

"That's right", García nodded. "And I take it as a good sign for the healthy spirit of our students that two of his own roommates are keeping off him, as if he were the devil in person. Juan de Peña and Francis Xavier."

Don Diego smiled. "Neither of them is likely to have much patience with mendicant ideals", he said. "Let's leave it for the moment. But as soon as there is any definite reason for action, believe me, I shall act."

*　　*　　*

There was definite reason for action the very next day.

There was a tumult in the room occupied by the suspect and an alarm was given. The Rector himself, who was having a nap, had to be waked up. He found the whole corridor buzzing with excitement.

The center of the excitement was Juan de Peña, shouting at the top of his voice that he was not going to share his room with a plague-infested man.

"Silence", commanded Don Diego de Gouvea. "What is all this about, de Peña?"

Juan de Peña was shaking with rage. "That fool Loyola", he spluttered. "He's been out all afternoon, nursing a man who is down with an infectious disease. The physicians think it might be the plague. And then he comes and wants to sleep in the same room with us."

The Rector's eyes narrowed. "Where is he?" he asked.

Everybody stepped back as Iñigo de Loyola appeared and

19

many of them turned away, so as not to inhale the horrible death he was carrying with him.

"He has endangered the entire college with this bit of criminal foolishness", cried Professor García, tugging at the sleeve covering his ulcers. "I implore you, Don Diego, do not tolerate such behavior. This is the finest college of the finest university in the world, and not a stinking hospital."

The accused, pale as death and with bowed head, said nothing, although Don Diego looked up at him as if waiting for his defense.

The Rector drew himself up. "Tomorrow at dinner Iñigo de Loyola will submit to the punishment of the hall", he declared. "Tonight he will sleep alone in the attic. The room he shared with other students will be washed with vinegar. That is all." He withdrew with angry dignity to resume his nap.

Iñigo de Loyola was marched off to the attic. The others dispersed.

"What's that—the punishment of the hall?" inquired Juan de Peña resentfully. "Just a public reprimand, eh?"

"No", said Laynez, his dark eyes smoldering with indignation. "They'll strip him to the waist, tie his hands behind his back and let him run the gauntlet between two rows of teachers and students, armed with sticks and cudgels and whips. That to a man of almost forty—and what a man! And what for? For doing what Christ taught us all to do. Priests and Levites you may be—but not Samaritans." He turned abruptly and walked away.

"I still say he earned every stroke of it", said de Peña sulkily.

"The man has debased himself", said Francis stiffly, "but he's still a gentleman by birth and this is no way to deal with him."

"You don't agree with Don Diego's judgment? I hope that pious sniveling rascal gets exactly what he deserves", said another student, a favorite of García's.

"I don't agree with anything", said Francis hotly. "I don't agree with Don Diego—I don't agree with that hypocrite of a García who points at the poor man with an ulcerous hand—and I don't agree with you, you idiot. If that displeases you, you can have a little fencing match with me on the Île-aux-vaches. Maybe you, too, will need a little Christian nursing after that."

The student withdrew rather hastily.

"Now we shall have to sleep in a room stinking of vinegar", said Francis to no one in particular. "What a nuisance pious people can be."

*　　*　　*

It was the talk of the college. Opinion was split, but on the whole the students were looking forward to the show. The temperamental Bobadilla, defending the culprit hotly, almost got into a fight with some of Professor García's minions. He, Laynez, Salmerón, Rodríguez and Favre tried to go and see the Rector. But Don Diego had expected something of the kind and refused to receive the deputation.

They held council after that and decided to surround Don Iñigo when he entered the hall, and to protect him with their own bodies. Gentle Favre warned that they were going to be attacked by the students in a body if they did that, but Bobadilla shouted, "Fine, then we shall have a free-for-all." Laynez said thoughtfully, "Pity we can't get Don Francis to help us—he's the best athlete of the college, I'm told." They tried. But Francis would have nothing to do with the matter. It disgusted him.

Many of the students—and teachers—appeared at dinner, armed with whips and sticks of all kinds.

Professor García himself supervised the forming of the double row through which the delinquent had to pass. One student was chosen to march before him, very slowly, to prevent him from escaping any of the blows by sheer speed.

Francis looked on in utter disdain.

When the stick of the major-domo announced the entry of the Rector, everybody rose and looked at the door.

A gasp of astonishment went through the large hall.

Don Diego appeared with the delinquent arm in arm.

Iñigo de Loyola, instead of being stripped to the waist, was dressed in his usual black habit.

Slowly and solemnly Don Diego accompanied him to his chair, bade him sit down, bowed to him and walked back to his own chair.

Whips and sticks began to disappear. Professor García looked so crestfallen that some of the students laughed. Apart from the laughter—and it was a mere tittering—no voices could be heard. Then the Rector began to recite the Benedicite. The dinner started.

It was the most silent dinner in the history of the college.

Afterwards, of course, the waves of excitement rose high in the corridors and rooms.

How did he do it? How did he get the Rector round? It was discovered that he had seen Don Diego in the afternoon. But what did he tell him, what could he have told him to make the grim old Principal change his mind so completely? A Sicilian student swore that he had the evil eye. "No one can resist a man with the *mal'occhio*. I should know. There was an old woman in my hometown . . . "

"Old woman yourself. The man's a saint."

"Yes, I heard Garron say that Don Diego's servant said after a quarter of an hour of talk the Rector fell to Don Iñigo's feet and asked for forgiveness."

"Forgiveness for what?"

"I don't know, but he did."

"I don't believe a word of it."

Miguel Landivar gave his master a significant look, when he came to clean his clothes. "What did I say, master?"

Francis frowned. "Well, what did you say? And what do you mean?"

"Magic", said Miguel in a low voice. "Remember what I told you about the book he keeps hidden? That's where he's got it from. He's in league with the devil."

"You're a fool, Miguel", said Francis. "Take the clothes and get out."

Miguel slunk away.

It was strange, all the same. How did he do it? And—perhaps stranger still—he did not seem to regard it as a victory, a triumph at all. He did not look up at dinner—not once—to savor the moment that made him the mysterious hero of the entire college. He just sat there and ate, with his eyes on the plate, pale and indifferent, no, not indifferent—aloof. Was it all self-control? If so, the man must be of iron. There was something about him that one could not fathom. Men like Miguel always thought it must have something to do with the devil. And men like Pierre Favre always thought it must have something to do with God.

Francis decided that he did not care which was which and that in any case it was not his business.

*   *   *

It was not Don Iñigo de Loyola's business to help Don Francis Xavier with his difficult letter to the King, but he did. It happened because Francis swore impatiently that he could not find the correct expression for a particularly difficult passage. Don Iñigo happened to be in the room, turned his head towards him and smiled indulgently. Had he objected to the use of barracks language, Francis would have given him a very sharp answer. But an indulgent smile was unbearable. Francis explained angrily that he could not find the way to express himself and Don Iñigo asked for his permission to read the passage. With a shrug, Francis let him read it, and Don Iñigo suggested a small alteration that put the whole thing right.

"It seems so stupid to ask solemnly for what is mine by right in any case", complained Francis. "But I need the nobility certificate for later on."

Don Iñigo nodded. "There was a time when I thought just as you do, Don Francis."

I'm not going to ask him what made him change, thought Francis grimly. Or else he'll tell me his life story.

"What made me change my mind, is a long story", said Don Iñigo quietly. "But you can find it in two lines—in the 8th chapter of Saint Mark—verse 36."

23

"Thank you for your help anyway, Don Iñigo", said Francis dryly. The older man gave him one of his dignified little bows and walked away.

What was Mark 8:36? Never mind what it was, the letter had to be finished and sent off. Professor at the college of Dormans-Beauvais was good, but canon in the chapter of Pamplona was better. He wrote a few more words and stopped. What was Mark 8:36? Oh well, let's get it over with. He took the book off his shelf and looked it up. Here it was: "What shall it profit a man if he gain the whole world and lose his own soul?"

This was sheer impertinence. What reason had that over-pious nurse of the sick to assume that Don Francis Xavier was losing his soul? Let him guard his own soul.

Dormans-Beauvais was a good Christian college. The chapter of Pamplona had worthy men as canons. Who said that one must be a holy beggar if one did not want to lose one's soul? No wonder the fellow had got himself into trouble with the Inquisition.

Francis was so angry that he finished the famous letter in one spurt and sent it off the same day.

*   *   *

"The Sieur Sarpillier has been here again", said Miguel Landivar sullenly.

"Who is he?"

Miguel sighed. "The horse dealer, master."

"And he wants money again, does he?"

"Yes, master."

Now Francis sighed, too. Twice he had written home for money and no answer had come. "Have we got any money, Miguel?"

"No, master."

"I don't know what this Sarsaparilla wants of me. I paid him some money a year ago and some more six months ago and again a third time—will he never have enough?"

"The Sieur Sarpillier says the horse is not paid for in full yet", reported Miguel. He was used to his master's habit of twisting names around.

"Then tell him I paid for everything but the hind legs—if he insists, he can come and take back what still belongs to him. The hind legs, no more."

"The Sieur Sarpillier", said Miguel, "says he'll come again tomorrow morning, and if he does not get the rest of his money, he will take the horse away in the afternoon—with the help of the authorities, he says."

"I'll box his ears, when he comes", exclaimed Francis, furiously. But he knew that the matter could not be solved so easily. Debts were perfectly admissible at Sainte Barbe—as long as there were no difficulties with the authorities about them.

"Miguel—do you think we can borrow the money somewhere?"

"No, master", said Miguel.

"That man Sarsaparilla is a brute", said Francis. He was so bad-tempered that day that even Pierre Favre could not cope with him. In the afternoon he went to the stable to say goodbye to the horse, a nice five-year-old roan. He loved horses and he had become attached to the roan.

There Don Iñigo found him—in tears. "Forgive me disturbing you, Don Francis. I am told that your horse dealer wants to take the animal away because it is not paid in full. Will you permit me to frustrate his plan?"

"Frustrate his plan?" Francis stared at the shabby little man. "How?"

"What does he demand of you?"

"Eleven ducats."

"The horse is worth fifty," said Don Iñigo, patting the roan's proud neck. "Here, give the man his eleven ducats and he will have to thank you, instead of taking your horse away."

"Has a rich uncle of yours died?" asked Francis, looking with stupefaction at the roll of gold pieces Iñigo had pressed into his hand. Then, a little ashamed of his rudeness, he added lamely: "I didn't know you had so much money."

And he thought, This makes it worse. What is the matter with me?

"I have only what I am given", said Iñigo. "And I don't need it myself."

"But why give it to me?"

"There was a time when a horse gave me much joy, too, Don Francis. We love horses where we come from, you and I."

"I do not belong to your circle of friends", said Francis uneasily. "I—I feel not drawn to it either. If there is anything else I can do for you . . . "

"Please, do not trouble your mind", said Don Iñigo, quite unruffled by the younger man's clumsiness. "Need I tell a man of your rank that no condition can possibly be attached to the service one nobleman renders another?"

Very red in the face Francis bowed.

"But if it is my motive that you question", went on Don Iñigo, "you will find it in the Gospel of Saint Matthew, 25th chapter, verse 40." And he walked away, limping a little and yet with a natural dignity that evoked in Francis a kind of grudging admiration.

But what was he up to? A quotation from Saint Matthew. Another piece of impertinence, more likely than not. Anyway, the roan was safe.

"You're safe, my little beauty", said Francis, caressing the horse. "But I had to pay a great price for you and I don't know whether I like it."

Later, he looked up the quotation. "Believe me, when you did it to one of the least of my brethren here, you did it to me."

Once more he was annoyed.

*   *   *

In the sickroom of the Convent of the Poor Clares in Gandía two nuns were lying side by side.

One was Mother Agnes, a woman of sixty-five, tall and bony, of peasant stock.

The other was the Abbess, Magdalena de Jassu y Azpilcueta.

Both were dying.

The nuns assembled, praying the prayers for the dying, called down all the forces of heaven for the protection of the two souls about to leave. Father Lamberto, the chaplain of the convent, was leading the prayers.

The older nun writhed in the agony of the last stages of cancer, for which the science of her time had no means of alleviation whatever. Her breath came in gasps and each gasp ended in a low howl like that of a pain-racked animal.

Magdalena, wasting away, was only dimly aware of it. She, too, was suffering, but she was still capable of praying. She prayed for her mother, who had gone four months before, and for her brothers Juan and Miguel. And for young Francis, all alone in Paris, that he would become a valet of God and a horse of God and that he would let God come into his heart and his mind and his life. Still troubled about him, she prayed that she would be allowed to help him from the other side, whenever there was need.

It was a very great thing to ask for, she felt, and suddenly she was gripped by a most urgent desire to render some last service in exchange.

At the same moment she became aware of the heartrending cries of Mother Agnes beside her. Had not Christ said that whatever one did for anyone, even for the least of his brethren, was done to him?

Bracing herself, she prayed that she might be allowed to take over Mother Agnes' pain.

An instant later a thousand knives seemed to pierce her body and she gave one single loud moan.

Beside her, the body of the elder nun became very still and her cries stopped.

On and on went Father Lamberto's voice and the responses of the nuns, but between them and Magdalena was a curtain of fiery pain that enveloped her from head to foot to meet the counter-fire of that other pain radiating from deep inside her.

It was unbearable and essential, it could not last for longer than one pulse beat and it lasted for hours.

Shortly before midnight both nuns died at the same time. There was a calm smile on the face of the Abbess.

But when she was laid out, it was found that she had bitten her tongue to pulp to prevent her nuns from knowing in what pain she was dying.

*   *   *

"For the love of Our Lady", said Francis, "tell me, Laynez, what do you see in him? And what are you grinning about?"

Diego Laynez beamed. "Now what", he asked, "makes you inquire about this?"

Francis stamped his foot. "I'm in no way attracted towards your circle, your magic brotherhood or whatever you may call it. On the contrary. It makes me annoyed and irritated."

"An excellent sign", said Laynez cheerfully. "Annoyance is a hot feeling. It is not those who are too hot or those who are too cold, it is the tepid ones that God has spat out of his mouth."

"I can just hear him", exclaimed Francis. "Except that he only gives chapter and verse and makes you look it up, because he knows you can't resist ordinary curiosity. Going about, hitting people over the head with quotations from Scripture. He's forming you in his image. But why, why, why should you all wish to become holy beggars? I know there are always some more or less strong personalities in university colleges, each with a following of his own—like García, too, in his way, rather dirty way, I admit, but there it is. But what he's doing is more. You—you all *look* like him, you and Favre and Bobadilla and Salmerón. . . . "

"Salmerón went with me through the whole thing", said Laynez. "It's done wonders for him. They say it's done wonders for me, too, but you never see it so clearly in your own case."

"What are you talking about? What thing? What wonders?"

"Maybe your time will come one of these days", said

Laynez evasively. "Not much good talking about it before it happens."

"Look here", said Francis. "Has it anything to do with that book he keeps in his knapsack?"

"What do you know about that?" asked Laynez.

"So it has, has it?" Maybe Landivar was not so stupid after all.

"Well, yes, it has. There has never been anything like it. Of course, you must be ready for it and he alone can decide whether you are or whether you aren't."

"And then you give away all your possessions and dress like a beggar and create a scandal—like Peralto, Castro and Amador."

"Perhaps they weren't quite ripe for it", Laynez agreed. "And in any case they were people with a circle of their own—not unlike García's—and their friends interfered in a very noisy way, as you know. The poor Principal had to be inconvenienced again. There is no scandal now, is there?"

"I'm told the Inquisition took a hand."

"That is quite true, Don Francis. Some silly ass thought fit to raise a complaint and naturally they had to check up on it. Don Iñigo saw the Inquisitor and everything was settled. It's happened to him before, you know."

"Yes, I heard that, too, Laynez, and I don't like it. It's not exactly a good sign, is it, when a man gets into trouble with the Inquisition wherever he is."

Laynez frowned. "I'm from Alcalá", he said. "I was a student there, when Don Iñigo arrived and began to preach. I heard him. They accused him there and he was put into jail. Everybody came to visit him, including the Archbishop. A learned doctor wrote to a priest friend of his that he had seen Saint Paul in chains."

"Well, well . . ."

"I think he was right. The world hasn't changed as much as it ought to, Don Francis. We still resent it when a man preaches Christ to us, and if we cannot crucify or burn him, we try at least to put him behind bars. The better

a man is, the more enemies he will have. It's inevitable,
I suppose."

"I can't see why a man can't be a Christian without running
after Don Iñigo de Loyola", exclaimed Francis angrily.

"He can", said Laynez, smiling. "Just as a man can be a
Christian without being a priest. But to some of us it seems
that God has a total claim on us. It's rather frightening
when you realize it first. It frightened me out of my wits.
But then . . . "

He broke off. "You'll hear more about all this, when the
time comes", he added.

"I doubt it", said Francis stiffly.

As Laynez left, he passed Miguel Landivar. The servant
gave him a black look. "So they're sending him now", he
said, as soon as Laynez was out of earshot.

"Eh? What do you mean?" asked Francis.

"Well, he's easily the most intelligent among them, isn't
he, master? And they know you don't like talking to the
holy beggar himself. So they send his lieutenant."

"What for?"

"To win you over to their ways, master. To make you a
beggar—as they are."

The hatred in the man's voice made Francis look up.

"The idea doesn't seem to please you", he said jokingly.

"My master", said Landivar, "is a great man—he will be a
professor in a few weeks and he will rise and rise. . . . Who
knows but he will be a duke or a prince of the Church.
Everything is open to my master. Nothing is open to these
beggars. So they try and drag my master down to become a
beggar with them."

"That'll do", said Francis, frowning. "If I need your
advice again, I shall ask for it. You may go."

Miguel Landivar left without a word. But his whole
attitude spoke of rebellion.

He's more ambitious for me than I am myself, thought
Francis. No—that was not quite right. Sometimes he also
thought of a duke's sword, a marshal's baton or the red hat

of the cardinal. Sometimes. And then the chapter of the canons of Pamplona appeared to be all too peaceful and quiet. One of these days he would have to make up his mind.

*   *   *

"Sometimes", whispered Francis, "I think of a duke's sword, a marshal's baton or the red hat of a cardinal. And then the chapter of the canons of Pamplona seems all too quiet and peaceful."

"I know that feeling", whispered the man on the palliasse only two yards away. "All this and more I wanted for myself when I was just about your age."

"All this and—more? How more?"

"I wanted to conquer new countries for the King and rule them for him—I wanted to gain the love of a queen, once my sword had won me the rank I desired to fulfill my ambition."

A pale man with a little pointed beard, balding. A man to whom gentle Pierre Favre had to give lessons in the rudiments of Aristotelian philosophy. A limping little cripple, who spent his college holidays begging—in the provinces, in Holland, in England. And then suddenly paid out gold pieces so that a nobleman need not sell his horse.

"You had great dreams. Why did you give them up?"

"Because they were not great enough."

"What?" exclaimed Francis almost too loud. He looked and listened. But no one else stirred. Favre and de Peña were fast asleep.

"Not great enough", repeated the man on the palliasse next to him. "A duke is less than a king and the king may be unjust to him. A queen is a very great lady, but she may give and withdraw her favor as the whim takes her. But a man who serves the King of kings and the Queen of Heaven has nothing to fear but his own shortcomings and he will receive rewards beyond all human ambition."

"But on earth—must he lead the life of a beggar?"

"When a man's ambition is boundless, he must not waste

it on trivialities. He needs no possessions. In God he possesses everything. He needs no rank. In God he has the highest rank of all. To serve God is to rule."

Francis shook his head. "That doesn't sound like Aristotle. It is not Peter Lombard either, or Aquinas. . . . "

"I found it in the canopy room of Loyola, when they had broken my leg for the third time and reset it. I found it in my vigil on Montserrat and in a little cave near Manresa, where I wrote my book."

The book. The magic *claviculum,* the thing that Landivar feared so much and of which Laynez said that there was nothing like it, if one was ripe for it. What could it do to people, that mysterious book? He dared not ask about it, lest he would be told that he was ripe for it.

"Why did they break your leg?"

"I was wounded in the siege of Pamplona", said the man on the palliasse. "The French surgeons treated my leg badly and the Spanish ones, later, no better. I had it broken again and then once more, because a piece of the bone showed as a lump on my kneecap and it would have been an ungainly sight, especially on horseback. It was nothing but vanity. Yet in that time I decided to serve God instead of the King. It was a new life. And every new life has its infancy and childhood. Mine was at Manresa. Then I went to the Holy Land."

"But you had given up your possessions. How could you get the passage?"

"God got it for me. It is all in the Sermon on the Mount. God willing, I shall go back to the Holy Land, and this time with others, serving him in the same way."

"As beggars?"

"The beginning is only a very small part of the matter. It is good for our humility. It is good also for the charity in the hearts of others. Poverty makes a man free. People will not envy him—except for a few and they can easily satisfy their envy by imitating him. A man who is not carrying possessions has his mind free as well as his hands. People who serve Mammon call us mad. They forget that a mad

32

man has greater strength than a sane one, not because his muscles are stronger, but because he does not think of protecting himself. He can use all his strength to smash his enemy."

"Thought like a soldier", said Francis.

"I *am* a soldier", said the man on the palliasse. "And so are those who are going my way. Good night, Don Francis."

"Good night", echoed Francis. Only then did he realize the polite abruptness with which the strange man beside him had brought their discussion to an end. His "good night" had been like the clanging of the school bell, announcing the end of the lesson.

Here ended the first lesson.

He wanted to be annoyed. But there was no room for annoyance.

Then he heard the man on the palliasse breathe evenly and regularly. He had fallen asleep.

*   *   *

"Professor", said Landivar, showing all his teeth in a triumphant smile. "Regent of the College of Dormans-Beauvais. It is a great day, Professor. It is the first of many great days. Now I shall always be able to borrow money for my master, but my master will not need the money, because he will be paid in good, solid ducats by the bursar."

"The ducats are the main thing, eh?" Francis smiled.

"When are we going to take up our abode with the other professors of the college?" inquired Miguel.

"Why?"

Miguel shifted from one foot to the other. "Surely," he said, "it is not meet that a professor should sleep with three students in the same room. . . . "

"You forget", said Francis, "that they also passed their examinations. And your pet enemy, Don Iñigo, has outdone us all. He has become a Master of Arts."

Miguel pursed his lips. "It will not change his ways", he said with a shrug. "Nothing will change that one."

"Miguel," said Francis gently. "I'm afraid, this will come

as a disappointment to you. I'm not going to take up my appointment at Dormans-Beauvais."

"No?" Miguel Landivar's eyes became shifty and his hands twitched a little. "My master has changed his mind?"

"I have", said Francis quietly. "And the way I am going is not a way you will like. I'm afraid our ways will part, Miguel."

Landivar avoided his eyes. "The holy beggar", he said tonelessly. "It is the holy beggar, master, isn't it?"

"It is Don Iñigo de Loyola", said Francis. "And I also shall be a beggar. That is why our ways must part."

Landivar nodded. After a while he said, "Tomorrow is a feast day, master."

"Yes, the Feast of the Assumption."

"It is the day when the holy—when Don Iñigo and his disciples will swear the oath, is it not?"

"It is", said Francis. It was astonishing how that fellow managed to find out things. As a spy he would have been invaluable. But why should he be interested in Don Iñigo's plan? Suddenly he felt sorry for the man who had served him faithfully all these years, more ambitious for his master than the master was for himself. "Don't take it so much to heart, Miguel. Go home now, and come back tomorrow afternoon. I shall have some money for you by then."

"Thank you, master", said Miguel hoarsely. "Good night, master."

"Good night."

A minute later Landivar was forgotten. Tomorrow life began anew. It was not going to be pleasant, the way he had thought of pleasant things so far. It was going to be the greatest of all great adventures, though. He had a natural urge for adventure; it was that, perhaps, which made him doubt again and again that he could be happy among the worthy canons of Pamplona. And yet his enthusiasm, great as it was, seemed puny when compared to the radiant expectancy of Favre, Laynez, Salmerón, Bobadilla and Rodríguez. Now Bobadilla at least, had a hankering for adventure, too, by nature. He was an impulsive hothead like—other people. And Favre was a man ready to jump into a burning volcano if it could further the cause of Christ on earth. With him it was all devotion and love. But Laynez, for instance—an intellectual, a man of whom one would expect that he did nothing but what cold, logical intellect dictated—how was it that such a man could glow like a lover? And Salmerón and Rodríguez, at an age when a man's mind was still playful like a kitten. What was it that made them so keen and fiery, each one of them in a different way—bursting with energy and zeal and, despite all modesty and humility, so absolutely sure of their aim?

Of course, all of them had passed thirty days with Don Iñigo and—the book. All of them. Only in his own case, Don Iñigo had waited and was still waiting.

Something happened to people who underwent that— test, or whatever it was. After the thirtieth day a man, quite simply, was no longer the same man he had been on the first day.

Strange, that he, Francis, should be allowed to share the oath tomorrow, although he had not yet passed the test.

And yet not so strange. Perhaps in his case, there was no need for transformation. None of them ever spoke about what happened to him in those thirty days; at least no details were given. But Francis knew now that it was some kind of military manual. Maybe that was the solution of the riddle. Don Iñigo himself said that he considered himself a soldier of Christ. But none of his little band of followers was a soldier, none of them even came from a soldier's family. So they had to go through some sort of exercises. But he, Francis Xavier, did come from generations of soldiers. To him this sort of thing was natural. And Don Iñigo, with his subtle understanding of human nature, had seen that straightaway. So with him, there was no need for that particular kind of test or exercise or whatever it was.

And only thirty days! How could a man be shaped in so short a time? The glowing zeal, the keenness and energy they now showed—was it going to last, when they met with real hardship? Now a man who came from military stock . . .

He stopped abruptly. Something was wrong. *He* was wrong. Lord! One only had to think whether Don Iñigo himself could have thought what he had been thinking these last minutes, to know the answer. It was all nonsense. He just did not want to have it true that he was not *ripe* for the test yet—that young Salmerón and dear, simple Favre had gone through it and great, courageous, noble, wonderful, pompous, proud, vain, idiotic Francis had not.

He probably needed it—whatever it was—much more than anybody else. . . .

*　　*　　*

Miguel Landivar went home. Once or twice, when he passed a wine shop he stopped for a moment, jingling the few coins in his pocket. But each time he turned away again and marched on. When he reached his quarters—not far from the Hospital of Saint Jacques—he threw himself on his bed. He did not sleep. He stared at the shabby, gray ceiling. After a while he began to hum, a dreary little song, as monotonous as the creaking of a wheel. He got up, went to his knapsack and fumbled in it, till he found what he was looking for. It was a knife with a four-inch blade. He tore a curly, black hair from his head and tested the blade on it. The knife was sharp. He smiled and put it back. Then he undressed and went to bed.

*　　*　　*

Francis slept badly that night. Once the thought that he was not really worthy of the brotherhood had entered his mind, it would not be banished. He slept fitfully and was awake before the clanging of the bell, still wrestling with his problem.

Pale and exhausted, he decided to go to Don Iñigo before the appointed time and to leave the decision to him.

He could have asked him during the night—they were still sleeping in the same room with Favre and de Peña—but his sense of etiquette would not permit it. It was not the kind of decision a man could make lying in bed. Besides, Don Iñigo had not been well. Once or twice during the night he heard him sigh deeply. Either he was completely wrapped up in some meditation or he was suffering, as he sometimes did, from that sharp pain in his side which the physicians had tried in vain to diagnose.

Suddenly Don Iñigo rose and silently left the room. It was his habit to spend half an hour in the college chapel every morning before the rising bell and long before the community Mass.

Francis got up and followed him.

In the pitch darkness of the corridor he suddenly bumped into a man and knew at once that it could not be Don Iñigo, who by then must be a dozen or more paces away. The man uttered a foul oath. By sheer instinct Francis reached out to grasp the fellow's arm. Something clattered on the floor—something metallic.

"Who are you?" asked Francis, seizing the man by his throat. "And what are you trying to do?"

"Santísima," gurgled the man, "it's you, master. . . . "

"Miguel—have you gone mad?"

The sound of light steps. A tiny flame flickered. Don Iñigo had turned back and lit the stump of a candle.

His dark eyes took in the whole situation: Francis, holding the servant in a bearlike hug—Landivar's despairing face—and the long, sharp knife on the floor.

"Not you, master", gasped Miguel. "Him . . . the seducer . . . "

"Let him go", said Iñigo in a low voice.

"But . . . "

"Let him go."

Francis obeyed. All strength seemed to have gone out of Landivar. With his head bowed, his arms dangling down and his whole body swaying slightly, he was the picture of helplessness.

"I forgive you", said Don Iñigo gently. "Go in peace."

Landivar fell on his knees, babbling incoherent words.

"Do not talk to me", said Don Iñigo. "Talk to God. Come with me, Don Francis."

They both prayed in the chapel. When they returned to their room, Landivar had vanished.

Then the bell clanged and Favre and de Peña awoke.

Only when Laynez, Rodríguez, Bobadilla and Salmerón arrived at the door, did Francis suddenly remember that he had not asked Don Iñigo the decisive question.

*　　*　　*

The bells of all the churches of Paris began to intone their song of joy, as the little group mounted the slopes of Monmartre. It was crowned by the Benedictine Abbey of Saint Pierre, surrounded by gardens and trees.

There were not many houses here. The arms of a few windmills were at rest, their shape a symbol for the close relationship between Cross and Bread.

The seven men did not ascend to the mighty abbey. They entered a wayside chapel, named after the martyrdom of Saint Denis, the patron saint of France.

There was one priest among them—Pierre Favre had been ordained a little over three months ago.

They were received by the under-sacristan of the Benedictine nuns, Mother Perrette Rouillard, who gave Father Favre the keys to the crypt, where he vested.

Salmerón, the youngest of them all, only eighteen years old, served as an acolyte.

Only the length of a Mass now separated them from their vows, which would bind them irrevocably to the service of God and their neighbor, to poverty and chastity and to a pilgrimage to Jerusalem, there to reconsider and to decide by vote of majority whether they would stay and spend the rest of their lives preaching Christ to the Mohammedans or whether to return to Europe.

They had discussed their vows for many weeks. Nothing was left to chance. Things political could stop them from reaching the Holy Land, even from starting their voyage. In that case they would wait in Venice for a whole year. If within that time no ship was available, they would go to Rome and put their fate into the hands of the Pope. Wherever he would send them, they would go, "preaching the gospel anywhere at his discretion, whether it be the land of the Turks or of other tyrants hostile to the Christian name", as Iñigo put it.

Jerusalem still meant much to the Christian mind, after centuries of crusades. Christendom had won it and lost it again, battling as the individual soul was battling for the state of grace.

Islam had started the war, more than eight centuries before, when Tarik's hordes swept across the narrows near the Pillars of Hercules into Spain, stormed the steep mountain that would never be stormed again and called it after their leader, Gibr-al-Tarik, Tarik's mountain; when they overran all Spain and were halted only in France. And Christendom had counterattacked, and driven the war deep into the countries of the Green Flag of the Prophet. Yet it was not until a few decades ago that Spain could be liberated completely from the Moslem yoke, and even now the Grand Turk, the terrible successor of Selim, Suleiman the Magnificent, was threatening Christendom again. No country was safe from the onslaught of his janizaries, the raids of his swarms of cavalry on their fast Arabian horses, and his artillery, which was the best in the world.

And Christendom was divided, split up in three camps: Protestantism was fast becoming a power to be reckoned with, a power that may have come to stay; and the Catholic camp too was split, politically, with Charles the Fifth on one side and Francis the First, of France, on the other.

No armed crusade was possible in such circumstances, except one that was armed only with the Gospels. And that was the crusade these seven men planned. Seven men . . .

"It is folly", Laynez exclaimed, when Iñigo talked about it the first time.

Iñigo nodded gravely. "It is the folly of the Cross." And

suddenly they all felt the shadow of St. Paul in the shabby room in which they were sitting. But long since they had all come to share his folly, and as Laynez put it, they had the strength of madmen, who were stronger than others, because they never thought of protecting themselves.

And Mass began, the Mass of the Assumption of the Blessed Virgin Mary into Heaven, the feast observed by Christendom since the fifth century.

They all knew about Don Iñigo's very special attachment to the Queen of Heaven. It was not surprising that he should have chosen her feast for the foundation day of their brotherhood. It was Mary who had put him on the road, that day when he was lying on his bed of pain in Loyola. It was on the Feast of the Annunciation that he renounced the world, holding his night's vigil in the church on Montserrat.

Even so, they were stirred to their depths when the lesson of the day was read, not as usual an excerpt from the letter of an apostle, but from the Old Testament, from the book Ecclesiasticus. "I have sought rest elsewhere in vain; it is among the Lord's people that I mean to dwell. He who fashioned me, he, my own Creator, has taken up his abode with me; and his command to me was that I should find my home in Jacob, throw in my lot with Israel, take root among his chosen race. So, according to his word, I made Zion my stronghold, the holy city my resting place, Jerusalem my throne. My roots spread out among the people that enjoys his favor, my God has granted me a share in his own domain, where his faithful servants are gathered I love to linger."

And then it was as if Mary herself were speaking: "I grew to my full stature on Mount Zion as a cedar grows on Lebanon, or a palm tree in Cades, or a rosebush in Jericho; grew like some fair olive in the valley, some plane tree in a well-watered street. Cinnamon and odorous balm have no scent like mine, the choicest myrrh has no such fragrance."

And the Gospel spoke of that other Mary who "has

chosen for herself the best part of all, that which shall never be taken away from her."

And the Offertory sang jubilantly: Mary is taken up into heaven, the angels rejoice and join together in praising and blessing the Lord, alleluia!

They, too, had chosen the best part and it would never be taken away from them, come what might.

And Christ came down into the Host and was the Host and Favre, the priest, broke it, as Christ's body had been broken on the Cross, and partook of it, and came down to the six others to let them partake of it, too.

Each one of them, before receiving it, recited the oath, binding him to what they had decided, and then let Christ enter under his roof. In the end Favre, the Host in his right hand and the ciborium in the left, recited the oath, too.

A quarter of an hour later they left the crypt and the chapel and found the morning sun gilding the roofs of the city. The bells were still ringing everywhere. For a while their hearts were too full to speak. They sat down by the little spring, where Saint Denis was said to have suffered martyrdom. There was no need to return to the college. This was a feast day. They unpacked their morning meal, bread, an egg and some fruit. Then only they began to talk, as men will when they feel the reaction of a tremendous upheaval of mind and soul.

And then only Francis remembered that he still had not mentioned his problem to Don Iñigo—the problem now overtaken by action. He was still trying to formulate it, when Iñigo swung round to him: "I have found a quiet room for you. We shall go there tomorrow and begin the Exercises."

*   *   *

"I wish he were through it and out safe and sound", said Laynez.

Young Salmerón gave him an inquiring look. "We've all been through and come out safe and sound, why shouldn't he?"

41

Laynez grinned wryly. "I fasted for two days and then took only bread and water", he said, "and so did you. But we have a sense of moderation. Francis hasn't."

"But surely, Father Iñigo will be with him all the time and . . . "

"Not all the time. You should know that. If it weren't for his supervision and direction, Francis would never get through. But God alone knows what will happen when he is left alone. The first week is bitter enough, but in the third—the Third Prelude for instance and the Sixth Point—I shall never forget them. I know what it evoked in me, and when I think what it is likely to evoke in Francis . . . "

"We have not sworn obedience", said Salmerón, shaking his head, "because we're not an order. But surely Iñigo is our Father, our Captain. If Francis cannot obey him . . . "

"He will learn—he will learn. But I wish he were over the third week."

*   *   *

It was Simon Rodríguez who wrote down what happened in that third week, when Francis was wrestling with angels of light and of darkness. The military manual of the soul that is called *The Spiritual Exercises,* under Third Week, First Day, says under Point Five: "To meditate under what condition the Divinity of Christ is hiding itself, and does not destroy his enemies when able to do so, but permits his humanity to suffer cruel punishments." And under Point Six: "To think, since Christ so endured for our sins, what we ought to do or to suffer for his sake."

What ought he to do? What ought he to suffer?

Was it not only a very short time ago that he thought he would be a better man than his brothers, he, the man from a warlike family, he, the best athlete of the school? He had spent months and months in training his body, and what for? To be best at the high jump, to win at wrestling and fencing, to be applauded for his animal abilities. . . .

He roped his upper limbs so tightly that he could no longer move, and so trussed up, made his meditations.

When Iñigo found him, his arms had swelled and covered the cord he had used beyond any possibility of cutting it.

They tried everything they knew but nothing helped. They prayed, fearing that at least one of his arms would have to be amputated. But after two days of terrible agony the cord, so deeply embedded in the flesh, broke suddenly.

Simon Rodríguez wrote: " . . . by the singular mercy of God, in a way utterly beyond my comprehension, he became completely well."

*   *   *

One year later on the Feast of the Assumption of Mary into Heaven the little brotherhood renewed its vows in the same chapel. Three new members, the Frenchmen Claude Le Jay, Paschale Broët and Jean Codure, swore the oath. But one member was missing. Don Iñigo had left for Spain, to visit not only his own family, but also those of his Spanish brothers Laynez, Bobadilla, Salmerón and Xavier and to render them an account of the new life their sons, brothers and nephews had embraced.

Three months later the others also left the city.

Their goal was Venice, where they hoped to see their spiritual father again and to leave with him for the Holy Land.

By now they had got rid of all their belongings. Each one took with him: his rosary, a leather wallet containing a Bible, a breviary and his private papers. And they carried with them their Masters' degrees.

They were dressed as usual in black cassocks and wore broad-brimmed hats, the regular outfit of the Paris student. Well-meaning men of the college tried to stop them from their foolhardy undertaking. If they wanted to work for God, they could do it here, in Paris. Why go, unarmed, into a den of angry lions? They would be stopped by the French troops, by the Spanish troops, by the police and the secret service of Francis the First, of Charles the Fifth, of dukes and counts and towns. In a week, in two weeks, they would be dead.

They were all very polite about it—and completely intransigent.

On the day of departure, a special courier arrived asking for Don Francisco de Jassu y Xavier. He found him cleaning his boots with great gusto. "A man must keep his servants in good shape, if they are to perform their duties well", explained Francis gravely, when the courier eyed him with some astonishment. He was given a letter on heavy parchment, sealed with a seal the size of a man's palm. The courier bowed with the courtesy due to a nobleman and Francis bowed back. When the man had gone, Francis broke the seal and read:

> We, the Emperor . . . by this present definitive sentence pronounce and declare
>
> Don Francisco de Jassu y Xavier
>
> to be a nobleman, hidalgo and gentleman of ancient lineage, and as such empower him and his sons and descendants in direct line to use and enjoy all the prerogatives, exemptions, honors, offices, liberties, privileges, landed property and dueling rights which appertain to gentlemen, hidalgos and noblemen in our Kingdom of Navarre and everywhere else.

The famous document had come at long last. Francis grinned broadly and cleaned the other boot.

He was still grinning when he joined his companions. "I have one piece of luggage more", he said. "Shall I leave it here or take it with me?"

Laynez looked at it. "Better take it with you", he said cheerfully. "It may help, when we encounter Spanish troops."

Francis nodded. He had not thought of that. It was just like Laynez to think of it. "There is some good in everything", he said contentedly.

* * *

Three days walk from Meaux a couple of students caught up with them; one of them was Carlos, the brother of Simon Rodríguez. The other was also a Portuguese. Both were horrified at the folly of the travelers. "There is war all

44

around you, you dear fools. You have no arms, you have no money. Be reasonable and come back with us."

"You come with us", said Simon Rodríguez.

"Thanks very much", said his brother, lifting his hands. "I have no wish to starve."

"Have a radish then", said Simon, offering him a whole bunch he had been given an hour earlier by a farmer's wife who was almost as large as her own cow.

The two well-meaning students withdrew, shaking their heads in despair.

A few days later they ran into French troops and the fun started in earnest.

They tackled Francis whom, as the tallest of the lot, they took for the leader, and Francis, only too well aware of his hard, Basque accent, just grinned at them, without saying a word.

Little Jean Codure came to his help. "What is it we can do for you, *mon sergent*?"

"Who are you?"

"We are students from Paris."

"Where do you come from?"

"From Paris."

"I mean, from what country?"

Jean Codure looked very much offended. "Don't you know that Paris is in France?"

The soldier eyed him distrustfully. "Not so much lip from you, my fine bird. And those others—are they also good Frenchmen?"

Jean Codure looked very solemn. "We are all from Paris", he stated with great dignity.

They were allowed to pass.

Later, near Metz, they first encountered streams of refugees and then Spanish soldiers. Francis brandished his royal certificate under their astonished noses and addressed them in a torrent of Spanish.

Both times they escaped death by a hair's breadth. If the soldiers had found out that the little group consisted of two nationalities, they would have made short shrift of them. Both trees and ropes were ubiquitous. It was a death none of them particularly cared for. To die for the Faith, as a martyr, was one thing; to be hanged because one was falsely taken for a spy quite another.

On one occasion they were allowed to pass because they gave an impression of invincible stupidity.

But then, perhaps it was not easy to detect Masters of Arts and Professors of Philosophy in the nine shabby, bedraggled young men, stalking and squelching through the perpetual rain and mud of a northern French November.

When they entered Germany, the three Frenchmen among them had to become deaf mutes. Germany was pro-Emperor, where it was not Protestant. This latter aspect, however, was a very different thing. At no point did they disguise the fact that they were Catholics.

A delightful middleaged Protestant pastor challenged them to a debate in a Constance inn, quoting (of all things) Virgil at them and promising them as a kind of special treat to introduce them to his children. Laynez took him on and spiked the German's guns so adroitly that he had to admit he could not answer the questions. "What?" asked Laynez severely. "How can you hold opinions that you cannot defend?"

That was too much. The German rose wrathfully. "Tomorrow I'll have you flung in jail. Then you'll see whether I can defend my side or not."

They left Constance that night.

"You've eaten him", exulted Salmerón. "You won right through."

"Maybe," sighed Laynez, "but we had to make a strategic withdrawal all the same."

They crossed into Switzerland, where they had similar experiences. Zwingli, Farel and Oecolampadius had done their work in Basle, Berne and other towns.

"We should really stay here", grunted Francis. "There is a great deal of work to do."

"We should have remained in Germany", said Broët.

"There is one great difference between the two countries, though", declared Laynez gravely.

"What difference?"

Laynez shivered. "It's colder here", he said.

*   *   *

When they entered Venice, after a journey of six weeks, the bells were ringing for the Feast of the Epiphany, and for once it was neither raining nor snowing.

The sacristan of the Church of Saint Mark told them the address that meant more to them than all the glories of the glorious jewel of the Adriatic that is Venice. They had no eyes for the lagoons, the *palazzi,* the incredibly rich shops exhibiting the most precious and costly goods of three continents. They cared nothing for the very special elegance of the Venetians, aped by all the fops and worldly ladies in Christendom. They had no interest in the Palace of the Doge and the Bridge of Sighs, leading to the notorious "chambers of lead" from which there was no return. All they sought was the modest house of an old Spaniard, in a very unfashionable part of the city.

There they found a frail, thin, pale man, bald and limping, with deep-set, hooded eyes who opened his arms to them. They embraced him and pressed around him as children will when they see their father again after a long separation.

The little room was awhirl with black cassocks and beaming faces and even Laynez, the most controlled of them all, had tears in his eyes.

The three newcomers, Le Jay, Broët and Codure, were introduced and welcomed and then all of them wanted to know how their father had fared on his journey and the Spaniards among them wanted to know how he had found their families and what they had said about their decision, and Don Iñigo wanted to know how they managed to escape the French and the Spanish and the other dangers, how far the stories were true that were told in Spain about the growing heresy in Germany and in Switzerland and whether they had stuck faithfully to his rules of examining conscience twice a day and going to confession and receiving Holy Communion once a week, and they all spoke at the same time and Don Iñigo's poor old Spanish host, a good and learned man, thought the house was coming down on him.

Gradually they found out that Iñigo had arrived in Venice a long time ago and that he had met with many adventures on his way here from Spain; that their families were well; that Iñigo intended to go on to Rome and yet at the same time for some reason seemed to vacillate.

It was fairly late in the day when Francis managed to speak to Don Iñigo alone for a few minutes.

He already knew by then that his only surviving brother, Miguel, had married a wealthy girl and was living very comfortably. But he knew also—or rather he felt—that Don Iñigo's reception had not been exactly glowing.

He began to understand why the nobility certificate, addressed originally to his home at Xavier, had been forwarded to him by a special courier. It was Miguel's way of trying to steer him away from a life as a beggar. How could a hidalgo be a beggar!

"They don't like it", he said with a sad smile.

Don Iñigo smiled back. "You will find the answer in the Gospel of Saint Matthew, chapter 10, verses 37 and 38."

Francis looked it up that evening. "He is not worthy of me, that loves father or mother more; he is not worthy of me, that loves son or daughter more; he is not worthy of me, that does not take up his cross and follow me."

Book Two

THERE WAS NO ship. Beyond vast stretches of wintry sea the Holy Land was waiting, but there was no ship.

And still Iñigo hesitated about going on to Rome. They knew why, by now. The fierce Bishop of Chieti, Gian Pietro Carafa, had become Iñigo's enemy. The reason was dark, but had something to do with Carafa's love of pomp and circumstance and Iñigo's love of poverty. There must have been some grave provocation for Iñigo to write to a man much older than himself, and a bishop: "When a man of rank and exalted dignity wears a habit more ornate and lives in a room better furnished than the other religious of his Order, I am neither scandalized nor disedified. However, it would be well to consider how the saints have conducted themselves, Saint Dominic and Saint Francis, for example; and it would be good to have recourse to light from on high; for, after all, a thing may be licit, without being expedient."

And now Carafa had gone to Rome, there to receive the red hat of the Cardinal. And in Rome, too, was Dr. Pedro Ortiz, Ambassador-Extraordinary of Charles the Fifth, and Dr. Ortiz had been opposed to Iñigo's ideas and aims from the early days in Paris. His business in Rome concerned the divorce of King Henry VIII of England from Queen Catherine of Aragon. The air of Rome was dangerous, with two such powerful enemies present.

On the other hand, Iñigo had won new friends and followers. There was Diego de Hoces, two brothers named Eguia and a number of high dignitaries who all had gone through the Exercises. One was an Englishman, a Master of Arts of Oxford and a refugee from the regime of persecu-

49

tion raging in his country, John Helyar by name. Another was the prelate Gaspar de'Dotti.

But there was no time for anything in the nature of social intercourse. Now that the ten fighters were together, they gave battle to the enemy straightaway. That enemy, like the Lernaean hydra, had many heads: lack of faith, lack of morals, spiritual ignorance, misery, illness and dirt. And they went where most of the evils could be found together: to the Hospital of Saint John and Saint Paul, and to the Hospital of the Incurables.

They attacked with a vigor that changed the whole atmosphere of these two terrible places practically within a day. Never before had there been so much sweeping and cleaning. Every patient was treated as if he were Christ himself. Food and drink were begged, nightwatches were established. Above all, service was rendered with so much gaiety that it spread like a new kind of infection.

To most of them this kind of work was not new; they had done similar things in Paris in their free time. Even so, it was not always easy to bear, especially in bad cases of the French pox and of—leprosy.

An old man, covered with horrible ulcers, asked Francis to scratch his itching back and Francis obliged, although his hands were trembling with disgust. He thought of that other Francis, the glorious Fool of God, who was so ashamed of his horror of a leper that he ran after the man to embrace him. Bending down, he touched the ulcerous places with his lips and even sucked them. Rising, he saw Rodríguez, his face white, looking at him.

Francis grinned wryly. "Don't you remember that our Lord said, 'Deadly poison will not hurt them'? Ask Iñigo— he'll give you chapter and verse."

*　　*　　*

Still there was no ship. At long last Iñigo decided to send his sons to Rome, while he remained in Venice. Their task was to approach the Pope, ask him for his blessing for them all, and, if possible, for his permission to be ordained priests, before they set out for the Holy Land. None of them had incurred the wrath of a powerful cardinal, so there was hope that they would not meet with too much opposition.

They traveled without any luggage, as before. On their three-day march to Ravenna they did not meet a single soul, and therefore had nothing to eat. They lived on the seeds of pine cones. In Ancona they had to pawn Laynez' breviary to pay for their passage from Ravenna, and then they begged till they had enough money to get the breviary back.

They prayed at the shrine of Loreto; they traversed the Apennine and Sabine mountains, sleeping in cattle barns and abandoned shacks, hungry most of the way.

In Rome one surprise followed another. The much-dreaded Dr. Ortiz was practically the first man they encountered. The huge, fat man in his rich robes stared at them. "That strange gentleman from Loyola sent you, eh? Never thought he would get anywhere with his methods. Seems to have collected a whole company of recruits, eh? All Masters of Arts, too—although you don't exactly look the part, eh, eh? What do you want here?"

Laynez gulped twice and then told him. No one could fool a man like Ortiz as they had fooled the French and Spanish troops. This might mean that their mission would come to an end before it had started.

"See the Holy Father, eh?" chortled the Emperor's Ambassador. "Nothing less than that, eh? Well, we'll see what can be done, we'll see, we'll see. Better wash your cassocks, before you go to the Vatican, though. Where do you stay? The poorhouse? You would. No worse than a certain stable in the Holy Land anyway. You'll hear from me. Promise."

And the portly prelate waddled off, leaving them in a state of complete confusion.

"Something tells me he's going to keep his promise", said Favre.

Francis nodded. "Oh, he'll keep it all right. We'll hear from Dr. Orcus. He'll tell the Governor of Rome to have us thrown out before we are a day older."

However, nothing happened for a few days. Then a Vatican official appeared at the poorhouse with a letter, requesting their presence at the Holy Father's dinner table. "Dr. Orcus" had been as good as his word.

"What's our Father going to say to that?" Laynez demanded, with a beaming face.

*   *   *

He was delighted. Delighted all the more since not only that first visit of his sons to the Pope, but several others that followed it became a chain of successes.

The formidable gentleman on the seat of Saint Peter, Paul III, looking a little like a patriarch of ancient Israel with his long white beard, hooked nose and dark eyes, enjoyed a lively theological or philosophical debate at dinner and he certainly got his money's worth. He was moved to give the ardent young pilgrims sixty ducats from his own pocket. The many bishops, prelates and abbots present added a collection of another two hundred.

It was supposed to serve them as passage money to Jerusalem, although the Pope seemed a little doubtful whether they would be able to get there in the near future.

Paul III had taken over a burden a lesser man could not have carried for a week. England, large parts of Germany and Switzerland were in open rebellion against the established Faith, and rebel groups had been formed in practically all countries. There was deadly enmity between the powerful princes on the Catholic side. And the whole of Christendom was threatened by the Turks, whose next onslaught could be expected at any moment.

The Papal State and the papal power were only just beginning to recover from the terrible blow inflicted on them by the Spanish and German troops under the Duke of Bourbon ten years ago, when Rome was taken, burned, looted and reduced to a little town of less than thirty thousand inhabitants.

Such was the state of affairs when Paul III took over from poor Clement VII, who had been kept a prisoner more than

52

six months in the Castello Sant'Angelo, while outside the walls soldiers were raping, killing and robbing to their hearts' content.

And Paul was sixty-seven, and gravely ill—they said he had only been elected Pope because the cardinals could not agree on any other man and Paul was supposed to serve as a kind of interregnum, since no one expected him to live more than a year or two longer.

But Alexander Farnese, who was now Paul III, did not die. Against all expectations he recovered instead of breaking down under the Triple Tiara and he resolved to deal with all the urgent problems at hand at the same time.

He moved heaven and earth to bring about a reconciliation between Charles the Fifth and Francis the First. He was forming a Holy League of all Christian princes against the Turks. He fortified the ports of the Papal State.

Reforms inside the Church were necessary—he knew that. But they had to come from the inside, not from the outside.

Men were what he needed—men, filled with apostolic zeal, ready to go anywhere at his command, ready to die, if need be, for the restoration and propagation of the Faith.

Quietly he observed the nine young men—the brilliant debating technique of Laynez, the disarming charm and winning kindness of Favre, the youthful enthusiasm and adroitness of Salmerón, the sparkling vitality and energy of Bobadilla, the zeal in the eyes of all the others, Xavier, Codure, Rodríguez, Broët and Le Jay. Something could be done with those men.

Willingly he gave them the permission they asked for: that those among them who were not yet priests, would be ordained at once "at any place no less than forty miles outside Rome". As for their voyage to Jerusalem, he had dropped a hint or two that it was not likely to take place. There was no harm in giving his permission and blessing to the project. He knew that they had as much chance to get to the moon as to the Holy Land. Here—here was their

Jerusalem. But let them find out for themselves. A man always worked better when he worked voluntarily.

* * *

They found out for themselves.

On their return to Venice, they first resumed their work at the two hospitals.

On June 24 they were ordained. But none of them said his first Mass. They decided to prepare themselves for that by a forty days' fast and prayer, split up in groups of two. After that they reassembled in the ruins of an old monastery near Vicenza. Then and then only they said their first Mass.

Except for Iñigo de Loyola. Quick as he was, whenever action was required, when it came to his own spiritual evolution, he was painstakingly slow. It would be a whole year after his ordination before he felt himself ready to say his first Mass.

* * *

Francis fell ill. The poisonous breath of the Pontine Marshes was too much even for the strongest of the little group. The quartan ague made him intolerably hot at one moment, and shivering with cold in the next. He emerged as weak as a kitten, just as the year they had agreed to wait for the pilgrim ship had elapsed, and Iñigo gave the order to proceed to Rome without delay.

Francis should have stayed behind, but nothing short of a direct order could have made him do so. As usual, they traveled on foot, as usual without money, in little groups of three or, as in Francis' case, singly.

Rodríguez arrived first and managed to find a house that could serve as a home for the whole community. It was a wretched little place near the Trinitá dei Monti. But the rent was so cheap that Rodríguez rejoiced. It would always be possible to get the few necessary silver pieces by begging. His first night in the house showed him why it was so cheap. Quick feet seemed to clatter up and down the stairs, furniture seemed to move about by itself and pots and pans came sailing through the air, thrown by invisible hands.

But Rodríguez had not learned logic at the College of Sainte Barbe for nothing. He reasoned it all out. If the noise was made by thieves, it did not matter, because there was nothing to steal. If it was made by demons, surely they could harm him only if God permitted it, and if God permitted—the will of God be done. After which he turned over and went to sleep.

The noise did not cease when the others arrived, but they took the same philosophical attitude.

Francis came late, completely exhausted by the long and arduous journey, a shadow of himself. His night, too, was troubled. "Never mind", he said to Rodríguez with a grin. "If they're ghosts, they'll take me for one, too."

In the morning, when he came down, he found Iñigo standing in the open door and before him a man on his knees. He rubbed his eyes still heavy with sleep. He could not believe what he saw.

The man on his knees was Miguel Landivar.

"See my contrition, Don Iñigo", said Landivar in a broken voice. "See my contrition. I've made all the way to Rome on foot. Don't reject me, Don Iñigo. Let me stay with you and my—my former master. I'll do everything you say—everything. I know how good you were to me in not calling in the authorities, when I tried to—to take your life. But do not reject me now, I beg of you."

Iñigo made him rise. "You did not try to take my life", he said slowly. "I am no longer Don Iñigo de Loyola. I am Father Ignatius. If you are looking for a master, you will not find one here. We are all servants. In Paris we were a company of students and of Masters of Arts. Now we are priests."

"I know I am not worthy", stammered Landivar. Then he saw Francis. "Master—Don Francis—Father Francis—won't you put in a word for me?"

"Come in", said the man who now was Father Ignatius. He spoke quickly, giving Francis no time to say anything. It was an act of supreme tactfulness. He wanted to spare

Francis the dilemma of rejecting the plea of a wretched man, or putting in a word for a would-be murderer.

Miguel Landivar entered. And now there really was a demon in the house.

* * *

As a general sends detachments of troops to the various strategic places of a fortress, Father Ignatius sent out his one-man battalions to as many churches as possible. The Pope had told him through Laynez that Rome was "as good a Jerusalem as any", and Jerusalem had to be conquered.

He himself preached in Spanish at Nuestra Señora de Montserrat; he would not leave that to anyone else. Favre spoke at San Lorenzo in Damaso, Laynez at San Salvatore *in lauro*, Bobadilla at San Celso, Rodríguez at Santi Angeli, Salmerón at Santa Lucia, Le Jay, alternating with Francis, at San Luigi dei Francesi.

Much had happened in the ten years since that terrible day when the Eternal City had been looted and raped by barbarian soldiers. Life had flooded back, all the churches had been consecrated anew, but even so, Rome's morals were down to a very low level, so much so that good Christians in all the countries of Europe agreed that it was dangerous "to come too close to the kitchen of God". A spirit of fresh zeal, of enthusiasm for the cause of God was needed more than ever.

Francis preached either in good French or in bad Italian. He had no inhibitions about speaking in a language of which he knew only a couple of thousand words, if that many. Somehow they understood him, he knew that.

Landivar invariably listened. He was sharing the life of the "Iñiguists", as Salmerón had dubbed the little company, he begged and worked and prayed with them—but his former master was still the center of his interest.

* * *

It was in San Luigi dei Francesi, during a sermon by Francis that Landivar first met the Countess Vanozza Morini. He had been observing her for some time, a beautiful woman, still young, and exquisitely dressed. She had been in church twice before, when Francis was preaching, a regal figure, a creamy white face, fiery-red curls—genuine, and not a wig as so many ladies sported nowadays. Secretly he made his inquiries. She did not come from a noble family, but she had married Count Morini who had died ten years ago in the sack of Rome. His death was not exactly peaceful. While defending his lady against the attack of four drunken soldiers he had managed to kill one, before he himself was killed. Only one . . .

The Countess, apparently, did not find it too difficult to survive.

In the years that followed she managed to retrieve a good part of the money and treasures that had disappeared at the time of her husband's death, and moreover she was said to be on excellent terms with a number of personages in very high positions, although they took care not to visit her too openly. A lady of means, a lady of resources . . . More than once such a lady had helped an unknown little priest to acquire the necessary connections which in due course led to a great position. And when a man became a prelate, and wore the purple silk of his office, he could no longer go about begging. If necessary, others did the begging for him. But there was no reason why it should be necessary at all.

There was little doubt that Don Francis appealed to her, despite his shabby black cassock. And why not? Don Francis (it was much easier to call him that than Father Francis) was a fine figure of a man, anyone would know that he came from noble stock.

It was worth while to see what could be done.

Miguel Landivar made the acquaintance of Countess Vanozza Morini by giving her holy water, when she was leaving the church, and saying that it was gratifying to see a great lady take so much interest in religion. Like every member of the Iñiguist household, he wore a black cassock.

The Countess gave him the gentle smile she reserved for priests. "He is the most wonderful preacher in Rome", she murmured. "You must be very glad to have him in your parish."

"Oh, I am not a priest", replied Miguel modestly. "I am only a serving brother of the community to which Don—to which Father Francis belongs. When he was still in the world, I used to be his servant, as befitted his rank."

"He comes from a noble family, then", exclaimed the lady. "I knew it. Only breeding can produce such beautiful, eloquent hands. I knew it all the time. I never miss his sermons. So uplifting, so heartwarming, even when he threatens us all with terrible punishments for our sins. Does he hear confessions?"

"For hours on end, every day", said Landivar.

The Countess became pensive. "I don't think I can bring myself to go to him", she murmured. "There is something so dreadfully impersonal about a confessional. . . . Would it be possible to see him where he lives?"

Miguel thought of the ramshackle community house, of the street urchins coming to learn the catechism or to get a plate of soup, of Father Ignatius. . . . It was unthinkable.

"I don't think that can be done, noble lady." Boldly he added, "But perhaps I may be able to persuade him to come to you."

"Oh, but that would be wonderful", exclaimed the Countess. "I would be so grateful to you. . . . "

She offered him a gold piece. After some show of reluctance he accepted it. She gave him her address and he wrote it down carefully, although he had known it for some time.

*   *   *

There was great excitement in the community house.

For some time the Iñiguists had been paying close attention to the sermons of one of Rome's most famous preachers, the monk Agostino Mainardi of Saluzzo.

There was little doubt that the man was preaching—in a very subtle way—rank heresy. There was no doubt at all that he was an extremely popular orator and that he enjoyed the admiration and the support of many clerics in very high positions. What was to be done? They had tried to reason with the man in private, and he had conceded the points they made and promised to change his sermons accordingly. But instead, he had again and again repeated his errors, and supervision by ecclesiastic authority was so lax that no one else took him to task. Few men would have dared to do so anyhow.

"It's simply vanity", said Laynez. "Preaching always contains that temptation. "The false logic of his thoughts has a glittering appeal to the poor man and he succumbs to his own eloquence."

"That", said Father Ignatius, "is up to his conscience and to his Father Confessor. What we must be concerned with is the people he is misleading. He would not listen to you, when you remonstrated with him. You have done what Saint Paul told us to do: you corrected him like a brother — you did not treat him as an enemy. But now the time has come to oppose him and the evil he is spreading."

When one of his sons warned that Mainardi was a man of great influence and high connections, he replied, "Here again Saint Paul gives the answer: 'If, after all these years, I were still courting the favor of men, I should not be what I am, the slave of Christ.'"

The next Sunday the attack against Mainardi began.

Ignatius himself went to warn the preacher's most ardent admirers, two Spanish priests, Mudarra and de Castilla.

Burning with anger, they reported immediately to Mainardi. Then the Iñiguists began preaching against the monk from the pulpit and the real battle started in grim earnest.

* * *

When Miguel told Francis that a lady wished to confess to him, who could not get herself to join the queue at his confessional, he was quite willing to visit her, as she requested so anxiously.

People had many weaknesses, scruples and fancies. There was the woman who could confess the worst kind of sin easily, but hedged to shield some shabby little action or thought that hurt her vanity. There was the man who would not go near a confessional, because he could not stand being closed in. The little box was like a coffin and he could not breathe. That sort of thing. . . . A priest had to be patient and indulgent.

He was pleased with Miguel's eagerness, too. The poor man tried so hard to adapt himself to the austere life of the community.

So he went to what Miguel called the Palazzo Morini.

The Countess received him with a kind of demure joy. She was quite unhappy when he refused the wine and the tidbits she offered him. She talked of her past, of her marriage to Count Morini. He was a fine man in many ways, but he never really understood her. Not her soul . . . Now life was so empty. Friends—yes, more than enough. But women were cats, and men—they were all the same. All out for what they could get. How wonderful it was to find a man like Father Francis who was living an ideal life. . . . Really not a single goblet of wine? Such a pity, it was good wine, from the Frascati vineyards, Prince Urghino had given it to her. A nice, young man, very elegant, women fell in love with him right and left. But she knew how to cope with that flighty, empty-headed type. He had given her the sapphire ring on her little finger; it meant very little from him, although the ring had once belonged to his mother. It was pretty, wasn't it?

Francis interrupted. He had come to hear her confession.

Of course he had. Only, it was not easy for her to start talking of such things right away. Men were all so direct. Even priests, sometimes, did not know how sensitive she was. She could not, no, she could not possibly confess to a priest she scarcely knew and who did not know her at all. She had to feel that she was understood.

She felt better already, through his mere presence. So soothing.

Francis interrupted. Had she prepared herself? Had she searched her conscience?

60

She could not. She could not do it alone. He would have to help her—when she was ready. It was so long ago since the last time she had confessed. She was so glad that Father Francis was obviously a nobleman. It made things so very much easier. . . .

Every priest was a nobleman, inasmuch as he was a man set apart, Francis told her. And that was the only kind of nobility he wished to claim.

Ah, yes, yes indeed. She knew that. Nevertheless there was a great difference between an ordinary sort of priest and Father Francis, and only a man of gentle birth could understand her, although her husband had not.

When she saw Father Francis in the pulpit, she knew that he was the man, the priest who could help her.

These beautiful hands. One of the great painters should paint them for her as the hands of Christ. . . .

She had taken his hands into hers.

But it was the comparison she dared to make, not the physical fact that made him flush with anger.

He opened his mouth, to tell her in no uncertain terms what he thought of her remark, when he saw that she was leaning towards him, her painted mouth smiling, her nostrils flaring greedily.

With a jerk he released his hands.

"I came to free you of your sins", he said, rising. "Not to add to them."

He marched towards the door.

The disappointed laughter behind him made him turn round once more. "Repent", he thundered. "Repent. Repent!"

Then he walked out.

He was in such a towering rage that he did not even see the man who was standing in the doorway opposite. It was Father Pedro de Castilla, the admirer of the monk Mainardi.

*　　*　　*

The next day rumors began to be whispered in Rome. A group of alien clerics had dared to insinuate all kinds of lying things about Father Mainardi. Everybody knew that the great orator was a saintly man, admired and respected by the highest in the land. It was envy, jealousy. Or no, it was much worse: these people tried to shield themselves by accusing Father Mainardi. It was they who preached heresy. They were hypocrites, too; one of them had been seen, coming out of the house of a notorious courtesan, Vanozza Morini, a woman who changed her lovers as she changed her dresses.

Something of the kind was to be expected, but Father Ignatius took the trouble to check up whether one of his sons had really met that woman anywhere, be it only for a few minutes.

Francis, horrified, told him the whole story as he knew it.

"It was imprudent", said Ignatius severely. "You should have inquired about the woman before paying her a visit in her house." Then he took Miguel Landivar to task.

Landivar listened to his reproaches for a while. But instead of apologizing, he fell into a rage. Sputtering and stammering, he accused Ignatius, Francis, everyone in the house of hating him, of finding fault with him for everything he did. "I wish I could tell you what I think of you", he screamed.

Ignatius, icy cold, dismissed him from the community.

"I was going anyway", shouted Landivar. "And I know where I'm going, too. You'll hear from me! All of you . . . "

He was in such a fury that as soon as he had found himself a place to stay, he wrote a letter to Ignatius. Ignatius was the ruin of Don Francis. He, and he alone, had befuddled him into joining his sorry troop of beggars, when Don Francis was just on the verge of making a real career for himself. He—Landivar—had not been able to look on any longer. The Countess Morini was a great lady with excellent connections. Through her Don Francis could have gained such connections, too; he could have become a prelate, a bishop, perhaps a great cardinal, if only he had known how to seize his opportunity. But no, he had to insult the poor woman and go back to his beggarly life. It was too late to extricate him from the jaws of Ignatius, but not too late for him, Landivar, to withdraw from them forever.

Coolly, Ignatius put the letter away in a safe place. It might be useful someday.

Soon he found out that Landivar had not uttered an empty threat, when he said that he knew where he was going.

He had joined the Mainardi camp and now a whole flood of new rumors went through Rome. That man Ignatius was nothing but an escaped convict. He had been in jail several times. He posed as a saint, but in reality his teaching had got him into trouble with the Inquisition time and again—in Alcalá, in Salamanca, in Paris, everywhere. Even in Venice there had been painful scenes.

People began to ask themselves whether it was safe to send their children to such men to be instructed in the Faith. Many of the children did not come back.

*   *   *

Benedetto Conversini, Governor of Rome, was not exactly happy about the visit of a pale, bald, limping priest in an old black cassock. He knew who Father Ignatius was, of course—Rome was seething with rumors about him and thus the visit had a certain amount of curiosity value. But it was not agreeable to be drawn into the maelstrom of theological arguments and accusations, especially as Mainardi had friends in such high positions.

The pale little man put him at ease with a couple of sentences. One gentleman, a caballero, informed another gentleman about a little matter of honor. It was just not good enough to be accused indirectly. Let those people who accused him and his companions come forward and accuse him openly, here and now. Conversini, after all, was the competent authority to deal with the case. Who exactly were the accusers?

Conversini hemmed and hawed. It was not easy to fix this kind of thing on any particular person. However, there were the Fathers Mudarra and de Castilla and there was a man called Landivar, who seemed very emphatic about the fact that he knew all about the community in general and Father Ignatius in particular. Much of what the two priests said was due to information received from that man Landivar, as they admitted themselves.

Father Ignatius suggested with a kind of persistent courtesy that he should be confronted with Landivar, and Conversini agreed, not without some relief. Landivar, at least, was not a man whose connections could make trouble.

He did not know that he was up against a mind with a genius for strategy. He had no idea that the confrontation with Landivar was only the essential prelude, the first cannon shot in the battle, and that the next half-dozen moves had been calculated and fixed with painstaking accuracy by the mild little man before him.

Landivar was summoned and made his appearance. He blustered and spluttered. After half an hour he had contradicted himself often enough to discredit completely his own testimony. Then Father Ignatius coldly produced Landivar's letter, from which it became evident that Landivar had an axe to grind and that it was he who had tried—and tried in vain—to bring about friendly relations between Father Francis Xavier and the famous Countess Morini.

Conversini made short shrift of him and banished him from Rome straightaway. In doing so, he believed that he had killed two birds with one stone. He had pleased Father Ignatius—and at the same time he had got out of the way a witness whose character and action could only endanger the Mainardi party.

But as soon as Landivar had departed—white with rage and muttering curses—Father Ignatius demanded that he be confronted with Mudarra and de Castilla.

Conversini could not very well decline, nor could the two Spanish priests. Their method was the very opposite of Landivar's. They simply denied everything. They had never said anything. They had never done anything. It was not at all their fault, if some strange and possibly quite unfounded rumors pervaded the city. A fellow named Miguel Landivar had indeed approached them and made certain statements, but he was not in their employ, nor did they intend to employ him. On the contrary, he had been a member of the community around Father Ignatius. *They* had nothing to do with him. They could have taught slipperiness to an eel.

It was still not good enough. Conversini, of course, seized the opportunity to dismiss the whole affair, rather than get himself into unnecessary difficulties with the Mainardi party. Even the Pope himself received Mainardi and was said to have a weakness for the man's gift of eloquence.

Father Ignatius knew only too well that this could not be allowed to be the end of the affair. Unless his and his companions' honor, righteousness and orthodoxy were clearly reestablished, his entire work was imperiled. The children still stayed away. Here, there and everywhere clever, subtle remarks were made against the community, and occasional direct and potent attacks. There were some who said loudly that "these alien priests" ought to be burned at the stake for heresy, or sent to the gallows.

In vain Father Ignatius tried to press Conversini to initiate an official inquiry; that was precisely what the worthy Governor most wanted to avoid.

The big guns were called on now.

Father Ignatius mobilized his auxiliaries. Letters flew to all the bishops of the dioceses where he and his companions had worked—in Alcalá, in Salamanca, in Paris, in Venice, in Vicenza, Bologna and Padua. Letters went to the directors of hospitals, to vicars-general and to eminent laymen in half a dozen cities and towns. And each of them asked for a testimony about the character, the morals and the teaching of the Iñiguists.

A mobile unit consisting of Laynez and Favre was sent in forced marches to the Holy Father, to plead their case. Pope Paul III had just secured one of his most pressing aims—a ten-year peace between the Emperor and the King of France—and was trying to find a little rest in Frascati. He promised them that all would be well, but weeks passed and nothing happened.

In the meantime Ignatius had met Cardinal Contarini, a man of great calibre, and the two men had become friends almost at once. To Ignatius' joy, Contarini accepted his suggestion to go through the Exercises.

When it became clear that Laynez and Favre had failed to stimulate the Pope into action, Ignatius himself sought an audience. Once more it was fat Dr. Ortiz who procured it for him. There had been a time (not so long ago) when the Inquisition of Salamanca found fault with his teaching and had paid for it with a defense that really was a theological sermon of almost three hours' length. Paul III did not fare much better. Ignatius told him not only the story of his case, but everything, down to the smallest detail, that had led up to it—and that was a goodly part of his life story. He explained every single bit of trouble he had had with the Holy Office, in Alcalá, Salamanca, Paris and Venice. Rarely, if ever, in the history of the papacy was a pope so well briefed about what to him must have seemed a very minor matter. And Paul, ordinarily not the most patient of men, listened and felt that here was more than a Mainardi.

What is more, he felt that Ignatius was telling all this in order to clear the decks for action. He wanted to have his arms free, unfettered by the calumnies and whisperings of his adversaries. And Paul, too, like all farseeing people confronted with Ignatius, knew that it was impossible to remain neutral. One had to be for him or against him.

He gave formal orders to Governor Conversini to go ahead with an official investigation.

And now the replies to the scores of letters Ignatius had sent out began coming in. The Governor's desk was inundated with letters of praise from bishops, vicars-general, priests, monks and laymen. The very extent of the inundation enabled him to stall still further. Until Cardinal Contarini sailed into his office and demanded progress . . .

And strangely enough, practically all the members of the

Holy Office, in front of whom Ignatius had had to prove his innocence before, happened to be present in Rome. Figueroa of Alcalá, Matthew Ori of Paris, Dr. Gaspar de'Dotti of Venice, to say nothing of Dr. Ortiz. All of them came forward, ready to give evidence.

Before such a formidable array of witnesses and material the Mainardists began to withdraw, reluctant step by step at first, then quicker and quicker.

When the official verdict of the Governor was published, declaring all rumors and accusations against the Iñiguists groundless and false, stating that their life, morals and teaching were deserving only of praise, and exhorting the faithful to consider Ignatius and his companions as good and learned priests, Mainardi hastily canceled his next sermon, and, after a while, left Rome and Italy. And the children streamed back to resume their catechism classes. The position of the Iñiguists had been securely established.

A few weeks after his victory Father Ignatius at long last celebrated his first Mass in the Chapel of the Manger in Santa Maria Maggiore. That was on Christmas Day.

*　　*　　*

The winter of 1538–39 was one of the worst ever known. People perished by the hundreds of cold and starvation. Many were found frozen to death in the open streets. The Iñiguists, pilgrims without pilgrimage, went to work on that problem.

They had left the haunted little house near Trinità dei Monti and were now living in a large, if ramshackle, building near the Torre Melangolo. It soon became a hospital and hostel for the poorest of the poor. They gave the poor their own beds, they begged for them and gave them comfort. Sometimes they had three hundred, four hundred wretches under their roof and each was treated with such love and respect as would be accorded to Christ himself. They fed another two thousand starving people. The community still numbered just ten men.

Ever since the Pope had mentioned that Rome was as

good a Jerusalem as any, a new idea had come into the minds of the ten men. It was the idea to form a new Order.

Salmerón's enthusiasm and love for Ignatius had made them call themselves the Iñiguists. But Iñigo had become Father Ignatius, and besides they knew that he had never liked the idea that the community should be called after him.

Many a time, on their wanderings they were asked who they were. And when it was no longer necessary to reply "students of Paris", they came to say, "We are companions of Jesus", or, "We have nothing to fear—we are in the company of Jesus."

The phrase had taken root in Father Ignatius' mind. Once, when they were talking about it, he said slowly, haltingly, "We are in the company of Jesus, to be sure. But we also are his company. His soldiers."

Francis' eyes sparkled. To him, the descendant of generations of soldiers, there was a clarion call in the words. He repeated, in Spanish: *"La compañia de Jesús".*

Ignatius smiled at him. Suddenly he knew that the name of the new Order had been found.

* * *

But not only the name of the new Order was a bold innovation. They planned for an Order without a choir—something hitherto unheard of. And beside the third vow—obedience—a fourth was to be included in their charter: that of "absolute obedience to the Holy Father" who could send any member of the Order wherever he wanted at a moment's notice. They did not discuss some of these points among themselves. As Ignatius suggested, they carefully abstained from influencing each other, "keeping their souls poised and in absolute dependence upon the divine will". Only in plenary session they debated and then decided, unanimously. One further revolutionary idea was accepted: the Order would have a head and that head was to hold office for life.

Condensed into five terse chapters, the Charter of the

68

Compañia de Jesús or, according to its Latin name, the Societas Jesu was submitted by Ignatius to Father Thomas Badia, Master of the Sacred Palace, a Dominican. Father Badia then submitted it to the Pope, and there was great joy at the ramshackle house at the Torre Melangolo when Cardinal Contarini told Ignatius that the document had been received with benevolent assent. Even so, they knew (at least Ignatius knew) that this was not final. Soon they heard that the first man, Ghinucci, who was requested to draw the necessary papal bull of approbation, had flatly declined to do so. The next was, of all people, Cardinal Guidiccioni, of whom it was known that he held no brief for any new religious Orders and even wished to reduce those already existing to four: Benedictines, Cistercians, Dominicans and Franciscans.

Of the ten men assembled at their frugal dinner, nine had clouded foreheads. They could not understand how it was that Ignatius remained serene and smiling. The very fact that the matter was in Cardinal Guidiccioni's hands could mean, was exceedingly likely to mean, the end of their plan, perhaps the end of their Order even before it came to life.

Later, Ignatius said to Laynez: "If everything I planned failed, all my wishes were thwarted and all my fighting were in vain—a quarter of an hour in prayer would reconcile me and leave me as cheerful as I was before."

*　　*　　*

The Order was not established, but the Order worked. The papal bull was not yet drawn up, but the Pope made full use of the new rule that every member of the Order was to be at his disposal, to be sent wherever he wished at a moment's notice.

Paul III sent Father Broët to Siena on special mission.

He sent Laynez and Favre to Parma.

He sent Bobadilla to Calabria.

He told Codure and Salmerón that their services would be needed in Ireland.

Only Francis Xavier and Rodríguez stayed with Ignatius at headquarters.

*   *   *

The Portuguese Ambassador in Rome opened a letter, just arrived by special courier.

> Dom Pedro Mascarenhas, my friend.
> I, the King.
> As you know, my principal purpose, as that of my father before me, God reward him, in the enterprise of India and the other conquests which I made and maintain with so much peril, toil and expense, has ever been the increase of our holy Catholic Faith. For this I have gladly borne everything, and it has been my constant preoccupation to secure for my dominions lettered and virtuous priests to exhort and instruct those newly converted to the Faith.
> This by God's grace I have been enabled to do so far, but now that the work is developing I feel it my bounden duty to obtain new workers. I was recently informed by Mestre Diego de Gouvea that certain clerics of good attainment and virtuous life had departed from Paris, after vowing themselves to the service of God, and that, living solely on the alms of the faithful, they went about preaching and doing a great deal of good.
> One of them wrote to the same Diego at Paris on November 23 last, saying that, if it should please the Holy Father, to whom they have vowed their services, they would go to India. I enclose a copy of the letter ... and commission you with all earnestness to inquire into the lives of these men, their learning, their habits, their aims, letting me know the result, so that I may be sure whether their purpose is to increase and profit the Faith by their prayers and example.
> As the sanction of the Holy Father is necessary in the case, you will petition him in my name to have the goodness to issue the order required.

Mestre Pedro de Mascarenhas sighed with relief. The main purpose of his business in Rome was to press the Pope for the recognition of the Inquisition which King João had set up all on his own, and in that purpose he had so far been singularly unsuccessful. In over a dozen audiences he had not got one step nearer to the fulfillment of his mission. It seemed as if the Pope had very little liking for any energetic measures against those who imperiled the Faith, although of course, it would never do to say as much.

In any case it was most welcome to receive a new order, and one a man with enough connections and some diligence could easily carry out. He had been too long in the diplomatic service of his master not to know that an ambassador's first and foremost duty to his sovereign was to be successful.

*　　*　　*

Ignatius had to send Rodríguez to Siena for a time, and he and Francis Xavier held the fort in Rome all by themselves, although supported by a few priests, some of whom hoped to belong to the community.

"Dukes, princes and towns have plagued the Holy Father for trained men", said Ignatius, "and now it is a king. If I had ten men for every single one I have, they would not suffice to fulfill all the tasks that must be done."

"And still no news from Cardinal Guidation", said Francis.

"Guidiccioni", corrected Ignatius mechanically.

He recalled Rodríguez from Siena and Bobadilla from Calabria.

Rodríguez was a Portuguese; King João had some sort of a claim on him for that reason. Father Paul, a young priest from Camerino was also willing to go. A cheerful soul, he would get on well with bubbling Bobadilla.

*　　*　　*

Bobadilla returned from Calabria pale, ill, desperately thin. He found Ignatius ill, too. Twenty hours of work and four hours sleep are not conducive to good health, and that went for both of them—except that Ignatius was also suffering, as so often before, from sharp pains in his side, and that Bobadilla had a severe attack of sciatica.

It was a hard time for Francis as well. With so many of the companions away, the duty of doing secretarial work fell on him. It would have been easier for him to walk a tight rope, and much easier to go in for athletic feats again, as in the old days. Father Ignatius' correspondence was growing by leaps and bounds, it was quite impossible for him to cope with everything himself. But under Francis' hand all names had the habit of being utterly transformed, and what was more, when he once fixed his own version on a man's name, he somehow never got away from it again. Thus the unfortunate Cardinal Guidiccioni remained for ever "Guidation", Dr. Ortiz was "Dr. Orcus" once and for all, and the energetic matron Fausta Jancolina who wished to give them a house, but attached half a hundred stipulations to her gift which made it practically impossible either to enter or leave it, was lucky to escape with the top-slice of her name cut off, as "our dear Ancolina".

But the obedience not yet vowed kept Francis to his post, although he dreamed night and day of India, and had been doing so for many months. Long before the impressive figure of Dom Pedro Mascarenhas had made its entrance, he told Laynez that he dreamed of having to carry an Indian on his back, who proved so heavy that he could not lift him. "Now what on earth makes you dream of an Indian?" Laynez wondered.

But modesty forbade Francis to mention how great was his desire to be shot like an arrow into the wild heart of Asia, and he had himself so thoroughly under control by now that he did not even bite his lips when Ignatius sent one companion after the other on special missions, keeping him at headquarters, as if—yes, as if he could not be entrusted with such work.

His heart leaped, when Mascarenhas, with the sanction of the Pope, demanded two companions for India, and yet he did not go to Ignatius to offer himself. And when Ignatius chose two other men, without so much as taking him into consideration, he said nothing. The two men had to be recalled from other missions—he was here. It was obvious that Ignatius did not wish to send him. And Ignatius had reasons, good and wise reasons, for everything he did.

Rodríguez was quite fit. And Bobadilla, God willing, would soon recover. He would be just the right man for the task, too, with his incredible energy and his firm belief, his most justified belief, in his own abilities.

After all, what was India? A faraway, dark country of pagans, speaking countless tongues and worshiping countless gods. There was no more merit in spreading the gospel there than anywhere else. As Ignatius said, Jerusalem and the Holy Land were wherever work was to be done for the greater glory of God, in Siena or Calabria, in Ireland or in Parma, in Lisbon or in India. Even at this old desk in this old room . . .

He told himself that many a time, but he never quite convinced himself. More than most of the others he had been disappointed when the pilgrimage to Jerusalem had to be given up.

And India . . . India meant a direct attack against the demon of paganism, it meant fighting in the front rank, instead of remaining here like—like a secretary.

It was different for Ignatius, of course. A general must stay at headquarters where he can see everything and give his orders accordingly.

Besides, Laynez had told Francis what had happened to Ignatius at the little chapel of La Storta, on the way to Rome. Laynez, the dry, the unemotional, could only speak of it in a whisper. "Father had a vision just as he was entering the chapel. Since then he knows: he will be favored in Rome."

Rome was where Ignatius belonged. And Rome was where Francis Xavier belonged, as long as Ignatius did not say otherwise.

And he did not. He did not.

*   *   *

A messenger in the livery of the Portuguese Ambassador came to see Ignatius—still ill in bed—and left a few minutes later.

Shortly afterwards Francis was summoned to the bedside.

73

"The Portuguese Ambassador can wait no longer", said Ignatius calmly. "He is leaving tomorrow. Rodríguez is going. But Bobadilla is unable to travel."

There was a pause.

"This is your enterprise", Ignatius said crisply. He spoke in Spanish.

"Right", said Francis, a little hoarsely. "I'm off."

"They will start from the embassy tomorrow morning at ten o'clock", Ignatius said. "You will ride, of course, so as not to impede their progress."

"Right", said Francis again. He was beaming now. He could not help it.

Back in his room, he packed. A few books. A set of spare linen. He remembered that his trousers were torn and there were a couple of holes in his cassock. He sat down and began to mend his clothes.

*   *   *

He woke up in the morning while it was still dark. He prayed. He washed, dressed and went to the community chapel to say his Mass. He had breakfast. Then he sat down and wrote three short letters. Secret letters. In the first he gave full assent to any decision made by the companions in his absence. In the second he gave his vote for Father Ignatius in the future election of a Superior for life. In the third he asked Father Laynez to make in his name the vows before the Superior elected.

Shortly before nine o'clock he went to see Father Ignatius to say goodbye.

He found him out of bed and just finished dressing. Ignatius put his arm round the younger man's shoulders and limped with him to the door. "Rodríguez left a quarter of an hour ago", he said.

It was a very beautiful morning.

"Who is going to do all those letters now?" Francis blurted out.

Ignatius smiled—without answering.

And suddenly Francis knew that he would never see this

74

man again, this incredible man whom he loved more than he had loved anybody else on earth; he knew that there was between them a very special love, beyond all the ties with the other companions, born of the air and soil and blood of their country, born out of the very hardships of the battle Ignatius had waged to win him over during all those long years in Paris.

And he knew that the gateway to heaven could look like a man and be a man, a small, frail, bald man, who was for Christ on earth what Saint Michael was for God in heaven.

"Go", said Ignatius. "Go and set all afire."

Book Three

THE TWO shabby cassocks in the magnificent audience hall of the royal palace caused a certain amount of sensation.

There was no court in the whole of Europe more magnificent than that of Portugal, then at the very height of its power and glory. Not even France could compete with its splendor. The spoils of all the world had been more or less peacefully divided between Portugal and Spain since the Borgia Pope, Alexander VI of terrible memory, drew with his pen the straight line that divided their spheres of influence. The wealth of four continents had contributed, and contributed lavishly, to the picture of magnificence in the royal audience hall, where Singhalese princes and Indian rajahs displayed their priceless jewels next to gold-glittering courtiers.

What, in comparison to all that, was the poor Emperor, Charles the Fifth? King of Spain he was, to be sure, but most of the time he was traveling over Europe, trying to settle the countless disputes of countries that were subject to him in name only.

"I am getting quite accustomed to it", whispered Rodríguez. "I know so many of them personally by now. Do you see the duke over there — in the black velvet dress? I am putting him through the Exercises. A wonderful man." He gave a short laugh. "Bobadilla would plume himself on knowing some of the people I know."

Francis did not reply. He had arrived only four days ago whereas Rodríguez, traveling a different way, had been here for weeks. Francis felt hot. Lisbon was stifling at this time of the year, much hotter than Rome, to say nothing of the fresh, cool breeze he had enjoyed on the way through his own homeland. He had not seen the old castle, where he was born, or the place where his mother and brother were buried—or the tomb of his holy sister, the Abbess. Dom Pedro Mascarenhas, a good man, but an impatient one, pressed forward. It was perhaps just as well. They were buried on earth, but living in heaven. It was better to travel towards the living. Besides, let old dreams be buried there, dreams whose fulfillment would have made him at best one more courtier like those crowding around him now.

Why was dear Simon Rodríguez—like brother Bobadilla—so proud of meeting dukes, when he met God himself every morning at Mass?

How hot it was! What was it going to be like in India?

Lisbon was a foretaste of what to expect, in more senses than one. He had seen hundreds and hundreds of black slaves, imported from African possessions. He knew that Portugal lost the flower of her sons to all those faraway countries of unlimited possibilities. Either they perished there, or they returned corrupted by the vices of the Orient or by the very power they had become accustomed to wield over peoples and races they did not even try to understand.

"Dom Pedro Mascarenhas, Ambassador-Extraordinary to the Holy See, and Fathers Rodríguez and Xavier to their Majesties' presence", called a master of ceremonies.

Stared at from all sides, they marched behind the Ambassador. He was walking like a dancer.

Their Majesties, King João and Queen Catherine, were large packages of brocade, silk and jewels, benevolent packages, speaking softly and gently. Despite Francis' scanty knowledge of Portuguese, he could understand them.

The King was delighted, quite delighted. He had heard so many good things about the Reverend Fathers. It was very necessary to have priests of such wisdom, learning and purity of life at court.

"You would oblige us by becoming *patres confessores* to our pages—there are just a hundred of them—and by taking over the supervision of their conduct."

Rodríguez beamed, but Francis said quietly, "Your Majesty intends us to go to India, I believe."

"Ah yes, yes, most certainly. Though it is a pity really, when your work is needed here so very urgently. But in any case, no ships are going at this season of the year—they would never arrive. The winds of those regions are very dangerous and permit sailing only at a certain time." The King was obviously proud of his nautical knowledge. "They always leave at the end of March", he added. "And meanwhile we feel sure that the Fathers wish to help us in our most pressing tasks. The youth of our country is particularly dear to us."

The end of March! That was almost nine months away.

The two men in the black cassocks bowed.

"Which reminds us", King João went on, "that we wish to have your blessings on our own children—the only two God has left us in his mercy." He gave a sign and in marched two more packages of brocade, silk and jewels, hiding a little girl of twelve, the Infanta María, and a tiny boy of three, called João like his father.

They received their blessings and a few kindly words and withdrew again.

"The Reverend Fathers will be lodged in the palace, of course", said the King.

Francis stepped forward. "If Your Majesty please," he said firmly, "we should go on living, as our rule demands: in the hospice of the poor, and begging for our daily bread."

Mascarenhas drew in his breath sharply. "One does not contradict the King", he murmured.

But the King smiled. "You will still permit us to send you food from the palace, I hope", he said.

Francis bowed. "The patients at the hospice will much appreciate Your Majesty's kindness."

*　　*　　*

When some time later the King told Rodríguez that he was going to give the learned Fathers of the new Order a college in Coimbra as well as residences in Lisbon and

Évora, Rodríguez, overjoyed, wrote to Ignatius in Rome. The soil here was fertile beyond all imagination, the King the most wonderful man, who did everything he could to make them stay and reform the whole country. They heard the court's confessions day and night, so many and so often that they had practically no time for preaching. There were many young men who were being taken through the Exercises, some of whom had already expressed the desire to join the Compañia.

Francis, too, wrote in rather the same vein, but giving a factual and detached report, carefully omitting anything that seemed to point to wishes or desires of his own. Rodríguez' letters, however, made it abundantly clear how much he preferred the idea of staying here to that of leaving for India, even if he did not explicitly say so.

Ignatius pondered over the matter. He knew that both his sons were perfectly sincere and truthful. He could see the enormous advantage of having at least one good man stationed in a country whose King was so much in favor of the Compañia.

He suggested a compromise. Rodríguez was to stay, and Francis, if it could be done without incurring the King's anger, was to go to India with Paul of Camerino.

Rodríguez, a born organizer, started at once to put the King's ideas into practice by enrolling suitable young men for the college in Coimbra.

*   *   *

Visiting various hospitals of the city, Francis encountered in no less than three of them a curious-looking man in a long, gray soutanelike garb. He was a large fellow with a fleshy, goodnatured face, a turned-up nose and a pair of childlike blue eyes. His hands and feet were enormous. It was difficult to say how old he was—twenty-six, thirty, perhaps even thirty-five. There was something bearlike in the way he went from one bed to the other, both in the awkwardness and the softness of his movements. He was nursing the patients, and it was incredible how gentle the thick, clumsy

80

fingers were. Whenever he approached a bed, he uttered a deep, grunting noise, just like a bear. The patients seemed to love him. There was something calming, comforting in his deep grunt, as if he were saying, "All right, all right, we'll look after you now, so stop worrying."

The third time Francis saw him, he walked over and spoke. "I am glad to see you working here, too, Father . . . "

The large man became purple with embarrassment. "I'm not a priest, Father", he said slowly.

"Brother, then . . . "

The purple deepened. "I'm not even a lay brother, Father. Just a man."

"But a man with a heart for sick people", said Francis.

"Best I can do", grunted the large man. "I—hmmmm— tried to be a priest—hmmmm. . . . "

"You did? Well?"

The large man shook his head slowly. "Too stupid", he declared. "It's the verbs. . . . "

"The verbs?"

"The irregular verbs. In Latin. The regular ones were difficult enough. But the irregular ones." He was still shaking his head. "They wouldn't have me", he added sadly. "I tried. Excuse me." He turned away, to an old man who needed fresh bandages for his ulcerous leg.

Francis watched him putting the bandage on. "Well done", he said, when the large man stepped back. "Was your Latin really so bad?"

The head-shaking started anew. "Very bad, good Father. I can say the Pater and the Ave, and the Gloria, and the Creed. But even in the Creed I mostly stumble over the Holy Ghost, Spiritum Sanctum, *dominem et vivicantum . . .* "

"*Dominum et vivificantem . . .*" corrected Francis.

"There you are, Father—*vificantem.* I knew I was wrong."

"Well, Latin isn't everything", said Francis gently. "What else can you do?"

The large man grinned sheepishly. "Nothing", he declared. "Nothing, except what man can do with his hands." He became embarrassed again. "The Fathers at college said God had forgotten to put a brain in my head", he confided. "Do you think that can be true, Father?"

"I don't think so", said Francis gravely. "I don't think God ever forgets anything—or anybody. But I think perhaps the Fathers forgot something: ordinary Christian charity."

"Oh no", protested the large man. "They said it was out of charity that they asked me to go away. I would only waste my time at the college, they said. I was only good at lifting heavy things, they said. So I went to the hospitals. A man can do a good deal of lifting in a hospital. I lift all the patients, before I do their beds."

"But why hospitals?" asked Francis. "Men make good money at the port, when the ships are coming in."

"Barrels", said the large man contemptuously. "Chests. Patients are people. I like people."

Francis smiled at him. "What is your name?"

"Mansilhas", said the large man. "Francis Mansilhas."

"My name is Francis, too. Francis Xavier."

"We have a very wonderful saint, we two", said Mansilhas, beaming all over his enormous face. "Saint Francis of Assisi—he could talk to the birds, they say. What a man! And to a wolf—he talked to a wolf, too. Fancy that!" Suddenly his face darkened. "Wish I could do him more honor", he muttered.

"I think he is very pleased with you", said Francis, turning away.

He inquired about the man. He really had tried to study for the priesthood, but was thrown out after a few weeks. He tried again at another college with the same result. Latin was his main obstacle, though not the only one. His teacher in philosophy gave him up after the second lesson. Mansilhas just sat and looked at him with large, oxlike eyes. Once he said, "Is it really so necessary to know all that? I'd rather try to learn by heart what Our Lord said."

When Francis met him again, he asked him pointblank whether he would be willing to come with him to India.

Mansilhas' eyes widened. "India", he said. "That's where those brown men come from, with bandages round their heads, and stones all over their dresses, isn't it?"

"Yes, but there are others who have no stones at all, poor people like those here in hospital. And they are heathens. I'm going there to bring them Our Lord. Will you help me?"

"I think Saint Francis would like that," said Mansilhas frowning deeply. "But what can I do? I have no brain. Or none to speak of."

"I'll try to teach you a little more", said Francis. "If you listen carefully and put your heart in it, maybe we can make you a priest after all, in a few years."

Mansilhas' eyes began to shine. "That would be a miracle", he exclaimed, overjoyed. "Like talking to the birds."

*   *   *

At the beginning of March Francis was introduced to the new Governor of Goa, who was sailing on board the same ship to take over his office.

Dom Martim Affonso de Sousa was a bluff, hearty man, with twenty years' experience in colonial service. "Been to India before, of course", he said. "Brazil, too. That's real life, Father; life in the raw. Anybody can sit in Lisbon and squash the shape out of a velvet cushion. Mind you, a voyage like ours is not like sitting in a monastery and teaching the boys the catechism—though the boys on board could do with a bit of catechism, too. Glad if you can provide it. Very welcome."

Francis said he did not expect it to be a time of recreation.

"Ever been on board a sailing vessel before?" asked the Governor. "No? Well, you're in for a few nasty surprises, Father. Ours is a big ship—almost five hundred tons the *Santiago* has—but even so. Remember that everybody must bring his own food—*and* see to it that it is not stolen from him. And most food goes bad in the heat round the equator. Bread gets green and full of weevils. Often think the devil must have made weevils—can't imagine God making the blasted things, forgive me, Father. Must learn to be careful about my language. His Majesty is very emphatic about it. Mustn't be tolerated on board, either. There also we count on your help. You a Benedictine?"

Francis explained that his was a new Order and that the main purpose of his mission was to propagate the Faith.

The Governor nodded. "Excellent. Excellent. There is an island South of India, called Ceylon. You'll find no Moslems or Jews there, only heathens, and the King is a reasonable man, they say. You'll have a rich harvest there. On second thought, don't bother about your food. I'll provide it myself, for you and your companions. You'll eat at my table. Anybody told you what to take with you, clothing and other stuff?"

Francis told him that the King had asked him to see one of the great men of his court about that, a Conde de Castanheira.

"Good. He should know. Very refined gentleman, the Conde. Travels in great style—when he travels. I'll see more of you in the near future, Father. . . . "

He could not have been kinder, thought Francis. It was lucky, too, that the Governor had been in India before. From him he could get invaluable advice about how to tackle his problems. It was a matter that made him lie sleepless at night. He knew all kinds of Christians, in all stages of sinfulness. But what if these heathens thought quite differently, felt quite differently? What approach was to be taken? He had written to his Father Ignatius about it, but had received no answer. It was really not right, to put the burden on Father Ignatius; after all, he had met only Moslems, not heathens. It was good that now he had found a man—and a man in such a responsible position and with so many years of experience—of whom he could ask questions to his heart's content.

He did not know that Dom Martim Affonso de Sousa,

like most Portuguese, had met Indians only in two positions: attacking him in arms, till he killed them; and standing before him with their backs bowed, till he gave them what orders he chose to give.

Francis' visit to the noble Conde de Castanheira took a very different course.

Castanheira's functions were those of the major-domo of the King. He was a man of supreme elegance, exquisitely dressed and perfumed and his manner of speaking had the peculiar affectation used by the elegant set at court.

"Delighted to help you", he fluted, "quite delighted, Reverend Father. His Majesty the King has written to me on your behalf—here is the letter. I will read it to you. 'Conde, my friend . . .'—His Majesty is indeed too kind and condescending, to address me like this, and I would never dare to tell it to anybody, but in this case I must read his letter just as it is, must I not?—'Conde, my friend, as you are aware, Mestre Francisco and Micer Paulo, clerics of the Order of Saint Peter'—a new Order, I take it, Father?"

"Ours is a new Order." Francis nodded, not quite knowing whether he should correct the royal error or not. He decided not to. After all, the King could not be expected to know the name of an Order not yet formally established.

"Ah, wonderful", exclaimed the Conde. "Very well then: ' . . . clerics of the order of Saint Peter, are going this year to India. I strongly commend them to you, and request you to issue orders concerning their embarkation and hospitable reception aboard ship. See that each of them is given two suits of clothes, one for the voyage and one for use in India. Let them have such books as they request and need, and also give instructions for the provision of medicines and everything else requisite for the journey.' You see, His Majesty has thought of practically everything."

"His Majesty is most kind", said Francis and meant it.

"You have a good *moço de camara,* I trust?" asked the Conde.

"The one who suits me best", replied Francis, smiling. "Myself."

The Conde smiled too, but it was clear that he was not pleased. "Surely you must have a personal servant in a decent livery", he said. His tone was that of a mother, trying to persuade her son to use knife and fork instead of his fingers. "I shall see to it myself", he added.

"For the love of God", begged Francis, "spare me such an encumbrance, Senhor Conde."

The elegant man threw up his hands. "A lackey an encumbrance!" he ejaculated. "Why, he is a necessity. But if that is how you feel, I will not—eh—encumber you. You will have an ordinary servant, then."

"I will have no servant at all", Francis said firmly.

The Conde pushed back his chair. "My dear Father, this is quite impossible. Perhaps you do not realize how we feel in this country about such things. You cannot possibly do all the menial work necessary on such a voyage. It would greatly diminish your credit and authority with the other passengers."

"But . . ."

"Passengers, whom it will be your duty to instruct! I shudder to think what they must feel when they see you washing your clothes at the side of the ship or preparing your own meals. After all, you are a priest, not a cook or a tramp."

Francis seemed to grow inches taller. "Senhor Conde," he said hotly, "it is credit and authority of the kind you suggest which have reduced the Church of God and her prelates to their present plight. The right way to acquire them is by washing one's own clout and boiling one's own pot, without being beholden to anybody, and at the same time busying oneself in the service of souls."

The Conde de Castanheira had not received such a rebuke since his childhood. He gasped for breath.

Before he recovered, Francis had bowed himself politely out of the room.

Back in the streets with their honest, vulgar smells of onions, garlic, wine and sweat, Francis' indignation vanished

and he grinned contentedly. It was just as well that he had
not mentioned the letter in the right pocket of his shabby,
patched cassock—not to the noble Conde of Castanheira
and not to good King João—though perhaps the King
knew about it. One could never be quite sure about what
kings knew.

The letter, on very stiff parchment, had arrived that
day from Rome, together with a few lines from Father
Ignatius.

To be quite exact, it was not an ordinary letter. It was
a bull, a papal bull, nominating Father Francis Xavier
"Apostolic Nuncio to the islands of the Red Sea, the Persian
Gulf, and the Indian Ocean, as well as to the provinces and
places of India this side the Ganges and the promontory
called the Cape of Good Hope, and beyond." There was
also a personal letter from the Pope to "the princes and
rulers".

*   *   *

Dr. Cosmas de Saraiva was a little drunk when he came on
board the *Santiago* and fairly drunk when the ship sailed
majestically down the Tagus.

"It's the best way to paralyze seasickness", he explained to
Father Xavier. "I can only advise you to follow my example."

Francis looked at the big, black-bearded man with distaste.
He said nothing.

The Doctor grinned. "Never been at sea before, I suppose?"

"No."

"I thought so", the Doctor went on grinning. "I give
you a couple of days—no, let's say a week. Then you'll
come and ask for my advice. More likely, you'll send for
me. It isn't alcohol that makes legs unsteady at sea, Father."

Francis pressed his lips together. This was an entirely new
world, a world by itself. A little island, floating, overpopu-
lated—and only by males, as far as he could see. "There are
no women on board, it seems", he said casually.

"You ought to be grateful for that, Father", The Doctor
grinned. "If there were, you'd have to hear confessions all

around the clock. It's bad enough as it is, I should think. We never carry women on these ships, and that suits everybody: the government, the crew and the passengers. The crew is glad to get away from their wives. The passengers to India are all in search of riches and a man who is still searching for riches cannot expect the senhoritas to give him their favors. And the government does not believe in married men going to India. Let them marry over there—if they feel like it. Some do. Many. Politics, Father. Disseminating Portuguese blood. It's getting a bit mixed up in the process, but that can scarcely be avoided, can it now?"

Francis knitted his brows. He was not quite sure whether this physician was trying to shock him or whether he was just too drunk to care what he said.

"I've heard of you", said the Doctor. "You're going to sit at the captain's table, with the Governor and his retinue. Met our new Governor yet, Father?"

"Yes."

"A lucky man. Did himself very well in Brazil, five years ago. And now Viceroy of Goa. Means about half a million pieces of gold, on the average. Ah yes. Fabulously wealthy country, India. Prize plum. You sell posts, jobs, titles, everything. You collect taxes. No questions are asked at home about how much you collected as long as you deliver a large enough sum. Well, de Sousa knows his business. The only trouble is how to get it all home safely. Now the *Santiago* is as good a ship as any—this is my third voyage on her. And she carries the Viceroy. But the sea is no respecter of persons. . . . "

"The sea, too, is a servant of God", said Francis quietly.

The Doctor shrugged his shoulders. "A strange servant", he said. "Moody—greedy—unreliable . . . "

"No worse than we are", said Francis.

"You don't know her yet, Father. I've known men so bad they would kill their own mothers for a piece of silver—a drink. But I never met anything as cruel as the sea. And she in turn makes men cruel. . . . " He gave a short laugh. "I'd better stop, or you'll think I want to frighten you with my stories."

"But I am not frightened", Francis said, smiling.

Again the Doctor laughed. "Well, remember what I said. In a few days you'll be at your wits' end. Then you'll come to me. They all do. Good day, Father."

He marched off on somewhat stiff legs, but quite steadily.

Francis took a deep breath. The air seemed fresher now that this drunkard no longer befouled it with his breath.

All around him spread the glory of a wonderful April day. That, too, was a present from God, was a divine courtesy. He was allowed to set out to India on the same day of the month on which he had drawn his first breath, thirty-five years ago. He had been angry when the ship's departure, scheduled for the last week of March, was delayed, presumably on account of a storm raging in the Viscaya. He was angry then, because the last words of Father Ignatius were burning in him: "Go and set all afire." He would have liked to be shot into India from a giant bow. But God did everything in his own good time and now the *Santiago* was sailing on Francis' birthday.

He looked at the hundreds of men standing around on deck, a disorderly mass of soldiers, sailors, merchants and officials, adventurers and servants, with many a jailbird among them. This, for many months to come, was his flock, almost seven hundred souls, given into his care. It was a beginning.

Slowly the big ship made its way downstream, its shrouds painting lazy shadows on the deck. From the array of ships moored right and left came thin, raucous cheering. The galleons, galleasses and galleys, the carracks, caravels and cromsters, the hoys, sloops, zabias, canters and coasters greeted their big sister, leaving for the voyage of voyages to the land of gold and slaves, of precious stones and almond-eyed women. To the land where countless millions knew nothing of the birth and death and resurrection of the Lord.

The fort at the mouth of the Tagus fired a gun.

The good luck gun they called it. A thin wisp of bluish smoke drifted across the harbor mouth, hiding the mighty tower of Belém, monastery, church and all.

There was a commotion among the crowd. As if on command, a circle had formed around two men. Above the shouts and the laughter Francis heard the clatter of steel. He sailed into the circle with such vehemence that everybody recoiled.

Two stalwart fellows were slashing away at each other with knives a foot long.

Francis stepped between them, gripping their armed fists, and they stared at him in a dull rage, their eyes bloodshot and dangerously glittering.

"What is your name?" he asked one of them. His tone was gentle, but his grip was very firm.

"Oliveira, Father", gasped the man.

"And yours?"

"Ortao—at your service, Father."

"And you're on your way to India. What for?"

Oliveira grinned sheepishly. "Why, Father, to make my fortune there, if I can."

A grunt from Ortao's tooth-gaped mouth seemed to indicate that this went for him, too.

"And the best way to achieve your purpose", said Francis, still holding them both in a tight grip, "is to cut each other's throat on the first day out, is it?"

"But, Father, he said I was a . . . "

"Never mind what he said. Why did he say it?"

"Because he pushed me", cried Ortao angrily. "He deliberately pushed me so that I almost fell overboard, and . . . "

"I didn't, I . . . "

"Be still", said Francis, doubling the strength of his hold, from which the two men were straining to get free in order to fly at each other's throats again. "If you go on showing so little reason, you'll be too stupid to make your fortune, even if you walk over diamonds and rubies. And that which is against reason, is mostly not only stupid, but also a sin

90

against God. Now, make it up with each other. Shake hands—shake hands, I say! That's better. And come with me, both of you, and I'll hear your confessions."

He released them and stepped briskly towards the poop deck, less crowded than the other parts of the ship. They followed him slowly. He seemed to take for granted that they would, not even bothering to turn his head.

Dr. Cosmas de Saraiva watched the whole performance from afar, a half-filled goblet in his hand and an amused smile on his lips.

*　　*　　*

"Strange table manners, by my faith", grunted Senhor Diogo Pereira. "I don't know whether Your Excellency noticed it, but I just saw that friar, or whatever he is, making off with most of his dinner wrapped in a napkin."

The Viceroy laughed indulgently. "You must not mind him, Senhor Pereira. He's done the same thing at the King's own banquet, I was told."

"Has he made a vow to eat alone?"

"No, he's uncommonly fond of the rabble on the forecastle. Feeds them whenever he has an opportunity—and as you see, he is adept at seizing an opportunity. He's a good man."

Pereira emptied his goblet and wiped his mustaches. "All the same, I regret that Your Excellency has no better ecclesiastic company on this voyage. Why, the good Father scarcely speaks at all, and as for his two companions—that Father Paul of Camerino is not much better and the fellow who reminds me a little of the animal elephas, *he* isn't even a priest, as he admitted when I asked him."

Dom Martim Affonso de Sousa gave the merchant a quizzical look. "I'm sorry that the company at my table is not to your liking, Senhor Pereira."

The merchant's neck above his enormous ruff became as red as the wattles of a turkey. "There is no greater honor than to sit at the table of the Viceroy", he said hastily. "But surely such a table should be graced by spiritual advisers higher than a couple of monks or friars. There was some rumor that the Apostolic Nuncio himself would travel on board of the *Santiago.* . . . "

"Father Francis Xavier", said the Viceroy, "*is* the Papal Nuncio." He enjoyed the sensation his words created all around the table.

"If that is so", remarked Pereira, when the exclamations of surprise had calmed down, "then the Holy Father must once more be in dire straits. He cannot even afford to equip his Nuncio properly, or give him a retinue worthy of his rank. It is sad to see things come to such a state."

Dom Martim caressed his beard, carefully adorned with little seed pearls. "I'm not sure", he said. "You may be right, Senhor Pereira, but I'm not sure. Incidentally, you will all oblige me by not making any use of the intelligence I just gave you. His Majesty was good enough to tell me about it, but it looks as if Father Francis prefers to be Father Francis, at least for the duration of this voyage."

"I understand, I understand . . . " Senhor Pereira nodded emphatically. "The Papal Nuncio is traveling incognito, like the Caliph Harun al Rashid of old."

"For shame, Senhor Pereira. Would you compare a good man of God with an infidel—even if it is the Caliph of the infidels?" The Viceroy emptied his goblet.

"*Mea culpa*", bowed the merchant. "I should not have said that, certainly."

"Incognito", said the Viceroy slowly. "There at least you've found the right word. Incognito. A man comes to my station in life only if he knows something about men— their strength, their weaknesses, their whole makeup. And I don't mind telling you, friends, there is something about this new Nuncio that I do not understand at all. No, I beg of you, don't ask me what it is. If I knew, I'd also know the answer."

*   *   *

"One, two, three—four—" counted Mansilhas, poking holes into the air with his enormous finger. "But where is the fifth?"

"What are you doing?" asked Francis.

"Why, I'm counting our ships, and one has been lost. There were five of us, when we set out, weren't there? Now there are only four. One—two—three—four."

"You've forgotten our own ship", said Francis. His smile was a little weary.

Mansilhas opened his mouth. "So I have", he said, bewildered. "Thank God. Then the ships are all safe after all."

Francis pressed a well-filled napkin into the man's huge hands. "Take that to the old man with the broken leg. Tell him I shall get him some wine, too. Where is Father Paul?"

"Still hearing confessions, Father."

"Right. Run along, then."

Mansilhas stalked off. He still did not know the Credo well enough to recite it without a few mistakes and a good deal of hemming and hawing. But the voyage had only just started.

Francis glanced at the sinking sun. Time for evening prayer.

He walked towards the poop deck, passing a number of open fires surrounded by little circles of men, cooking their dinner. They were late. Probably they were the weaker ones who had been made to wait till the others had finished. Better let them have their meal first.

He climbed up the ladder to the poop deck. The sails of the four ships behind the *Santiago* seemed to blossom forth from the ocean like strange marine flowers, white, yellow and golden under the touch of the dying sun. Five ships— that was all Portugal sent out during a whole year, and often enough only two or three arrived at their destination. It was good to see them, though. Without them, the *Santiago* would have been a lonely little world in that immensity of blue and gray that was the ocean.

He shook off the thought.

For a while he prayed silently and alone, to give the poor fellows around their fires a chance to finish their meal. Then he raised his arm and made a sweeping sign of the Cross.

His voice rang out: *"In nomine Patris et Filii et Spiritus Sancti...."*

Ten, twenty, fifty heads turned in his direction and as many hands made the sign of the Cross, passengers and crew alike, as Francis began to recite the Lorettine litany that closed the day on every ship of the Royal Indian fleet.

"Lord have mercy ... "

"Lord have mercy ... " responded the men.

"Christ have mercy ... "

"Christ have mercy ... "

They turned towards him or they drew closer, from the forecastle, the quarterdeck, the second, third and fourth deck, their hands folded, their faces upturned.

"Holy Mary ... "

"Pray for us."

"Holy Mother of God ... "

"Pray for us."

"Holy Virgin of virgins ... "

"Pray for us."

Merchants and officials, adventurers and jailbirds, officers in brocade doublets, with starched ruffs, sailors with golden rings dangling from one ear, the gentlemen of the Viceroy's retinue, their hands folded over the cross of their swords, the Viceroy himself, a lonely figure in black velvet at the door of his cabin.

"Mother most pure ... "

"Pray for us."

"Mother most chaste ... "

"Pray for us."

Many of them would rarely if ever show mercy to an enemy. Many of them were not pure and not chaste. But at least they knew they were not. At least they knew that they themselves were in need of mercy, the first step toward recognizing the need of others. At least they knew that they all had a spiritual mother in heaven. They loved her and praised her.

"Mother of good counsel ... "

"Pray for us."

The whole ship was praying. The invocations seemed to fill her sails, to be the very power that made her move across the endless blue, a living ornament on the Madonna's blue cloak.

*   *   *

The blue cloak had vanished. Instead, the ship danced dizzily across a landscape of mountains gone mad, mountains rising and sinking, mountains of a sinister, foam-tipped gray.

The other four ships had vanished. But there was no need for the *Capitana,* the Admiral's ship, to fire a warning shot as she did when one of the ships strayed behind. There was no danger now of a bold corsair of the Barbary Coast turning up to attack a straggler. Even if a corsair had been near he could not possibly board in this sea, and just to fire at him would have been a waste of good ammunition.

Francis was ill, and so were Father Paul and Mansilhas, whom a howling gust of wind had thrown down a ladder. He was indignant about it. "I'm not sure whether it's right for a man to travel across the sea in a ship", he moaned, patting his bruised head. "If God wanted us to, he would have made the sea nice and solid like the earth." Father Paul wanted to remind him that there were such things as earthquakes, but did not have the strength to do so. Crawling on all fours, Francis was able to provide a jug of fresh water for them, only to find that they were unable to drink it. Through the porthole he saw the endless procession of crazy mountains pass by, dancing and swirling, changing suddenly into valleys full of glittering foam and then erupting into dizzy heights again. The whole of creation seemed to have gone mad. The ship, another Ark, was lifted up to heaven and cast down into hell three times, before one could say one Our Father. It shuddered like a human being, its stout timbers creaking and crackling under the impact of the sea's attacks. The bulkhead beside Francis rose to become the ceiling and sank to become the floor. The bunk under him gave way and then stopped his fall by rising under him with such force that all the bones in his body began to ache. There was no rhythm, no symmetry, no order of any kind in these hellish movements, and breathing itself was drawn into the maelstrom, cut in two and all but suppressed.

Not only those new at sea, but old mariners as well were convinced that the end was in sight. Curses and prayers alternated, accompanied by the screams of those who were wounded by falling spars and cases and barrels that had torn loose from their lashings.

Inch by inch Francis crawled to the help of a man whose legs had been mashed by the fall of a huge crate. When at last he reached him, he saw that the man's skull had also been hit and that he was beyond help. His face was waxen, his breath stertorous—quite a young man, one of the many who were going East in search of riches. He recovered consciousness for a few moments, long enough to ask for and receive absolution. It was impossible to give him the Viaticum or to apply the blessed oils of the last sacrament. With demoniacal force the gale prevented it, howling in dismal triumph.

Cries for confession went up from all parts of the ship and Francis crawled from one man to the other. Twice again he had to close a man's eyes forever.

The storm raged on during the night, and for the next twelve days and nights. Fires were not allowed inside the ship and on deck it was impossible to kindle them. Thus even those who were in a mood to eat, could not cook a meal, but subsisted on salted fish, ship's biscuits and water.

A falling barrel hit and killed one da Silva only three paces away from where Father Paul and Mansilhas were huddled together. The man, a notorious drunkard, died instantly. They prayed over him and Mansilhas, despite his illness, undertook the shrouding of the body. "It was a barrel of Canary wine that killed him", he said to Francis. "He told me he had been warned many a time that the wine would kill him sooner or later. He joked about it. Now God has joked back at him."

Francis opened his mouth for a sharp answer and then said nothing. From the lips of any other man such a saying would have been well-nigh blasphemous. But Mansilhas was quite incapable of blaspheming.

A few times he saw the ship's physician giving medical aid to the sick. Dr. de Saraiva seemed to be little affected by the terrible rolling of the ship, although he too had to crawl on all fours to get from one patient to the other. Perhaps he was drunk again. It was impossible to tell, for the movement of the ship made it almost impossible to stand upright. There were only two things the Doctor seemed to prescribe: a purge or a bleeding, but either one was carried out very thoroughly.

On the afternoon of the thirteenth day the storm abated.

But as all wood on board was soaked, it was still not possible to kindle a fire, and by now both crew and passengers were ravenous. Fights broke out all over the ship and several times the Viceroy's own bodyguard—a dozen men, armed to the teeth—had to interfere with swords and halberds.

When the first bits of wood were sufficiently dry, the stronger passengers fought their way to cooked food like enraged tigers and one almost killed Francis, when he calmly walked up and took some of the cooked food to carry to those of his sick who needed it most.

The captain had the man put in irons, but Francis begged till he was freed again, "under the condition that he accepted whatever penance the good father chose to give him". Francis made him abstain from cooked food for a week and carry it to the sick instead.

It was discovered that five men had used the general confusion during the storm to steal the valuables of other passengers. The captain set up a court, listened to the evidence and condemned every one of the five to a hundred lashes. In vain Francis begged for mercy. The captain was adamant. "A ship without discipline is lost, Father, and it's up to me to see that there is discipline. I must beg of you never to ask for such a thing again on this voyage."

Four of the wretched men survived the ordeal. The fifth died in the night, with Francis at his side. A few days after that the Royal Indian fleet entered the Region of Death.

*   *   *

The Region of Death was the name given by the great explorer Vasco da Gama to the coast of Guinea.

"You are now learning", said Dr. Cosmas de Saraiva, "that the sea can be more deadly when she is calm, than when she rages like a thousand whipped demons."

Francis did not answer. He went on mixing the medicines and ointments for the eighty-odd patients on board. Both he and Mansilhas—always astonishingly clever with his enormous fingers—helped the physician, who could no longer cope with the work alone. He knew that de Saraiva was right, although scarcely more than a week had elapsed since they had entered the dreaded region.

There was no wind. The sails hung lifelessly, without the slightest movement. The ships seemed to be anchored in the middle of the sea.

The whole world stood still. To walk up and down seemed like breaking the laws of nature. The Region of Death demanded immovability and it had ways and means of enforcing its demand.

Always the same portion of the ship was exposed to the sun—and what a sun! It burned the skin, it scorched the throat, it wore blood red circles before a man's eyes. It made people delirious, like the two brothers Gómez deep down in the hold now, where the heat was stifling, too, but of a different kind. Everybody demanded water, but the captain had the precious liquid rationed. It was precious beyond price, although it had become tepid and tasted brackish.

Food was beginning to spoil. There were weevils in the bread, maggots in the meat.

"We shall soon have the first cases of scurvy", said Dr. de Saraiva placidly. "Are your teeth getting loose yet, Father?"

Francis went on mixing medicines. After a while he asked, "How long does this last, Doctor?"

"Don't ask me", said the black-bearded man. "And for heaven's sake don't ask the captain. God alone knows."

* * *

Another week passed and another and still another. Each day Francis felt that another like it could not possibly follow. The *Santiago* had become a ghost ship.

The ocean, bluish, leaden, was the wraith of an ocean.

The only things that moved were the little animals in bread and meat—and in the drinking water. Even so, the men could hardly wait for their next ration, and when it came, they fought for the yellow, brackish stuff. It was the elixir of life. It was more desirable than all the gold of Cathay. One goblet full every four hours from sunrise to sunset. Nothing at night. Many a strong young fellow snatched away the goblet from the lips of an older and weaker man.

A dozen times within the last weeks Francis had seen it happen and had taken the goblet away from the robber. Only twice did he have to use force—what force was left in his own limbs, which was not much. His own ration he usually shared with somebody who had been cheated out of his portion in some other part of the ship.

"You can't go on doing that", warned de Saraiva when he saw it happen for the second time. "Not if you want to arrive in India alive." There was an undertone of grudging admiration in the doctor's rough voice.

He was right, as Francis found out when things went black and began to spin all around him. He woke up in the Doctor's cabin. A burning pain in his back made him wince.

"That's nothing", de Saraiva reassured him. "I've had to bleed you a little. May have to do it again in a few days. Got a big gobletful out of you, Father. Feeling better?"

He felt better. But three days later de Saraiva had to bleed him again.

"He's put the leeches on me three times so far", declared Mansilhas sulkily. "I think he drinks the stuff. Does a man get drunk from drinking blood?"

And still there was no wind. The Region of Death held the *Santiago* in a strangle hold. Slowly, slowly, the heat was sucking the life out of them all. They were lethargic now, sitting around in dull silence. Only when the water came, they woke up to a short galvanized kind of life, groaning and gasping and fighting each other.

It became more and more difficult to share one's ration with anybody. One had to do it quickly and one must never let oneself think, "Another four hours before there is water again."

The Our Father and the Ave became confused in one's mind, the letters of the Office jumped about as if they too tried to snatch a drop of water for themselves.

Day before yesterday five people died. Yesterday eight. Today?

They could not pray the Lorettine litany in the evening. Words would no longer come from the parched throats.

Francis nodded to them, to the many emaciated, patchy, desperate faces with the unnaturally gleaming, sunken eyes. "Don't worry", he said hoarsely. "God knows how you feel. I will say it for all of you."

There were always a few who still tried to croak or whisper the responses and he stretched out his arms in compassion for them.

Again and again he went to the citadel, as he called the quarterdeck with the captain's cabin and the three cabins of the Viceroy and his retinue—always in order to beg for something he needed for some wretch whose life hung on a thread. Mostly he begged for wine, made them sacrifice a quarter of a goblet each, poured the liquid into a jug and hid it under his cassock, till he had reached the man who needed it.

Even in the citadel the mood was very grim, although these gentlemen had taken ample provisions with them to safeguard them against shortages of any kind, and although they had awnings erected to protect their cabins from the sun. Down on the lower decks men often enough fought for place in a patch of shade and two, who had not been able to get such a place for several days, went mad and jumped overboard, where the sharks caught them before anything could be done to save them.

"They are all around us", said Mansilhas, shuddering. "I've seen them. There are so many, I couldn't count them. Looks as if they expect us all to end like these."

That was last Tuesday — or was it Wednesday? No, Tuesday, the day when de Saraiva had had to bleed both Mansilhas and Francis again.

Francis stopped a duel between two gentlemen of the Viceroy's retinue. When he questioned them, neither of the two remembered how the quarrel had started — but each felt that he had been mortally offended by the other. "Just imagine that you would have to appear before Our Lord with such a silly story", he told them, shaking his head.

It became impossible to remain below deck at all. One might as well have stayed in a red-hot oven. Butter melted to oil, tallow candles melted to oil, the very pitch and tar of the decks melted and the ship began to show tears and splits in all parts above the waterline.

Then came the rain.

When the passengers first saw the cloud gathering on the horizon, they began to cheer weakly. Salvation was coming at last. But the faces of the crew remained grim.

The rain came. It was warm, almost hot. It drenched the whole ship in the course of a single minute. And after that single minute it stopped.

In the evening there was a second burst, lasting about ten minutes.

The next morning de Saraiva was busier than ever. About half of the people on board had swellings under their armpits and in their groins. "No, it's not the plague, thank

God", he told Francis, who had seen similar cases in the hospitals of Venice and Rome. "But it's painful enough. Even the rain here is rotten with disease."

Four horribly hot days followed and cost the lives of fifteen people. Then the force of the Region of Death succumbed to the onslaught of huge, billowing black clouds that seemed to appear from nowhere. A low, metallic sound like that of a very high trumpet came across the water and ripples showed where oily stillness had reigned for forty consecutive days and nights. The ripples began to swell up to the size of hillocks, then to hills.

The sails of the *Santiago* began to fill, became taut.

"We're moving", gasped Mansilhas.

"Thank God", groaned Father Paul of Camerino. "I knew I couldn't have stood it one single day longer."

Dr. de Saraiva grinned at them. "It's not a question of what you could stand or not stand", he said grimly. "The heat has loosened up the ship. What matters is whether *she* can stand what is coming now. Pray to God that she does or the sharks will get us all."

*   *   *

The ship stood it. A thousand times in the weeks to come it looked as if she could not possibly do so, but she did.

The crew had to work feverishly to repair the damage the Region of Death had done in a hundred different places.

Now that the ship was moving again, the heat was no longer quite so oppressive, but the food and water did not improve. A dreadful depression hung over the passengers like an invisible cloak. It did not matter any longer to them whether they arrived or not. Many withdrew into the dark belly of the ship as if they wanted to go back to the womb of their mother, to the time when no courage had been demanded and everything had been provided. It was among these that mortality was especially high. They offered little or no resistance to the many diseases caused by spoiled food and scummy water.

Francis joined them, whispering comfort, cleaning and

bandaging ulcers, performing every kind of menial task and praying over them when they were dying despite his efforts and de Saraiva's purges and bleedings.

Then storm set in again. Its brutal force hit them and knocked them about so terribly that it dwarfed all their personal ailings and welded them together to one suffering body. Bleeding gums, ulcers, long worms in the drinking water, lice, boils and even the hopeless, all-embracing depression—all that vanished from their consciousness before the stark danger of death. It was as if a demon made sport of them, trying to show them how much they still cared in the root of their souls for sweet life itself.

Waves of a height they had never seen before crashed down over the ship, hiding it under cascades of foam.

"This is the test", said de Saraiva, bleeding Francis for the sixth time. "Maybe we'll get out of it and maybe not. You won't—unless you become a little more sensible and stop behaving as if you were the father and mother of every single man on board."

"That", said Francis weakly, "is exactly what a priest is." Then he fainted.

De Saraiva swore blasphemously. "I wish I really knew something about the art of healing", he shouted, as Mansilhas crawled into his cabin. "I don't and no physician does. We're all hopeless bunglers, God knows. But I wish I really knew something, if only to restore this man to health, this idiot, this damned saint, blast it all. He's too good to rot on board this blasted ship. Do you hear me?"

"No", Mansilhas said stolidly. "Because if I did, I would have to tell you off for swearing. As for Father Francis, you don't need to cure him."

"Oh, I don't, eh? Why not?"

"He'll get well."

"Oh, really? How would *you* know?"

"Because God needs him here", said Mansilhas and he began gently to massage Francis' arms and shoulders.

*   *   *

When the storm abated, a small army of scarecrows came up from the ship's belly, carrying with them all kinds of things, bedding, books, clothes, baskets, personal effects of all sorts, to dry them in the sun. There was not a single corner in the ship where water had not leaked. An hour after the sun became visible again the decks of the *Santiago* looked like a junk sale with no one buying or selling.

The sea was still high, but there was a new rhythm about its movements and the ship no longer rolled and pitched, but was riding the waves.

"We've got through the worst, I think", said de Saraiva gruffly. "But you haven't, Father, unless you take it easy for a few weeks. We're sailing round the Cape now."

"How do you know?" asked Francis.

The Doctor grinned. "See that old fellow there, with the leathery skin? That's Marquez, the second steersman."

"The one who is just changing his shirt?"

"Exactly. Hi, Marquez!"

"Yes, Senhor Doctor."

"Changing your shirt, eh?"

The old sailor gave a quizzical look to the shirt he had taken from his back—a gray rag, stiff with dirt. "Yes, Senhor Doctor", he replied gravely. "I always change my shirt, when we're rounding the Cape."

"You see?" said de Saraiva to Francis. "That is how I knew."

In the evening they saw the Southern Cross for the first time, no longer veiled by the clouds of storm.

Mansilhas was delighted. "I didn't know that God has a pectoral cross, too", he said. "And it's much more beautiful than that of the Benedictine Abbot who chucked me out of the seminary."

*   *   *

At long last the five ships were together again and on board of each there was jubilation when it became clear that the others had also escaped.

There was one last chain of dangers to be met: the straits

of Mozambique. There were opposing currents; there were hidden reefs. The lead would tell fifty fathoms at one moment and fifteen the next. The wind changed constantly, often as much as twenty, thirty times in one night. The crew were exhausted by furling and unfurling the sails. The captain could not leave the bridge for a single moment.

And by now food had become scarce and what little was left was almost uneatable. Beans in oil alternated with bread in oil. The last of the meat had to be thrown away and Mansilhas declared if only there were more of it, it would cleanse the ocean of all sharks.

There was a last storm on the Feast of the Assumption.

But Francis preached, as he had preached every Sunday.

"No one is going to turn up and listen this time", muttered Father Paul of Camerino. "Not in this weather."

"They'll turn up", said Mansilhas confidently. "This is Our Lady's day." After a while he added, "If they wouldn't turn up, the fishes would come up and listen."

They did turn up, they huddled together, hundreds of scarecrows, wet and hungry, and they listened.

It was as if Francis were speaking to each one of them individually, and what he said, what he preached, was joy.

They forgot the whistling of the wind, the rolling of the ship, the downpour of the rain. Men with their teeth loose in their gums, men racked with fever, men with broken legs and arms sat there, smiling with radiant eyes.

"How is it that his voice carries so effortlessly in all the noise of this storm?" murmured Father Paul.

"How is it that Saint Francis of Assisi could talk to the birds?" said Mansilhas happily.

*   *   *

Three days later they saw land.

"Don't expect a tropical paradise", warned Dr. de Saraiva. "Or you will be bitterly disappointed. Mozambique is a tiny coral island with a pestilential climate, just the right thing to kill off those who are between life and death now. No wonder we're using it as penal colony."

"There'll be work to be done", said Francis.

"But not by you", said de Saraiva. "You are to take it easy for some time. Man, do I have no authority at all? It is almost a miracle that you can walk. You're as weak as a kitten. Don't you want to get to India alive?"

"If it's necessary, you can always bleed me again", said Francis cheerfully. "I'm getting quite accustomed to it."

"No work for the next six or seven days at least", insisted the Doctor. "After that we shall see. There will be plenty of time for you, Father. We won't get off that confounded island that quickly, don't you worry."

"How long do you think we shall have to stay there?"

The Doctor snorted. "We're late. We set out late and we've taken more time than usual, thanks to those . . . to those storms. We shall have to wait for the April monsoons to carry us off."

April—and three days ago it had been the fifteenth of August.

*   *   *

The Doctor was right; Francis did not feel well at all. But there was no question of resting six or seven days, not with all the ships spewing their poor, ill, dying people out on land. The hospital of Mozambique was overcrowded within a few hours after the arrival of the Indian fleet.

When Mansilhas tried to remind him of what de Saraiva had said, Francis replied, his eyes blazing: "If Our Blessed Lord were here, wounded, dying once more—would you have me stay in bed and look after my own health?"

"N-no, Father, but . . . "

"Our Lord is in the suffering of every one of these."

He caught the fever from one of the patients in the hospital, but he would not lie down. One of the men from the *Santiago* saw him falter and almost fall with weakness.

"You can't go on like this, Father", he said kindly. "You're ill yourself. It's you who needs nursing, more perhaps than most of these."

Francis passed a weary hand over his burning forehead.

"There's just one more job to be done", he said hoarsely. "A little business with a poor fellow who is at death's door and not quite right in the mind at times. When I've finished with him, I'll sit back a little. Don't worry on my account, Mestre João." He chuckled quite happily.

But Mestre João did worry. He came back to the hospital the next day and went to Father Francis' cell. It had two occupants. One was a sailor from the *Santiago* and he was lying on Father Francis' bed, an ingenious construction of leather thongs with a straw-filled pillow and a bit of old cloth for a coverlet. Up against the bed was a piece of wood, taken from a gun carriage and on this Francis himself lay, in an eager conversation with the sailor who seemed to have recovered his senses. Neither of the two took any notice of Mestre João. They were much too engrossed in their subject to be aware of his presence. The subject was God's readiness to forgive.

Mestre João slipped away quietly.

When he came back to the hospital the next day again, de Saraiva told him that Francis was ill.

"As if I didn't know", exclaimed Mestre João. "He was ill yesterday and the day before. . . . "

"Certainly", replied the Doctor grimly. "But this time I put my foot down. He wouldn't even use his bed any more. . . . "

"I know. He gave it to a sailor. . . . "

"That fellow died yesterday night—not before Father Francis heard his confession and gave him the Viaticum, of course. I knew that man. Used to scoff at—well, many things. The Father got him round. He'd get the devil himself round, if he had the ghost of a chance. But it's taken the wind out of him. Fell in a dead faint. So I had him carried over to my own lodgings and by all the saints and all the devils, there he is going to stay, till he is well again."

* * *

For a while it looked extremely doubtful whether he was going to get well again.

Both Father Paul and Mansilhas went to the Doctor's lodgings several times a day to inquire about him and each time the Doctor shrugged his shoulders and would not promise anything—except that he would send a messenger, if things took a decisive turn for the worse.

From behind the thin bamboo wall they could hear Francis' voice at times, babbling incoherent words.

Once they both went into his room. "It won't harm him and it won't do him any good", snapped the Doctor. "He's in a state of delirium."

"Bad", said Francis. "Easy for you, Magdalena—you don't have to eat it. Never mind, never mind, I'll get along."

"You see?" said de Saraiva. "You can talk, if you wish. He won't hear you. He's not conscious."

"I don't understand why God permits this to happen", said Father Paul in a low voice.

Francis sat up. "Are you trying to sit in judgment over what God should permit and what not?" he asked sharply. "Come now, you should know better than that."

They saw that his eyes were firmly closed. The next moment he was on his back again, muttering. " 'Set all afire—set all afire.' "

"He's been like that for two days and two nights", said de Saraiva. "If only I could get some ice. What an island this is! I dare not bleed him any more, he's lost too much blood as it is."

"The Moors are quite hopeless, I can do nothing with them, Magdalena", Francis said plaintively. "Let the others come in, if you wish, all of them."

"Poor Father Francis", murmured Mansilhas, tears overflowing his eyes.

"There is no reason to have compassion for me because I am poor", said Francis quite clearly. "Our Lord has blessed the poor." Then he began to mutter again. "Mustn't forget old mischief . . . mustn't forget old mischief. . . . "

"That's what he used to call an old sailor on board ship",

explained Mansilhas. "His name was Misopoulos. A Greek. He died two days before we arrived."

De Saraiva shook his head. "I can't make him out. He's not conscious, you know. Definitely not conscious. He's talking nonsense. But each time he says something about God or things of God, he's as lucid as ever."

"With most people", said Mansilhas, "it's the other way round."

"And some are never lucid at all", said the Doctor rudely.

* * *

Two days later Francis was out of danger. Another three days and he wanted to resume his activities. The Doctor fumed. When all his persuasion came to nothing, he declared Francis to be his prisoner, locked him in his room and took the key with him when he went to inspect the hospital.

For one day he succeeded. On the morning of the second day Francis cut a hole through the wall and escaped. He went straight to the hospital. De Saraiva raged when he discovered him there, but he was intelligent enough to see that work seemed to give Francis strength rather than to tire him.

The amount of work to be done, now that the whole Indian fleet was at anchor in Mozambique was such that over three months went by before Francis found time to send a report to Father Ignatius.

* * *

There was considerably less for His Portuguese Majesty's new Viceroy, Dom Martim Affonso de Sousa to do. In fact the necessity of having to spend the whole of eight months on that godforsaken island of Mozambique was in his opinion about the worst thing that could have happened to him. Eight months wasted, eight months in which he could have reorganized the entire colony of Goa, to say nothing of the money lost by the delay. Life on Mozambique could not have been more boring. There was the "governor"—it was ridiculous for the captain of a hundred men to insist on that title, but Dom Alonso was just the kind of man who would insist on it. His "palace" was not much better than a chicken coop, but it was the best house on the island and one would think that he might offer it to the Viceroy, now that unforeseen circumstances had stranded him here. Not that de Sousa would have accepted the offer—but the damned fellow should have *made* it.

As it was, de Sousa went on lodging in his suite on the *Santiago,* till, after a few weeks, his sailors had built a house for him and his retinue. There was no sport. There were no pretty women—well, almost none. As long as he was in a small place like this, where everybody knew everything about everybody else, he had to use a certain amount of discretion. The younger officers of course used no discretion at all, and that included Dom Alvaro d'Ataide da Gama, God rot his impudent soul, the youngest brother of the new Viceroy's predecessor, Dom Estevam da Gama, of whom everybody knew that he had spent the whole time of his administration robbing people right and left and who now had eight months prolongation of his rule on top of it.

A bamboo hut, instead of a palace in Goa. No women—well, practically no women. No news from home, of course, and no news from India either.

His Excellency the Apostolic Nuncio, of course, had a rare good time nursing the sick, teaching children the catechism, preaching in church and altogether working himself to death. It was almost enviable. Almost . . . But he was quite a man, this strangest of all apostolic nuncios, quite a man. The kind of man one would like to have on one's side, when things went wrong. Of course, what figure he was going to cut in Goa . . . but that was his affair. In the meantime it was best to help him in whatever way one could, when he came with another of his thousand and one needs—a dozen more beds for the hospital, medicines, wine, food, the permission to build a school for the half-caste children swarming all over the island. Where did they all come from, these children? The "governor"—ridiculous title—only had a hundred men under him.

Well, His Excellency Father Francis had the chance to

make a model colony out of Mozambique and he certainly seemed to be taking it.

For His Excellency the Viceroy there remained only drinking, dicing and the swapping of stories, all quite delectable activities, but not if there were no others—well, practically no others—in the course of eight months.

Such was the situation and such was Dom Martim Affonso de Sousa's mood, when he received the report that a ship was approaching the island.

A ship—now? In February? Two months before the southwest monsoon started? And not a coaster, not a felucca, but a full-rigged ship.

He ordered a general alarm. It was unlikely, extremely unlikely that it was a Turkish corsair, although these devils were practically omnipresent—and if it were, he would think twice before trying to attack five well-armed ships of the Royal Indian fleet, even if they were lying at anchor. But the Viceroy was not going to take any chances.

On four of the five ships the guns were run out and ammunition stacked on the decks. It was senseless to do the same on the *Santiago*—she was lying too far inside the port. Her guns could not be trained on an incoming ship from any angle.

After a while word came from the *San Pedro* that the incoming ship was of Portuguese build, and shortly afterwards that it was the *Coulam*.

This was far more interesting than a brush with a Turkish corsair gone berserk. The *Coulam* was a merchantman and a small one at that. She had been stationed in Goa. What had brought her here at this time of the year?

*   *   *

The *Coulam* was not able to enter port, not with five large ships filling it beyond capacity. She was anchoring outside. There was a good deal of maneuvering.

Dom Martim Affonso de Sousa was waiting for the report of the *Coulam's* captain, who by now was bound to know that the Viceroy was here, if indeed he had not known that when he left Goa.

A good hour after the *Coulam's* arrival a boat showed up, rowed by two natives of Mozambique. Its passenger was a gentleman in elegant clothes who gesticulated violently and from time to time looked back as if he were a fugitive and expected his pursuers to turn up at any moment.

"Take the man on board and let him come in here", snapped Dom Martim.

A few minutes later the stranger was bowing and scraping and obviously extremely relieved. His name, he said, was Dom Suárez de Mello. Yes, the *Coulam* came from Goa. Her captain was Luiz Méndez de Vasconcellos. No, he did not *know* why the captain had not yet come to render his respects to the Viceroy, but he had his ideas about it and could he speak to His Excellency alone?

Dom Martim gave the man a sharp look. Not the type to use a dagger or a pistol, unless he had made sure that he would escape unhurt after using it. Did not seem to be armed at all. And Dom Martim had his sword and a couple of pistols within reach. He nodded.

"Your Excellency," said Dom Suárez, as soon as the door had closed behind the last man of the Viceroy's retinue, "I have come to render you the greatest service any man has ever rendered you."

"A very promising start", Dom Martim said skeptically. "Pray go on."

"The ex-Viceroy of Goa is—not exactly my friend", said Suárez de Mello. "Nor could he be—for he is the enemy of every honest man in Goa and his actions are such that he is in the gravest possible danger of being arrested on his return to Lisbon—if not before."

"Grave accusations", said Dom Martim, in a carefully casual voice. "Such things can happen—but it is usually extremely difficult to have proof of them."

"There is a conspiracy against you, Your Excellency", Suárez went on, quite imperturbed by the Viceroy's skepticism. "Things are to be hushed up before you can reach Goa. Everyone knows that you will not be able to leave here before the southwest monsoon, so there is time—time to do many things, and especially to get the most dangerous witnesses out of the way. Once that is done, Dom Estevam da Gama hopes that no one will dare to pursue the matter and he trusts that the name of his late father will protect him against what then will seem to be unproven accusations."

"Dom Vasco da Gama was a great man and a great Portuguese", said the Viceroy attentively. "Unfortunately the sons of great fathers do not always follow their example. But the proof I referred to . . . "

"The proof", said Suárez de Mello firmly, "is in a number of letters written in Dom Estevam da Gama's own hand to his younger brother, Dom Alvaro d'Ataide da Gama, now a passenger on board of one of your ships, Your Excellency. That I know. And the reason why the captain of the *Coulam* has not yet rendered his respects to Your Excellency may be that he first wishes to deliver those letters safely into the hands of the man to whom they are addressed, Dom Alvaro d'Ataide. This I do not *know*—but I think it is so."

The Viceroy's hands twitched. He had great difficulty in hiding his excitement. "Dom Suárez, if you're lying to me . . . "

The elegant gentleman smiled. "Ships have yardarms," he said, "and there are always many ropes on board. I happen to be rather fond of my neck; it is the only one I have."

The name of Suárez de Mello was not unknown to Dom Martim. It was the name of an unscrupulous, wealthy man.

"Captain Luiz Méndez de Vasconcellos is—in this—conspiracy, Dom Suárez?"

"Yes, Your Excellency. He has received five thousand pieces of gold for the delivery of the letters."

"You are extremely well informed, Dom Suárez. . . . "

The man smiled. "I would hardly dare to come to Your Excellency with such a story, if I had not made sure of my facts first", he said, with a flashing smile.

"If I find this confirmed, your reward will be very handsome", said the Viceroy.

Dom Suárez smiled again. "I'm not asking for anything", he said. "All I want is to keep the privileges to which my firm is entitled and which Dom Estevam wishes to rob me of."

"You will not be robbed of anything, Dom Suárez", said the Viceroy. Then he bellowed for his aides.

They rushed in so quickly that it was obvious that they, too, had thought of the possibility of a physical attack against their master.

"Dom Marcello," said the Viceroy, "I want you to take thirty men and board the *Coulam*. You will arrest the captain—Dom Luiz Méndez de Vasconcellos—and take temporary command of the ship. Dom Luiz is to be brought here, if necessary by force. I want his cabin searched very thoroughly. Every scrap of paper you find, you will seal up and bring to me. In no circumstances is the *Coulam* to be permitted to leave port."

Dom Suárez cleared his throat. "Dom Luiz may no longer be on board," he said. "He may have . . . "

"I'm aware of the possibilities, Dom Suárez. Dom Henrique, you will go to the *San Pedro*. My compliments to the captain and he is to permit any arrest or other legal act you are to perform on board of his ship. He is to give you a guard of ten men. You will arrest Dom Alvaro d'Ataide de Gama. You will search his cabin and collect every scrap of paper you find there, seal it up and bring it to me. If you should find Captain Dom Luiz Méndez de Vasconcellos of the *Coulam* on board the *San Pedro*, you will arrest him also and bring him here. No explanations of any kind will be given to the prisoners, except that you are acting on my orders. Off with you both, gentlemen."

*   *   *

"They've been kept in solitary confinement for three days", said de Saraiva out of the corner of his mouth. "And it is said that the Viceroy has been sitting up in his cabin day after day, studying a mountain of papers, conferring with his aides and with Pereiva—remember him, richest merchant on the *Santiago* — and falling from one fit of rage into another. They're all going on tiptoes on board the *Santiago*."

"But what is it all about?" asked Francis, shaking his head.

De Saraiva laughed. "The dirtiest business on earth, Father — politics. Every new Governor wants to make a big success out of his time in office, and one of the most important things is to prove how badly his predecessor has done. If he then leaves his office with the country in a so-so state, he will always be able to point out how very much worse it was when he took over. That's elementary."

"Dom Martim has been exceedingly kind to me in every way, and he never struck me as being the kind of man you describe now, Doctor. I cannot imagine . . . "

"No, I suppose you can't", de Saraiva said kindly. "You are probably the last person who could imagine it. But that's how it is, take my word for it. Incidentally, there is very little doubt that Dom Estevam was not, shall we say, overscrupulous? What I don't understand is how the business could leak out. You see, it seems that Dom Estevam has written a letter or a number of letters to his younger brother, and the Viceroy intercepted them. So somebody must have told him about it. Now that by itself wouldn't be so surprising, there is always somebody who will play the Judas. But that it's happened so quickly, that is the surprising thing. The *Coulam* had only just arrived and in the wink of an eye both d'Ataide and Vasconcellos were arrested."

"How glad I am that I'm not an official", said Francis with a sigh. "What about the case in room number eight? Is he better today?"

"He is. Rather surprising. You gave him the Viaticum yesterday, didn't you?"

"Yes. They often get better after that."

The Doctor rubbed his chin. "I wonder . . . "

"What about?"

The Doctor looked embarrassed. "It sounds quite mad,

Father, but I sometimes wonder whether there isn't some sort of—of interplay between mind and body. When you have shriven a poor fellow and he knows he's safe, even if he dies—it makes him feel more confident, doesn't it? He gets fresh courage. He doesn't feel as if all is lost. On the contrary. Now if that feeling could somehow give fresh strength to his body to resist the illness—oh, well, it's probably all nonsense. Hola—whom do we have here?"

An aide of the Viceroy entered, gaily dressed, with his sword clanking at his side. It was a most unusual sight at the hospital.

"Father Francis," he said, bowing respectfully, "His Excellency the Viceroy requests your presence on board the *Coulam.*"

"The *Coulam?*" asked Francis, astonished. "You mean the *Santiago,* surely."

"No, Father, the *Coulam.* And His Excellency asks you to take your things with you, too. The *Coulam* will sail for India this afternoon."

* * *

"What is the meaning of all this?" asked Dom Alvaro d'Ataide furiously. "Why has Your Excellency given orders to arrest me? Why have my belongings been tampered with? Why have I been brought on board this ship?"

The Viceroy remained seated. He gave the excited man a cold stare. "You ought to be very grateful, Dom Alvaro. I am only trying to make up for the time we lost in Lisbon, when we sailed on April the seventh instead of on the Feast of the Annunciation. Thirteen days' difference may not be much, but it easily becomes much more, if one has the misfortune to miss the trade winds. I have decided to risk the voyage on the *Coulam,* instead of waiting for the monsoon. This will reunite you with your noble brother much earlier than you could hope for otherwise. You do not appear to be grateful. Why not, I wonder? Could it be that our delay suited you? Could it be, by any chance, that it suited your brother, too?"

Dom Alvaro d'Ataide turned white as a sheet. "I do not understand your riddles, Dom Martim. And I demand an explanation for this unworthy and humiliating procedure."

"You do not know Senhor Pereira, perhaps", said the Viceroy, beckoning the merchant to his side. "He is a man of much experience with our trade to the East Indies. He has ships of his own and factories of his own. He has been very helpful to me these last days, when I tried to figure out the riddles, as you so aptly put it, Dom Alvaro. Now it seems that our delay in Lisbon was due less to a storm in the Viscaya, as I was made to believe then, than to the machinations of certain gentlemen in Lisbon who seemed very anxious that the fleet should wait for a number of goods they were shipping out East. Goods, by the way, which never arrived. But it seems that some persons connected with the port authorities were paid extremely well—and not by the government, Dom Alvaro—for services rendered: the services consisted in spreading the news that there was a violent storm blowing in the Viscaya and in warning the fleet not to leave port before it had abated. The port authorities, of course, believed the story of the goods. They thought it was really a matter of some anxious merchants, trying to get valuable goods ready in time and needing a few more days. At least, so it seems. Of course, when the matter is raised in court, we may find out more. In any case I have reason to believe, Dom Alvaro, that you know a good deal about this affair."

"I have no idea what Your Excellency is talking about", declared d'Ataide.

"You haven't? Let me refresh your memory, then. The firm who was so keen on getting their goods belatedly on board and who then did not deliver them, although they succeeded in delaying the Royal Indian fleet by thirteen days—and by now by many months—is that of Ambrosio Valdez."

"I don't know them", said d'Ataide contemptuously.

"No? How did it happen, then, that Senhor Pereira saw

you together with the senior partner of the firm three days before you left?"

"I have not met Senhor Pereira before", said d'Ataide, "although I have heard his name and I know that he has amassed some wealth, probably by questionable methods. I also know that he started his career as a valet of Gonzáles Coutinho, and it surprises me that his word should be taken in evidence against a da Gama. Doubtless my brother Dom Estevam will have something to say about that."

"Ah, but your noble brother has already said a few things about it", said the Viceroy with a grim smile.

"I saw him. . . . I swear I saw him. . . . " spluttered Pereira, sweating profusely. He looked as if he were going to have an apoplectic stroke any moment.

The Viceroy gave him a gracious nod. "Thank you, Senhora Pereira. You have rendered me and your country a service and I shall not forget it."

"Nor will I", said d'Ataide darkly.

An aide announced the arrival of Father Francis.

"Ask him to come in", said the Viceroy after a short moment of hesitation.

Entering, Francis found a small, grave-faced assembly in the Viceroy's cabin. Pereira and d'Ataide were the only civilians among them. The Viceroy rose. "Gentlemen, the time has come to inform you officially that Father Francis Xavier is the Apostolic Nuncio to the Indies and entitled to be addressed as Excellency."

There was a ripple of surprise. Not all those present had known the secret. Francis frowned.

"You must forgive me for this disclosure", said the Viceroy courteously. "But the matter we are dealing with here is very serious and I welcome the opportunity of your presence in your official capacity. A chair for His Excellency, Marcello."

But Francis preferred to remain standing.

"Very well then", said the Viceroy. "I told you, Dom Alvaro, that your noble brother has already said a few things about the case. I did not express myself well. He did not say anything. He wrote. He wrote two letters—addressed to you."

"Where are these letters?" asked Dom Alvaro sharply.

"In my possession", replied the Viceroy coolly.

"You . . . you dared to intercept them? Read them?"

"I certainly did. May I remind you, Dom Alvaro, that I am here as the representative of His Majesty the King both in matters of military and civilian authority? I had reason to believe that these letters contained treason. . . . "

D'Ataide opened his mouth—then did not say anything. He shrugged his shoulders.

"What do you know, Dom Alvaro, about the sum of five thousand cruzados found in the possession of Captain Luiz Méndez de Vasconcellos?"

"I know nothing about it. How could I? I have never met the man before in my life. But perhaps Senhor Pereira has seen me with *him* also—in a dream, maybe."

"Surely it is an unusually high sum for the captain of a small merchantman", pursued the Viceroy, imperturbably.

"Large or small, it has nothing to do with me", replied d'Ataide sullenly.

"Hasn't it? But perhaps it has something to do with your noble brother. I shall have to question Dom Estevam about that as soon as we arrive. About that and about many other things. In the meantime you will remain in your cabin, Dom Alvaro—under guard. So will Captain Luiz Méndez Vasconcellos. Can't have you two making up a story together."

The Viceroy turned to Francis. "For your information, Father—Your Excellency, I should say—this is not a trial. Not yet. It is a—first examination, no more than that. But already I know that there has been a conspiracy. I am glad to have you here at my side, as a witness that the matter is being investigated. The delay of our departure from Lisbon was not due to the weather—it was due to this conspiracy. I cannot at present show you the letters of Dom Estevam da

Gama to his brother here, but all that will come out in the open when we arrive in Goa . . . at least two months before we are expected there. Marcello! the prisoner Dom Alvaro d'Ataide is to be taken to his cabin. Put a sentinel before the door, day and night, same as with Vasconcellos. Captain Vargas will take over the *Coulam.* Now leave me alone with Father Francis."

"Upstarts and criminals!" d'Ataide cried, his eyes flashing. "The King will hear of this, and . . . "

"Take him away, Marcello", interrupted the Viceroy, "before he forgets himself so far as to insult the Apostolic Nuncio as well."

D'Ataide looked from one face to the other. "I won't forget any one of you", he said. "You may rely on that—I swear it by the wounds of Christ."

"Whether you are receiving justice or injustice", said Francis, "do not invoke Our Lord when you are thinking of vengeance."

By then they had dragged the struggling man to the door. Once more he turned back, his face distorted with rage.

"You're all in this", he gasped. "Every one of you. I will remember. I will remember. . . . "

Then the door closed behind him.

"I am sorry that you had to witness such a lamentable scene", said the Viceroy suavely. "But I did want you to see that he was being interrogated without undue pressure. It is a sad affair, Your Excellency. Apparently my predecessor, Dom Estevam da Gama, played a very clever trick on us, to keep us out of India—and to keep himself in power considerably beyond the end of his term of office. It is clear that he has a bad conscience. The letters to his brother contain a whole chain of innuendos—they are almost in code. He must have thought of the possibility that they might fall into my hands."

"May I visit the prisoners?" asked Francis.

The Viceroy thought it over. "They may wish to confess

to you", he said. "And that would make it impossible for you to give evidence in court, if that should be required. However, as you are the only priest on board, I cannot forbid it."

"The only priest on board! Then my two companions . . . "

"They cannot come with us. There is not enough room in this ship. They will have to follow later, on the *Santiago.* It's only a difference of a few months. I would have gladly left you together, but, frankly, I would not feel happy without having you on board. The *Santiago* has had only forty-odd dead on this voyage so far. The other ships had double that number and one almost treble. Our journey will be dangerous, as you can see from the fact that I do not wish to risk it with the entire royal fleet. It's good to have you with us. And if we should run into a Turkish felucca, there must be somebody to look after us and give us the last blessings, before those infidel dogs finish us off. We're practically unarmed, you know. We can't afford to take the direct route. We must sneak along the coast to Malindi and from there to Socotra. With a bit of luck and with your prayers we'll make it. Is it agreed?"

He would have to bid farewell to Father Paul, of course, and to Mansilhas. He must tell Father Paul to go on where he had left off with Mansilhas' theological lessons. Not that it would help much, but it had to be done. And de Saraiva—he must say goodbye to him. The patients in the hospital—there were four who were in danger now, he must tell Father Paul all about them. Old Morao had to be spoken to with firmness, he was the kind of man who never did anything unless he was pushed into it, he *wanted* to be pushed into it, but that was as far as his willpower would go. He would miss de Saraiva. And Mansilhas. And Father Paul, of course.

Francis nodded. "It is agreed, Your Excellency."

* * *

A cross. A gigantic, golden cross was the first thing he saw in the light of the early morning, when the *Coulam* approached the port.

Profoundly moved, he prayed in a crystal clear silence, as the palms of Malindi drew nearer. The world was enchanted. Beyond the wings of the gulls, circling and recircling the ship, the angels of God, archetypal birds, were flying in glorious arcs. Earth, marked by the "fool-ishness" of the Cross, could not be lost, was attuned to high heaven.

"Old Vasco put it there", said a voice beside him.

He finished his prayer. The man beside him was Marcello, the right-hand man, the henchman of the Viceroy, a tall, bullnecked man with only one eye. He had lost the other in Brazil, they said. An Indian arrow, fortunately not a poison-ous one.

"Vasco da Gama", repeated Francis. Slowly he came back to the voyage—to hearing d'Ataide's and Vasconcellos' confession—and Vasconcellos' sudden death. A stroke, said the ship's physician, a foxy little man, shifty, with a curi-ously plaintive, high-pitched voice.

"I wish he could be as proud of his sons as of the other deeds of his life", said Marcello. "None of *them* is worth much. But old Vasco—he always planted a cross like this wherever he had been. It is our cross, the Portuguese cross. Where you find it, is Portugal; even when the natives do not know it. They know it here, though. Their little king has sworn eternal friendship with us. He'd better! We could blow his old walls to smithereens with a couple of nine-pounders."

"Are the people here Christians?"

"Faith, no, Father—Your Excellency, I should have said. They're Moslems—infidels."

"Moors", said Francis and his mouth hardened a little, as every Spaniard's mouth did, when he pronounced that fateful word. The German crusaders, the Italians, the French and the Dutch—none of them would ever grasp what that word meant to a Spaniard. Seven hundred years of Moorish occupation. For seven hundred years the raucous cry of the muezzin went up five times a day to assemble the people for prayer to a god who through his prophet Mohammed commanded them to spread his law by fire and sword. Part of Mohammed's teaching was that killing a Christian was a deed particularly pleasing to God, and assured a place in paradise for the killer. For seven hundred years women (whose status Mary, the Mother of God, had raised from that of a chattel to a position commanding respect and reverence), were kept in abject subjection, were taught that they had no souls and that all they were good for was to give birth to sons. The spirit of a softer race would have gone to pieces under the yoke of such conquerors as these. The Spanish spirit had hardened. It would take another seven hundred years to soften it again.

"I shall go ashore, for the burial of Captain Luiz Méndez de Vasconcellos", said Francis stiffly.

Marcello nodded. "There's a good cemetery just outside the town. A few hundred of our merchants live here—till they assemble there. I shall give you an escort of thirty men. Not that the Moors would try to harm you. They're peaceful enough. People usually are, when they have had a visit from old Vasco. But it makes a better impression. Our merchants like us to keep up their prestige. Helps them to drive a harder bargain, I suppose. Merchants will be merchants. The Moors would do the same, if they could. We'll land in half an hour. I shall see to it that all is ready. On second thought—I'll come with you myself."

The gulls, circling and recircling the ship, uttered short, sharp cries, greedy for the remnants of food flung over the side.

*　　*　　*

Captain Luiz Méndez de Vasconcellos had been buried. Father Francis, in surplice and stole, had said the requiem Mass.

All around the cemetery, hundreds of men in flowing white burnouses were watching, and when Francis left, one of their number stepped forward, an old man with a straggly white beard.

"I know that fellow", whispered Marcello. "He's Ali ben Mottaleb and the one following him is an imam, a priest among the infidels."

The old man stared at them out of rheumy eyes. "Peace be with you", he greeted. "Will the *khassis* permit an old man to ask him a few questions?" He did not wait for an answer, but burst into a torrent of lamentations. Allah was his witness that things were bad, very bad. He was an old man but he had never thought to live to see such a state of affairs. Seventeen mosques there were in Malindi, but no more than three of them had worshipers and these were few in number. He could not understand it. How could it be? Why was there such a hardening of the hearts, such negligence and indifference? Surely it must be because of some great sin they had committed. . . .

"The sin that was committed", Francis said sternly, "is that God's revelation brought to us by Our Lord Jesus Christ was not accepted by you."

"Isa ben Marryam", said the old man, "is to us a prophet—a great prophet—though not as great as Mohammed."

"There is your sin, old man", said Francis, "and the sin of you all, Moors and Saracens, Turks and Arabs. You are not like the poor heathen who have never heard of Our Lord and thus have had no chance to accept him in their hearts. You heard and you rejected him, you give a mere man preference over him. No wonder then, that God does not abide with you and takes no pleasure in your prayers."

The old man shook his head. "Allah is merciful", he murmured, "it cannot be that."

The imam, dark-faced, his beard dyed with henna, threw up his arms. "Mohammed has promised to send us the paraclete, the Mahdi", he cried. "Year after year we waited for him to appear. He never did. And behold, our community is dwindling. How can we remain faithful, if the Prophet himself does not keep faith with us?"

Old Ali ben Mottaleb seemed shaken by the outburst of the priest of his own religion. There was a brief, but almost violent exchange of words between them in Arabic. The imam shook his head and fell back into Portuguese. "No, no—it was a firm promise and it was never kept. If the Mahdi does not appear to us within two years, we may as well give up believing. Allah will not test anybody beyond his strength and endurance."

"God has revealed what he wishes you to believe", declared Francis. "And Our Lord has said: He that is not for me is against me."

"We must go back to the ship, Father", muttered Marcello. "They'll go on debating like this for days and weeks. No good wasting your time on them. And His Excellency is waiting for us. Please, come."

It was not easy for Francis to tear himself away, but he remembered that the Viceroy was in a hurry.

The two Moslems salaamed to the departing procession and remained silent till the Christians were out of earshot.

"He had the eyes of a prophet", wailed old Ali ben Mottaleb. "Surely he could have given us a word of encouragement and comfort. Last Friday twelve people were with me in the Mosque of Omar. Twelve people! This Nazarene should have been more gentle. But that is how they are. It is always everything or nothing with them."

The imam gave a bitter laugh. "How right he is and how wrong you are, O Ali ben Mottaleb!"

"Allah!" The old man stared at him, aghast. "You, a Moslem can say such a thing?"

"I can say it, because it is the truth. When we were children, O Ali ben Mottaleb, we learned that two and two is four. Not seven. Not one. Not even four and a half. Just four. And when the teacher asked us how much two and two made and we gave any other answer but the answer four, he would punish us, because we were wrong. Now if this is right and true in an everyday matter, how much more so must it be so in the things of Allah? Either we are right and the Nazarenes are wrong, or the Nazarenes are right and we are wrong. Of course, we may both be wrong. But one thing is certain: we cannot both be right! It is not possible that at the same time Mohammed is greater than Isa ben Marryam and Isa ben Marryam greater than Mohammed."

"That is true, but . . . "

"And it so happens that that Nazarene believes he is right, O Ali ben Mottaleb! So he must declare us to be wrong. It is true that his eyes are those of a prophet—because his soul speaks through them with conviction. He feels sure that he has got the true answer. So how can he make any concession? By the beard of the Prophet, it is impossible! Don't you see what is wrong with us? It is that we no longer have real faith. If we had, we would not ask him questions. We would try to win him over to Mohammed and kill him if he resisted our attempt."

*   *   *

Four weeks later the *Coulam* landed at the island of Socotra, at the mouth of the Red Sea.

As Francis was going ashore, Marcello gave the Viceroy a quizzical look. "I think I know what's coming now", he said.

"What do you mean?"

"He'll want to stay here."

"Here, of all places? Why there's nothing here but dates, aloe, very meager cattle and the Socotrans."

"Exactly, the Socotrans. He'll be after them. There was a moment in Malindi when I seriously thought I couldn't get him away from *there*. That man is as greedy for souls as some people are for gold or titles. More so."

The first thing Francis discovered was that most of the natives he saw had a cross hanging around their necks. There were wooden crosses, coral crosses, mother-of-pearl crosses, metal crosses. . . .

He addressed them in Portuguese and they answered in the same language. Yes, they were Christians, of course they were. And he? Was he a Christian priest? No sooner had he admitted it than they drew themselves up to a solemn posture and began to recite prayers. Francis could not understand a single word of what they said. It was not Portuguese, it was not Spanish or any other language he had ever heard. It was what they had been taught by their priests when they were children, yes, by their *khassis,* and he had it from *his khassis* and so on, back to the Apostle Thomas himself.

Francis listened carefully. "What does it mean?" he asked when they had finished.

They grinned sheepishly. "We don't know, Father. But these are the holy prayers we pray."

They began afresh. This time he caught one word he knew: alleluia. It was repeated a minute later, and then again. Apart from the sprinkle of alleluias the prayers remained completely enigmatic. Was it Aramaic? Was it Chaldean?

He walked around with them, entered one of their churches.

They went to church four times a day—but there was no Mass. Instead there was a veneration of the Cross which they incensed very solemnly and then anointed with—melted butter.

They seemed overjoyed at the landing of a priest. From all sides they came with presents, mostly dates, and when he offered to baptize their children, they fairly danced.

The children were sweet, with large, dark eyes and smiling faces. Only once did he meet with a protest. There were about a dozen children milling all around him, when a woman with heavy golden earrings appeared and shrieked that her children must not be baptized. She spoke Arabic and her words had to be translated to him. "We are Moslems", cried the woman. "We want nothing of your baptism."

"She is quite right, Father", an elderly man agreed. "Let her take her brats away. She is a Moslem. You should never baptize Moslems, Father. They're not worth it."

It was a novel point of view.

Of course there was no sense in baptizing any child here,

if he did not stay and teach these people so that they in turn could teach their children.

"Do you want me to stay with you?"

A general outbreak of noisy enthusiasm was the answer.

"It would make much good difference", said the elderly man in broken Portuguese. "So much good difference. We very much plagued by Moslems. They come over in felucca and dhau from the coast of Araby, they take away what we have, they threaten us, if we do not recognize Mohammed. When my father was alive, it was better. Then General Albuquerque came, drove out Moslems, poof-poof-bang, make life safe for us. But now very bad. Very bad. You stay with us, Father, give us baptism and everything."

When Francis returned to the *Coulam,* he asked at once to see the Viceroy.

Dom Martim received him immediately. There was a broad grin on Marcello's piratical face, when Francis suggested that he be left here, at least for the time being. The Viceroy gave his lieutenant a nod.

"There is a rich harvest on this island", concluded Francis.

"That may be so", said the Viceroy, "but there are no barns to store the grain. It would be destroyed by the next rain. The kind of rain that comes from Arabia, Father—and the only kind that ever came from that accursed land. Marauding, looting, and altogether extremely disagreeable Arabs, Father. We have no Portuguese garrison on Socotra. The dhaus come fairly regularly and the Arabs will get you the very first time. Even if your friends tried to hide you. Too many informers. No, Father."

"But this is intolerable", exclaimed Francis. "There are thousands of men and women—and children—living here who regard themselves as Christians—who want to be Christians. Why don't you put a garrison on Socotra, Your Excellency?"

The Viceroy smiled indulgently. "When you have been out East a little longer, Father, you will realize what it means to keep our empire together. For every Portuguese soldier there are a thousand natives, and more. We cannot be everywhere at the same time. This isn't Portugal. I'm a soldier, Father—but I also wish for the propagation of our Faith. You are a priest—but if you wish to succeed, you must adopt the methods of a soldier."

Francis thought of Father Ignatius. "Go on, Your Excellency", he said. "Please, go on."

"Strategy", said Dom Martim. "That's what I mean. It isn't good strategy to attack headlong the first objective. We must attack where it is likely to lead to lasting success. An attack on Socotra is bound to peter out. Come with us to Goa, Father. And when you've been there a while, and have seen a little more of what is going on, then . . . I know an objective for you that is worthwhile. The region around Cape Comorin. In southern India. There are tens of thousands there, waiting for you. The Paravas. Poor people. Pearl fishers, most of them. They're a caste by themselves. Most of them were baptized a few years ago by priests we sent out from Cochin—Franciscans, some of them, I think. Mind you, many of them probably came round, because they hoped that by becoming Christians they would gain our protection. They needed it bitterly. Both Moslems and Hindus harassed and exploited them for all they were worth, thirty villages of them all along the Coromandel Coast. Shortly afterward the Arabs came again, with a large fleet and the Paravas screamed for help."

The Viceroy was interrupted. Marcello wheeled round, his eyes sparkling. "Your Excellency, please permit me to take it up from here. This part I—I can tell better than anybody else."

Dom Martim smiled. He looked a little embarrassed. "Very well then, Marcello", he said affably.

"At that time", began Marcello, "His Excellency was Grand Captain of the Sea in the Malabar area. He was in command of the fleet. But you couldn't really call it a fleet. One galleon and three caravels were all we had, and the infidels had over fifty large feluccas. When we got there, we found a dozen villages burned to the ground, people massacred in droves, and we were told that many hundreds of them had been carried off by the Arabs, to be sold into slavery on the markets of Mascat and Baghdad and other infidel towns. We set sail at once and pursued them. Now you try and pursue a fleet of feluccas with a galleon and caravels, Father! But fortunately they were overladen by their own greed and they had to stick together and so we caught up with them eventually and what a battle it was, four against fifty! And how we beat them! It was the most glorious day I can remember, Father, there was nothing like it ever! We sank half of them and fished out the Paravas and pushed back the Moors, and a dozen feluccas were driven on the reefs and foundered and again we picked up the Paravas and pushed back the Moors and . . . ”

"All right, Marcello, that will do", said Dom Martim. "But that battle was the main reason why I was given the post as the next Viceroy, Father. The battle for the Paravas. They have no priests now. We had to withdraw the few we had there, because the Arabs would have murdered them all. Now you know what a harvest is awaiting you in India. And the Paravas are not the only ones. Does that put your mind at rest?"

"I shall come with you to India", said Francis.

"Excellent", said Dom Martim. "Have a look how far along they are with taking meat and water on board, Marcello."

Both Marcello and Francis left his presence.

"Mind you, don't think that we're safe here on board this little ship, Father", said Marcello. "It's a straight enough run from here to Goa. But you never know whether we're not going to run smack into a Turk, and we're practically unarmed."

"When I set out from Lisbon", said Francis gently, "I did not expect to go on a pleasure cruise."

Marcello grinned, showing two rows of excellent teeth.

Francis went to his cabin. He knew that the voyage

would take about another month. But there could be storms again with the ship rolling and pitching. Better do it straightaway. He sat down and wrote a long letter to Father Simon Rodríguez at the College of Coimbra, imploring him to go and see the King and ask for permission to send priests to Socotra.

Book Four — 80 pages long!

INDIA WAS ASLEEP as the *Coulam* slowly drifted into the harbor of Goa. All over the giant continent the lights had gone out. They were sleeping, the millions who had prayed to Brahma and Vishnu and Siva, to Lakshmi and Ganesha, to Hanuman and Durga, and to the terrible Kali of the six arms, dancing on the bodies of her slain enemies. They were asleep, the millions who believed in the Eightfold Path of the Gautama and the many millions more who had combined the mild teaching of the Buddha with the adoration of demons. The yogis and sannyasis, the nautch-girls of the temples, the wandering fakirs, the great rajahs and the lepers, the brahmans and the harijan, the merchants of the bazaars, the soldiers and the whores, the hunters and the pearl fishers, the horse dealers and the slaves—all were asleep.

The *Coulam* dropped her anchors. There could be no disembarkation before morning. The double splash and the clanking of the chains caused no stir in the Golden City.

For a long time Francis stood at the rail, looking toward it. The only lights he could see came from the stars, and all of them seemed to form a most glorious setting for the Southern Cross, the "pectoral cross of God" as Mansilhas had called it.

Thirteen months of voyaging. But never before, in all that time had his longing for India been as great as it was now—now that he had reached it and yet could not go ashore.

There was a night of many thousand years between paradise and the advent of the incarnate God on earth, said the stars.

But they had been waiting so long, those sleepers out there in the darkness.

Francis sighed deeply. It was the sigh of the lover for the beloved.

As in the ancient games of Olympia one runner pressed the flaming torch into the hand of the next, so Ignatius had passed the torch on to him. Go and set all afire.

But India was asleep, and he must wait for the morning.

*   *   *

The arrival of a ship was always an event. It meant mail. It meant new faces. It meant goods coming in, from home, from Cochin or the Moluccas or many other places.

Who was on board? What did they say?

The first to know were, as usual, the half-caste women, idling in their doorways in gauze blouses, flowered skirts and loose slippers. They always picked up everything first, from the coachmen, the palanquin carriers, the clanking soldiers and anybody else in the streets. They were pretty women, most of them, with tawny skin and almond eyes and soft little snub noses, many of them mistresses of soldiers of the garrison. Each cooked for her man, housed him and paid his debts. Goa was cheap enough, but even so a soldier's pay did not go very far.

It was not the Royal Indian fleet that had arrived, it was only the *Coulam* on its way back from Mozambique, but with the new Viceroy on board, and the old Viceroy had gone in state to receive him and the two great men had been very friendly with each other, very friendly indeed. Like brothers they were. Ah, and the new Apostolic Nuncio had been on board too, the special envoy of the Holy Father in Rome, and when they heard about it in the Bishop's palace, a delegation went to fetch him, and what a sight it was, all those palanquins, the Governor's in red and green with the carriers in red and green liveries and the Bishop's in white, with the keys of Saint Peter embroidered on front and back and then there was no envoy at all, no archbishop or bishop, not even the tiniest little prelate, only a monk, and a very shabby one, and *he* would not use a palanquin. Poor man, he was probably afraid it would cost him money or that they might drop him or something. Anyway, he refused to enter and walked away.

One-eyed Marcello was there, the new Viceroy's lieutenant and very fierce he looked and very strong.

The next batch of rumors said that there was a prisoner on board the *Coulam,* but that no one had seen his face so far, and that the new Viceroy and the old one were having a *very* long conference at the palace.

It was superseded by the news that young Terreiro had died, the "husband" of little Inez and little Inez, of course, was as heartbroken as the situation demanded. The police had been in for a while and then had gone again. Another of those young men who took too much datura. There were furtive smiles and comprehending glances among the women. There were few among them who had not put datura into their lovers' food on some occasion; not too much, of course, just enough to keep them in that wonderful state of trance and forgetfulness that datura caused, so that a girl had time to enjoy the embrace of another man. You had to be a little careful about the dose. And Inez was not the careful sort.

But who was to blame her? Terreiro was such a tiresome young man, always around instead of going about with his comrades to the gambling houses or the cock fights, which gave a girl opportunities. He was jealous, too.

Oh, and Andrea de Castro had a new mistress—no, the two others had not left his house, he knew how to handle such things, such a successful man in so many ways, over twelve thousand fanams he made in that deal with Captain de Paiva down at Tuticorin. Not that de Paiva did not make a tidy sum himself, and what a great gentleman he was, with his waistcoat buttons real rubies from Burma and his sword hilt full of rubies, too, and whole strings of pearls round his neck, all matching, the best quality, but then that was not surprising with him lording it over the Parava district.

And the Moslems in the city were all smug and supercilious again, because the troops had not yet left against the Rajah of Bijapur. The counter-order had come this morning. Everybody knew what *that* meant.

It was discussed all over the city, in the barracks, the gambling dens and the whorehouses, everywhere. The new Viceroy had arrived much earlier than expected. How so? Surely, he was late. Ah, of course he was late, but Dom Estevam expected his arrival even later, that was well known. His personal valet had told it to the Master of the Horse and the Master of the Horse had told it to his mistress and what Ana Figueroa knew was always known throughout Goa within a day or two. Dom Estevam had cursed wildly when the arrival of the *Coulam* was announced to him, or rather when he was told that Dom Martim was on board of the *Coulam.* Whatever else Dom Martim's arrival might mean, it certainly meant the end of Dom Estevam's rule and that's why the troops were ordered to stay.

*   *   *

Senhora Ana Figueroa was at Mass in the cathedral. She wore a gown of silver brocade, glowing under a mantle of the finest silver gauze and she knelt on a beautiful little carpet from Bokhara. At just the proper distance behind her four slaves in scarlet petticoats and yellow smocks were sitting on their haunches, carrying the lady's prayerbook, handkerchief, parasol and fan.

The church was very dark; the windows of mother-of-pearl transformed the glaring sunlight to a mild yellowish glow. It was most becoming, as long as one was wearing heavy makeup, and Senhora Ana Figueroa did. This was the Mass the new Viceroy was attending with his men to thank God for a safe arrival, and it was the best possible opportunity to see what kind of a man he was and what the men were like whom he had brought with him. Pedro was on such good terms with the old Viceroy, it was not very likely that he would retain his position under the new one, although neither was he likely to lose it straightaway, not as

136

long as there was no one who knew how to handle his office properly. Four weeks, six weeks, three months, and Pedro would be replaced—very likely by one of those gentlemen in the benches just behind Dom Martim. That was going to happen to most of the leading officials, of course. And once without office they had to go back to Portugal, or live here on what money they had made. Now Dom Carlos Gomez, for instance, could afford that very well. After three years as head of the Viceroy's household, with all the buying and the keeping of the books in his charge, a man had to be an absolute fool if he did not become well off, to say the least, and Dom Carlos was by no means a fool.... Ah, Mass had started—

Dom Carlos was by no means a fool, but he was absolutely besotted with Lolita Pérez and Lolita was not an easy woman to dislodge.

"*Confiteor Deo omnipotenti....* "

Senhora Ana Figueroa rose to the Credo last and the graceful way she did so did not remain unobserved, as might have happened had she risen when everybody else did. It was as if she made a fresh entrance altogether, and yet she managed to make it appear charming and even modest; Oh, Madre de Dios, everybody is standing, there I was, dreaming again, up I go....

From the Offertory on, when the church had become fairly well filled, Senhora Ana Figueroa took her fan from the hands of the demure-looking little creature in yellow smock and red petticoats behind her and began to fan herself.

By now she was fairly sure that Dom Martim himself had been looking at her once or twice and quite sure that several of his gentlemen had and now it could be left to them to make inquiries about the lady in silver. Pedro was rather a darling, but he did take her just a little bit too much for granted, and it was his own fault, really, if he was too lazy to go to Mass.

In the third from the last row Senhora Violante Ferreira

was sitting with her daughter Beatriz. Senhora Ferreira was a widow of forty-five, though she looked considerably older and not only because her hair under the black veil was gray; there was a network of wrinkles around eyes and mouth, the wrinkles of suffering and the wrinkles of laughter. Beatriz shared with her mother an expression of quiet nobility and she had the freshness of youth. Even so, it was easy to see that her mother at her age must have been more beautiful. Both women were dressed almost alike in black and wore no jewelry except for a small golden cross on a thin chain around the mother's neck and a still smaller one pinned on Beatriz' dress.

As so often before Senhora Ferreira had not been able to wait with her very personal prayers till the suitable moment came with the "Prayers for the Living", but unburdened herself to God from the very start. "I know I shouldn't," she prayed, "but there *is* so little time during the Prayers for the Living and I do have so much to ask—again!" There was her bad leg which made it painful to do all the errands she had to do for so many people—"Oh and for myself and Beatriz, of course. I'm not trying to tell you that I am living an unselfish life, far from it, as you know very well." There was Beatriz, who was very nearly twenty and still unmarried, for who would marry a girl without a dowry, in Goa? Young men wasted their own money on worthless women all over the city, whom they would not marry, and Beatriz was quite right *not* to accept old Senhor Portao, everybody knew what kind of life he was leading and he was suffering from the French pox to boot. "Surely, dear God, old Portao is not the only man who will ask her?"

She had not seen the cathedral so full for a long time, except of course, at Easter—but the new Viceroy was here and perhaps that made some people curious. . . . She should not have thought that—it was most uncharitable. "Please forgive me, I should have remembered that there is only one soul I know anything about and that is my own and therefore I am the worst sinner I know."

She stopped herself energetically from praying about her own problems and, raising up her heart, began to listen to God instead of babbling to him.

Beside her Beatriz prayed that God would cure old Inez López so that she could work again and mother need not take her food every day at the other end of the city when her own leg was bad—or that her own leg would get well quickly; that she receive grace to prevent her from wandering off in her thoughts at Mass and that old Senhor Portao would not succeed in persuading the Viceroy's Master of Pensions to cancel her mother's pension as he had threatened to do when she refused to marry him; and that she would find a nice, handsome husband—not *too* old—before she was *quite* hopeless herself with old age, because she was not much good for anything else and what convent would take a postulant who could not concentrate on prayer even for half an hour, without her thoughts wandering at least twice and sometimes more often. . . .

When the Mass ended, everybody rose, but no one left, as courtesy demanded that the new Viceroy leave first, which at the same time gave a welcome opportunity to have a good look at him.

Perhaps it was only natural that the ladies and gentlemen in the first rows managed to get through immediately after him; after all it was not easily discernible whether they also belonged to the Viceroy's retinue or whether they did not.

Thus it happened Senhora Ana Figueroa left the church before Senhora Ferreira and before most other people, so that the Viceroy's retinue—perhaps even Dom Martim himself—got a good glimpse of her as she walked gracefully down the steps towards her palanquin, whose two bearers, sturdy Negroes, salaamed deeply as they were trained to do.

The four maids helped their mistress into the palanquin and she was just going to pull the thin silken cord whose other end was tied to the little finger of the bearer in front, when she saw Senhora Ferreira come out.

"Tell her to come here", she snapped at one of the maids. When Senhora Ferreira approached the palanquin: "How nice to see you, my dear woman. Had a look at our new Lord and master?"

"The Lord I went to see is still the same, Senhora Figueroa", replied Violante Ferreira quietly.

"Oh? But the old Viceroy wasn't there at all, was he? But how stupid I am, that's not at all what you meant, of course, I understand, what a good answer, too! You *are* such a good woman, I often wish I were as good as you are, really I do. And so clever. You did this dress for me so well, I just love wearing it. What would I do without you? Do come and see me at the beginning of next week, will you? I've had such a *lovely* idea for a very special veil. I must say the new Viceroy looks *very* impressive, don't you think? Of course, one would have thought that our new Apostolic Nuncio would have said the Mass, and not our dear old Bishop Albuquerque, but he does not seem to be very interested in us, does he? I mean, it's all very nice to be so interested in the *rabble,* but surely that need not prevent him from preserving some kind of etiquette at least, if nothing else. But it's quite in keeping with the first things we heard about him, don't you think?"

Violante Ferreira said that she knew nothing about the arrival of an apostolic nuncio, but seemed rather interested.

"My dear woman, how is it possible that you haven't heard *that?* Why, it's the gossip of the whole city! They sent a very solemn delegation to fetch him from the *Coulam,* the whole thing was very solemn—what with the Viceroy arriving. Dom Pedro was there, of course, as Master of the Horse, and Dom João and Dom Felipe, everybody—and the episcopal palace sent a prelate—I forgot who it was, well, it doesn't matter, really. They came in palanquins and had a very special palanquin ready for the Nuncio. And then, my dear, no Nuncio! The only cleric coming out was a very shabby monk. So they asked him about the Nuncio and he said, 'I am he', just like that and they all shrank back in their surprise, Dom Pedro saw it all with his own eyes. My dear, they had expected at least a bishop, more likely an archbishop or a cardinal, and now this!"

"If he is really a simple monk, he must be a very exceptional man to be made Apostolic Nuncio", said Senhora Ferreira more to herself than to the silvery lady.

"He certainly is a most exceptional character," said Senhora Figueroa. "He flatly refused to mount his palanquin. So they very courteously said they also would walk with him, in procession, to the episcopal palace, where lodgings were prepared for him. They were quite proud of that, really, because after all, they themselves had been told only an hour earlier, by a special messenger from the Viceroy, that the Apostolic Nuncio had arrived with him. Now believe it or not, but the Nuncio refused to come with them! All he wanted was to be shown the nearest way to the hospital. So, of course, they thought he was ill and Father Almeida said that it would be so much better if His Excellency would come with them to the palace, as he would be much better looked after there, and the Bishop's own physician would come and see him at once. The conditions at the hospital were quite impossible for a man of exalted rank and the doctors there accustomed only to the riffraff of the streets who had no one to look after them. So the Nuncio said, 'Then that is a reason more for me to go there at once', and he insisted and they had to give in and to that putrid, smelly, horrible place he went, and took his lodgings there! The Nuncio!"

"And—and then?" Senhora Ferreira's voice shook with excitement.

Senhora Figueroa felt just a little flattered. The Ferreira woman was no more than her dressmaker, but apart from being exceptionally good at it, there was something about her that she admired, she did not really know what it was; perhaps her calm, unruffled aloofness and a kind of—of modest self-assurance, if there was such a thing. Usually Senhora Ferreira did not show much interest in gossip and just said "yes" or "no" or "really?" as if it did not matter to her at all whether Lolita Pérez had a new lover, or even if Dom Pedro was unfaithful. But now she seemed very interested.

"Then? My dear, he just stayed at the unspeakable place. They have the most horrible cases there, even lepers and worse—it is positively *dangerous!* Of course, he had to pay a formal visit to the Bishop, and he did, but I cannot imagine that poor old Bishop Albuquerque can have been very pleased to sit cheek by jowl with somebody who just came from that pesthouse. He might have caught bugs or lice, if nothing worse! The Nuncio, my dear Ferreira, the Apostolic Nuncio! After the visit he returned at once to the hospital. They say he says his Masses at Nossa Senhora do Rozario, which is near by, and he gives catechism lessons to little children he picks up in the streets! My dear, I am quite sure there has never been an apostolic nuncio like him before *any*where!"

"I daresay there hasn't", said Senhora Ferreira and the tone of her voice made Senhora Figueroa look up in astonishment. But the calm, dignified face of the elderly woman was expressionless as usual.

"Of course I did think at first that it must be all a mistake," the silvery lady ran on. "I mean that he was not the Nuncio at all—that there was some kind of misunderstanding or something. But after all he did pay that visit to the Bishop and he is still being referred to as His Excellency, so he must be what he says he is, even if he is a little—a little mad. What do you think?"

"I am sure he is what he says he is", said Senhora Ferreira. "Although it may well be that he is—more."

"*More?* How could he possibly be more?"

But now the Ferreira woman curtsied a little, in that funny way of hers, not *really* respectfully at all, but keeping the formality of the fashion, and Senhora Figueroa nodded curtly and tugged at the silken cord, and the bearers snapped into action. More than a papal nuncio! Perhaps the Ferreira woman was a little stupid after all. It was not a bad idea for a stupid woman to be very quiet and reserved—it was not so easy to be found out then. But no one could bluff Ana Figueroa for very long. More than a papal nuncio. What did she think the wretched man was, the Pope in disguise?

*   *   *

Senhora Figueroa and her kind were not the only ones who gossiped about the new Nuncio in Goa within the next weeks. In fact, there was more gossip about him than about anybody else. Even the rumors about the relations between the old and the new Viceroy paled in comparison. There were some who said that there had been a furious clash between the two, but if that was true the two gentlemen certainly concealed it extremely well. They were seen together at several banquets, and in at least two speeches spoke of each other as, "my most highly esteemed predecessor" and "my famous and renowned successor, the best man His Majesty could have chosen for a post of such grave responsibilities".

There was a new Controller of Revenue and there might be a new Master of the Horse and Master of the Household, and other posts might undergo certain changes, but on the whole most things were more or less as they had been before and there were some who even maintained that the old Viceroy would not leave with the *Coulam,* but would wait for the arrival of the ships of the Royal Indian fleet, to return with them.

But the Nuncio!

Father Almeida told Father Campo that he had made over fifty visits to parishioners within the last ten days, to get as many children as possible together for a catechism class.

"Over fifty visits! You can't have done all that in the cool hours only."

"Indeed, no. I have been sweating my life out. I am a shadow of my former self. But as it was, the parents were too lazy to do anything about religious instruction, and I was afraid if I did not take matters in hand, I might have to buy myself a bell."

"A bell? What do you mean?"

"Don't you know? His Excellency the Papal Nuncio goes through the streets every day with a large bell, ringing it for all he is worth and laughing, and when people crowd around him, he picks out the children and asks them whether they want to come and hear him tell them the most wonderful story!"

"Santa María!"

"So of course the brats shout yes and he takes them with him to the Church of Nossa Senhora do Rozario and tells them the story of the Gospels. But what am I saying! He doesn't tell it to them—he sings it to them. He has put it in rhymes so that they can remember it better."

"Does the Bishop know?"

"I told him myself. He just smiled."

"And is it true that our new Apostolic Nuncio goes barefoot?"

"It is. It is causing some scandal with some of our dear diocesans, of course, but you see, Father, the trouble is that the scandalized ones are the kind of people whom I for one wouldn't like to be applauded by. If I were, I'd think there must be something wrong with me. Altogether . . . "

"Yes, Father Almeida?"

"Well, I don't know. I have forty-two children in my catechism class now and three weeks ago there were seven. They make so much noise, I cannot hear my own words at times, but—but they do need instruction, you know, and they did not get it, and . . . I might have thought of it earlier. You haven't met him yet, have you, Father Campo?"

"No. And it wouldn't help much if I did, I daresay. I can't sing."

*   *   *

When Sergeant-at-arms João da Silva asked Father Campo to put the marriage bans up for him and Lucía González, the grizzled old priest looked at him with a certain amount of suspicion. But the man was quite coherent and he did not smell of alcohol.

"You have known the girl a long time, haven't you?"

"Yes, Father."

"There are—children, aren't there?"

"Three", said da Silva proudly. "Two sons and a daughter. She's just getting her first teeth. Two of them."

The priest blinked a few times. "And now you want to marry the girl. A little late in the day, isn't it?"

"That's exactly what I said to Father Francis", the sergeant grinned. "But he said better late than never. Besides it'll be Lucía's birthday in a few weeks."

"W-what's that got to do with it?"

"Well, I told Father Francis I didn't have much to give her as a present, so he said, 'You go and marry her, that's the best present you can give her—and yourself. She's a good girl and she should be married.' Well, he's right, somehow, don't you think, Father? And Lucía, she could have fallen on his neck, if she'd dared to. So I said, 'Tell you what, Father Francis, you're right and you marry us', but he said, 'No, the priest of your parish must do that', so here I am."

"Father Francis", said Father Campo. "Now who is he? Do you mean Father Francisco Gumaya of Saint Pedro's or . . . "

"No, no—I mean Father Francis—Francis Xavier. The new one. The Nuncio. He had dinner with us yesterday night."

Father Campo gulped. He sat down. After a while he said, "Why didn't you come to me long ago, when you fell in love with the girl—or at least when you had your first child?"

The sergeant grinned sheepishly. "You'd have thrown me out on my ear, Father."

Father Campo shook his head.

"And anyway it never really occurred to me", said da Silva. "Why marry? I always gave Lucía enough money—

half my pay first and two thirds when the brats came. But she's sort of grown on me, if you see what I mean, Father, and when Father Francis suggested it, she looked so happy, so I thought what the devil—beg your pardon, Father—I thought what the saints, I'll go and do it."

Father Campo took paper and quill. "Name", he said, probing the quill on his thumb. "Rank. And where stationed."

* * *

Within the next ten days no less than fourteen couples came to see Father Campo for the same reason. All of them had been living together for some time and almost all had children. It was clear that Father Francis could not have had dinner with all of them, but a few shrewd questions made it clear that little Lucía González' example had stirred the girls into taking action. Little Lucía was showing off a bit and for once showing off had happy consequences.

Perhaps it would be a good idea to visit some of those whom little Lucía did not know and tell them, quite offhand, what was happening. If Lucía could show off, so could Father Campo. Perhaps some more girls might wish to take action.

He decided to do it and in the course of a week bagged three more couples. He told Father Almeida, not without pride.

Father Almeida grinned. "So he's made you sing after all."

"Who?"

"Father Francis, of course. And he's taught you without having to meet you. The man's incredible. Now, of course, friend de Borba is after him."

"Father Diogo de Borba?"

"That's right. He and his people founded a small school, as you know—he's got about fifty or sixty boys together, all between thirteen and seventeen."

"But no money."

"Very little money. But he has got courage, our friend de Borba. He even started building a church for his school and he has all kinds of wild dreams. When he heard what the Nuncio was doing here, he ran to him straightaway. Father, it was like pouring oil into a fire. A school? A seminary it must be, says the Nuncio. We need native priests, says the Nuncio. Where do your boys come from? What languages do they speak? So de Borba tells him they are Bengalis, Malagasy, Singhalese, Malays, Paravas, everything under the sun and he can talk to them either in Portuguese or in Konkani. Excellent, says the Nuncio. Now all we need is money and teachers."

"No more than that", Father Campo nodded ironically.

"So the Nuncio writes home to the Pope and to the King and to heaven knows whom else, send us trained men. He'll get them, too, you'll see. He'll get them. He'll get anything he wants, though God alone knows how."

"He hasn't got the money", said Father Campo with a shrug.

Father Almeida laughed. "That's what I thought. But he went to see the Viceroy. He spent two hours with him. So the Viceroy gave him money. I don't know how much, but it seems to be quite a lot. He also gave him three hundred workmen and all the material that is needed for the completion of the church."

"In two hours", said Father Campo, shaking his head.

"Give him two and a half and the Holy Father will give him a dozen cardinals to teach Father de Borba's boys."

"But how does he do it?"

"I wish I knew."

"I suppose he flattered de Sousa. . . . "

"Don't you believe it. Though I have actually heard him make flattering remarks. . . . "

"Well, there you are."

"Yes, he told a man I know that he was a wonderful fellow and extremely intelligent and sure to have a fine career and that it was sheer waste of time for him to sit day and night at the gambling table, where he could only lose. The man had lost eighty fanam, which was all he had. So

Father Francis told him he was going to finance him for exactly half an hour but then he would have to quit gambling and concentrate on making a living in a different way."

"But—where was this?"

"In Tumala's gambling den at the river."

"You mean to say the Apostolic Nuncio went *there?*"

"He certainly did. Well, the man accepted the challenge—because that's what it was—and Father Francis gave him money to play with. After half an hour he had won back his eighty fanam and another fifty on top of it. 'Stop', said Father Francis. 'Time's up.' And the man stopped. One of Tumala's guests saw the two sitting outside on the bamboo terrace for a while and he swears he saw the fellow kneel and receive absolution. He must have made his confession then and there."

"No wonder some people are scandalized", said Father Campo.

"Oh, that story went round like wildfire. So some people, whose concern it isn't at all, went to see the Bishop, full of moral indignation and their own importance."

"So?"

"So the Bishop told them to go home and look up Luke 5:30–32. Afterwards he told me that that was what Father Francis had told *him* to look up, when he tackled him about visiting Tumala's house."

"Luke 5 . . . "

"Well, I've learned it by heart since then", Father Almeida smiled. " 'Whereupon the Pharisees and scribes complained to his disciples, How comes it that you eat and drink with publicans and sinners? But Jesus answered them, It is those who are sick, not those who are in health, that have need of the physician. I have not come to call the just: I have come to call sinners to repentance.' "

"And how", asked Father Campo, "did the Bishop enjoy being compared to a Pharisee?"

Father Almeida frowned. "There is no question of that.

The Bishop did not complain to Father Francis. He asked him whether he thought it was wise to go to such places, as it was bound to make people talk unfavorably and Father Francis quoted Luke in his defense."

"They get on well, then?"

"When Father Francis paid his first visit to the Bishop, he knelt and kissed the ring. The first thing he said was that he had no intention of making any use of his powers as Nuncio, except in accordance with the Bishop's own wishes. He even asked to have his rank kept a secret wherever possible."

Father Campo chuckled. "Keep anything a secret in Goa! It's about as easy as to transform all the women in Goa into saints."

"Not even Father Francis could do that", Father Almeida nodded. "But he is changing a good many mistresses into wives. Yours is not the only parish where this sort of thing is going on, you know. Nor is it the only thing that's going on. He's got himself a number of catechists lately, trained them and sent *them* out with bells. He's even got himself a woman catechist, although he doesn't seem to like having anything to do with women. He's made an exeption of Violante Ferreira. I know of her and he's probably quite right. She's instructing women only, of course."

"And where is this paragon now?"

"Let me see, what time is it? Nine. That means he is in the Sala das bragas."

"In jail?"

"Yes, he goes there every day. Either to the Sala das bragas or to Al Jabir."

"Good heavens! There are only the galley slaves and convicted murderers in Al Jabir."

"That's right. It is a pretty fearful place. When I got there first, I frankly didn't think I was going to get out alive. The stench alone was bad enough to kill anybody. However, as you see I survived it."

"You went there too?"

"Well . . . " Father Almeida looked a little embarrassed. "I couldn't very well let him do everything by himself, could I? So I offered to go there once a week and he agreed. When I go to the Al Jabir, he goes to the Sala das bragas. He's contaminated me all right. What can you do?"

"He told you to go?"

"Lord, no. He wouldn't. He does not remonstrate with you or preach to you or anything of the sort. He—he just *does* things, and after a while you feel like a pig for not doing them yourself. 'I was in prison and you did not visit me'—you know."

*　　*　　*

Father Campo could not quite decide whether he wanted to meet Father Francis or not. He went to the Sala das bragas and waited for the Nuncio to come out. Three or four times he told himself that this was a silly thing to do, that he was behaving like one of the stupid men who gape at anything or anybody out of the ordinary. Yet he stayed.

But when Francis came out, a tall man with bushy black hair and a short black beard, in a shabby old coat, and carrying a bundle, he did not go up to him. Instead he trotted after him, to see where he was going. Perhaps he was going back to his hospital or the Church of Nossa Senhora do Rozario. There Father Campo could introduce himself and talk to him and see what kind of a man he really was.

But apparently Francis was not going there. He passed the palace and the wharves and walked through the Northern Gate, where he talked for a minute or two with one of the soldiers who then knelt down and received his blessing.

It was damnably hot by now, and Father Campo was sweating profusely. But with a kind of dogged obstinacy he kept on. Where was the Nuncio going?

Francis passed a few huts just beyond the gate and then turned into a small road leading in a westerly direction.

Father Campo had never been there before. However, the Nuncio would have to return, surely, and then he could talk to him. At least a dozen times Father Campo told himself that he was a fool for traipsing through the hot sun like this, and yet he went on.

Then he saw the camp. It had no walls and no gates. It was just an accumulation of a few dozen ramshackle old huts and he could discern a number of men and women standing or sitting about. As he came nearer he saw that most of them were wearing bandages around their arms or feet and some had their heads bandaged, too.

Then he heard the clapper and suddenly he knew and he stood still. All the blood drained from his face. His mouth was dry and his hands and knees shook with a life of their own.

But Francis was not standing still. He walked on, as if the wooden sound of the clapper meant nothing to him. Now the people in the camp seemed to recognize him; they uttered strange hoarse sounds and began to mill around him. Others began coming from the huts. There must be a hundred of them now, or more. He was waving his arm, greeting them, then went up to what looked like a heap of stones, set down his bundle and unwrapped it.

His heart in his mouth, Father Campo took a few more steps towards the camp. He could see Father Francis taking out alb, maniple, stole and chasuble and beginning to vest.

Mass. He was going to say Mass for the lepers.

Father Campo was now near enough to see hands swollen up to double their size, faces with gaping holes in them where nose or mouth should have been, shoulders and breasts covered with large ulcers. Again he stood still. Despite the sun he was shivering.

Mass began. A little boy with bandaged hands served as an acolyte.

Father Campo crossed himself and prayed, and as he prayed, he had the strangest thoughts. The whole world was leprous and the worst lepers were those who did not even know that they were ill. For with many of them the disease did not show on the outside, not on the skin, nor did it mutilate their fingers and toes as it did with the young woman over there, but inside they were worse to look at than even that old man whose face was one whitish mass of swellings and who was crouching on the ground, because he no longer had any legs, except for bandaged stumps. Father Campo, for instance, was leprous inside. He was covered with the ulcers of indifference and sloth and lack of charity, with the sores of self-righteousness and lukewarmness in the service of his Lord, and he confessed to Almighty God, to Blessed Mary Ever-Virgin, to Blessed Michael the Archangel, Blessed John the Baptist, the Holy Apostles Peter and Paul and all the saints and to Father Francis Xavier that he had sinned greatly in thought, word and action through his fault, through his fault, through his most grievous fault. . . .

As Mass went on he wondered whether it would be safe for him to kneel down on ground trodden by countless leprous feet, but when all backs bowed as Father Francis was calling the Second Person of the Blessed Trinity down from High Heaven, he forgot all about it and dropped on both knees and stayed there.

When he saw that the moment for Holy Communion had arrived, he felt that it was up to him to do something and at the same time fear shot up in him as he had never felt it before. But he knew that this was a decisive moment— that it might well be, no, that it was *the* decisive moment for him and he forced himself up and marched forward, his legs only barely carrying him, till he reached the horrible circle of the lepers and some of them turned their dreadful faces towards him and once more he had the strangest thought: the thought that it would be unbearable if they did not let him through, if they excluded him from their midst, as if *he* were the leper. . . .

But they withdrew just a little, right and left and he marched through, till he reached Father Francis at the altar, just as he was turning to his community, the ciborium in his hand.

Once more Father Campo knelt. Then he took the plate

from the bandaged hands of the little acolyte who looked at him with large, black eyes and he held it under the chins of those who were now receiving the Host from Father Francis' hands. Faces from a hundred nightmares, mouths without lips, suppurating sores and stinking ulcers, eyes whose lids were almost eaten away, ulcers on the very tongues on which Father Francis put the blessed Host with a swift, gleaming movement, old men, young men, women, girls and children. All of them received Holy Communion, every single leper. There seemed to be thousands and thousands. There seemed to be no end of them.

But there was an end, and the little acolyte got his plate back and Mass went on to its finish and Father Campo helped Father Francis disrobe and the bundle was packed again and the thanksgiving prayer said, and the lepers talked to Father Francis and he talked to them, and then the two priests walked away and back towards the Golden City.

They did not talk. They did not say a single word. Only when they had passed the gate, Father Campo suddenly stopped and Father Francis stopped with him and turned towards him.

"There is just one thing I want to say", said Father Campo and he had to repeat his words, because his voice faltered so. "I want to say that only now I know what the Incarnation of Our Blessed Lord means."

Father Francis smiled.

* * *

"There is constant war in this country", said the Viceroy genially. "Only yesterday I dispatched six hundred men to make a counterattack against the ruler of Bijapur. Best I could do at the moment. Things have been very slack here and I haven't been able to clean the stables of Dom Augias — Dom Estevam I mean — in the few months I've been here."

Francis said that everybody felt very glad of the fact that the — misunderstanding between His Excellency and Dom Estevam da Gama seemed to have been cleared up quickly and without disagreeable consequences.

"It has and it hasn't", said Dom Martim enigmatically. "No good making a big show of it in public, anyway. It was very good that I arrived before I was expected, Father, that much is certain. I released Dom Alvaro d'Ataide, of course—you may have seen him since. You haven't? Well, he's free, and as you put it, the misunderstanding has been cleared up. I hope—I say, I hope—the da Gamas will keep their mouths shut when they get home. Incidentally, I'm not even sure whether Dom Alvaro will go home, though his elder brother will, of course; no good having a man around who has been Viceroy, only makes bad blood. I may give Dom Alvaro a post in the not too distant future. Nothing has been settled about that yet, though. Have some wine? We shall be sorry to see you go, Father. Sure you have made up your mind?"

"It was you, Your Excellency," said Francis, smiling, "who first told me about the Paravas and the coast near Cape Comorin."

"True. But since then I have seen what one man can do in this unspeakable nest of vice and treachery that is our most glorious Majesty's good and faithful city of Goa. You have practically turned it upside down. There's a new wind blowing. It's—it's as if all these people had waked up to the fact that they are Catholics and that it's about time to do something about it. Still going around with your bell, Father? In any case you're still going around without shoes or sandals. You can't do that on your journey to the coast, you know. You would be a dead man on the second day of the journey, at latest. Bugs and snakes of all kinds, and not the sort we are all accustomed to but the kind that kill you with one sting or bite. Better get some shoes. Tell you what, I'll get you a pair of new ones."

But Francis declined. He had a pair somewhere, and if they were no longer new, one could always patch them. Would the Viceroy promise him to see to it that Father Paul of Camerino and Brother Mansilhas followed him to Cape Comorin as soon as they arrived with the Indian fleet?

"Of course, of course. They may come in any time now.

Should have arrived, really. Now remember this: my administrator for the Parava country is Captain Cosmas de Paiva. Paiva. You won't find him very easy to handle, I suppose. Has been in the country for many years and is very much accustomed to have things his own way. You may not find that way much to your liking. A man who lives out there goes through all kinds of things we never so much as dream of. Has to protect himself—*and* his interests. May go a little far—too far—in doing so. The Parava district is not Lisbon or Rome—it isn't even Goa. Far from it. You must see how you get on with him—I'm afraid I won't be able to do much about it. Six hundred miles may not sound such a terribly great distance, but it is, when one realizes that most of it is jungle. It's a different set of dangers and pitfalls and troubles from here, very different. It's no bed of roses here either, as you've found out, I'm sure."

The Viceroy looked at the ceiling. A few large, green geckos were running along it. "They don't do any harm", said Dom Martim. "But I'd like to know how they manage running across the ceiling, upside down. Mad country. But the people are madder still. D'you know what the first Viceroy—old Albuquerque himself—wrote to the King? 'There is not a single man in India whom I can trust, not one who would not tell a thousand lies for a ruby, or break a thousand oaths for a bale of silk.' That's still true, and perhaps more than ever."

"I have found a good many people whom I trust", said Francis calmly.

Dom Martim looked at him. "They aren't trustworthy", he said gruffly. "You make them so. Don't know how. Between you and me, Father, I wouldn't mind telling Dom Estevam as many lies as there are fleas in Goa, but I'd hate to tell you a single one. How many men are you taking with you?"

"Three Tamil students from Father de Borba's school. From Saint Paul's."

"Is that all? Well, you must know what you're doing.

Nothing surprises me. Not since I've heard men in the streets—soldiers amongst them—going about, singing rhymes of the Ten Commandments and the Credo. I know you are behind that, Father, no need to say anything. Well, I'll see you before you go. You'll need some money. Later, Captain de Paiva is the man from whom you must ask for money. Also I want your blessing before you leave."

On his way out Francis had to pass the large audience hall, where hundreds were waiting for the Viceroy's appearance. A hundred guards in blue uniforms, gleaming halberds in their fists, lined the steps.

He was going to write to Father Ignatius again tonight. So many letters—and no answer. But there could not be an answer. No ship had come, no ship could have come as yet. In fact his earliest letter could not even have arrived in Rome. But he would write. He felt so lonely. So utterly alone and forgotten. Six hundred miles of jungle. Once more an entirely strange country, full of unknown dangers, devilridden and infested by demons, as everybody here said. And he, he was nothing, no better than a little child sent out into the wild forest with a little crucifix round its neck.

He would write to Father Ignatius.

But first he would patch up that pair of shoes.

*   *   *

A ship again, a small merchantman, built at Goa, and serving the coastal route. The pepper ship, they called it, because it brought pepper from Cochin to Goa, pepper, that most precious article. The whole of the Portuguese Empire of the Indies was built on pepper. There were other spices, of course, and there was silk from the faraway, unapproachable land called China—unapproachable because every foreigner trying to land there was instantly killed, according to the standing orders of the Emperor. But pepper was the main thing.

Francis and his three Tamil students were the only passengers. He almost wept as Goa vanished in the mists of the morning sun. Somehow the rumor of his departure had got around and a huge crowd had come to see him off, Father Almeida and Father Campo and other priests, Violante Ferreira with her nice young daughter, both in tears, Father Diogo de Borba of course, with all his students, and hundreds and hundreds of others; they upset the entire traffic near the port. And as the ship left, they had sung the Credo, rhymed as he had taught it to the children. How they loved singing, these joyful people. They sang when they plowed their fields, sang when they worked on the wharves. And there were the children, his children, tossing hibiscus flowers at the ship, bobbing up and down. . . .

Leaving them was a kind of dying. And now started the voyage to purgatory.

Father de Borba had told him a good deal about the Paravas, and no one could have given him better information. Eight years ago Father de Borba had been there himself, in the course of the War of the Ear.

Every girl child on the Pearl Fisher Coast had the lobes of her tiny ears pierced. Little leaden weights were inserted into the ears and these weights were gradually increased, till at last they were large enough for the enormous earrings that would be put in on the day of the girl's marriage. They were the sign of the married state and a Parava woman's pride and badge of rank and dignity.

An uncouth, greedy Moslem trader—one of the many who cheated the poor pearl fishers out of their goods, won by so much effort and under constant danger from sharks and stingrays—tore such a ring off the ear of a young Parava woman, tearing her earlobe at the same time. Outraged, the Paravas killed him and everyone of his kind they could lay their hands on. Then came the armed feluccas to burn down the Parava villages and the pearl fishers asked for Portuguese protection.

And Dom Martim de Sousa, Gran Capitan of the Seas, arrived with his fleet. Francis had heard the story from Marcello, but Father de Borba had a few things to add. He and a few Franciscans had gone ashore with the troops, and the priests—numbering no more than six—had baptized twenty thousand natives. They tried to instruct them, too, but the fleet had to go on and priests were needed on board. . . .

Since then the Paravas had had to be left to themselves, except for a few priests going over at Easter, from Cochin.

And now it was eight years since the War of the Ear.

The little ship, the pepper ship, was careful not to sail too far out into the dangerous waters of the Indian Ocean. Hugging the coast, it stopped for a day at Mangalore, for two days at Calicut, for another two at Cochin. Then it sailed along the Travancore Coast and round Cape Comorin to Manapad.

There Francis and his three students went ashore.

"Flat country", said Coelho, the oldest of the students, and the only one who had received major Orders and was a deacon. "Good for us, because there won't be so many wild animals. Bad—because there is little shade." He opened his parasol.

They found a little grotto, where Francis said Mass.

Far away, to the north, a few catamarans stood out in the ocean.

"Pearl fisher boats", explained Coelho. "One of the men is diving now. Can you see, Father?"

"Yes—he's holding something in his mouth, something shimmery. . . . "

"His knife. For sharks."

Francis made his bundle ready and swung it over his shoulder. "You said you know the way to Tuticorin", he said.

"I know it, Father. I—I hope I do."

Rice paddies. A few laborers working in a millet field, with a number of completely naked boys jumping around and throwing stones at something, Francis could not see what it was.

"They're chasing parrots away", explained Coelho.

Coconut palms and banyan trees and limes and mangoes.

With those and the fish they can get from the ocean, at least they have enough to eat, thought Francis. Of course, fish had to be eaten at once; they putrefied at almost the moment they were taken from the water.

A cow appeared suddenly, seemingly from nowhere, and the workers in the field turned towards her and bowed their heads.

"They hope for the droppings", said Coelho. "It is a sacred animal, you know, and the droppings are a certain cure for a great many diseases, when mixed with the food of a man. That is what Hindus believe", he added hastily, as he saw Francis look at him with horror.

"But these people are supposed to be Christians!"

"Some of them, yes, Father. Many of them. Not all. And there is no priest. Things get mixed up . . . "

" . . . with the dung of cows", said Francis grimly.

He had to restrain himself from walking up to the men and tackling them then and there. It would have been foolish. The thing to do was to go to the heart of the country and to work from there towards the periphery. That was what Father Ignatius would do, he thought.

They closed their parasols, as they entered a forest—if the maze of trees of all kinds and sizes, of high grass and strange plants could be called a forest.

"Look out for snakes, Father", warned Coelho. "Most of them will not attack—except when they believe that they have been attacked. You must be careful not to tread on them. They will never believe that you didn't do it deliberately."

Mansilhas might have said that. Mansilhas. Perhaps he and Father Paul had arrived by now. They should have arrived long ago.

Suddenly he stopped. From a tree something was hanging upside down, an animal, not unlike a huge bat. But surely there could be no bats of that size! It had a horrible head, black or dark brown, with large, pointed ears. It looked like a devil.

One of the younger students jumped up and clubbed it to earth with his parasol. A few more strokes and it was dead.

"What did you do that for?" asked Francis with disgust.

"Verrie good to eat", the student grinned. "Flying fox, Father. Wonderful, when cooked."

A country where they held cows sacred and cooked devils. He gave a wry smile. "Let's go through the Credo in Tamil again, Coelho", he said. "I must learn it. *Visuvasa manthiram—paralogath iyum—pulogathiyum—sarvesar—anai athiokia—bhaktiyaga...*"

"*Visuvasikirain*", Coelho helped out.

Francis sighed. "Why must every word in Tamil have at least six syllables", he complained. "*Avarudya—yega—suthanagya—namudaya...*"

"*Nathar Yesu*", said Coelho, beaming. "*Christuvayum...*"

"Ah yes, now I know: *athikiya—bhakthiyaga visuvasikirain—ivar ispirithu santhuvinalai karpomai urpavithu archayasishta kanni Mariyaiyidathilai nindru piranthu—*"

"Wonderful, Father", said Coelho. "You are making great progress."

"I know the Ten Commandments", said Francis, "and the Pater and the Ave, but I'm hopelessly lost with the exposition of the Faith and the story of the Gospels. Tell me, Coelho, I know there are those who speak Hindi and Konkani and Tamil, but tell me, quite honestly and frankly—how many other languages are there in India?"

"Oh, quite a few", said Coelho, looking away. "There is Pushtu and Urdu and Gujarati, and Telugu and Kanarese and Bengali and Singhalese and Gondi and Malayan and..."

"That will do", said Francis. They went on silently for a little while. Then Francis said, "Let's get on with the Credo where we left off. *Ponchu—pilathinkizhai—padupattu—siluvaiylai araiyundu—marith—adakappattar....*"

*　　*　　*

The names of the villages they passed were of the same ilk. Alantalai, Periytalai, Tiruchendur, Talambuli, Virapandianpatnam, Punaikâyal, Palayakâyal, Kayalpatnam and Kombuturé.

He did not stick to his original idea, to start working only when he had reached Tuticorin. He could not wait. It was bitter to see the shrines and temples on the way, with obscene gods of stone performing obscene actions on temple friezes, with phallic symbols abounding; bitter to see trembling villagers watching overfed cows eating all their food without daring to disturb the sacred animals; bitter to hear that the pearl fishers paid a good percentage of their catch to sorcerers for spells and talismans against the bite of sharks, and paid still more for *mantrams* against any other kind of danger, trouble and illness.

At Kombuturé they told him about a woman who had been three days in labor and was dying, although her husband had paid the sorcerer for all the aid he could give and the house was full of mantrams of all kinds.

Coelho shook his head sadly. "The demons are more powerful than the sorcerer and the mantrams", he murmured.

Francis exploded. "Where is that house?" he asked.

Coelho and the other two students tried to hold him back, but they might as well have tried to stop the monsoon with their hands.

Francis stalked into the house.

The sorceror, with two apprentices, was squatting on the floor; all three of them were drumming on some kind of musical instruments and chanting invocations at the top of their voices. They had put a kettle on the floor, filled with some burning substance that sent up clouds of stinking smoke. In a corner of the room the husband and at least half a dozen youngsters of all ages were crouching, moaning and rolling their eyes in abject fear.

A grotesque figure of clay and half a dozen mantrams were tied to the body of the suffering woman.

Francis took one look. Then he seized the kettle and swung it at the sorcerer and his helpers. They did not wait for what might happen next, but jumped up and raced out. Francis threw the kettle after them, untied the idol and the mantrams and threw them out as well.

A midwife, sitting at the feet of the woman, looked up at him as if she were seeing a demon. The woman herself kept her eyes closed. Now that the noise had subsided, Francis could hear her moaning softly.

He knew nothing of childbirth. The hospitals in which he had nursed his patients in Paris, Venice, Lisbon and Goa were only for men. He thought the woman was dying, as he had been told that she was. She certainly looked as if she were dying. And into a dying woman's room he brought his Lord. It was all he could do and all he set out to do.

"Coelho—translate. Tell her that I am coming in the name of the Lord who made heaven and earth. . . . "

Coelho's lips were trembling a little. Perhaps Father Francis was not quite aware of the risk they were taking. Now if the woman died, as surely she would, the sorcerer would say that it was all the fault of these interfering strangers . . .

"Translate", ordered Francis. "I command you."

Coelho translated. The woman opened her eyes. She fastened her gaze not on Coelho but on the strange face of the white man with its complete absence of fear, with its tranquil smile. Being a woman, she recognized love when she saw it.

"Tell her, Our Blessed Lord wants her to live with him forever. Tell her what he wants her to believe. *Visuvasa manthiram—paralogathiyum. . . .* "

She stared at Francis. Her lips moved a little and then she echoed his smile.

"Are you ready to accept what you have heard?" asked Francis gently, when Coelho had finished translating the last part of the Creed. "Can you believe it?"

Oh yes, she could. She could.

He took the New Testament out of his pocket and read out the story of the birth of the Christ Child. Coelho translated again. From time to time he looked towards the entrance of the house. The crowd outside was growing larger and larger. They would never get away alive. He was sweating. But he went on translating.

"Water", said Francis. When they brought it to him, he baptized the woman.

Coelho, looking on, prayed for all he was worth. In a state of utter confusion he implored God to save their lives, to save the woman, to prevent the sorcerer from making the villagers storm the hut, to have mercy on him, on Father Francis—on everybody.

A sudden tremor went through the body of the woman, she threw back her head and gave a loud cry. Instantly the midwife sprang up.

Francis took a step backwards.

At first he did not know that labor had started again after hours of interruption. But he knew it soon enough.

Minutes later the child was there, and a few seconds later yelling lustily.

Outside the villagers broke into a howl of enthusiasm that shook the hut.

Two hours later Francis had baptized the husband, three sons, four daughters and the newly born infant, another son.

Coelho was grinning from ear to ear.

But for Francis this was no more than the beginning. He stepped outside, where the villagers were still howling their joy to heaven and asked for the headman. Coelho had to tell him that Father Francis wanted the entire village to accept Jesus Christ as their God and Lord.

The headman scratched himself thoughtfully. They would do so gladly, but they could not—not without the permission of the Rajah.

"Where is that Rajah?" asked Francis curtly.

Coelho passed on the question. The Rajah was far away, very far away, but there was an official here, who represented him. He had come to collect the taxes for his master.

Francis went to see him at once.

The tax collector was at first a little suspicious. If these people accepted this new belief, would they still be willing to pay their taxes to the Rajah? They would? Well . . .

Francis began to explain the tenets of Christianity to the man who listened politely. In the end he gave permission in the name of his master. He himself? No, no. This new thing seemed very good, but he himself could not accept it. He was the Rajah's man. The Rajah would have to give the order to him personally.

"It is a pitee—a great pitee", said Coelho, when the man withdrew, rather hastily. "We could have called him Matthew."

It took all next day to baptize every man, woman and child of the village and two days more to tell them at least the rudiments of what they must know.

As they left, they saw the woman with her newborn babe in her arms standing in the door of the hut, smiling at them and making the sign of the Cross.

*　　　*　　　*

The children came in droves. There was no holding them back. They beleaguered the hut in Tuticorin, they stormed it and sat all around Francis, chattering away, nudging him, clambering up on his lap. They chanted the Creed and the Ten Commandments, the Pater and the Ave and they went on chanting when they went home. The very air of Tuticorin was full of it.

"Ants", said Coelho disapprovingly. "Ex-actly like ants. You can do nothing. You can only go away or they eat you up."

Francis shook his head. "That's not the way you've been taught. What did Our Lord say about children?"

"'Of such is the kingdom of heaven'", quoted Coelho dutifully. "They will have to make less noise there, though. Perrrsonallee, I cannot see why it is good for the kingdom of heaven, if these brats do not let you eat or sleep ever!"

"They ask questions", said Francis, beaming. "They *want* to know, Coelho. They do not accept it, as if it were just another law of their Rajah's. They are full of it, God bless them and send me more of them."

He had his wish. In fact he could never go anywhere, without at least a hundred and often hundreds of young, shiny brown bodies milling around him. Soon enough he made teachers of them who brought the truth he had taught them to houses where he had no access as well as to their own homes.

The very first thing he uprooted in their young souls was the fear he saw time and again in the eyes of their parents — fear of the spirits and demons of the woods and sea and air and fire, fear of witches' spells and sorcerers' power. It was no more and no less than a revolution. Never in the history of the Paravas had demons been treated with such irreverence.

The children delighted in reporting to him when and where one of those ghastly meetings would take place, where black cocks and rams were sacrificed to Bhawani, Siva's bloodthirsty wife and where everyone cringed before the eye of the priest of the goddess, to whom she gave power to wish any evil he liked on those who did not sacrifice enough and particularly on those who for some reason or other did not turn up at the meeting.

When they told him about that for the first time, Francis looked around the crowd of youngsters: "Who's coming with me to help beat the devil?"

They were so enthusiastic that he had to warn them. None of them was to say a word about it to anybody else. None of them was to do anything, except on the Father's direct order.

They assembled just as silently as did the worshipers of Bhawani and they appeared at the meeting, sixty boys, all between ten and fifteen or sixteen, just as the fat and entrails of a black ram began sizzling in a copper vessel before the statue of the atrocious goddess.

They pelted Bhawani with stones, then rushed in and upset everything and everybody.

Francis himself walked in and pushed the six-foot statue off its pedestal. It was of wood. He poured the contents of the boiling kettle over the statue. "Such is the power of Bhawani", he said in a ringing voice. "From now on no Parava will serve her or any other demon."

The villagers were in a daze. They had seen their boys burning mantrams and heaping ridicule on the sorcerers, but never before had anyone dared anything like this. The priest of Bhawani had vanished with great speed, and the goddess herself did not seem to take any action.

Standing on the wooden image of the fallen foe, Francis intoned the Creed while all his boys chanted with him.

Many such raids followed. Sometimes Francis took several hundred boys with him, to the utter destruction of a temple dedicated to the monkey-god, Hanuman, or to the potbellied, elephant-headed Ganesha.

"You must plow the field before you can sow the seed", he told Coelho. "And you must uproot the weeds that are only good for the fire."

* * *

What happened in Tuticorin and Kombuturé, happened in five, ten, twenty, thirty villages, all along the seacoast. Everywhere Francis preached, admonished, won over, baptized. Everywhere the children streamed to him to become his friends, his catechists, his ambassadors and his army. It was a bad time for demons. It was a bad time also for those who were ridden by one of those demons for whom no statue was erected even by the idol-loving Paravas: the demon of arrack, the toddy made of the juice extracted from the palmyra palms. Francis made the headmen of each village responsible for the drunkenness prevailing in his domain, when he found that many a Paravas, under the influence of arrack, mistook his brother or friend for a shark and went at him with the long knife.

He raced up and down from Vêdâlai in the North to Cape Comorin, sometimes with Coelho or another of his three helpers, sometimes accompanied by the headman of a village. It was necessary that the whole tribe understand that he was never too far away not to appear quite suddenly.

166

He was like a sheep dog, circling the herd and keeping the flock together, the only sheep dog for twenty thousand sheep grazing on a field of one hundred and forty miles in length.

He knew only too well that his work was insecure and he also knew why. Not only human nature, weak and prone to sin ever since the Fall, even human habit which reverted time and again to haunting old fears and the thousand and one superstitions which were supposed to banish them, not only arrack and datura and other poisons that made a man forget his miseries instead of carrying them as a man should—it was a certain class of men who endangered his work.

His first encounter with one of that class had shown him the power these men had over the minds and bodies of the Paravas.

In Punakâyal, in the main street of the teeming village, while talking to the headman, he noticed a tall, emaciated figure sauntering down the street. It was a man of sixty with a well-kept gray beard and a caste mark just above a proud nose. People were drawing back right and left and bowing. He did not respond to their courtesy. He did not even seem to see them. A child of perhaps four years of age, a little boy, was sitting in the middle of the street, cheerfully playing with a few sticks.

The tall man gave it a single glance and then stepped carefully aside, passing the child at a distance of several feet.

"At least the fellow seems to like children", said Francis.

The headman shook his head. "How could a twice-born like one who is only a Sudra?" he whispered.

"A what? Why did he step aside then?"

"He must not be polluted by the shadow of a Sudra child. He is a twice-born, a Brahman. Don't you see the sacred thread from his shoulder to the waist?"

Francis gave the man a hard stare.

The Brahman passed him as if he were not there at all.

Then and there Francis decided to tackle the "twice-born". He did not know that he already had trespassed on their immediate sphere of power, when he first led his swarm of boys against the meeting in honor of Bhawani.

Coelho then gave him at least an inkling of what he was up against. The Brahmans were the spiritual aristocracy of India, initiates to the sacred mysteries, towering high above all other castes, untouchable in their exalted rank, as the harijan were untouchable because of their lowliness. They were so holy that they could not eat food if as much as the shadow of a man of low caste had fallen upon it. They were priests, sages and prophets and their influence was immense. All the pearl fishers were Sudras. The caste was hereditary. No Sudra could possibly stand up against a Brahman.

"We shall see", said Francis grimly.

* * *

The twice-born came to visit him that same day. The villagers recoiled and fled at the man's approach and to his astonishment and anger Francis saw that even Coelho was uneasy.

The Brahman was dignified and courteous. He had heard so much about the foreign sannyasi, who was such a great teacher and could cure men by just looking at them. He was delighted to make his acquaintance and to bid him welcome in the land of the Paravas. It was most kind of the foreign sannyasi to bother about the spiritual enlightenment of such ill-favored and low-caste dogs as the Paravas. The Brahmans knew only too well how difficult it was to teach them anything at all beyond the exertion of their natural faculties.

Four servants brought baskets full of presents: fresh fruit, meat, betel and, in a beautiful ivory box, a number of beautiful pearls—pearls conquered from the sea in the face of appalling risks by the ill-favored and low-caste dogs of Paravas and sacrificed by them to the Brahmans in exchange for a blessing or, more likely still, claimed and received by the Brahmans as dutiful tribute to potbellied Ganesha or bloody Bhawani.

"Please accept in kindness these little tokens", said the

Brahman, "tokens of our admiration and respect and the sign of the respect we servants of the gods have for each other."

"There is only one God", said Francis stiffly.

The Brahman smiled. "To the servant of Siva there is only Siva", he said. "To the servant of Ganesha there is only Ganesha. That is as it should be and as the wisdom of the gods has decreed it. But confusion would result if we were to teach the lower castes that they must listen to us alone and not to anyone else. We are resolved not to contradict your teachings, wise man from the West, and all we ask of you is that you will not interfere with pious men and women rendering their tribute to the gods in our temples."

"I have no intention to be bribed by you or by anybody else", said Francis, and a quavering Coelho translated it. "Truth makes no bargain with error. Take your presents. I cannot accept them. I shall not rest till all Paravas have become the servants of the one, true God. And I tell you that many of them whom you call low-caste dogs are more pleasing in the sight of God than those who strut about as you do, believing themselves to be so high and exalted. Instead of parading your arrogance before men, evoke in yourself humility towards God and you too will be pleasing in his eyes."

"Surely one gift is worth another", said the Brahman, without so much as batting an eyelid. "And if these presents are not good enough for a sannyasi of your rank, you must forgive us for not having recognized your true greatness."

Francis swung around to Coelho. "Tell him", he said, "all the wealth of India will not change the law of the one, true God and the will of his servant."

Coelho translated.

The Brahman shrugged his shoulders, gave a courteous greeting and left, slowly and dignified.

"This is war", said Coelho in a low voice.

"What else can there be between truth and lie? And what do we have to fear? If God wants us to go on spreading his holy law, all the Brahmans in the world won't be able to stop us. And if God wants us to die, how could we possibly live? They can do nothing."

Even so, Coelho told the other two students that in future they would have to do all the cooking and that all victuals would have to be inspected very closely. Father Francis could not be bribed, but a Parava woman could, more likely than not. And even a few bristles from a tiger's skin, hacked very small and mixed with food had the disagreeable quality of perforating the intestines and bringing about a protracted and very painful death.

*   *   *

His boys were the most faithful of all, and by far the most militant. They loved to argue and they loved to fight. They could now be sent to other villages to teach the children and to pray for the sick. Again and again reports came of patients who had become well after their prayers. Youth was on the side of God. No wonder then that God was on the side of youth.

But both young and old now assembled on Sunday for Mass, prayed daily, sang the truth while at their work.

And yet—the influence of the Brahmans was felt almost everywhere. When one of them was near, the villagers were reticent and sullen. Many would not open their doors to the white man. Some refused to talk or to listen.

After an experience of that kind Francis returned to his own hut and began to write to Father Ignatius in Rome, pouring out his lonely heart.

After a few moments of brilliant display the sun had sunk as a stone sinks in water. Darkness in India came as suddenly as death, and with it came the hooting of night birds and the faraway howling of jackals. The first mosquito began its monotonous, insistent buzz.

"There is a class of men out here", wrote Francis, "called *bragmanes*. They are the mainstay of heathenism, and have charge of the temples devoted to the idols. They are the most perverse people in the world, and of them was written the Psalmist's prayer: *De gente non sancta, ab homine iniquo et doloso eripe me.* They do not know what it is to tell the truth but forever plot how to lie subtly and deceive their poor, ignorant followers. . . . Thus they make the simple people believe that the idols require food, and many bring an offering before sitting down to table themselves. They eat twice daily to the din of kettledrums and give out that the idols are then feasting. . . . Rather than go short, these *bragmanes* warn the wretched credulous people that if they fail to provide what is required of them, the idols will encompass their deaths, or inflict disease, or send devils to their houses. They have little learning, but abundance of iniquity and malice. They regard me as a great nuisance because I keep on exposing their wickedness all the time, but when I get one or other of them alone they admit their deceptions and tell me that they have no other means of livelihood than those stone idols and the lies they concoct about them. They really think that I know more than all of them put together and they request me to visit them and take it ill when I refuse the gifts they send me to keep my mouth shut. . . . "

There was a stir and Francis looked up.

Coelho was standing in the doorway. "They have sent a message", he blurted out. "They want you to come to them. If you go it is certain death."

"What are you talking about?" asked Francis, frowning. "Who are 'they'?"

"The Brahmans, Father. They are having a full assembly at Tiruchendur. They want you to come there."

"Where is the messenger?"

"There were three of them—all Brahmans. But they would not wait. You know how they are. You won't go, Father, will you? After all it is sheer insolence, not to deliver their message to you in person."

"In other words, you don't want me to go", said Francis, smiling dryly. "And they will say that the strange sannyasi was afraid of them. And God will say that his servant

Francis out of pride or fear or sloth missed the opportunity to talk to all the Brahmans together. I will go tomorrow morning at sunrise. And I will go alone."

He did not finish his letter that day. Tomorrow evening there might be more to report, if he was alive to report it. It was quite possible—it was even probable—that Coelho was quite right and that the Brahmans had resolved to get rid once and for all of the nuisance that was Francis Xavier.

*   *   *

A man must step out briskly, if he wants to make the way from Tuticorin to Tiruchendur while the sun still shines. All is well in the neighborhood of the town, but there are a few stretches of forest and "forest" here means the jungle.

Despite his fear Coelho had begged to be taken along, when Francis departed, but the answer was a quiet shake of the head.

It was not that Francis wanted to punish his best helper. He wanted to be alone. By now his Tamil was good enough, he hoped, to cope with the Brahmans' arguments—if there were any arguments. He did not know what they wanted of him and he dismissed all surmise. He knew he had to go in the name of his Lord and that was all there was to it. It was much. It was so much that the man, walking alone through the jungle, paid no attention at all to the dangers around him. He did not even see the snakes slithering away at his approach as most snakes will. He paid no attention whatever to the long, brown shapes, like fallen trees, that lay quietly on the bank of a half dried-up river. The crocodile rarely attacks on land. But the very assurance of the man, walking alone, baffled a huge hamadryad into uncertainty and made it let him pass. And the hamadryad, the cobra of cobras, is ill-tempered and will attack without provocation. Parrots screamed and became silent. Monkeys chattered and became quiet. Silent eyes followed the wanderer all the way through the jungle.

*   *   *

They were waiting in the great hall of the temple beside the sea. Two hundred and four men, each one wearing the sacred thread of the twice-born, and in their midst Harit-Zeb, eighty-two years of age, priest in charge of the temple, and Devandas, of whom it was said that he was very learned.

On the other side of Harit-Zeb sat Ramigal, who came from the high North. He had vowed that he would go to the holy city of Benares on foot, following the seacoast. He was a young man, as the age of a single incarnation goes, no more than thirty-five years old. But for twelve years he had been sitting at the feet of an old man who had given up his name together with his heritage as the brother of a rajah and withdrawn to the mountains, and the ancient one had become Ramigal's teacher and taught him many things.

But even such as the ancient one must die. And Ramigal had burned the frail body of his teacher. It took him many days to carry up the wood he needed for the pyre, but the body must be buried where the ancient one had lived, facing the mountains at whose sight even a lower soul than his could see the smallness and insignificance of the busy activities of man.

Thus Ramigal had become a chela without a guru and he decided to go on pilgrimage to the holy city, to find enlightenment at another source. For alone he could not yet face the life the ancient one had lived.

Coming down into the valleys he found what the ancient one had told him he would find: men whose greed kept their souls prisoners, men whose hatred rode their souls with bloody spurs, and worst of all, men who used their sacred office as a pretext to deceive the unenlightened. "It is not from the rulers and their pomp, but from these deceivers that I fled into the mountains", the ancient one had said.

Passing through Goa and Calicut Ramigal had seen men not unlike the Parsee, though a little whiter, but their attention was given to the loud business on the market places, and they ruled under the protection of their arms—arms that could kill a man and even many men all at once with terrible force from a great distance. He had no interest in them.

Thus he arrived in Tiruchendur, where they received him with the courtesy due to his rank as a Brahman and asked him many questions about his life in the North and particularly whether his studies of yoga enabled him to perform certain feats that would astonish the unenlightened. The very question had shown him their mettle, and he declined to answer, hiding his disdain because he was their guest and because it was unbecoming to show disdain to someone less learned.

Then they complained to him about the workings of a foreign sannyasi who went about turning the people away from the service of the gods; but their main complaint was that so few people now came to bring offerings and that even threats did not always have an effect.

They told him that they had sent for the sannyasi, but were not sure whether he was going to turn up.

And now they were all waiting, over two hundred men of the sacred thread, for the arrival of the foreigner, a man who had never studied the Upanishads, who did not know anything about the sacred mysteries, a clever and glib demagogue, as they told Ramigal. What did they want with him? Surely, it was doing such a man far too much honor, to receive him in full assembly. He asked Devandas for the reason and Devandas smiled. "It may be that he has some knowledge. If so we shall soon know what it is. If not . . . " Devandas shrugged his shoulders.

They were inferior people. They were thinking in terms of tricks and hoping that the foreigner could teach them something new. Or—was there another meaning behind the idea of getting the man here?

It was senseless and purposeless to think about it. Tomorrow, Ramigal thought, he would go on towards the holy city of Benares.

Just as the sun went down and the slaves brought the torches, the foreigner appeared in the entrance.

*   *   *

The great temple had stood for many generations. Now that the sun had gone, the thousand and one obscenities performed by intricately carved stone figures on its many tiers were no longer visible. And the two hundred figures sitting closely together appeared like one huge body.

The thin man in black walked straight towards them, gave a curt greeting and at once asked in a loud and clear voice what their religion claimed from them as necessary for their salvation.

Old Harit-Zeb raised his hand a little and smiled. Would it not be better if the foreign sannyasi told them what commands the God of the Christians had for his adherents?

If this was a polite way of reminding the foreigner that it was not for him to ask questions of the assembly, it was lost on the barbarian from the West.

"I will tell you that, when you have answered my question", he said.

Again old Harit-Zeb smiled. "The two main religious duties are to abstain from killing cows and to show honor to Brahmans", he said.

Ramigal gave him a sharp look. Was this gross ignorance or was the old man trying to insult the stranger?

"If that is so," said Francis, "a murderer, thief and oppressor of the poor could be a man who still fulfilled his main religious duties. After what I have heard, I feel no wish to know more about your religion."

Ramigal winced. The subtle insult had been answered by a stroke with a heavy club. When the stranger walked up to them, he looked like a man who had some knowledge of things known only to the initiated. But now he went down to the level of those who were living in the plains. It was a pity.

"You have asked me what God demands of those with whom he is pleased", said Francis. "This I shall now tell you."

One by one he recited the articles of the Creed, always with a short, poignant interpretation of the meaning. Then he gave them an exposition of the Ten Commandments.

Old Harit-Zeb went on smiling all the time.

Devandas looked bored.

All this is extremely simple, thought Ramigal. It is a good teaching for children. But he thought it with only a part of himself. There was another part—and he was far enough on the way to know what it was—that fixed itself on the man who spoke and enjoyed his sincerity as a thirsty man will enjoy a drink of cold, fresh water. And there was a third part of himself—and here he was no longer quite so sure what it was—that felt a great and rising longing. Twice only in his life he had felt it before. Once, when he first met the Ancient One, the day before he became his chela. And a second time when the Ancient One was dead and his body burned. Then that longing had welled up, strong and demanding, and he suddenly knew that he must leave and go on his search till he reached the holy city. The first time the Ancient One had evoked that longing in him—either the Ancient One or something or somebody which in turn worked through the Ancient One and made Ramigal wish to follow him and become his disciple. The second time—he had often meditated about it—it must have been the soul of his teacher urging him on to undertake that search. But now? What could it mean now?

When the stranger had finished, Harit-Zeb thanked him. No doubt what he said was beautiful and true. All search for holy things was sacred and bound to lead to truth and all religion was searching. And therefore all religions were true. Now if a Brahman was eating the food offering of a Sudra—after due purification of the food, of course—it was by no means untrue for him to say that the god ate it. For was there not a spark of the god in him and did it not need nourishment as long as it was a prisoner in its present incarnation? And yet, how could this be made clear to a mere Sudra, still so much at the beginning of the long journey? Surely he could not possibly understand—therefore he was simply told: the god ate your offering. It was not just that the great foreign sannyasi should go about denouncing the Brahmans and it was hoped, very much hoped, that he would not continue doing so. In this hope all the brethren joined. Also it was not just that the great foreign sannyasi told his young men to destroy the sacred images of the gods. After all, the Indian gods had been in India long before the Christian God and there should be respect for that which is old—especially in the souls of young men. It was to be hoped—very much hoped—that they would in future abstain from such works of destruction. Because if the hopes he, Harit-Zeb, had expressed did not find fulfillment, the gods themselves were likely to take a hand and things then would happen over which even Brahmans had no control.

Francis listened carefully. His Tamil was not good enough to understand every word, but sufficient to understand the essential trend and he easily guessed the rest.

"When God was incarnated on earth", he said, "and became Jesus Christ, my Lord and your Lord, he told those who showed him the great temple in Jerusalem: tear it down and I will build it up again in three days. But he spoke of the temple of his body. And when they killed him on the Cross and buried him, he rose again on the third day. The idols that my young men destroyed did not rise again and more and more idols will fall. For there is only one God and he is not pleased with idols. It is because he wishes his law to be obeyed in India that I am here. And under his law there is no difference between a Brahman and a Sudra, but only a difference between those who obey his law and those who sin against it. Listening to you, one would think that it is you who demand equality. But the only equality you demand is that between truth and error and that can never be. The equality I demand in the name of Christ is that between man and man before God. And I have found more honesty and goodness and above all more humility and

177

faith in the Sudras than I find in you who are supposed to be learned and holy men. The vengeance of the demons you call your gods I do not fear. If you wish to accept the law of my God, I shall teach you and baptize you. If not, you must know that Christ has said: 'He who is not for me, is against me.' "

He gave them a greeting, turned and walked away.

Ramigal saw Devandas lean forward and whisper with Harit-Zeb. The old man nodded and Devandas rose and walked quickly, till he had caught up with the stranger.

"I am Devandas", he said politely. "Please permit me to accompany you to the hut we have prepared for your stay at night. I shall keep you company, if I may. There are some questions I want to ask of you."

Francis accepted. It was impossible to return to Tuticorin at night, when the jungle woke up. Besides, he was very tired, and he still had to say his Office. He was under little illusion about Devandas' questions, but one could never know for certain. . . .

Behind them, the assembly in the wide courtyard broke up into little groups. Then a steady flow of white-robed figures began to disappear inside the main building.

A short, thickset man bent down to Harit-Zeb and muttered something.

Ramigal saw that he had a sacrificial knife in the folds of his dress.

Harit-Zeb gave him an angrily hissing answer and the man, reluctantly, withdrew.

Ramigal said, "What is this foreign sannyasi doing?"

"He is the first and only of the Portugi who will not come to terms with us", said the old man sullenly. "He does not understand the law of give and take. But he will pass away—sooner or later. There are many teeth in the jungle and some of them are poisonous."

After a while Ramigal said, "That is not what I meant, my old brother. What kind of life does the sannyasi lead?"

"There is little doubt that he is possessed", said Harit-

178

Zeb. "Many say he never eats anything at all and he drinks only water, except when he celebrates his ritual in the morning. He goes about teaching and pouring water over the heads of the Paravas, invoking his God. He continually interferes when some of the people start a quarrel. He prays when they are ill and it is said that his demons hear him and that many walk again who should have died. This is particularly upsetting to us, because there has been no healer in the temple for many years now and they all go to him."

"He charges them heavily for the healing?"

The wrinkled, old face twitched in annoyance. "He does not charge them at all. Nor does he charge them anything for his teaching and the Paravas are too stupid to understand that anything given away cannot be valuable."

"What is his gain then?" asked Ramigal quietly.

"Ah, if only I knew! We thought it might be power. But power goes with display. Yet he has never been seen but in the same coat and he does not wear any precious thing on his body. He refused to accept our presents, and we sent him some good pearls. He does not accept presents from the Paravas either. They call him Father. It is bewildering, Ramigal—he really is treating these lowborn dogs as if they *mattered!* As if he could instill into them the understanding of mysteries, due to them only after another two or three incarnations. He tells them that his God *loves* them. As if it were possible to love a Sudra! We have had him under sharp observation, Ramigal. He does not pretend about the kind of life he is leading. He lives the same way even when he believes himself unobserved—unless, of course, his demon tells him when he is watched and when he isn't. And he sleeps no longer than two or three hours at night. The rest of the time he either reads a book he always carries with him, or he kneels in the middle of his hut and holds converse with his demon."

"When a man is thirsty for power", said Ramigal almost inaudibly, "he will kneel only before himself."

"What did you say? Ah yes, power. But what itch can it

179

satisfy in him, to be the father of many thousands of Sudras? Well, Devandas has gone to ask him certain questions. Perhaps we shall soon know more. There are some who recommend very simple ways of dealing with the problem—I am not for that."

Harit-Zeb broke off. He suddenly felt that he was saying far too much. After all, this Ramigal was a stranger himself. Devandas would have said he was being garrulous again— the impudent young man—if he had been present. But then he saw that Ramigal was no longer at his side. He was walking towards the entrance of the courtyard, very slowly and with his head bowed, deep in thought.

*   *   *

"We *know*", said Devandas eagerly, "that there is only God the Creator of all there is. This is one of the great secrets Brahmans know about. This is one of the things we are told by our great teachers. But it is not for the uninitiated. We must swear a most solemn oath never to reveal it to them, nor any of the other great mysteries. Yet I will tell you all. And in turn you will tell me all the secrets of the Christian religion and I will swear to you that I will not reveal them to anybody else."

"I will gladly tell you all the Christian mysteries", said Francis, "and I will hold back nothing—but only if you promise *not* to keep them secret, but to spread them as best you can. And the first is: he who believes and is baptized will be saved."

Devandas wrote it down. "I will write it all down", he said, "and you will baptize me. But you must never tell anyone that I have become a Christian."

"There is no need for me to tell anybody," said Francis, "but you must never deny that you are a Christian."

Then he saw Devandas smile, a crafty, cunning smile, the smile of a man who knew how to circumvent a dangerous situation, and he sighed and said wearily, "If you deny Christ, he will deny you."

"It must remain a secret", murmured Devandas. "No

Brahman can become a Christian, unless he can be sure that it will remain secret."

"I cannot accept you into the Church under such conditions", said Francis sadly. "Pray that God will give you courage to overcome your fears. At least you can teach those who come to you for advice that there is only one God, the Creator of heaven and earth."

"Teach that to the Sudras?" asked Devandas, startled. "I would break my oath and a demon would surely kill me. Siva has many servants." He caught himself. "I will pray", he said. "Most assuredly I will pray. But tell me, what incantation do you use that makes ill people well—even dying people? Or do you use a mantram of great strength? You do not accept payment in money or pearls, they say. But perhaps they must give you their children in payment. What do you use them for?"

"Go, Devandas", said Francis quietly.

The Brahman gave a short laugh. "I knew you wouldn't tell me your real secrets", he said. "But perhaps we already know them."

He left.

*   *   *

After a while Francis became aware of a shadow, darkening the entrance of the hut. He made the sign of the Cross and rose from his knees. So the man had come back. Perhaps they had given him fresh instructions.

But it was not Devandas.

"I am Ramigal", said the tall, young Brahman. His eyes shifted to a corner of the room, where a plate with rice cakes and some fruit was lying on a low table of brass. Something was moving on that plate.

A small, flat, triangular head appeared, raising itself high on a slim, stalklike body. It darted first to one side, then to another and now it slid down to the floor.

Francis saw it, too. Neither of the two men moved.

The snake hesitated for a few moments, then made its way right across the hut. Still neither of the two men moved. It was a krait, its bite deadly within a fraction of an hour.

It passed noiselessly between the two men and reached the entrance and was gone.

"What is it you want of me, Ramigal?" asked Francis.

After five heartbeats the Brahman answered, "When you told those men about what Christians believe, I thought it was a very beautiful thing to teach children. But then I thought who would dare to teach children things that are untrue? Then I saw that you yourself believed in your own teaching. And I heard from the lips of an enemy that you are living it. For the sake of my soul and for the sake of the soul of India, answer me: if God became incarnate on earth and suffered for all men, be they Brahmans or Sudras or any other caste, then is final salvation possible for a man even if he has not achieved perfection by himself?"

"No man can achieve perfection by himself", said Francis gently. "But by cooperating with Our Lord and on the strength of Our Lord's death on the Cross a man will be acceptable to God."

"If he can do that, there is no need for him to be reborn on earth", said Ramigal slowly.

"A thief died on a cross next to Our Lord", said Francis. "Surely a man who had not reached perfection. But he begged Our Lord to remember him when he came into his kingdom and Our Lord answered him: 'I promise thee, this very day thou shalt be in paradise.'"

Ramigal took a deep breath. "It is clear, then, that you have come to teach people how to cooperate with the incarnate God. It is not surprising that the basis of such teaching is simple. Great truth of its very nature must be simple."

"God", said Francis, "is simple."

The man who had been sitting for years at the feet of the Ancient One in the faraway North understood at once, and he knew that there was now no need for him to go to Benares, because he had found the holy city. "I have been searching for God a long time", he said. "Now I come to you and I beg of you: teach me, as you would teach a child."

* * *

When Francis returned with Ramigal to Tuticorin, he found so much work needing immediate attention that he had no time to go on with his letter to Father Ignatius. Several weeks went by before he could resume writing.

"The *bragmanes* tell me that they know right well there is only one God. . . .

"I let them have my views of their behavior; and I expose their impositions and trickeries to the poor simple folk, who out of sheer terror alone remain attached to them, until I become tired out with the effort. As a result of my campaign, many lose their devotion to the devil and accept the Faith. Were it not for these *bragmanes* all the heathen would be converted. . . .

"Since I came here only one *bragmane* has become a Christian, a fine young fellow, now engaged in teaching the children Christian doctrine."

Coelho slipped in. "The Captain has come back, Father."

Francis rose. At last. The official in authority for the Parava district seemed to have the gift of making himself invisible. He had a magnificent house in Tuticorin—magnificent at least in comparison to the other houses—and a great number of servants. But in all the months here Francis had never been able to set eyes on him. He either was "just gone" or "not yet back". Francis had written to him several times, but never received a reply. He was not going to let this opportunity pass. He put on his broad-brimmed straw hat and left the hut.

But it did not prove to be so easy to meet Captain de Paiva, even when he was at his headquarters.

For one thing, the entire approach to his house was blocked by the most unusual sight: a whole herd of horses. Twenty servants were trying to get them off the streets and into a corral adjacent to the Captain's house, but it took them a long time, and there was a great deal of yelling, and cursing, and loud orders roared from the direction of the house.

Francis knew that de Paiva had his hand in many different kinds of business and that horse-dealing was one of them. But never before had he seen such a large transport of the beautiful animals. To the best of his knowledge de Paiva bought them in Goa or Cochin and sold them to the neighboring rajahs, especially the Great Rajah or Maharajah of Travancore. What did he want with so many horses here at the Fishery Coast? The Paravas were not likely to buy them.

He had to wait for almost half an hour, before the way was free again, and then he saw the Captain near the door of his house, apparently giving instructions to a number of men.

Patiently he waited till the men disappeared. The Captain at once turned away and walked towards the door. Either he had not seen Francis or he did not wish to appear as if he had.

In no way discouraged, Francis went after him. "Captain de Paiva . . . "

The man turned round again. He was a sturdy, thickset individual, with glossy black hair, perhaps forty years of age. His eyes were a little too close together, the mouth full-lipped. In his right earlobe he wore a large diamond.

"Ah," he said, "Mestre Francisco Xavier, I believe. My house is honored. Please enter." The grating tone of his voice belied his courtesy.

Francis entered. He had not seen a house like this since he left Goa. It was full of precious carpets, vases, furniture inlaid with mother-of-pearl and golden trinkets of all kinds. There was so much of all this that it looked more like a warehouse than the home of a government official. He was made to sit on silk cushions and a servant offered arrack with lemon juice and sugar.

De Paiva grinned as Francis declined. "You haven't by

any chance become a Moslem, Father?" he inquired. "It is they who are not allowed to drink strong drinks, not us. Mind you, they drink it too, when there is no one to report them to *their* priest."

"Where do you encounter Moslems in this country, Captain de Paiva?"

"Not in this district. But up in Madura you find a great number of them and of course also in Cochin and Calicut. I do a good deal of business with horse traders there and a shrewd lot they are, believe me, Father. You have to keep your eyes open all the time. But I get along with them. I have to. Animosity is bad for business. Speaking of animosity, Father—I hear with great regret that you do not seem to get on very well with our Brahmans. Old Harit-Zeb is very— sad about it."

Francis told him exactly what he thought of the Brahmans in general and old Harit-Zeb in particular. De Paiva grinned. "I quite understand", he said genially. "The spirit of competition. But you know, it may be wiser to compromise a little more. Personally I am quite fond of old Harit-Zeb. And the temple of Tiruchendur gets some of the finest pearls of the coast from the Paravas. Gifts, of course. They give them to old Harit and he sells them to me. I would be very—grateful, if you could see your way to treating them a little better."

Francis managed to remain quiet. He remembered what the Viceroy had told him. "The only business I have here is to spread the Faith", he said. "Both in your capacity as a Christian and as an official of His Majesty the King I must count on your assistance. I have trained a number of men to be *kanakapullai*—catechists, teaching in the various villages. These men must be provided for and I have no funds."

"Why, let the Paravas pay them in pearls", said de Paiva. "If they're any good, I'll buy them from you."

"I am here to bring Our Lord to the Paravas", said Francis. "Not to sell him to them. My catechists are under strict orders to accept nothing for themselves."

"A sad mistake, Father", said de Paiva. "They'll never

believe that it's any good, unless they pay for it. I know them. Don't count on me for subsidies or whatever you may call it. I must give an account of all my official transactions to Goa. I don't want any trouble with the Controller of Revenues there. He's a sharp one."

"The Viceroy", said Francis, "told me that I should come to you for such things."

"In that case", said de Paiva cooly, "he should have informed me. But he didn't. And if he does, he will have to send me the funds for it. Sorry, Father, but I can do nothing for you on my own. Times are not easy. There is trouble brewing, too. We may have a bit of a storm in the near future. Let the Paravas pay in pearls. That's the best advice I have for you."

"Never", said Francis. He rose. "As you have no news from the Viceroy, Captain de Paiva, you may not know that I am the Apostolic Nuncio for all Portuguese territory in the East."

De Paiva rose too and bowed slightly.

"I am here", Francis continued, "on the explicit wish of His Majesty. Am I supposed to report that you have no intention to be of any assistance to my mission?"

De Paiva raised his hands. "I would gladly help you, if I could, Your Excellency, but what can I do? Without orders from the Viceroy my hands are tied. And I do so wish you could see your way to get on better with the Brahmans. It does not make life easier here, if you stir up trouble with them. You do not know this country as I do, Your Excellency. Compromise is essential, compromise. Too much interference is decidedly bad for business, and with all due respect to your rank, His Majesty does count on his revenues from India, you know, in fact very much so. My old friend de Sousa is new in his position. He will have to rely on the reports of his officials. . . . Incidentally, Your Excellency, it is a little unusual, is it not, that the Apostolic Nuncio is not at least a bishop. You have your credentials with you, I suppose—Your Excellency?"

"My credentials are in Goa", said Francis icily.

"Oh, really?" There was open irony in de Paiva's voice. "Sorry you are already going — *Father.*"

"You will hear from me again, Captain de Paiva", said Francis in a very low voice. And he left.

*   *   *

When Francis suddenly turned up in Goa, he took everybody by surprise. It was like the arrival of a whirlwind. People trying to see him at the hospital, found that he had been there, but had gone to see the Viceroy. A crowd assembling at de Sousa's palace was told that he had left there half an hour ago to see the Bishop.

At the hospital he found his mail. And one of the letters was in Father Ignatius' handwriting.

He opened it on his knees. For a minute or two he could not read a single word, the tears in his eyes blurred the text.

When he had recovered sufficiently the love radiating from the very first lines made him cry again and he kissed the letter, his trembling hands almost unable to hold it.

And then came the news, the tremendous news: the papal bull *Regimini Ecclesiae Militantis* had been signed by the Pope and Father Ignatius elected the first General of the established Order of the Society of Jesus, elected unanimously, with the exception of one vote — his own. Among the votes was of course that of Francis, left in charge of Father Laynez.

It was news two and a half years old; it had happened when he was still in Lisbon. What did it matter? In the mystic moment of joy a man lives, like God, outside of time.

The news electrified him. All worry, weariness and bitterness fell off him as so many scabs. He raced down the stairs, out of the hospital and into the street. He raced through the streets as if he were back in the old days of athletic feats in Paris, and people stared and recognized him and word went from mouth to mouth. "The saint is back."

He reached the palace. One of the sentinels knew him and went down on his knee for his blessing. The other just gaped.

He told the major-domo, beaming, that he had to see the Viceroy and the major-domo told him that the Viceroy was busy, but he could not help smiling, and Francis beamed still more and said it did not matter, he would have to receive him whether he was busy or not and the major-domo, infected by such overwhelming hilarity began to beam too and, babbling something about "absolute necessity", went to announce him.

A minute later de Sousa came out of his study, his arms wide open. "It's good to see you back and alive."

Arm in arm they went to the study, where Marcello stood, grinning.

"I haven't got much time", said Francis. "I must go back to my children on the coast, but I had to see you first. I need money. I need a great deal of money. And I must know whether that man de Paiva is evil or only greedy."

"He is as they all are", said Marcello. "Perhaps just a little more so. What's he done to you?"

Francis told him. "So you see", he concluded, "I must have money."

"You know," said de Sousa, shaking his head, "I think, if I were to give you some now, you'd run straight to the next ship out and leave at once."

"No," said Francis, "I must talk to the Bishop first."

De Sousa and Marcello burst out laughing.

"I've written to Lisbon about it", said Francis. "To the Queen. From Codim. There are four thousand fanam set aside for her, every year, from the revenue of the pearl fisheries. . . . "

"That's her slipper money", said the Viceroy, aghast.

"I know," Francis said. "And I told her she can have no better slippers to climb into heaven than charity towards my children at the Fishery Coast."

"You said that in your letter?" cried de Sousa.

"In so many words", said Francis. "But I need it *now*."

"And by the slippers of all the saints, you shall have it", said de Sousa. "I'll send four thousand fanam over to you this afternoon. I *had* written to de Paiva, of course, but I'll do so again. Mind you, he is not an easy man, I told you that before. And he's right at least about trouble brewing, I think. There's an old quarrel between the Rajah of Madura, Vettum Perumâl, and the Maharajah of Travancore, Udaya Marthanda Varna . . . "

"No," said Francis, frowning, "that's not his name. He's called Iniquitriberim."

De Sousa stared at him. "Iniqui . . . oh, I know what you mean. They call him Ennaku-tamburan. Means 'our King.' "

"That's what I said", said Francis. "And which of the two is in the right, Iniquitriberim or Beterbemal?"

"Vettum Perumâl, you mean. I don't know. I don't think even a political or legal expert would be able to answer that question. It's extremely complicated. Personally, I like them both as much as a sick headache. Trouble is, I can't come down to clear up the situation. My hands are tied up here, with His Infernal Nuisance, the Rajah of Bijapur. Paiva seems to think that old Vettum might be an easier man to deal with, but I have my doubts. Paiva is very vague about it, anyway. He complained bitterly about you, incidentally. You are stirring up the whole country. . . . "

"Captain de Paiva flatters me", said Francis, smiling grimly. "One day I hope I shall merit his flattery. What he says is what the Roman pagans said about the first Christians in Rome, is it not? I wish I could stir them up as much as Saint Paul did." His smile died. "Captain de Paiva seems to think the Portuguese are in India only for pepper and pearls. If his belief is shared by men in positions of higher authority, God will not allow the Portuguese Empire to stand for very long. The Fishery Coast could do with a better man than de Paiva. But this is your business, not mine, Your Excellency. With your permission, I will now go and see the Bishop."

"There he goes", said Marcello. "Look at him, sir, racing away like a boy. Well, he's got his four thousand fanam."

"And won't spend a single one on himself", said de Sousa. "I know that man. And I'll get the money back, too.

Yes, from the Queen. Do you think she can resist that letter of his? He's a wonder."

"And a great nuisance", said Marcello.

"Of course he is", assented the Viceroy cheerfully. "And so is religion, and for exactly the same reasons. We want to do one thing and we must do another. But what would we do without it? Besides, a real man is always a nuisance to somebody. He wants things done *his* way." He became serious, then grave. "I wish I could dislodge de Paiva, Marcello."

"De Paiva", said Marcello, "is nothing. But the men behind him . . . I need not mention any names, you know them as well as I do. And they need de Paiva. Do for Father Francis whatever you like, give him all the fanam he wants—but don't cross the men behind de Paiva. The da Gamas are against you as it is. If you antagonize the 'Great Web' . . . "

"Is that what they call it now?"

"Yes. And that's what it is. A web from Lisbon across Goa and the outer provinces to Malacca and the Moluccas and perhaps farther still. It's the Great Web all right. . . . "

"I am the King's Governor", said de Sousa hard. "I'm the Viceroy."

"But for how long?" asked Marcello. His voice was almost gentle. He had been with Dom Martim in good times and bad for over twenty years. "And the King—the King is far away."

*   *   *

"I've laid the foundations", said Francis. "There are cate-chists now in all thirty villages of the coast. Now what we need is priests. Priests. Priests."

Beside old Bishop Albuquerque, propped up with cush-ions in his heavy chair, stood Vicar-General Vaz, a tall, slim man with a high forehead and beautifully regular features.

"Of course you do", he said, after a brief moment of hesitation. "And we know full well that we should have sent you at least your own two men when they arrived with the royal fleet. You have seen them, of course . . . "

"Not yet", said Francis, "I didn't have time to go to the college. I shall go there from here. But I knew that they are here. They told me when my ship landed in Cochin."

"I've kept Father Paul of Camerino busy", said Vaz apologetically. "Father Francis, he is such an excellent teacher for our seminary. He is made for it, the answer to a thousand prayers, both of His Lordship and myself. And how could I send you that poor good fellow Mansilhas alone?"

"I thought that was it", Francis nodded. "Has Mansilhas been ordained?"

"Ordained?" Vaz raised both hands in mock horror. "How can you ordain a man who tries to tell me that he is now studying the difference between mortal and *veneral* sin!"

"Simplicity", smiled Francis, "is not even a venial sin, as you know. I shall take him with me. And I have brought two men with me—the Tamil Coelho who is ripe to be ordained and a young Brahman, Ramigal, who is now called Pedro. They're both at the hospital. And I think it will not be long before Pedro can receive ordination, too. Coelho I must take back with me. In the meantime I hope the Society will soon send us new men. If not, it won't be for lack of trying on my part, I assure you."

"Letters", said the old Bishop sadly. "How many letters have I written, year after year. . . . "

Francis' eyes sparkled. "I know, Your Lordship. And up to now your Order alone has come to the rescue of the East. But from now on this is no longer so. When my General, Father Ignatius, sent me out he said to me: 'Go and set all afire.' I am trying to carry out his order, but I know I need help, and that means that I must also try to set afire some of those at home. So I wrote home that I should like to go through the universities of Europe, shouting like a madman about the souls that are being lost. How many there are in such places, who think only of getting a high position in the Church through their reputation for learning, instead of using their acquirements for the common good. If only they would leave their miserable ambitions and say, 'Lord,

here I am — send me wherever thou wilt — even to India!' —
how much better their own state would be when they come
to die."

"A call to arms", said Vaz and now there was a sparkle in
his eyes too.

"At my arrival", said Francis, "I found a letter from my
General. The Order is established at last. I left my vows in
writing in the hands of one of my companions in Rome.
But if Your Lordship consents, I would like to make them
now before you."

"Thank you", said the old man, "for thinking me worthy
of it."

*   *   *

When Francis arrived again at the Fishery Coast, he left
Mansilhas at Manapad. As the dumb giant did not speak a
word of Tamil, he gave him an intelligent Parava boy as an
interpreter. He himself with Coelho went straight back to
Tuticorin. He found out very quickly that his absence had
done his children little good. They really were like children,
needing supervision all the time. At Kombuturé he found
that they had erected a little statue of "Kurami", as they
often called Bhawani, in a hut. He ordered the hut burned,
gave first the catechist and then the whole village in a mass
assembly a piece of his mind, gave the headman fresh instructions of how to deal with drunken women, married fourteen young couples, heard confessions, prayed over the
graves of the eleven villagers who had died during his
absence, baptized a number of newborn babies, told the
villagers the exact amount of revenues the government
claimed from them, thereby cutting Captain de Paiva's
demands as official collector of revenues practically in half,
laid the corner stone for a village church, said Mass at
sunrise and walked on to Tuticorin.

*   *   *

The two Tamil students he had left in Tuticorin greeted
him with overwhelming relief. They were very near a
breakdown from overwork and besides there was a strange

atmosphere of unrest and fear all over the town. "I know that feeling", said the older of the two. "It is just like before an earthquake."

"The earth may quake, heaven doesn't", said Francis cheerfully and threw himself into the work to be done. In the afternoon of the next day he went over to Captain de Paiva's house, but that worthy, as usual, was not at home and the servants did not know when he would be back.

Francis found them nervous and shifty. Their master, he thought, has no doubt a heavy hand.

On his way to a sick call he turned into the street of the fruit sellers and was halfway up the street, when he heard the piercing scream of a woman. He stopped in his tracks.

A sudden hush fell over the busy street. Merchants and bargaining women, even the children at play, all stopped and listened.

The scream came again, long drawn and horrible—and again and again.

In the dust of the street, perhaps a hundred yards away, two women appeared, and at first Francis thought they were drunk, since they seemed to be reeling.

Then he saw the blood streaming from the shoulder of one of them and he saw the other fall and he rushed up to them reaching the wounded woman just in time to keep her from collapsing, too. To his horror he saw that there was a deep cut across her shoulder and her left arm.

The other woman was writhing on the ground and when he looked at her even he reeled for a moment. She was pregnant and right across her belly ran a long gash, so deep that he thought for a moment he could see the child in her womb.

The woman he was holding up had begun to scream again and now he could hear that she was screaming a word:

"Vadagars! Vadagars!"

Among the cluster of terrified brown faces Francis recognized a man who had some knowledge of medical things and he shouted at him to help carry the woman into the next hut. "Get the midwife for this one—get bandages—get hot water."

But instead of obeying, the people recoiled, their faces twisted with fear.

"Have you all gone mad?" he shouted. Then he heard the noise—the noise of hooves, of horses galloping.

The villagers turned and ran.

"Vadagars!" screamed the woman at his shoulder.

Then he saw them—five, ten, thirty, forty men on horseback, all with red turbans and swinging long, curved swords.

"The Vadagars", howled the villagers, running for their lives.

The woman became suddenly very heavy and began to slide down. He saw an arrow sticking out of her back. Another arrow buried itself in the road right at his feet.

"In the name of Christ", roared Francis, wheeling round and facing the attackers. Half a millennium of crusades thundered in that ejaculation. He drew his own weapon—a black cross, six inches long—and raised it high.

There was such rage in him as he had never felt in all his life. It filled him to overflowing and under its tremendous impact he felt himself growing and spreading and filling the whole road with his body. The cross in his hand was the handle of a sword, whose blade reached to the very sky.

The commander of the raid saw a tall man—why! a gigantic man in black—barring his way. In a dead white face eyes burned like little suns. He had never seen a man like that before. And the man was shouting something, some terrible and incomprehensible curse.

He pulled at the reins with all his strength and his bay horse reared on its hind legs. Around him his men followed his example, there was a salvo of clattering hooves and the troop came to a standstill.

Francis said nothing. The whole troop to him was one entity, one foul, woman-murdering entity, born of the nethermost hell, and against that hell he set himself and his cross and it could not prevail against him.

The commander of the Vadagars bit his lip. This was either a demon or a sannyasi of a kind he had never encountered. If the man in black opened his mouth again to complete his curse... He tore at the reins, forced his champing, foaming horse to turn and made off, followed by his men. After a few seconds even their hoofbeats were heard no more.

Slowly Francis dropped his arm. He also turned, to look at the two women. They were both dead.

Wild screaming came from afar, from an entirely different direction. Perhaps it was another troop of raiders.

He rushed back to his house, to see whether Coelho and the others were safe.

On his way he had to pass Captain de Paiva's house. He isn't there, of course, when he is really needed, he thought grimly. He saw a number of servants carrying out large chests. One of them they had opened. There was something metallic in it. Well, it was only natural that de Paiva's men should try to carry his ill-gotten riches into safety. But where would they take them? To the ship, of course. One of the Captain's two little ships was lying at anchor in the small bay, a couple of hundred yards from the house.

Then he saw that the metallic glint was neither gold nor silver. It was steel. The case contained arms. Firearms. Again, that seemed natural. De Paiva's men were arming themselves. But were they?

If they were, why did that shifty-eyed fellow hastily close the chest as soon as he saw the missionary Father approaching?

Suddenly Francis stopped. The horses! The horses of the Vadagars. That bay horse their commander was riding— had he not seen it before? De Paiva. De Paiva had sold horses to them. De Paiva's horses carried those infernal raiders against his defenseless children. And these arms?

None of the servants made any move to transport the chests to the ship. None of them was arming either in defense of the Paravas or even in defense of de Paiva's house. Did they know, then, that nothing would happen to that house? Had they stacked up these chests as equipment to be used by the raiders?

He walked up. "What are you doing with these arms?"

They stared at him sullenly. They said nothing.

"Were you going to give them to the Vadagars?"

He had to repeat his question, before one of the men said defiantly, "Must obey Captain's orders."

"You'll obey my orders now", shouted Francis, and the man recoiled as if he had been shot. "Take up those chests—all of them. Get going—you, too, there! Lift them up. Now carry them to the ship. Get going, I say. Into the ship with the chests. There is murder enough going on here, without you adding to it by selling arms to the killers."

They obeyed. They could not resist him.

"When all the chests are on board, the ship must leave the shore", commanded Francis. "I shall hold you responsible, if these arms fall into the hands of the Vadagars."

Then he hurried on towards the mission house, where he found his three men nursing half a dozen wounded, both men and women.

"They just rode over them", Coelho told him, with tears in his eyes. "Now they're looting the shops."

"How many are there?"

"I don't know—I have seen three different troops of about fifty men each. They're Vadagars. . . . "

"Belonging to the Rajah of Madura?"

"Yes, Father."

"Get women to look after these. We must go out and stop bloodshed, where we can. If only I can get hold of that Rajah . . . "

They picked up a few wailing women in the next houses and sent them to look after the wounded. Then they ran on. Some houses were burning. Soon they came across the body of an old man, clasping a little boy to his chest. They were both dead of saber strokes.

"Up that hill. I must see what is going on."

It was a hill from which he had often preached to two or three thousand people. It overlooked the entire neighborhood. In the fresh clean air he felt as if he had been having a bad dream. Off there was the pure blue of the sea, the branches of teak and peepul trees were swaying in a brisk wind, the forerunner of the monsoon.

But below he could see the grotesque little heaps lying in the open streets, lying very still. And over there were men on horseback, men galloping—south, in the direction of Kombuturé. Not fifty or a hundred. At least four hundred of them and maybe more.

"Can any of you ride?"

They could not.

"We cannot get to Kombuturé in time, then. But we must get through to the other villages and we must warn Brother Mansilhas."

A terrible explosion shook the air. Turning, Francis saw a billowing cloud from the direction of the little bay near the Captain's house. The ship, he thought. The ship has gone up. It could mean that the chests had been handled without care and that one or more of them had contained powder. But it might mean something else.

He raced down the hill and his men followed him.

Several times he stopped, to help up a wounded man, or to chase a few children back into the houses.

They found the mission house still untouched. Francis sat down and scribbled a hasty note to Mansilhas. He gave it to the younger of the two Tamil students. "You're off with this to Manapad. See that you get there as quickly as you possibly can. On your way, warn all the villages, but keep out of the way of the Vadagars, do you hear? Brother Mansilhas *must* get this. And wait in Manapad, till you hear from me. Don't come back here. Whenever you pass a village, tell the people to be on their lookout for the Vadagars and when they approach, to take to their boats, *tônis,* catamarans, anything they have. They'll be safe in their boats. Ah yes—wherever there are little islands near the coast, tell them to go there with *all* their boats. Tell them I shall do what I can to help them. Is that quite clear? Good. Off with you—and may Our Lord be with you."

The young man sped away.

Next, thought Francis, what next? He was a general with neither troops nor arms. There was a moment when he had thought of arming the Paravas out of de Paiva's chests. But this would have been direct interference in a war between two Indian tribes or nations; and the Paravas with pistols in their hands—people who had never fired a shot in their lives! They would harm themselves more than anybody else. And above and beyond all such reasoning, that was not the right way to respond to what happened, much as the military instinct in him desired it.

He spent the better part of two days and two nights in Tuticorin. There was no more fighting, because there were no more Vadagars. They had all gone by now, leaving in their trail over thirty dead, half of whom were women.

He tried to organize the men, instructed them to post sentinels at the outskirts of the town who were to blow horns as soon as they saw another troop of the Vadagars approaching. At the sound of the horn, they were to take to their boats—in short he gave them the same instructions as he had given Mansilhas in his letter. If only he got it in time! And if only the Paravas obeyed him, who could not talk to them in their language!

He soon saw that the Paravas were hopeless in any kind of warlike activity. Their sentinels left their posts whenever they felt like it, and when he tried to drill them, they fought among themselves and two boats sank because of over-crowding, while six others were left empty on the beach. He appointed a number of men to supervise them, but was in some doubt about the firmness of character of the supervisers.

On the third day he received a letter from Captain de Paiva. It was extremely abusive. Apparently the Vadagars, furious at not finding the arms destined for them in the appointed place, had set fire to the Captain's house, manned a number of light boats, rowed out to the ship and set it afire, too, with fire-arrows. Francis gave a sigh of relief. In their blind fury the Vadagars had blown up the ship, instead of boarding it and finding their own arms on board. De Paiva did not, of course, admit in so many words that he had sold them the arms. Instead, he complained bitterly about the damage he had suffered through Francis' interference. Francis and only Francis had brought about all the misery. "Due to your scandalous behavior I am now stranded on a barren little island not far from Manapad. There is almost no food, and my very life is in danger, if I am caught here."

So the Vadagars were swarming about in the South now.

Again he dispatched a hasty note to Mansilhas, asking him to see to it that de Paiva got help. "Try to get as much food as possible to the islands where fugitives are."

A swift runner went off with his letter. Then Francis himself set out south, leaving Tuticorin in the care of Coelho. He found that the Vadagars had passed through Kombuturé, killing and looting as they had done in Tuticorin. The villagers had fled in confusion, old men had died on the roads, women given birth to their children in the open fields. Now the poor people pressed all around him and he helped, comforted, gave instructions. A runner arrived from the headman of Punnaikâyal. He brought a note.

Francis read it and the blood mounted to his temples. The Vadagars—thank God for that—had bypassed the village. But a number of Portuguese gentlemen, whose names the headman did not know, had been there and had forced four young girls to stay with them. Relatives of the girls had been chased away with pistols. In the morning the Portuguese had gone on, taking the girls with them. They had gone in a westerly direction, perhaps towards Quilon.

This was one of the moments when the humble member of the Jesuit Order had to remember that he also was the

Papal Nuncio. Francis sat down and wrote two terse notes, to the Vicars-General of Quilon and Cochin. "You will establish the identity of the ravishers by threatening major excommunication to them from the pulpit, unless they come forward to confess and unless they give up their victims into safe Christian hands."

He was beside himself. First de Paiva, then this! How could he expect people to accept the Faith if this was the example Christians gave them! It was there and then that he first conceived the idea of having the Holy Office established in Goa, the "Inquisition" as people had come to call it. A sharp instrument was needed to curb the gross appetites of certain Portuguese, calling themselves Christians. Vaz was the man to discuss that with.

Notes flew back and forth between him and Mansilhas. A fresh swarm of Vadagars had been sighted moving towards Cape Comorin. The headman had the villagers evacuated to a string of small islands, but of course they had *not* collected enough food, despite all warnings, and now they were near starvation.

Francis raced to Manapad. He drummed together all the men he could find, collected a fleet of twenty *tônis,* packed them full with food and sailed off towards the Cape, all in two days. A week later he was back again, driven back by the howling monsoon. In the meantime so many fugitives had arrived in Manapad that he had to distribute the food among them.

A very short note arrived from the Viceroy. "Travancore has been in touch with me. It would be good if you could see the Maharajah to discuss terms for an alliance; but if possible do not call him 'Iniquitriberim'. The gentleman who brings you this note is Senhor Pedro Vaz, a distant cousin of the Vicar-General of Goa. Please remember me in your prayers."

Pedro Vaz was a sharp-faced young man with keen, intelligent eyes. "There are two ways to the Rajah's capital", he said. "We can take my ship, sail to Calicut and go overland from there. Or we can go straight through overland from here. It's shorter, of course, but it's extremely dangerous."

"It is as dangerous as God permits it to be", said Francis. "We'll go the short way."

Pedro Vaz grinned. "From what His Excellency told me, I rather thought that would be your decision."

Just before they left, news came that Captain de Paiva had returned to Tuticorin and—arrested a slave belonging to the Maharajah of Travancore and carried him away in chains.

"That man!" exclaimed Francis in desperation. "Will he never do anything but mischief? How can we go to the Maharajah now?"

"He may have us chained in reprisal, or worse", Pedro Vaz nodded. "No good trying to chase after that slave. By now he is likely to be in the hands of the Rajah of Madura."

"But how can de Paiva dare to side with that man", stormed Francis. "Doesn't he know that his own government is opposed to him?"

"Oh, he knows that all right. After what you told me, it's probably his little way to get into the good books of the Rajah of Madura again. If he were alone in this, de Sousa could break him easily, of course. But it's an open secret that he isn't."

"But who is with him in this treachery?"

Vaz shrugged his shoulders. "A fair number of *very* rich men. Viceroys come and go, Your Excellency, but these rich men stay on."

Stay on—siding with the Rajah who sent his murderers into Christian villages. For the second time Francis thought of the Holy Office.

"Of course", said Vaz dryly, "we may never arrive even if we go to see the Maharajah. De Paiva is bound to hear about it. He has agents practically everywhere."

He could have said nothing better calculated to bring Francis to a decision. "We shall start at once", he said curtly.

They set out early in the morning, just the two of them. It was Francis' suggestion. "The more we are, the easier it'll be to see us." Vaz had suggested a disguise, but that Francis refused. They saw a man plowing a field. The bullocks moved ponderously, their huge horns nodding a little. The man was singing. He was singing the Creed.

To hide his tears, Francis strode out at a quicker pace.

It was this picture, this little event that somehow settled the whole issue in his mind. From now on to meet the Great Rajah of Travancore was as inevitable to him as to meet God at the end of life's journey.

He was under no illusion about the dangers and obstacles of the way. It came almost as a surprise that the first day passed without incident, except for the ludicrous one of picking up half a hundred leeches when they crossed a ford. It was not easy to pluck them off and by the time they had succeeded, most of the little brutes had had their fill. "It's just like Dr. de Saraiva bleeding me again", Francis laughed.

They spent the night at the house of a peasant who gave them a bowl of rice and some vegetable curry. "*Jai ram, huzoor*—it's all I have." He would not accept payment, although he was not a Christian. This ought to have made them suspicious, but they were too tired to think much about it.

Francis awoke with two strong hands dragging him up. Struggling against them, he suddenly saw that it was Vaz and then he smelled the smoke. His bed was on fire. He rolled off quickly and jumped to his feet.

"Are you all right?" whispered Vaz anxiously. "No, don't try to extinguish the fire. It was deliberate. I saw the man who did it. Our host."

Francis looked about. "You are certain? Very well, then we must leave quickly. Where is the man?"

"Somewhere outside, and I very much fear he isn't alone either. I told you, our journey might be known very quickly to de Paiva."

"We have no proof. . . . But let's get out first, or we'll both be burned to death."

They slipped away. At the door Francis said: "Careful now, they may *want* us to come out. We'll rush over to the trees, heads down."

It was still very dark, and there was grass all around the hut. Even so their steps must have been heard. There was a sharp swish-swish and a dull plop and Vaz heard a muffled groan. He could see Francis very dimly just in front of him, running and he kept up with him. The edge of the jungle was near enough. There were voices behind them, one barking something, the other answering. Then the trees engulfed them and they had to slow down.

"Father Francis, are you all right?"

"Yes", Francis said, panting. "But if you could kindly get that arrow out of my shoulder . . . "

"Mother Maria . . . "

"Shshsh. She'll hear you even if you don't shout and then these fellows will *not* hear you. It's nothing, just a scratch. There, it comes out quite easily. Now let's find some place where we can sleep, without somebody setting fire to our beds. And thank you for noticing it in time and waking me."

Vaz looked about. "A place where we can sleep—that's easier said than found. And if these men follow us . . . "

"They won't."

"What do you mean? Why not?"

"They won't enter the jungle by night. It's too dangerous. This is leopard country. There might be a tiger or two."

"A comfortable thought."

"Yes, isn't it?" Francis gave a short laugh. "I wish I could see a little more. Here. This will do splendidly."

"What? Oh, the tree. It's hollow."

"Better make sure first that it isn't somebody else's quarters." Francis cut a stick off the next tree and began to probe the hollow with it. "Seems to be uninhabited. And it's large enough for the two of us. No, don't worry about that arrow wound, it really is only a scratch. I'll climb in first."

They woke up to the shrill concert of the birds. They were cramped and stiff and Vaz had to help Francis who could not make much use of his left arm. They found a spring where they had a morning meal of water and chapatties. "Just as well I left them in my cassock", said Francis cheerfully.

Vaz looked at him. He said nothing, but he was worried about that wound. And for some time now they would have to keep off the beaten track.

They did. They circumvented three villages, always keeping to the edge of the jungle and well in the shadow. Twice they had to climb a tree to escape from the fast-footed boars in which the Tinnevelly jungle abounded. There were no more chapatties, but there was fruit enough and once Vaz, alone—a much less conspicuous figure—bought a whole stock of food from the headman of a tiny village.

On the morning of the tenth day, during their slow ascent of the Cardamom Hills, they saw soldiers. But their turbans were blue and Vaz recognized them as men from Travancore.

*   *   *

"Alone and unarmed", said Udaya Marthanda Varna whom his subjects called Ennaku-tamburan. "He must have powerful demons to do his bidding, to escape from all those dangers."

"They did not protect him from an arrow wound in his shoulder and from a scorpion sting in the leg", said Asanga Varna sulkily. "All Portugi are the same to me."

"It is good that I am the firstborn and not you", said the Maharajah. "Or else Travancore would be ruled by a prince without brains. It is precisely because all men in Hindi are the same to the Portugi, that they will always make mistakes in this country—which in due course will bring about their ruin. But until that happens, there is much to be done. We may not live to see it happen. And it would never happen at all if more Portugi were like this man, whose coat is in shreds and who looks as if sleep had not touched him for years."

"My elder brother is wise", murmured Asanga Varna, biting into a luscious mango. "I suppose he has decided what is to be done. So what good is it, if I talk."

"I have decided", said the Maharajah crisply. "I shall make the alliance the man Vaz proposes, because Vettum Perumâl will keep the peace, if he knows. And he knows it already, I think — the Vadagars are returning to their mud huts. He will no longer contest our ownership of that strip on the coast. Also this alliance will give us many guns, and it is cheaper to buy them at the source, instead of buying them through the man de Paiva."

"I hear he is very upset", said Asanga, grinning.

"How could he not be, when he hoped to sell arms to both sides and now finds that there will be peace."

"That is what the man said, whom you praise so much — the Great Father, as you call him."

"I have given order that everyone in Travancore is to call him that", said the Maharajah. "Even you, Asanga. And you will give him permission to enter your province and to teach the Macua his mysteries. It has done no harm to the Parava, it will do no harm to them."

"Are my subjects to forsake the gods?" asked Asanga angrily.

The Maharajah smiled. "If the gods are not strong enough to hold their believers, it is time for a change."

"And you?" Asanga leaned forward. "Are you going to become a Christian too?"

"Would it please you, little brother? Do you think the priests of the Macua will side with you against one who has forsaken the beliefs of our fathers? Do you, by any chance, have hopes . . . "

"I am my brother's slave", said Asanga Varna quickly.

"A ruler must be above such things", said the Maharajah quietly. "Or else how should he be able to make use of them? No. I shall not become a Christian. And that is why I will not see the Great Father again. But you will not interfere with him in your province. It pleases me—at present—to let him work."

*　　*　　*

The tall man with a bell in his hand walked through the country of the Macuas, and first the children came to him and then their parents, hundreds of them and soon enough thousands.

Once more the rumor spread that he never ate, or only, on very rare occasions, a little soup or a little piece of chapatty.

Once more many were cured when he bent over them, praying to that incredible God who cared for a Macua as much as for a Portugi and still more incredible, for an Untouchable as much as for a Brahman.

Once more the statues and shrines of ape-faced, elephant-faced and sword-swinging gods and goddesses were smashed to pieces.

There was peace again at the Pearl Fishery Coast, despite de Paiva's machinations.

The people of Vêdâlai and of the tiny island of Manar, between the southern tip of India and Ceylon, had sent messengers, *asking* for a priest to instruct them about "the new God who loves us".

Francis sent an urgent letter to Goa about it. It arrived a week after the ordination of two new priests. One was... Mansilhas. His Latin was still execrable. But he would not be asked to debate fine theological points before an assembly of scholars. The other man ordained was Ramigal, and it was he who was dispatched to Vêdâlai and the island of Manar.

There was news from Lisbon, too: the College of Coimbra, wrote Simon Rodríguez, had sixty students; and three Jesuit Fathers were on the way to India and must by now have reached Mozambique.

*　　*　　*

Chekarâsa Sêkaran, Rajah of Jaffna, knew perfectly well why his minister had demanded the special audience, and he was bored, because of the new girl lying before him, prostrate as befitted a girl who was given the greatest of all honors. She was lithe and beautiful, they had chosen well, for once, and he was looking forward to many things in which he had been a master many years. "Be brief, Tikal", he said grumpily, and the minister bowed, and spoke for a few minutes about the Rajah's subjects of the island of Manar.

"I do not care what the dogs believe in", said the Rajah. "You are wasting my time." Squat and obese and dressed in pink silk he looked like an enormous pink balloon.

"The Manarese", said Tikal, "have adopted the religion of the Portugi. This is not a religious fact. It is a political fact. Manar is a steppingstone between India and Ceylon. No man does anything except to gain an advantage. The advantage here is Portugi money, obviously—and Portugi protection. Portugi protection means Portugi rule. They also want an advantage. I have never seen a Portugi give something for nothing."

The pink balloon wobbled weakly. "You mean . . . "

"Sedition", said Tikar. "And I must have my Rajah's decision in the matter."

Chekarâsa Sêkaran thought about it. Tikal's eyes waited. The girl's eyes, too, were waiting. He drew himself up. "You will send troops. They are to retract their belief."

"And if they resist?" asked Tikal smoothly.

The Rajah was looking at the girl. "It is not advisable to resist the Rajah of Jaffna."

*   *   *

"My little church was completed last week", wrote Ramigal to Father Francis. "And so was my missionary work on this island. All its inhabitants are baptized, all over the age of seven instructed in the Faith, over sixteen hundred. Like ripe fruit they fell into the hand of God, joyful to serve. I am still not quite accustomed to being called Father Pedro.

Do you remember the first talk we had, in Tiruchendur, when I mentioned reincarnation, and you taught me that by the grace of God all could be achieved in a single life? Now that I am Father Pedro, I can see so clearly that more than one incarnation can be compressed into a single life. In a sense, a new life started for me when I joined an ancient and wise man high up in the North. But in baptism I was truly reborn from water and in confirmation I was truly reborn from the Holy Spirit. But now I know that it is not so much the matter of reincarnation that is the fundamental difference between Brahmanism and Christianity. The difference is first and foremost Our Lord himself—and the two commandments he gave. The word sacrifice is no stranger to us, but now I know that its spirit should be love and not fear. And whilst the yogi is bent only on his own sanctification, working on it incessantly and with great zeal, we, who must love our neighbor as ourselves, must extend our love in all directions. Nor is there any reason to fear that by doing so, our love will be diminished—for it is filled again to the brim, however often it is poured out like life blood. . . ."

He stopped. From far away across the sapphire sea a number of black dots were moving towards the island. Ten—twenty—thirty and more. Ships. Coming from Ceylon.

*   *   *

Good Father Gaspar, custodian of the sanctuary of Saint Thomas, the Apostle, in San Thomé, received his guest with a joy well mixed with curiosity. Rumors about the barefoot Nuncio had reached him years ago and each year had added to them.

His first impression was one of disappointment. Francis had always been described as a restless, joyful, dynamic personality, indefatigable, and of such charm that no one could resist it.

The man who came to stay with him for a while was pale, slow moving, his black, unruly hair mixed with gray, his eyes circled by purple rings. He was courteous and gentle, but there was an invisible wall around him. Day after day passed without the guest speaking a single word. Either he stayed in the tiny guestroom or he went to the sanctuary. Even at night he slipped out to go to the sanctuary. He seemed a ghost rather than a man—a ghost seeking the company of the spirit of the Apostle Thomas, at the place where the saint had died a martyr. Ah yes, a martyr. For the pretty story the Indians told about the Apostle being accidentally shot by a hunter who was aiming at a peacock was no more than an attempt to save face—to pretend that the Apostle's death was an accident and not murder. Mylapore they called San Thomé—Mylapore, the town of the peacocks.

*   *   *

"Guidance", prayed Francis, "guidance is what I need, more than ever before in this land of yours, Holy Apostle. You love them as I love them. No, your love is a thousand times more than mine, the love of a man who has seen Our Blessed Lord eye to eye, the love of a man who was allowed to put his finger into the holy wounds and who, first of all the apostles, addressed him as we still do when we receive his Body: 'My Lord and my God' ".

When news reached him in Cochin that the community of the island of Manar was no more, he could not at first believe it. But then came confirmation after confirmation. Father Pedro had tried to have the people evacuated in time, he used every ship on the island, but of course there were not enough. And he and over six hundred men, women and children were massacred by the Rajah of Jaffna's men because they would not give up the Faith. Mothers held up their babies, crying, "These are Christians, too."

There were moments when he exulted in the glory of it. Six hundred Christian souls in heaven, anchoring India there for ever and ever. And the blood of the martyrs was the seed of the Faith and had been from the days of Stephen onwards.

The word "Manar" was written in golden letters on the Throne of God.

But there was another side to it. The Rajah of Jaffna. . . .

Francis sped north to see the Viceroy. The Viceroy was in Bassein. Francis followed. De Sousa exploded when he heard the story. A fleet would go out to attack the bloody tyrant. It was to assemble at Negapatam. Francis would go with it. Indeed, it was impossible to let this crime remain unpunished. No Christian in the whole of India was safe, unless Manar was avenged.

Vengeance was the Lord's. But the safety of Christians was the concern both of a Viceroy of Portuguese India and of Francis.

If the Rajah of Jaffna escaped scot-free, every prince and princeling in India would know that he could do what he liked with Christians, without anything to fear.

The fleet assembled at Negapatam. And then the news came that a ship, a large Portuguese merchant vessel had foundered at the Ceylonese coast and that all its cargo—an enormous load of the most valuable goods—had fallen into the Rajah's hands. The Portuguese owners were negotiating with the Rajah. If there was a military expedition now they could be certain not to see a single fanam's worth again. Rubies! Lacquer! Silk of the finest quality. The goods were worth millions. There were discussions, conferences, threats, and finally . . . whispers.

The fleet did not sail. The rubies had prevailed. The fleet had to be used for other purposes. As long as it stayed massed in Negapatam, the Rajah would never negotiate with the merchants. It was well known who the merchants were. Their backers were less well known.

"Holy Apostle Thomas, I dare not even say that I have to do with people worse than those you ever knew. For you did break bread with Judas of Kerioth. If he sold Our Blessed Lord for thirty pieces of silver, why should not these merchants sell the Christians of India for a shipload of rubies, lacquer and silk?"

He had not left it at that, of course. He knew now who the real enemies were. Not the Brahmans; not the pitiful shortage of priests; not the horrible, stupid habits of the people; but a band of human vultures, calling themselves Christians and praying to Mammon. Pepper was their god, rubies and silk and lacquer and spices and above all—gold. They had formed a kind of camarilla, they helped each other, they used the de Paivas as pawns in their game. And people cringed before them.

But there was one institution, at least, which did not cringe. And it had weapons against those who, for the sake of greed, endangered the propagation of the Faith and the very life of converts.

Francis had met Vicar-General Miguel Vaz in Cochin for a decisive conference. He spoke without mincing his words. An overall plan was needed to meet this danger and to defeat it. He himself could not leave his post. But Vaz could, and should, and must. He must go to Lisbon and see the King. He, Francis, had written to the King, entreating him to nominate a Minister of Missions and to give that post to no one but Vaz. He showed Vaz copies of his letters to the King. Vaz was a very courageous man, but he blinked as he read: "I seem to hear voices rising to heaven from India against Your Highness, complaining of your niggardly treatment of her, while your treasury is being enriched by immense revenues, from which you give back so small a pittance for spiritual necessities." There was another letter imploring the King to make Vaz and no one but Vaz the Minister of Missions to India. There was a third, to Simon Rodríguez in Coimbra, asking him to prepare the soil at the palace.

"Make it clear to the King", wrote Francis, "that he is a ruler not in his own right, but under God. That he is responsible to God for his stewardship. What happens here is his responsibility. And if the King fails us, there remains only one thing to do: to establish the Holy Office in Goa."

"You are right", said Vaz gravely. "I'll do it."

Francis embraced him. "Look after yourself, though", he pleaded. "They tried to burn me in my bed and they tried to shoot me. They may try to kill you, too."

And now Vaz had sailed and he must wait for him to return, with those special powers so urgently needed.

Until then he could do nothing decisive.

But when Vaz returned, he must be ready for him.

He decided to prepare himself by going to San Thomé. At the foot of the tomb of the Apostle was the only place for him now, the loneliest man in India.

*   *   *

The Vadagars . . . he had thought of them as of a calamity at the time, but only as a calamity, as murderers, looters. . . .

Yet, if it had not been for them, he would not have gone to see the Prince of Travancore and would not have been given a free hand to convert the Macuas.

The thought came to him at his thanksgiving after Mass in the sanctuary. God had made use of the Vadagars. It was his way, it was that Golden Thread of which Father Ignatius sometimes spoke, the Thread of Divine Providence, over and beyond all human threads and patterns.

He had longed to see Father Pedro and his faithful on Manar. But Manar was desolation now and Ceylon was closed to him.

Could that also be the Golden Thread? Did God not want him to spread his holy will? Or—or was it that Ceylon, so near, so easy, was too near and too easy? He was the Papal Nuncio for all Portuguese territories in the East. Yet he had never gone farther than India. Father Ignatius had told him to go and set *all* afire. Yet he had stopped at Cape Comorin.

It would be a long time before Vaz came back.

That day Father Gaspar found his guest like a different man. He was loquacious, he smiled, he even laughed. Something seemed to have happened to him; Father Gaspar had no idea what it could be in this barren, lonely place. Later in the evening his guest asked him, quite by the by, when a ship was likely to sail for Malacca and the Spice Islands of the uttermost East.

Book Five

THE TALL MAN with a bell in his hand walked through the streets of Malacca, and first the children came to him and then their parents, hundreds of them and soon enough thousands.

They came much more quickly than they had come in the land of the Paravas on the Fishery Coast or in the country of the Macua, west of Travancore. They knew about him, who can say how? Ships must have carried the message, travelers told tales about a saint whom snakes and rajahs obeyed, who never ate and yet was always cheerful. As soon as he arrived, word went from mouth to mouth, "The saint is here."

Moslems came and Jews came and many who did not believe in anything, save perhaps a demon here or there. To those who did not believe in Christ, he brought Christ. To those who did, he brought consciousness of how they had failed Christ.

He had the bells of the churches rung three times a day and the people were asked from the pulpits to stand and pray wherever they were and whatever they were doing: to stand and pray for the poor souls in purgatory and for those alive who were in the state of mortal sin. And who was not? For Malacca was to Goa, what Goa was to Lisbon, and Lisbon to a city where Christians lived like Christians.

He woke them up. It was said—and it was true—that the captain of the ship that brought him here was a changed man. It was said—and again it was true—that he asked a sailor he knew was living like an animal and worse than an animal, to go to confession and that the sailor spat out a stream of foul blasphemies. The saint did not curse him in return, nor did he withdraw from him in disgust. He went on walking with him, till they reached a place where they could not be observed and there the saint took off his coarse coat and his belt and kneeling down started scourging himself mercilessly, asking God for forgiveness for the sins of the sailor. At the third stroke blood began to flow. The sailor broke down, begged the saint to stop, and then confessed to him.

It was also said—but this he contradicted sharply, when he heard about it—that he had raised a young boy on the Fishery Coast from death.

Perhaps it was an even greater miracle that he did definitely raise the moral and spiritual level of Malacca.

Many people feared that they would never be able to approach him, except in the streets. But they found they could always reach him at the Church of Our Lady of the Mount.

The day after his arrival a thickset, black-bearded man was seen climbing up to the church, where he met Father Francis in the sacristy and fell into his arms, roaring with joy. It was Dr. Cosmas de Saraiva, ex-surgeon of the *Santiago,* now the best doctor in Malaya. Both Francis and he were guests, that day, of another man they had both first met on board that ship: Senhor Diogo Pereira, now one of the richest men in the East. The poor of Malacca had a feast day after that reunion, and Dr. de Saraiva was to tease his friend Pereira for years afterward, calling him Zacchaeus, for the usurer in the Gospels, who gave half of his possessions to the poor after a single visit of the Lord in his house.

It was on that evening that Francis met Cristoforo Carvalho, a young man to whom success had come early in life. Like so many young men in Malaya and India, he had a native mistress. Did he love her? Love—well, no, it was not what you call love. It was not really possible to love a Malay girl, not in the sense Father Xavier meant. The young man was embarrassed. It was not exactly a theme to discuss with a priest, let alone . . .

"On the contrary, Senhor Carvalho. It is very much a theme to be discussed with a priest. You would not think of marrying the girl in question? Or would you?"

"Heavens, no. I mean—you must not misunderstand me, Father, I know that many of my friends think quite differently about this, and some of them *have* married Malay girls and are quite happy, as far as I can see. But I—I want children, Father, and I don't like too much what I see of half-caste children. I—I can't express it very well. I know Our Lord died for a Malay just as much as for me—only the mixture—it doesn't seem to be a *sound* mixture. But what can I do? There are practically no white girls in Malacca. I've often thought, if I went to Lisbon for a year or so. . . . "

"There may be no need for such a long journey", said Francis. "Go to Goa. Visit Senhora Ferreira in the Street-of-the-shipbuilders. Her daughter Beatriz is charming. Good, as well as pleasant to the eye. Give Senhora Ferreira my kindest greetings and when you have met Beatriz and feel that it is the right choice, you may tell her mother that I think so, too."

Carvalho blushed. He began to laugh. "You know, it is an idea, Father. It is an idea."

"If you're the man I think you are", said Francis, "you'll take the next ship."

*   *   *

There was mail from Rome. He kissed the letter and read it on his knees. Blessings came streaming to him across the tremendous distance. Pierre Favre was teaching in Louvain, and in Cologne and everybody said he was a saint. Of course he was. And how right that he should be where he was, where the most erudite and intelligent men came together to be disarmed by his gentle wisdom. If one could be there just for one day, for one single day, for an hour. . . .

Mail from Lisbon. The College of Coimbra was steadily expanding. Soon they hoped to send more men out to India. Mail from Goa. Dom Martim de Sousa's time was up. He was being superseded by de Castro, who was predomi-

217

nantly a military man, wrote Father de Borba, "with little understanding of what we are doing. But an honest and a good man, I believe." And the three Jesuits had arrived in Goa, Fathers Nicolo Lancillotti, João Beira and Antonio Criminali.

*   *   *

On the way again. Still towards the East. It was as if someone were gently shoving him all the time, go farther, go farther. Go and teach ye *all* the nations.

It was the strangest voyage he ever made, a voyage between heaven and hell. Nowhere else had he seen such glorious sunsets and sunrises, such radiant blues and greens of the ocean, such lush fertility on the countless islands the ship passed. Their very smell was inebriating, sensual and spicy. But often a brown and yellowish mist hung from the mountaintops and at night the mountains belched flames and the rich, fragrant aroma of the Spice Islands mingled with the stench of sulphur. How close they were to each other, hell and heaven, how dangerously close....

In Amboina he found that the Moslems had forced the natives to accept Islam at the point of the sword, for such was the command of their Prophet. The Moors again . . . and they had gone farther, up to a group of islands of which even the wild natives of Kerama and Ternate spoke only in whispers, to islands they called Morotai, after the Moors. He was warned not to go there. "You will never come back. They are headhunters. They are cannibals."

He established a church in Amboina, he taught and instructed and baptized. Then he left for Morotai.

*   *   *

They *were* cannibals. They had the charming habit of putting their own parents at the disposal of their friends for a festive meal, as soon as the older generation could no longer be useful. They shot poisoned arrows from blowpipes eight feet long. Death followed in a few minutes.

To find them, he had to pass through the worst jungles he had ever seen, across swamps breeding swarms of mosquitoes and full of crocodiles, across land infested with the most poisonous snakes in the world, with pythons and black leopards. But the most fiendish of all were the ants, red, brown, black and white. They got into everything and they were everywhere.

Long before he saw a single native the sound of strangely formed drums had announced his arrival. Rounding a small hill of rocks, he suddenly came upon two or three hundred of them, men and women with low foreheads, sullen, suspicious eyes. The blowpipes were ready for him.

He had one interpreter with him, a half-caste. He told him what to say but it did not seem to register at all.

Then he began to sing. He sang the Creed, in Malay. He had learned that in Malacca.

The savages listened. After a while they began to swing their naked bodies to and fro in the rhythm of the singing.

*   *   *

"A year and a half", said Dr. de Saraiva. "A year and a half under savages, headhunters, cannibals—and on the seas. I don't know which is worse. And he comes back, as if there were nothing to it at all."

"Malacca does not share his opinion", Pereira smiled. "I'm told they fairly beleaguer him up there in the church. His confessional is crowded day and night. Everybody says he's a saint."

Saraiva looked up, grunted and said nothing.

"It would be a strange feeling", de Pereira went on, "to have traveled on the same ship with a saint. When we started out, I thought he wasn't good enough for the table of the Viceroy. I said so, too."

De Saraiva sipped a glass of the excellent Xeres wine that his host favored. He remained silent.

"Oh, in the name of all the *other* saints!" exclaimed Pereira. "Why can't you speak up, man? Don't you understand that I want your opinion?"

De Saraiva looked at his friend over the rim of his glass.

"I'm a medical man", he said wearily. "That makes it ten

219

times more difficult. But it's no good keeping my mouth shut, I suppose. They say no one can be called a saint before he's dead. That is as it may be. I'm no theologian. But I've seen what I've seen. On the other hand I may be a little mad."

"What have you seen?" asked Pereira eagerly.

"I wish I knew", was the enigmatic answer. "This is very good wine."

"Man, will you talk or won't you?"

De Saraiva leaned back. He stared at the ceiling. "Well, you see, I'm medical officer at the hospital where he's living. It was the same way back in Mozambique. Always living with the sick. Now I'm not much of a praying man, ordinarily, but he has a way of saying Mass, I don't know how to put it. . . . Well, anyway, I attended his Mass. Every day. And once, after the words of consecration, he seemed to me to be raised in the air, his feet not touching the ground at all."

"Maybe you were drunk", said Pereira, breathing heavily.

De Saraiva gave a short laugh. "At five o'clock in the morning? It's about the only time when you can be sure that I'm not. Of course I may have had a hallucination or something, brought on because I—well, because I love the man, damn it all. All I can say is it would be the first and only one I ever had. What do you think?"

Pereira emptied his own glass of Xeres wine. He cleared his throat. He said nothing.

"Speak up, man", said de Saraiva. "Don't you understand that I want your opinion?"

*   *   *

When the church bells rang incessantly before sunrise one morning in late August, the Malaccans had the uneasy feeling that this time they were not simply a reminder to pray for the souls in purgatory or for those living in a state of mortal sin.

They were right. And soon enough runners appeared in the streets, calling all men capable of military service to arms.

"The Achinese!"

It was a scream of terror. Everybody knew them, the hated pirates of the Straits, the deadly danger for every ship, even a fleet of armed galleons or carracks. The Achinese were Moslems, ready to die in battle with the Christians at any time. Their mullahs taught them that to die fighting against the infidel meant that they would instantly enter paradise.

They crept into Malacca Bay with their light fustas, plundered the shipping, landed and attacked A Famosa, "the famous one", the very citadel of the town. There was a massacre in the streets near the port. The big guns of A Famosa fired, but it was much too dark to see what they hit, or if they hit anything. Governor Simon de Mello repelled the attack. The invaders disappeared as quickly as they had come.

The Governor was having breakfast when Father Francis was announced.

*   *   *

There was a war council in the afternoon, attended by all high-ranking officers. "I think we have every reason to be satisfied", said the Governor, smiling. "The damage to our dear merchants is of course very regrettable and even more so the loss of life in the streets near the port. Even so—the attack has been repulsed. His Majesty the King will like my report, gentlemen. The only person who does not seem to be content with our efforts is, I regret to say, our esteemed Padre Maestro Francis Xavier." The Governor's smile broadened. "He came to me this morning and practically demanded that we should pursue the pirates. I said: "Why? And what with?"

"And what did Father Francis reply, Excellency?" asked Colonel Pinto, a slim, sad-faced man with a gray moustache.

The Governor shrugged his shoulders. "The opinion of a civilian cannot be of much interest to us, Colonel."

"The opinion of a saint always interests me, Excellency", said Pinto quietly.

The Governor drummed with his fingers on the table.

"Saints, my dear Colonel, are not infallible. However, as it seems to interest you: he thinks that the Sultan of Johore will be watching our efforts and might be stimulated into attacking us, if he finds that we let the Achinese get away without pursuing them."

"It is quite possible", said Pinto curtly. To his surprise de Mello found the other officers equally impressed. "Gentlemen, gentlemen", he said testily, "how can we pursue these dogs without warships? I could of course, write to the Viceroy and ask him. . . . "

"It would take eight or nine months before a single ship from Goa could be here", said Pinto.

"I cannot create an armada out of nothing", cried de Mello.

"Perhaps not, sir", Pinto began to smile. "But Father Francis can."

"What?"

"I was called to the house of Senhor Diogo Pereira, two hours ago", said Pinto. "Father Francis had persuaded him to put his two caravels at our disposal—captain, crew and all. Pereira asked me whether I thought we could give him a few more light guns."

"Santísima!" said the Governor.

"Father Francis himself was not present", went on Pinto. "He had gone to assemble volunteers. I saw him for a moment, down in the Street-of-the-jewelers, marching at the head of a thousand men."

"Santísima . . . marching where?"

"To the port. They want to charter fifty small private ships. By now, I think, they will have them."

"Who is the Governor of Malacca?" asked the Governor of Malacca angrily.

His officers kept a respectful silence.

*　　*　　*

"Not a word from the fleet", said Pereira wearily.

Dr. de Saraiva nodded. "Should have been back weeks

ago. Months ago." He drank his Xeres wine. "Never mind, Pereira. It'll come out all right."

"Will it? You should have heard what I heard. The people are getting very restless. I've heard them say nasty things about Father Francis, too."

De Saraiva laughed grimly. "Of course. It's always been Hosannah first and to the cross with him afterwards."

"The Governor said yesterday that he never really intended this adventure—that's what he called it—but that his hand was forced."

Again de Saraiva laughed. "I hope he said it in the presence of many witnesses. He won't be able to claim that it was his idea then, when the 'adventure' has come off."

He got up.

"Where are you going, Doctor?"

"To see Father Francis."

"You want to ask him whether he's still convinced that our fleet will come back?"

"No. I know he is. I just want to see his face. Does me good."

"You're right", said Pereira. "And I'll go with you."

They found him preaching in church. It was packed. But the people looked down and many were weeping.

Suddenly Francis broke off in the middle of a sentence.

"Look", whispered Saraiva. "Look . . ."

Pereira only nodded. After a while the people raised their heads and looked, too. Something like a long-drawn sigh went through the huge nave.

The face of the man in the pulpit was chalk white, his eyes, shining, looked into the void. But—was it a void?

Suddenly he spoke again.

"There are women and others here who practise divining and consult fortune-tellers, only to hear from them that our fleet has been destroyed and that their husbands are dead. Rather ought they to lift up their hearts to God in thankfulness and to say a Pater Noster and Ave Maria in gratitude, for I tell you that today, this very day, our fleet has won a great victory and scattered the enemy."

Then he left the pulpit.

Caught in the stream of people leaving the church, Pereira could see that most of them did not believe what they had heard. He whispered to de Saraiva, "Do you think he said that to comfort them or has he had information from the Governor?"

De Saraiva pursued his lips. "I think he has had information—but not from the Governor."

"W-what makes you say that?"

"He had that same look on his face when he—well, you remember what I told you."

Pereira gave a deep sigh. "My two beautiful ships", he said. "I hope he's right—indeed I do, but . . . Well, today is the fourth of December. We shall see. . . . "

*　　*　　*

A week later the church bells rang again—for victory. The town was in an uproar. Ships broke out their flags. Carpets hung from a thousand windows.

The fleet had returned. Admiral de Eça had had to sail up one estuary after another on the western coast, to find the hideout of the pirates, till he cornered the enemy. The Achinese fleet was destroyed by gunfire. More than a dozen of their proas were captured. Portuguese losses were three dead and twenty-five wounded. And the battle took place on the fourth of December.

In the midst of all the excitement the mail ship arrived almost unnoticed.

Huge crowds assembled before the Church of Our Lady on the Mount and before the hospital, singing hymns in praise of the saint.

In his little room in the hospital, Francis was on his knees, sobbing his heart out. The long letter from Lisbon was lying on his desk, unread but for the first few lines.

Pierre Favre was dead. Pierre Favre was dead. The sweetest, the most angelic soul, his friend from the very beginning.

224

He knew, when he left for India, he would never see any of his friends again. Not Father Ignatius—not Laynez, or Salmerón or Bobadilla, Rodríguez, Le Jay, Broët, Codure—and not Pierre. He had cut out their signatures from their letters and he kept them in a little leather pouch, together with a copy of his vows, over his heart. His friends in the Order—they were the only ties he had on earth.

But Pierre had gone. Pierre had gone. O Holy Mother of God! Pierre had gone.

*   *   *

Had he really gone? Teaching in Louvain he was thousands of miles away. Was he thousands of miles away now?

Infinity knows nothing of miles, nothing of figures, nothing of time.

And Pierre was a saint. He . . . he had been a saint even before Father Ignatius raised him up higher still in sanctity.

Still kneeling, Francis crossed himself solemnly and prayed: "Blessed Peter—pray for me."

Strength came back to him and he rose and sat down at his desk and read the letter to the end. Father Laynez and Father Salmerón were doing brilliant work at the Council of Trent. Francis Borgia, Duke of Gandia, the grandnephew of the terrible Alexander VI wished to enter the Order . . . good news, good news.

Then someone came to announce the arrival of Father João Beira of the Society of Jesus, and he ran to meet him. From Amboina he had written to Goa and to the Fishery Coast, and ordered Father Beira and Father Mansilhas to join him in Malacca straightaway. So now they were here.

But only Father Beira had arrived, a dark, slender man with a sensitive face. Mansilhas? Father Beira looked down.

"He is not—dead, is he? Or gravely ill?"

No. Neither. He—could not—he did not wish—he . . .

He had disobeyed. He had broken the vow of obedience.

There was a pause. Then Father Francis began to speak of the vast field ready for harvest in the East, all over the Archipelago. He talked of Amboina, of Ternate with its slippery, sensual Sultan who had no wish to give up Islam as it would mean giving up his harem: "But the people, Father Beira, the people are ready. And even in Morotai. . . . "

He gave Father Beira a short catechism he had worked out in Malay, "With the help of my topaz, of course."

"Your 'topaz'?"

"Ah yes, we call all interpreters topaz. They are usually halfcastes and look a little yellow, almost golden in color. . . . "

"And if they are not precious, they are at least semi-precious." Father Beira smiled, much relieved that his Superior had fallen into a lighter tone after the first shock of disappointment, and having no idea that Francis forced himself to it for his sake.

*   *   *

It was time to go back to Goa. Any moment now Father Miguel Vaz would return, with special powers. Eight more Jesuits were on the way there, Father Beira told him. Also he longed to see how his children fared at the Fishery Coast and in the Macua region, and whether the murderous Rajah of Jaffna had been punished, and he wanted to say Mass for his lepers and find out whether young Cristoforo Carvalho had married Beatriz Ferreira. . . .

In the meantime he had a marriage to perform. A young officer of the triumphant fleet married a charming half-caste girl. There were clusters of relatives, an abundance of flowers and a general atmosphere of gaiety.

Smiling, Father Francis accompanied the couple to the church door, where they took leave.

Half a minute later he looked into the face of Destiny.

*   *   *

Destiny had a small, yellowish face with slit eyes and high cheekbones; blue-black hair; a short, stocky body and short, muscular legs. Destiny smiled and drew a deep breath, rather sharply. It made a low, hissing noise. And Destiny bowed deeply, several times. Destiny was a young man of about thirty-five, of a race or tribe Francis had never seen before in his life.

Next to this man stood Captain Jorge Alvarez, grinning broadly. Francis knew him well. He had met him in Goa and at the house of Senhor Pereira.

"It's a joy to see you again, Father Francis—allow me to present a friend of mine: Senhor Yajiro. From Japan."

*　　*　　*

Marco Polo already knew about it, although even he never boasted that he had got there. "Chipangu is an Island towards the East in the high seas, fifteen hundred miles distant from the Continent; and a very great Island it is. The people are white, civilized and well-favored. They are idolaters, and are dependent on nobody. . . . "

Six years had passed since Francis set out from Lisbon. Never in all that time had he met a man with such a thirst for knowledge as this Japanese. Ramigal, the Brahman, had understood him from the start, without an explanation. The supernatural seemed to come naturally to him. Yajiro never tired of asking questions, and behind him hundreds of thousands of faces seemed to loom up, as eager as he for the greatest message the world had ever heard.

But the moment came to ask him a few questions, too.

"What made you come all this way to see me, Yajiro?"

The perpetual smile became just a little strained. "I killed a man, Father."

There was a pause.

"Why did you kill him, Yajiro?"

"He was a samurai—a nobleman, Father. And my wife was beautiful. I killed him."

"And—your wife?"

"I killed her, of course. But she was only a woman. I was sorry, afterwards, because he was—innocent. I found out. His blood was heavy. Also his family pursued me, to avenge his death. I hid. In a monastery. A monastery of my own religion, Father. A Buddhist monastery. But the monks could not help me. Still the blood was heavy on me. Long afterward I met Captain Alvarez. He told me of a God who could forgive bloodshed because his own blood had been shed and he knew. He told me that this God had a great servant, Father Francis. So I came to see Father Francis. A long voyage, very long. I come to Malacca. Father Francis, he has left for islands far away. No one knows when he will come back. Maybe he will not come back at all. Sadly I go home. But the ship will not go home. We run into a typhoon, a terrible, terrible storm. We turn round and round. We turn back. The ship has a will of its own. We go back. When I come here again, there is Father Francis. We have a song in my country:

> *Tomo ni narite*
> *Onaji minato wo*
> *Izuru fune no*
> *Yuku-ye mo shirazu*
> *Kogi-wakari-nuru!*

'Those ships which left the same harbor side by side, towards an unknown destination have rowed away from one another.' It is the opposite with you and me, Father. Our ships come from such different harbors and neither of us knew where we would land, yet they rowed towards each other."

During a long evening Captain Alvarez had told Francis all he knew about Japan—he had been there twice—yet in a few words Yajiro had told him more than Alvarez ever knew.

"She was only a woman." that was what all the peoples and all the nations and all the tribes said, who knew nothing of the Mother of God. Here was a man whose conscience was deeply stricken because he had killed a man—so deeply that he would travel thousands of miles to find a God who could absolve him from his guilt. Yet it meant nothing to him to have killed his wife.

"Christianity, Yajiro, is not just a thing you learn about. It is a thing to be lived."

Yajiro nodded eagerly. "It is logical. I believe it. You will teach me, Father?"

"I will teach you. And in due course you will be baptized

and your guilt will be taken away from you together with all other sins of your life. But you will have to do penance. Is it still dangerous for you, to go back to your country? Will they still be after you for having killed the nobleman?"

"It is a long time", said Yajiro. "But there are men who have a long memory."

"As a penance—will you go back to your country with me? I shall not ask you to give yourself up, for you will reenter your country as a new man. But I may not be able to shield you, if they come to punish you. Will you come, nevertheless?"

Yajiro's eyes sparkled. "You will be the *taishi,* the Ambassador of God", he said, "and I will be your servant."

"It will not be for some time yet, Yajiro. First I must go back to India, to Goa. Will you come with me there?"

"I will, Father."

*   *   *

The most terrible shock was waiting for him in India.

Not in Goa but in Cochin. They told him that Bishop Albuquerque had arrived and wanted to see him straightaway. He went to his house.

The old man had been frail and ill when Francis left; now he looked like a shadow. He had shrunk, his robes were much too big for him. "Have they told you?"

"I have only just arrived, Your Lordship. What has happened?"

"Father Vaz has been murdered."

It was the most appalling sentence. But the Bishop added another, that changed it all to the downright grotesque.

"They are saying that I had him murdered."

Then the old man burst into bitter tears.

*   *   *

At first Francis seriously thought that the aged Bishop had lost his reason. He tried to comfort him, talking to him as if he were a distraught child. But then the old man told him what happened—so far as he knew it himself—and the story was coherent. Later, Francis gathered more details from prelates of Cochin and officials of the civil service.

Miguel Vaz had come back some time before—and the rumor went that he brought practically unlimited powers with him, both from the King and from Dom Henrique, the King's brother and head of the Portuguese Inquisition.

There was some talk that certain officials were to be put on trial before him, for deliberately preventing the spreading of the Faith, for abusing their authority in order to fill their pockets, for the murder of natives and the seduction and abduction of native women who were Christians.

A number of names were mentioned in whispers, but no one seemed to be quite certain about anything and everyone seemed to be afraid—afraid of sharing Vaz' fate, apparently.

A few weeks after his return Vaz fell ill. There were symptoms of poisoning: vomiting, convulsions, bluish lips. Within half an hour he was dead. A police inquiry met with insurmountable obstacles. No less than twenty people, including some of the highest officials in the land, had visited Vaz that day. It was impossible to accuse these people. Some of them were high police officials, or held equal rank in other branches of the administration. But there was a very definite rumor (repeated with downcast eyes and much shrugging of shoulders) that old Bishop Albuquerque fiercely resented the new powers of his Vicar-General and that he had had him put out of the way.

Francis listened to it all, his face a wooden mask. Then he withdrew into the nearest church. He must be alone with God. He could not stand their voices any longer, their murmurings, the sight of their embarrassment, real or pretended, their fear, real or pretended. He could not endure any more malice, any more cowardice, the outpourings of souls poisoned with a poison as deadly, if not as swift, as the one that killed poor Miguel Vaz. As he was praying, a shadow fell across the floor before him and he heard a smooth voice say courteously: "I am sorry to disturb you, Father, but would you consent to hear my confession?"

Instantly Francis rose, genuflected towards the altar and walked to the nearest confessional. A minute later he heard the voice of the man who had spoken to him, through the grille: "Give me your blessing, Father, for I have sinned. It was I who killed your precious Father Vaz. At least, it was done on my order. You did not look at me when I spoke to you outside—priestly tact, I wager. You did not wish to see the face of the man who was going to tell you his sins. But it does not matter. Nor does it matter whether you know who I am or whether you don't. This is the confessional—and if you breathe a word, if you make the slightest insinuation of what I tell you here, you also will be out for good—excommunicated. Thus, as you see, it is possible for the saint to be in danger and for the sinner to be safe. But I am telling you this not just for the sake of satisfying the glorious itch to tell *somebody,* as many a lesser man might have done. Nor can I give your priestly heart the joy of thinking that I am telling you this so that no further doubt should be in your soul about the possible guilt of the good old Bishop. My reason, Father, is grave, and it concerns *you.* What happened to Vaz will happen to anyone trying to interfere with those who have the real power in India. There you have my confession. I do not ask you for your absolution, I know you would have to make conditions which I am not of a mind to meet. Remember! No further steps towards dragging an ecclesiastic court to India. Keep your Holy Office for heretics and infidels, and above all, keep it in Lisbon, not in Goa. Good night."

Francis sat motionless, long after the footsteps of the man had become inaudible. But when he left the confessional he knew exactly what he had to do.

* * *

King João of Portugal had received many an outspoken letter from Father Francis Xavier. He would not have countenanced such directness from anyone else. But even

Francis had never before written anything like the letter that now went on its way, threatening him with hell fire if things were not changed and radically changed in his Empire in the East, and practically ordering him to give a series of instructions to his officials. "Order the Governor to give you an account of Christians already converted, and of the prospects there are for the conversion of more, and tell him that you will give credence to his reports to the exclusion of all others. But should he neglect to carry out Your Highness' intentions of greatly promoting the growth of our holy Faith, assure him that you are determined to punish him, and tell him with a solemn oath that, when he returns to Portugal, you will declare all his property forfeit to the work of the Santa Misericordia, and besides put him in irons for several years. Disabuse him of the idea that excuses or pretexts will be accepted. ...."

It was the first of twelve long letters that went out within the next days. There was, of course, his report about the voyage to the Spice Islands and its result. But for the most part the aim of his letters was to bring about the most drastic changes in the government of Portuguese East India.

The Augean stable had to be cleaned.

He raced to Goa, where he found the new Viceroy, de Castro, a well-meaning, intelligent and efficient man, but aged before his time and already weary to death of the effort to get some action out of his pleasure-loving, luxury-ridden, money-grabbing officials. De Castro was preeminently a military man. He hated the soft atmosphere of Goa, the feline intrigues, the perpetual lies and jealousies. To him it was a sign that the Portuguese Empire he loved and had fought for in many battles, was sinking, and sinking fast.

"I won't live to see its downfall", he said with a sad smile. "That at least is a sign of God's grace."

He was ready to fall in with Francis' ideas, but he made one condition: "Promise me to stay here for at least another year. The physicians are not happy about me—I shall probably die before that time, and I want you to be at my side, when the hour comes."

Moved, Francis gave him his promise. They worked together, "separating the wheat from the chaff", as Francis called it. In a special letter to the King, Francis recommended no less than thirty-four officials for promotion, men who had kept clean of the intrigues and the corruption and were therefore disregarded and held down by the camarilla.

At the college he found Father de Borba shaken to the core over the death of Miguel Vaz—so much shaken, that he himself looked like a dying man. But the college was flourishing; more teachers were urgently needed, despite Father Paul of Camerino's almost superhuman efforts.

At the college he also met . . . Mansilhas.

The giant started to blubber as soon as he was alone with Francis. "I . . . I'm desperately sorry, Father, but I couldn't come to those places you wanted me to go to, I just couldn't. Hurry, hurry, all the time. No peace, no quiet. And I had just managed to learn everything in Tamil, the Credo, the Pater, the Ave, the Confiteor, everything—and then they told me that people where you wanted me to go, didn't speak Tamil at all, but Malay. I . . . I couldn't face it, Father, I just couldn't."

"I did not want you to come to Malacca", said Francis gravely. "I *ordered* you to come there. You have broken your vow of obedience. It was not for you to decide where your work is."

The goodnatured simpleton blubbered even more when he was told that he was to be dismissed from the Society of Jesus.

"An army without discipline is no army at all", said Francis. "But you will remain a priest, of course, as long as you live."

"And I shall love you and revere you as long as I live", stammered Mansilhas. "Please pray for me."

Francis embraced him. But he did not revoke his decision.

*   *   *

233

No fewer than nine Jesuits arrived with the Royal Indian fleet, among them Father Antonio Gómez, chosen by Simon Rodríguez in Coimbra to become the new Rector of the college in Goa. Much as Francis rejoiced over his fresh troops, he regretted that Rodríguez had made this appointment without consulting him. His own choice would have been Father Paul of Camerino, who knew the state of affairs in Goa so much better. What was more, Father Gómez had a very high opinion of the abilities of Father Gómez, and very definite ideas about how to run the college.

"You will see, Father Francis, this college will become the Sorbonne of the East. And all its students will become Jesuits."

"I shall be very happy if they become good Christians", said Francis dryly.

* * *

Cristoforo Carvalho had married little Beatriz Ferreira. She was expecting a baby. "I shall have him baptized Francis, of course", said the young woman. "Or Francisca", added her mother, energetically.

"Oh, Mother, you know as well as I do, it's going to be a son!"

"We have this argument every day", said Cristoforo Carvalho, beaming.

Francis smiled. "It will be settled in due course. But remember — only pagans have little regard for a girl child. Our Lady was a girl child. . . . "

* * *

De Castro died, as he said he would, and even sooner than he expected. He died as he had lived, a good and brave man, and one of the very few who had never tried to enrich themselves by abusing their powers of high office.

On Pentecost, old Bishop Albuquerque baptized Yajiro.

In his own way, and mainly by his personal attitude, Francis had succeeded in clearing the old Bishop of the absurd insinuations that he had engineered Miguel Vaz' death.

But the camarilla was still at work. The police got nowhere with its investigations.

Francis made a swift voyage to see how things were getting on in Travancore, where the Rajah was taking a much less friendly attitude—also due to the workings of the camarilla—and to his beloved Fishery Coast.

They almost killed him with their love. Wherever he appeared, vast throngs milled around him, with everybody trying to talk to him, to receive a smile, a greeting, even only to touch his old coat. "You are our father and our mother", they shouted. He had to stay on a while; it was impossible to disappoint them. In Punnaikâyal they carried him on their shoulders into the new church.

* * *

Word of Francis' death came to Goa through a group of merchants from Cochin. He had been murdered by the arrows of hostile Indians.

Something like an invisible cloud settled over the city. People talked to each other in whispers. Many cried unashamedly in the open streets.

A crowd assembled from nowhere and marched to the Bishop's palace, demanding that Francis should be declared a saint and nominated the Patron of Goa.

All places of amusement were deserted, all the churches were packed.

A deputation of wealthy merchants went to see the Bishop.

"Your Lordship, everybody says this man was a saint. We must have his body recovered, cost what it may. We are ready to collect thirty thousand ducats for that purpose."

Outside there was a crowd again, shouting and yelling.

The Bishop looked out the window. Looked again. His eyes widened; then they closed. The old man smiled and his lips murmured a prayer. Then he turned back to the little group of men in his room. "Your gift is most welcome", he said. "And if you were ready to give so much for Father Francis' dead body, I am sure you will do so far more joyfully for the living one."

"W-what does Your Lordship mean?" stammered the leader of the deputation.

"I mean that Father Francis is very much alive. I've just seen him making his way through the crowd—with some difficulty. He's on his way to me."

*　　*　　*

"You ought to keep them to their promise", said Francis, with a wan smile. "I wish I knew who started that rumor, though."

"I have a mind to keep them to it", said the old Bishop grimly. "And to give the money to the college."

Francis shook his head. "Not to the Order", he said. Then he inquired whether there was news from the King. There was none.

*　　*　　*

A few weeks passed in a frenzy of work. At long last Francis could send priests to the island of Socotra. He wrote detailed instructions for all the clergy under his orders. " . . . be careful never to criticize the native Christians in the presence of the Portuguese. Rather you must take their part and speak up in their defense, for they have been Christians so short a time and have so small a grasp of the Faith that the Portuguese ought to be surprised to find them as good as they are. Try with all your might, Fathers, to win the love of your people, doing whatever you do for them with words of love. . . . Any alms we receive from men or women, or offerings made in church, we must give entirely to the poor, reserving absolutely nothing for ourselves."

Then once more he wrote to the King, who apparently had not reacted to his previous letter.

"Senhor . . . it is a sort of martyrdom to have patience and watch being destroyed what one has built up with so much labor. . . . Experience has taught me that Your Highness has no power in India to spread the Faith of Christ, while you have the power to take away and enjoy all the country's temporal riches. You must pardon me for speaking so plainly, as the disinterested affection I bear you compels me to it. . . . Knowing what happens here, Senhor, I have no hope of their carrying out the commands and provisions which are needed in favor of Christianity, and therefore I am, as it were, fleeing to Japan, so as not to lose more time. . . . May Our Lord give you to know his holy will and grace to accomplish it perfectly, as would be your wish at the hour of death. . . . This hour is nearer than Your Highness imagines, so be prepared, for kingdoms and seignories finish and have an end. It will be a novel thing, unknown in Your Highness' existence, to see yourself at the hour of death dispossessed of your kingdoms and seignories, and entering into others, where you may have the new experience, which God avert, of being ordered out of paradise. . . . "

On Easter Sunday, after Solemn Mass, he left for Japan.

* * *

"Let's get on with the writing signs of your language, Yajiro", said Francis. "If the weather changes, we won't be able to do much. What is the next one—ah yes, the one underneath, of course. Why can't you Japanese write as we do, from the left to right, instead of from the top to the bottom?"

"Why do people in the West not write as we do?" said Yajiro, shaking his head with earnest regret. "It is much more natural. When you describe a man, Father, you describe him from top to bottom, going downwards all the time. Why not in writing, too?"

Francis threw back his head, laughing. "You're quite right, really."

In the bow of the ship the two Spanish clerics whom he had chosen as companions were sharing a large parasol.

"I love to hear him laugh", said Father Cosmas de Torres.

"And he loves laughing", said Brother Juan Fernández. "And when men speak of him, even if they are thousands of miles away, they smile, and it's a kind of shadow of his own smile. Father Rodríguez in Coimbra, for instance . . . "

"You were brought up there, I know. Why is it that you are not ordained? You are twenty-six, twenty-seven, I should say."

Brother Fernández chuckled. "Father Francis asked me that, too, but I begged him to leave me as I am—for the time being, at least. Someone's got to do the menial work and that's just what Juan Fernández needs. I'm from Córdoa and my father had too much money. Need I say more?"

"Yes", said Father Cosmas de Torres.

"Very well then. He gave me too much money. And I spent most of it on clothes, perfumes, jewelry. I was a prize fop. I was so wonderful, I could hardly tear myself away from the mirror. I was a leader of society. Then I met Father Estrada of the Society of Jesus—and he made me really look into the mirror. I saw myself suddenly as I really was. So I went to Father Rodríguez and asked to be accepted into the Jesuit Order. Do you really want to hear all this?"

"Go on. We've never had an opportunity to talk to each other for more than a few minutes."

"Father Rodríguez accepted me—on one condition. That I put on my best clothes and ride a donkey through the main street, facing the tail end of the brute and holding its tail in my hand."

The priest laughed. "And you did it?"

"I would have eaten the donkey's tail, if he had asked me to. Of course I did it. It gave much joy to the urchins and my friends thought I had lost my reason."

"They often think that—when a man has just found it."

"Quite. So here I am. And you? You are thirty-six or so, aren't you? But you never were at Coimbra. Did you come from Rome? But no, I would have seen you in Lisbon, before they put us all on different ships."

"I come from the other side of the world, Brother Juan. This time, that is. And I've been roaming the world for ten years and more—first in Mexico, then as a naval chaplain in the Spanish fleet, under Admiral Rodrigo López de Villalobos. We set out to explore the greatest of all oceans, the Pacific. You must have been quite a sight that day, riding on a donkey backward, but it was quite a sight, too, to see my Admiral mixing his pure hidalgo blood with that of a native chieftain on some island in the Pacific. The fellow had his nose pierced and a bone three inches long inserted into it and his hair stood up on his head like an enormous, woolly hood. I've never seen anyone who looked so much like the devil, though he was a gentle enough man when you came to know him better. Then a storm drove us southwest and we landed in Ternate. Leaving there, we ran into a Portuguese fleet and there we took a real beating. My ship was captured and they brought it to Amboina. And in Amboina I met Father Francis. He looked after all the Spanish prisoners. After three days I knew the man was a saint. After a week I knew that I wanted to follow him wherever he went. After two weeks I had the courage to tell him so and he said, 'Meet me at the Jesuit college in Goa.'"

"I wonder why he has picked us for this adventure", Brother Juan Fernández said thoughtfully. "He had a good many men to choose from. You, of course, have had experience in traveling...."

"But not in Japan. I have no idea why we were chosen. It's no use thinking that he has a special love for us. He has—but then he has a special love for everybody."

"Could it be... could it be, because he felt that we wanted it so very much, do you think?"

Father de Torres looked straight ahead into the blue of sea and sky. "With many a good, spiritual man that would have been a reason *not* to take us", he said. "But with him—it is possible."

*　　*　　*

Two months later they boarded a very different kind of ship in the harbor of Malacca.

"It's unbelievable that it can sail at all", said Brother Juan, "in spite of its three masts. Why, of all the great, big, clumsy, lumbering tubs..."

"Have you never seen a junk before?" asked Father de Torres. "The one thing I'm worried about is that little squat figure over there on the poop deck."

"What is it? A statue of sorts. Fat little fellow, grinning all over his face. What's he supposed to be?"

"The Chinese Neptune. They invoke his help with all kinds of ceremonies. And I'm worried because Father Francis won't like it and when he doesn't like something, he acts. And if he throws old Neptune overboard, we shall certainly not get to our destination."

"Good heavens, Father, you don't—you can't believe that this absurd thing has any power . . . "

"Unfortunately it doesn't matter in the least what I think. But if that fat little fellow goes overboard, not a single Chinese sailor will lift a hand and the steersman will abandon the rudder. They believe in the little fellow. And we are too few to steer the ship ourselves."

"I don't think I could steer it if the General of the Order commanded me to", shuddered Brother Juan. "Things have been going too well, Father. Something has to happen."

Things had indeed gone extremely well. During the whole voyage to Malacca they had good weather. No seasickness. No pirates. And in Malacca itself they found the new Governor, Dom Pedro da Silva, almost falling over himself to assist them. He gave them no money to cover the cost of the journey and the first months in Japan; but he gave them a magnificent present of five tons of pepper instead, which he then had sold for them on the market; besides that he gave them bales of rich material to be used as presents to Japanese rulers; and he found them a ship, not an easy task, as no Portuguese ship was sailing for Japan for months to come.

"Father Francis has written to the King about it", said Torres. "He spoke of Dom Pedro with glowing praise."

Brother Juan grinned. "That'll do the poor King good. I'm told Father Francis hasn't been exactly complimentary about him in his letters so far. At the Bishop's house they said no one had ever written such letters to any king, and lived."

*   *   *

The Governor had warned Francis not to interfere with the Chinese habit of sacrificing to their sea god. It would take generations to change that kind of thing and any attempt to do so would be met by utter hostility. At the same time he had warned the ship's captain that he was responsible to him, the Governor, for the safety of his passengers. And the gnarled old Chinese—everybody called him cheerfully Ladrao, "robber", not only because his real name was simply unpronounceable for a Western tongue but also because he actually had been a famous pirate for many years—promised by all his ancestors that he would look after the passengers as if they were his own parents and children.

"They're about the only people he wouldn't sell into slavery, I suppose", said Brother Juan cheerfully. "Well, I'm glad Father Francis has been warned, too. How the people in Malacca love him! Did you see that gray-bearded Portuguese who embraced him as if he were his own brother?"

"That was Dr. de Saraiva. Father Francis has known him for years. And yesterday he had a last bit of good news—Father Beira is getting on well with the headhunters and cannibals on the Morotai Islands. Father Francis says they are really children and respond to the gospel as children do."

"Cannibals . . . " Brother Juan made a wry face. "I don't know whether I envy Father Beira. And I wonder whether they'll stop eating man—well, perhaps they won't do it on Fridays."

*   *   *

Francis had come to like old Ladrao. Even so, the ceremonies before the "fat little fellow" on the poop deck were more than a nuisance. It was not only a question of sacrificing to the "god". Time and again the *ho-chang,* after much burning of joss sticks and bowing and scraping, threw lots with little pieces of wood in order to find out . . . what course the ship should take. "We are sailing about on the whim of a devil of an idol", groaned Francis.

Soon enough it became stormy. Manuel, the cook, who was a Christian, stumbled and fell twelve feet down into a water-filled hold.

Francis instantly jumped after him and, with the help of two sailors, dragged him out again. It was not easy, especially as the Chinese were sullen and did not seem keen on really helping, and hours went by before the poor cook regained consciousness.

And then just as he was reviving, there was a terrible commotion.

"Someone's fallen overboard", gasped Father de Torres.

"Yes, a woman", shouted Brother Juan.

"A woman?"

"Yes, it's old Ladrao's daughter. He always lets her travel with him. I heard it only this morning."

The junk had no lifeboats. But even if there had been any, the storm, now at its worst, would have made a rescue impossible.

Old Ladrao closed himself into his cabin and would not speak to anybody. But a few hours later they were burning joss sticks again and asking questions of the oracle and soon Father Francis heard that according to the sea god the cook should have been drowned. As he had been rescued against the god's will, the girl had been taken in reprisal.

"One of us must remain awake tonight", said Francis coldly. "I shall take the first watch."

He was under no illusions. At any moment the Chinese sailors might attack and throw them overboard, to placate their angry god.

There were evil looks enough and even a few threatening gestures. But the night passed quietly.

A few days later an island came in sight—Sancian.

It took Francis an hour of pleading and even threats to persuade the captain out of his plan to land and stay there, only a short distance from Canton. He knew by now that the Chinese had absolutely no sense of time. If they stayed in Sancian, they would miss the monsoon to take them on to Japan. It could cost them many months.

A little later old Ladrao was equally determined to land in Changchow.

"That's the port Marco Polo called Zayton", Father de Torres explained. "And it's where they make a particularly heavy kind of silk. They call it Zayton or Zatin even now."

"It'll be the same thing", said Francis grimly. "If he lands here, we won't get to Japan for months. . . . "

But this time he did not have to resort to threats.

A ship passed by, another junk, and its captain shouted a warning. The port was full of pirate ships.

Old Ladrao did not relish the idea of having his junk captured. He was all for turning and going back to Sancian again.

The three Jesuits stood their ground.

Ladrao sniffed the air. "Wind is changing", he said mournfully.

A glance towards the sails and Francis understood. The wind was against Canton. The wind was for Japan.

The wind—which had spun Yajiro's ship around, when he wanted to go back to Japan, despairing of finding the priest from the West—was now for Japan.

And the wind, a few weeks later, made it impossible for the ship to land anywhere except in Kagoshima, Yajiro's native town, a small port, off the main trade routes. Once more it was the day of Mary's Assumption into Heaven.

Francis intoned the Te Deum and Father de Torres and Brother Juan joined in.

The fat little Chinese sea god, defeated, went on grinning.

Book Six

"WHERE IS Father Francis?" asked Brother Juan Fernández, fiddling with the joints of a large panel of lacquered wood, "I don't know how this goes together. You'll see, in the end we shall have a cupboard instead of a house."

"Father is with Yajiro in the house of Señorita Precious Jade", said Father de Torres. "And if all goes well, she will be called Mary next week. He can't help us with the house building and that's only right. If he were alone, he wouldn't live in a house at all."

"And sleep better than we do", Brother Juan nodded. "I caught a streaming cold from the draft. . . ."

"And I burned my left foot when I stumbled over a brazier."

" . . . and if the devil has any sense, he'll copy the Japanese custom of using a wooden block as a pillow for a human head. It's exquisite torture."

"To say nothing of sitting on one's crossed legs."

"He learned that in India. Father Francis, I mean, not the devil."

"He takes to this country like a fish to the water. He even likes that brew they're so proud of . . . "

"Chaa, you mean?"

"Yes, those crushed little berries, formed like tiny twigs and thrown into hot water. What a fuss they make about it! As if it were the finest Xeres wine."

"At least they don't get drunk on it. Pass me the hammer, please."

"Here—but be careful—this stuff is so flimsy, you only have to breathe against it and it falls to pieces. They don't get drunk from chaa, but they do from rice wine."

"Such wine! I wonder why Father Francis likes it here as much as he does. How can a man trust a country where hell itself is constantly breaking through the mountaintops."

Father de Torres laughed. "You might have said the same thing about Italy. Have you never seen Vesuvius? Or Etna? But I think I know why he likes it so much. It's because it reminds him of Navarra."

Brother Juan fairly gaped at him. "Japan? Like Navarra? You don't mean that, Father. I can't think of anything more different. In Navarra all is large and upright while here everything is small and dainty, as if it were made for children. The houses, the very trees, the people . . . "

"Ah, yes, but consider: Father Francis let me read a letter he had just written home. It was the most enthusiastic letter you can imagine. The Japanese are people with an astonishing sense of honor, they are not wealthy, but poverty is not regarded as a disgrace. . . . "

"True."

"A nobleman would not dream of marrying a woman of the lower classes, even if she were rich. They are extremely courteous and have much esteem for arms, carrying swords and daggers from the age of fourteen onward. They will not endure insults or mockery."

"The points are conceded."

"They are moderate eaters—they despise games of chance as just another form of theft—they are monogamous—"

"Right. I can see it now. And he might have added that they are as obstinate as the Navarrese, too. Why, we haven't made more than a handful of converts—a small handful. . . . "

"Yes, Father Francis says we must fish with a line here, not with a net. He still hopes he will find the way to the King of Japan and work from the top downward."

"He didn't mention that to the Duke, the other day, at the audience?"

"The Daimyo, you mean. No. Not yet. But he seemed quite a well-meaning gentleman."

"Seemed", said Brother Juan. "That's just it. Seemed. You never really know where you are with them, do you? They're courteous enough, too courteous perhaps, bowing and sucking in their breath—but I can't help feeling that at heart they despise us."

"Of course they do", said Father de Torres cheerfully. "Excellent thing for humility. Ours, I mean. They think we're utter barbarians who have no manners at all. And we do use all the wrong forms of tone and address and so on, you know."

"Why do they have so many? To say nothing of their ideographs, instead of a decent alphabet. Ah, well, it's all in the day's work. Pass me that panel over there, Father, please—I must get this roof right. All the matting is laid, and if we get rain before the roof is ready . . . there. Now it's going to be easy."

"I wonder whether it is because they're so small", mused Father de Torres. "Or, if you wish, because we're so big. They do not want to be smaller, so they must feel that they are bigger. . . . Good heavens, be careful . . . I knew that was going to happen. . . ."

Brother Juan had used just a little too much force and roof and wall panels came clattering down, demolishing the work of four hours in as many seconds.

He emerged from the heap, sneezing and gasping, but completely unperturbed. "My very own, private earthquake", he declared.

"You're not hurt, are you?"

"No, it's all such flimsy . . . I believe you're laughing, Father."

"Oh no, no . . . "

"So would I in your place. But now I know where the mistake was."

"Most of us need some kind of an earthquake before we know that."

*　　*　　*

The lotus flower, sacred to Sakyamuni whom they called the Buddha, no longer opened at dawn, under the first kiss

247

of the sun. But the seven springs in the garden of the Zen monastery went on murmuring, and some of the chrysanthemums were still in flower, great golden, brown and white blooms, larger than a man's head. No obscene carvings, no phallic symbols were worked into the slender beauty of the tile-covered pagoda.

This was the Zen monastery in which Yajiro had found refuge, years ago, from his pursuers.

Monks were sitting in a triple row on the pagoda steps, in the perfect repose of the lotus posture, their eyes closed or looking into the void.

Francis was moved. "What are they meditating on?" he asked in a low voice. Yajiro translated.

Old Nin-jitsu, the Abbot, smiled dryly as he answered.

"Some are calculating how much money they have received in alms", translated Yajiro. "Some are thinking of the next meal or of a new robe, or of some amusement. None of them is thinking of anything that matters."

Francis said nothing. Many a time he had walked through the gardens with the man whose name meant "heart of truth" and each time Heart of Truth said something that contradicted what he had said the last time. Once he had spoken of *samadhi,* as the aim of all meditation, the direct cognition of the nature of the Universe, a kind of sharing of divine Consciousness at its periphery—the Threshold of Happiness, the highest stage of the Eightfold Path of Buddha. And now this . . .

But perhaps the old man was just having his little joke, looking back from the wisdom of his seventy-odd years to the time when he himself had sat in the triple row, not yet capable of the meditation he was now attempting.

"Which period of life", asked Francis, "seems preferable to you—youth or the old age that you have reached?"

The old man threw up his brittle hands, as Yajiro translated, and answered with a wistful smile: "Youth, for then the body is strong, and a man can do as he desires."

Francis stopped: "What is the best time for sailing from

248

one port to another? When you are on the high sea, exposed to the tempest, or when you are about to reach the haven you elected?"

Again the wistful smile. "I understand, I understand what you mean. But I do not know whither I am sailing—nor do I know how the goal is to be attained."

"In Zen Buddhism", Yajiro explained with some difficulty, "there is no place for anything beyond birth and death. It is different, somewhat, with *Shingon-*Buddhism and again with *Shin* and with *Soto* and *Shinto.* Not all are like these here. Some are better, some are worse."

The Shin monks married and many of the others indulged in unnatural vices both among themselves and with their pupils, although others lived austere and ascetic lives, striving earnestly for the "threshold" of the highest Path.

Yet none of them knew that the final goal of man was not a threshold, but the entering into the sanctuary and the life in it, and that by living in it they could still be themselves, instead of being absorbed by the "All"; none of them knew that Christ had opened heaven to man by descending into time and space and matter and dying for mankind on the Cross.

They were living in a twilight sphere, particles of the All, little drops of water striving dimly for absorption in the ocean—and when a drop of water was absorbed by the ocean, it certainly was the end of the drop as such.

And in a flash Francis understood that Buddhism could be anything. That by itself it could not satisfy the urge in man and would be mingled either with superstition or—with the truth of God, of which it was the forerunner. It could become, it could develop into anything. Therefore, it could become Christianity.

It was not absurd that this old man was called Heart of Truth. There was in that name a longing, of which the old man was no longer aware. . . .

*   *   *

"*Maria,*" said Francis, pouring water three times over the girl's glossy black hair, "*ego te baptizo in nomine Patris—et Filii—et Spiritus Sancti....* "

The tiny figure in the flowery black kimono stood immobile, eyes downcast, hands folded. But the smile on the beautifully curved lips was no longer the ready smile of habitual courtesy, offered to everyone and shielding the true emotions. This was a happy smile. For the girl who had been Precious Jade and who now was Maria stood at the threshold by the merits of Christ and the strength of her own will. Long years were ahead of her before she would reach the sanctuary. No flash of sudden enlightenment told her that twelve years hence she would be a member of a Christian community of two hundred souls—or that in another twenty years she would be the only Christian soul in Kagoshima, all the others either dead or fallen by the wayside. The only Christian, mocked, jeered at, persecuted for her faith and still clinging to it as she would cling to the simple rosary Father Francis gave her at her baptism, wearing it round her neck in the open streets, resisting the anger of the Buddhist bonzes and the entreaties of her own relatives that she invoke Buddha Amida and the *kamis,* the house gods. Thirty-five years hence, Brother Damian, a Japanese Jesuit, would find her and report about her to the Superior of the Jesuits in Japan who sent for her and transplanted her to Nagasaki, where there was a flourishing Christian community and where she ended her days in peace, and was buried with Father Francis' rosary round her neck.

* * *

The Daimyo of Satsuma and Kagoshima was sitting high on a raised dais when the spy Inari entered and crouched before him.

"Your news?"

"Lord, the Western *Tôdô* has gone to Hirado.... "

"Your news, I said. I know that he has gone. What has happened there?"

"Lord, he went there, because a ship of the Western barbarians is in port, trading . . . "

The Daimyo closed his eyes. He had advised the Western *Tôdô,* the head priest, weeks ago that it was unwise to go to Hirado at this season, because of the bad weather and the man had taken the hint and stayed in Kagoshima. Now he had gone. But why? Because of that ship. If he had been such an important man, the ship would have come to him in Kagoshima. Perhaps he was not an important man.

"Go on, dog. Am I to wait all day before I hear what happened?"

"Lord, the *Tôdô* was received by the barbarians like a great chief much honored. He was invited also to the castle of the Lord Matsura Takanuba. There has been much talk about trade between the Lord Matsura Takanuba and the Portuguese."

The Daimyo stiffened. "That is all?"

"It is all, great Lord. The bonze from Portugal is returning and will be back here in two or three days."

"You may go."

Inari crawled out of the sight of the Presence.

What fools these barbarians were to prefer the northern ports to Kagoshima. Takanuba, of course, was quick enough to make use of their presence.

This bonze from Portugal had the esteem of his people in some ways, but he did not seem to be a political factor. Or if he was, he seemed to give preference to Takanuba. For the Daimyo of Satsuma and Kagoshima the presents of a few bales of embroidered silk and a picture of one of their Portuguese goddesses with her child. . . . To the Daimyo of Hirado the trade agreements and visits from Portuguese ships.

A servant, prostrating himself, announced the arrival of seven bonzes from various pagodas, asking for an audience.

The Daimyo granted it with the ghost of a smile.

They were most dignified and humble. For a long time

they had been silent, while these bonzes from the West went about, preaching strange things and making the stupid people follow their ways. They could be silent no longer.

"Does the activity of these foreign bonzes then diminish the revenues of the temples?" asked the Daimyo. It was impossible to say whether his question was sympathetic or ironical.

Certainly, when the agency of foreign demons was at work, the natural generosity of the people suffered, but that was a minor point. The success of the barbarians was negligible. Many people went to see them out of curiosity, but few returned and fewer still accepted the foreign doctrine which compelled them to accept a barbarian name. However, once they were taken into this new sect, they were then initiated into very terrible things. It was part and parcel of that accursed foreign doctrine to eat human flesh and drink human blood . . .

"Mendo-kusai", said the Daimyo. And once more no one could say whether he called the activities of the foreign bonzes "smelly troublesome" or whether by pretending to do so he uttered his disbelief in the horrible story of the Buddhist priests.

Yes, there was no doubt whatsoever that these men committed foul crimes under the cloak of religion. And therefore—not because of the quite insignificant reduction in the ecclesiastic revenues—they had come to tell the great Lord what was going on. They were most sincerely worried. They were anxious to avoid the dire consequences of such activities. If these people were allowed to increase in number still further, there would be constant murder, to say nothing of the profanation and destruction of the pagodas, once the foreigners knew that they had enough people on their side.

"Ingé", murmured the Daimyo. *Ingé*—the chain of cause and effect. "What measures will be necessary?"

There must be no more preaching and there must be no

further acceptance of Japanese into this new belief. It would be better if the foreigners left altogether. Then their beliefs would leave with them.

The Daimyo smiled. *"Tsuyu no jono",* he said, *"tsuyu no yo nagara—sara nagara.* . . . Though this dewdrop world is but a dewdrop world—yet, all the same . . ."

It was good enough. The priests knew that their wishes had been granted and they retired, a little yellow cloud of respectful dignity.

*   *   *

Two weeks later Francis said farewell to Yajiro. "We are forbidden to go on working. We must go. But instead of fleeing, we shall march forward till we reach the capital and the King. It is as I thought: only by winning over the King of this country can we win altogether. Do you feel that you are still in danger here? If you do, I could take you with me and leave Brother Juan Fernández here instead. By now he can speak Japanese quite well—I wish I had his gift for languages."

"Brother Juan will be able to serve as an interpreter", said Yajiro. "This is my country. I will stay here, Father, and look after those who have accepted the Faith."

"You did not answer my question about the danger, Yajiro."

"All of us are in danger, Father", said the Japanese simply. "And yours perhaps is greater than mine. God alone knows."

*   *   *

Yajiro awoke in the middle of the night.

Three men were standing in his room.

He jumped to his feet.

The men smiled. One of them gave a hissing murmur: *"Irrashai!* Condescend to come . . ."

"Where to?" asked Yajiro. "Who are you?" The light of the little lantern was dim, but he thought he recognized at least one of the three—a man called Inari and known to be in the service of the Daimyo. He could be wrong, of course.

"There is virtue in obeying", said one of the men.

They led him away from the house. The streets were very dark. It was the time of the New Moon, the time when a man succeeds in his undertakings. It was fairly cold.

Outside the town, near a little brook murmuring garrulously, they killed him. It was done very quickly and efficiently. He had not even time to see that they had prepared his grave beforehand. All they had to do was to lower his body into the hole and cover it with the loose, brown earth.

A week later the rumor went through Kagoshima that Yajiro had run away to join the pirates and some time afterwards there was another that he had been killed in a brawl.

* * *

Father Francis Xavier and Brother Juan Fernández were on their way to the King. They had left Father de Torres in Hirado, where Daimyo Matsura Takanuba continued to be friendly.

They knew very little about the King. People would not talk much about him. Was it because he was regarded as a kind of sacred figure? Some at least seemed to think of him as that. He was the "Son of Heaven", the direct descendant of Amaterasu Omikami, the Sun goddess. But Daimyo Shimatsu of Kagoshima never spoke of him, and when asked directly, slipped off to a different theme. And he acted as if there was no one to whom he owed an account of his stewardship. Daimyo Matsura Takanuba told them the way to go, if they wished to find the Son of Heaven, but nothing more than that. The King was a mysterious figure. As the head of Shinto he was a religious figure. If it was possible to win him for Christ, if he would come out of his remoteness and declare the new religion . . .

Kyoto was his residence. Kyoto, a city of many hundreds of thousand houses, they said. There he reigned in incredible splendor, aloof and mystical, the ruler of sixty-six kingdoms on all the islands of Nippon.

*　　*　　*

They had to spend the nights under a roof of some sort for it was now too cold to sleep in the open. But the inns were very dirty and the food almost uneatable. For many days they lived on nothing but rice.

Only in a Zen monastery they found warmth and good food. But they left without spending a night there, when they saw what was going on between the monks. Francis—through the medium of Brother Juan—told them what he thought of them. They seemed to take it as a huge joke.

When they left it was beginning to snow.

*　　*　　*

Snow.

They crossed by sea from Moji to Shimonoseki, ragged beggars, stared at and despised by the other passengers of the little vessel. It was good to rest one's feet for a while. It was not for long.

Snow again.

Here on the island of Honshu people were different. Perhaps it was because foreigners never came here at all. Even the children were nasty and suspicious, pelting them with stones or filth, and shouting insults.

There was little left now of the daintiness and the charm of the Japanese landscape. It lay under its huge white blanket in a state of *rigor mortis*.

"Now I understand why white is the color of mourning in this country", said Brother Juan Fernández grimly.

There was no answer. Father Francis was walking as if he were in a dream, eyes downcast, arms folded. He was tired, of course. But was it only that?

"Do you think we shall find a place to spend the night, Father?"

Again there was no answer.

Brother Juan Fernández fell back a little. It seemed to him that Father Francis had grown, grown to such size that it was not right and meet to walk beside him. He was walking across the blanket of the tremendous corpse that was Japan.

255

He was walking barefoot and always there was a trace of red where his feet had touched the snow.

Blood. He was sowing his blood into the soil of Japan.

Would it bring the corpse to life?

Suddenly Francis stopped in his tracks. He bent down.

When Brother Juan reached him he saw a tiny, emaciated body in his arms, a newly born child, a girl, still alive but beyond all hope of recovery. Here, too, just as in India . . .

Francis gave her to Brother Juan to hold. With the warmth of his breath he melted a little snow, to baptize her.

The baby died half an hour later and they buried the tiny body under a maple tree and prayed the prayers for the dead.

Then they went on.

*   *   *

In the great wooden city of Yamaguchi the Daimyo Ouchi Yoshitaka listened to the ragged strangers, but would not give them permission to preach or baptize.

In the streets they met with open contempt and once more the urchins ran after them, throwing stones and filth.

"Chikushōmé! Kuso!"

"What do they call us?" asked Francis calmly.

"Beasts and dung", replied Brother Juan.

*   *   *

They followed the coastline to Sakai. But from here on they knew they would not be able to travel alone, if they were to reach their destination. It was the most lawless and danger-ous part of the whole country.

A samurai, on his way to Kyoto, gave them permission to travel with his servants.

The samurai was on horseback. His servants had to be quick.

But this was the last stage of the journey. A few more days and they would at long last meet the King.

Francis forgot his weariness. The nearer they came to Kyoto, the more cheerful he became. He was wearing a Siamese cap somebody had given him back in Hirado and now he gave it a rakish angle.

Brother Juan laughed.

The samurai's servants eyed the strange pair, half-bewildered, half-amused. Some said that they were from Siam, the Land of the Gods. Others knew that they were barbarians from the South—from India—and probably quite mad. As it was always a good thing to humor a madman, one of the servants gave Francis an apple. Francis promptly began to play with it as a child plays with a new ball. He threw it into the air, ran forward and caught it, threw it up again, caught it again. . . .

Now there was no doubt that he was mad—hopping about on his swollen, bleeding feet and laughing and singing.

*   *   *

The scarecrow that was the Papal Nuncio for the East and Far East and Ambassador-Extraordinary of the King of Portugal and his scarecrow companion stood before the Imperial palace of Kyoto. It was an enormous, sprawling, ramshackle building, a maze of buildings, rather, with gardens and parks, surrounded by a bamboo stockade. If it had not been for a few curious faces, peering at them from large holes in the stockade the whole thing would have given the impression of being utterly deserted. It was not yet in ruins, but it looked as if it soon would be.

A small door opened, creaking, and a soldier stepped out. Perhaps a sentinel? He wore a lacquered helmet, and a shabby breastplate and carried a rusty spear. He walked up to them.

"Who are you? What are you doing here?"

Brother Juan explained that they had come from afar to see the King.

"The Tenno?" asked the soldier. "The O? The Dairi? Why should he see you?"

Brother Juan explained that they were special envoys from a country called Portugal.

The soldier walked all around them and grinned. "It must be a strange country", he said. "Where are your presents?"

Brother Juan was prepared for that question. They had not brought their presents with them. They would fetch them after the audience.

The soldier laughed contemptuously. "You come without presents and you expect to be received? One would think you had come from China that you imagine all doors must open to you as soon as you appear."

Francis listened carefully to Brother Juan's translation.

"China?" he asked. "Why China?"

Brother Juan passed on the question. Again the soldier laughed. "It is the country of the great Dragon, the country of the middle of the earth. Even the Son of Heaven speaks of him who rules China as of his elder brother. All good things come from China. Who are you that you do not know what a child knows?"

"Tell him", said Francis, "even China cannot bring the King as much good as we are bringing."

The soldier raised his eyebrows. "You have money with you, maybe? If you have five hundred silver tael, the Son of Heaven may consent to sell you a poem he copied. If you have a thousand, he will certainly sell you a poem, perhaps even one he made himself. You have no money? *Baka,* fool, you are wasting my time. Go back where you came from."

He turned away and sauntered to the bamboo door.

"I understand now", said Brother Juan. "The King has lost his authority. Kyoto is a forgotten city. Did you see how many houses were in ruins? I'll wager there are no more than fifty people in that palace. The poor man is selling poems. And for this we have come all that way...."

Francis smiled. "It would have been enough to come all that way to baptize the child we found dying in the snow. But there is more, Juan. Perhaps that soldier is quite right...."

"What do you mean?"

"China", said Francis. It sounded like an invocation.

*　　*　　*

All good things came from China. The ruler of China was the elder brother of the Son of Heaven. The ruler of China was a real ruler, a real king, whose subjects obeyed him implicitly.

If the ruler of Japan became a Christian, it would not inspire his subjects to emulate him. Not he, but the Daimyos really ruled the country. But if the King of China became a Christian, his subjects would follow his example. And then Christianity would come from China to Japan— from China whence all good things came. . . .

It was worthwhile to march for weeks and months, just to find and baptize a dying Japanese child. But only if China became Christian first, would the whole of Japan adopt the new religion, too.

Surely that was what Father Ignatius would think.

Time and again he had heard the Japanese speak of China in a tone of awe and reverence. Yet it was a simple soldier who pointed out the way to him.

China.

*   *   *

After a few days of rest they left the magnificent squalor that was Kyoto. The way back to Hirado was even more difficult, with the winter at its height.

Plowing his way through the snowdrifts, Francis suddenly smiled.

"What are you thinking of, Father?" asked Brother Juan.

"Of the first church in Kyoto", said Francis. "It will be called the Church of the Assumption of Our Lady."

Brother Juan gasped.

*   *   *

Brother Juan gasped again in Hirado, when Francis declared that he would go back to Yamaguchi once more, before leaving Japan. "But that's where we were treated worse than anywhere else!"

"And that may well happen again", Francis nodded. "But this time we shall have a different approach. They like presents and trappings. They shall have both."

He had made friends with a number of Portuguese merchants, and they helped him to organize a caravan with presents that even the richest Daimyo would have to respect: an arquebus, three crystal vases, a bale of brocade, a Portuguese dress, mirrors for the ladies, several pairs of spectacles for restoring the sight of the short-sighted, a manicordia playing seventy different notes and above all a chiming clock.

Both Francis and Juan had new cassocks and surplices and Francis a stole of green velvet.

*   *   *

They did not ask for an audience. They just sent the presents. Daimyo Ouchi Yoshitaka was vastly impressed and sent them a large sum of money.

Francis promptly sent it back. "It is not money that we want, but your permission to preach and to baptize."

It was granted. Moreover, the Daimyo put a large deserted monastery at their disposal, "In order to develop the law of Buddha."

Francis winced when he heard it, but he understood: it was the Daimyo's way of covering himself against the bonzes.

Now the work started in earnest.

Once again Yamaguchi showed itself at its worst. Brother Juan's Japanese was still far from classical and the crowd jeered at him wherever he spoke.

"*Deus . . .* " ejaculated Francis.

"Dai-uso—big lie", howled the street urchins gleefully.

A brutal looking man stepped forward and spat straight into Brother Juan's face.

A sudden hush went over the crowd. This was a deadly offense. Death was hovering over the offender. The crowd waited.

"Jesus cured the leper", went on Brother Juan, "and he performed many more miracles. But in their hatred, they had him arrested and when he was in their power, one man spat into his face. Later they nailed him to a cross. But he did not curse them. He prayed: 'Father, forgive them—for they do not know what they do.' Then he died so that by his sacrifice man should be reconciled with God."

A crowd of common people did not observe the rigid self-control of the samurai. There were tears in many eyes now.

Another man stepped forward, with a queerly shuffling gait. He was bald and blind in one eye. Under a tiny button of a nose his mouth was as broad as a frog's. His ears were enormous. He had a *biwa,* a kind of mandolin, slung over his shoulder.

"I make people laugh", he said in a loud voice. "But you make them cry. You are my elder brother."

No one laughed. Juan saw that the man had tears in his eyes too. "Men are born to be brothers", he said gently.

"Tell me," said the queer-looking man, "is it true that you have come from very, very far?"

Brother Juan tried to explain the distance between Lisbon and Yamaguchi and the people all around them made little noises of admiration.

"And you traveled all that way", asked the man, "to tell us about your God? For no other reason?"

"For no other reason."

"Brother," said the man, "at long last I have seen men who live what they believe and who mean what they say. Such men must either be fools, like I am, or . . . "

" . . . Christians", said Brother Juan.

"You are living at the monastery on the Hill of the Little Pheasants. . . . "

"We are."

"Will I be allowed to come and see you there? I have many questions to ask, if your forbearance and patience will permit."

"You will be very welcome—and so will everybody else."

When they came home they found a man waiting for them. He was about forty and his dress, like the sword and dagger in his belt, showed that he was a samurai. "I was very much opposed to your coming here", he said after a courteous greeting. "But I was present today and saw and listened. I thought there could be, to such offense, only one of two reactions: that of the coward or that of the man of honor. I was wrong. There is a third reaction. It has nothing to do with cowardice, for cowardice will blanch and tremble. And it has nothing to do with honor, because the Fujiyama is not dishonored when the droppings of a dog fall on one of its slopes. Yet I know that no samurai would have been able to keep self-control as you did. Therefore I have come to find out more about the things you are teaching."

*   *   *

Six months later Father Cosmas de Torres came from Hirado to take over a community of five hundred Christians.

"There are two Portuguese ships in the port of Hiji", he told Francis. "I told them to wait for you."

Francis nodded. He introduced Father de Torres to his flock.

"He and Brother Juan will be your guardians. But remember to put your trust in God."

He embraced Brother Juan. But his final word was for a lay brother, a Japanese with a ridiculous face, blind in one eye, with a button of a nose, a mouth as large as a frog's and enormous ears. Nowhere else in Japan had he found a man of such gifts as this wandering singer and juggler.

"You can make people laugh *and* cry now, Brother Laurence", he said. "Now go and teach the people as I have taught you."

"I will, Father", said the man simply. "Just tell me where you wish me to go first."

"To Kyoto", said Francis.

*   *   *

They were waiting for him in the port of Hiji.

The two Portuguese ships ran up flags and fired their guns.

More important were two letters from Father General Ignatius. In the first Father Ignatius called him back to Europe. The second canceled that order and made him

262

Provincial for all the districts east of the Cape of Good Hope.

That meant that he would have to go to Goa.

He sailed in September. To his baggage was added one book. He read in it every day. It was a book about the Chinese language and its way of writing.

*　*　*

"Father Francis was here in Malacca?" asked Dr. de Saraiva. "Devil take that inspection tour. I must have just missed him."

"He was here only three days", explained Diogo Pereira. "Then he went on to Goa. Don't worry, you'll see him. He's coming back soon. Have some Xeres wine."

"It's first-rate wine", growled the Doctor, "but it's meager comfort for having missed Father Francis. When did he arrive?"

"Oh, about three weeks ago. On the *Santa Cruz.*"

"But that's your ship!"

"Yes, and I was on it myself. I picked him up in Sancian, on his way back from Japan. There is a good bit of trade going on in Sancian, as you probably know. . . . "

"Yes, I know. You can't get into Canton or any other Chinese port, but Sancian island can be used. It's about the only concession the Chinese ever made to the Occident, I believe."

"That's more or less the way it is—at present. It may not always remain like that."

"What are you grinning about, Pereira? I know you. There's something at the back of your mind. Out with it—but first tell me more about Father Francis. How did he look? How did he fare in the Land of the Rising Sun? What did he say?"

"As it happens, it's all one story", said Pereira cheerfully. "As I told you, I picked him up in Sancian—ran into him by sheer accident. . . . "

"He probably wouldn't call it that."

"No, maybe not. And maybe he'd be right, too."

263

"He usually is. Go on."

"Well, I was delighted, naturally, and he was quite happy about it, too. In any case it made it possible for him to sail for Malacca at once. He—he's changed a great deal."

"What do you mean?"

"His hair and beard are almost white."

"When we set out from Lisbon, ten years ago, he didn't have a single white hair. How old is he—let me think. He's forty—forty-six, that's all he is. And white."

"The years out here count double for all of us", said Pereira. "But for him they must count at least triple. Mind you, he's full of energy, more than ever, I should say. The way he talked, he made me feel young again. . . . "

"Now it's coming", said Dr. de Saraiva. "Did he make a Jesuit out of you or have you taken him into partnership with you in your commercial enterprises?"

Pereira threw his head back and laughed. "Neither", he said. "And yet . . . in a way . . . well, you know, I told him how regrettable it was that the Chinese secluded themselves so completely from the outside world. You can't get anywhere near them, not nearer than Sancian, anyway. If you show your face on Chinese territory, you're thrown into a dungeon before you even have a chance to explain who you are. I know of two men who escaped from there and they didn't have a pretty story to tell. And what a country it would be for commercial enterprise! Absolutely unlimited possibilities, I tell you. Even India can't compete with it. And when I told that to Father Francis, he looked at me very gravely and said he too regarded China as the most important country in the whole of the Orient to win for Christianity and that he had made up his mind to go there."

The Doctor shrugged his shoulders. "Perfectly hopeless, of course, as you know very well."

"Oh quite, quite. He then said he had made some progress in Japan, but not by any means enough and that he had arrived at the conviction that the Japanese expected all good things to come to them from China. If China was converted, Japan would follow, but never the other way round. Therefore he would have to go to China and try to reach the King of China, as he calls the ruler of the Central Kingdom. He really is an emperor, but Father Francis won't have any of that. There is only one Emperor for him, just as there is only one Pope."

"All very well", grunted de Saraiva, "but what's the good? Neither he nor you will be allowed to land in China."

Pereira rubbed his chin. "He's had an idea", he said. "A great idea. The kind of idea that can lead to historic consequences. He said: 'Senhor Pereira, there is only one thing to do. You and I must become special envoys, ambassadors of His Majesty of Portugal. As such we shall be allowed to enter the forbidden territory. Even the King of China sometimes receives embassies from other nations.'"

De Saraiva whistled softly. He said nothing.

"I just sat and gaped at him", went on Pereira. "It was such a glorious idea—and so simple. But then I came to my senses. 'How could we do such a thing?' I asked. 'First of all I don't know why the King of Portugal should make Diogo Pereira an ambassador. After all, I'm not an official, just a merchant. Then it will take years before he can be told about it, make up his mind and send us the necessary documents. But Father Francis was now in his inventive mood, or call it creative mood, if you wish. There simply were no difficulties of any kind. There was no necessity to approach the King. The Viceroy was fully empowered to fill out the documents appointing ambassadors in the King's name. And he himself would go to Goa and tackle the Viceroy. And why shouldn't the Viceroy agree to it, to such a tremendous chance of opening China to Portuguese trade—especially if the costs of the expedition were born by a certain Diogo Pereira!"

Again de Saraiva whistled. "And why should a certain Diogo Pereira hesitate to pay the costs", he said, "considering that it will make him an ambassador and at the same time the first man to gain access to the heart of China with all its unlimited possibilities of trade. . . . "

"Exactly", said Pereira, beaming. "And if it interests you, I have chosen the *Santa Cruz* as our ship and I've been buying up things ever since, the most wonderful presents for the Chinese ruler first and foremost. In fact, I have invested thirty thousand cruzados in the venture by now."

"That's more than I have ever seen in my life", The Doctor grunted. "Wasn't it a bit rash to do all that before you know that Father Francis has got the Viceroy to agree?"

"Father Francis said he would get him", replied Pereira simply. "That's good enough for me."

De Saraiva nodded. "Or for anybody", he said. "Ah well, I must be going."

"And do you know", said Pereira, "it isn't only the money—I'm fond of it, as you know, perhaps too much so, but this time it isn't only that. It's a grand thing for me to be a royal ambassador. But that also is not the whole thing. It's—it's like being young again, when you listen to Father Francis. You feel you can soar up to any height. . . . "

"He's got you", de Saraiva nodded. "And why not? He got me long ago. By the way, do you know who is the new Governor?"

"No. There hasn't been anything official about it yet and for once I've heard no rumors."

"But I did", said de Saraiva. "Do you remember the young noble whom Dom Martim de Sousa arrested in Mozambique? Dom Estevam da Gama's brother? A pale man with large, intense sort of eyes."

"Dom Alvaros d'Ataide", said Pereira, frowning. "You don't mean to say that he is the new Governor of Malacca?"

"He is", said Dr. de Saraiva. "And he should arrive any day now."

*   *   *

Francis came back with all the necessary documents.

Pereira, overjoyed, began to load the *Santa Cruz.* "Not even the great Ruler of the Central Kingdom will be able to resist our presents", he declared proudly. To his surprise Francis seemed much less enthusiastic than he had been a few months before.

"What is the matter, Father? When we met last time you were so sure of everything, and now that you have achieved what I thought was impossible . . . "

"The devil will spoil everything", said Francis in a strangely dry tone. "You will see. You will see."

But the day of departure was fixed at their first meeting. Perhaps Father Francis was just tired and worn out from the thousand and one things he had to deal with in India.

He had every reason to be. He had made the voyage from Japan to India in the record time of three months, arrived in Cochin at the end of January, and thrown himself into the administrative business both there and in Goa with whirlwind speed.

Just as he feared, Father Gómez had proved himself utterly impossible for the important position as the Rector of the college. He had treated the native students so severely that they ran away overnight and were seen no more. He had to be relieved of his duties and a new Rector appointed. Simon Rodríguez had sent another twelve Jesuits. Francis interrogated Father Núñez Barreto. "What are your qualifications?"

"Three years of philosophy and six of theology."

Francis smiled wearily. "It would be better if you had three of theology and six years of experience." He sent him to Bassein to get it. He liked the man. Father Baertz became the Rector, a man who had done excellent work at Ormuz. Two priests who had returned from the Straits without permission, Francis dismissed from the Society. He had to get rid of several unsuitable novices as well.

He felt profoundly sorry for Father Gómez. At first it was no more than a vague feeling, but then suddenly, in a flash, he knew that Gómez would not live long and that he would die on the high seas. These flashes came more and more frequently lately and caused him much suffering. It was perhaps not good to know too much. It was perhaps a sign that his knowledge in certain ways was outgrowing that which is permissible on earth. He did not know for sure, but he began to have a dim foreboding in regard to his own life.

New posts, new faces, appointments, petitions, work in the hospital—he would not give that up, of course—the negotiations with the Viceroy, the planning of a complete campaign in Japan, where everything would have to be prepared and ready when China came in. "Another ten years, O Lord, another ten years . . ."

Another ten years and the whole of Asia might fall into Christ's hands like a ripe fruit.

But the devil could spoil everything. That also was one of those terrible flashes. The devil could spoil everything.

On Maundy Thursday he went on board for the greatest of all his voyages. But the ship could not leave port. There was no wind. There was no wind for three whole days.

On Easter Sunday the ship sailed. Perhaps it was a good sign. Time and again he had departed or arrived on a great feast day.

With him he took a Tamil, baptized under the name of Christopher, and a Chinese—Anthony—a mere boy, who was to serve as an interpreter.

With him also—and that was a consolation for many things—he took the love of the people of Goa.

Easter Sunday. Exactly four years ago he had set out for Japan.

In Cochin he heard that the Vadagars had made another raid on the Fishery Coast and abducted a priest. The Paravas pursued them and rescued him, but they rescued a dying man. Francis dispatched two priests to take up his work. The wretched Captain de Paiva had been forced to leave and the new administrator was an excellent man.

Socotra, Goa, Cochin, Quilon, the Macua region, the Fishery Coast—the Faith was spreading everywhere.

Everything was set for the conquest of China. He should be happy and content. He was not.

Anthony, the young Chinese, watched him with worried

eyes, as he paced up and down the corridor in the rectory of Our Lady of the Mount. Only a week ago their ship had run into so terrible a storm that everyone had thought the end had come. Much of the cargo had to be jettisoned. Father Francis alone remained cheerful, telling them that there was no need for fear, that Our Lord would save the ship; then he mounted the poop, took a reliquary from his cassock and threw it into the sea, praying to the Most Holy Trinity to have mercy on them all. And the winds abated and the storm died away, but he still remained where he was, rapt in prayer. He always looked happy—but then he looked as if the heavens were open and he could see the land of bliss. And now—now, when all was quiet and no one in danger, he seemed to worry. . . .

"Father Francis . . . Father Francis . . . "

Francis stopped. Anthony saw that he had paled.

"Father Francis . . . " The voice was Diogo Pereira's. The merchant came up the stairs, two at a time. "Here you are", he gasped. "There is trouble, Father. Dom Alvaro d'Ataide has had the *Santa Cruz* requisitioned."

*　　*　　*

The days that followed were nightmarish.

A deputation of merchants, sent by Pereira, was told by Dom Alvaro that he did not regard the Chinese project as in the interests of the King. He would not allow the *Santa Cruz* to sail. A royal judge, into whose hands the case was given, was mobbed by the riffraff of the port. When the judge went to see the Governor to make a protest, Dom Alvaro told him bluntly that he would brook no interference from anybody.

Captain Marquez, the master of the *Santa Cruz* came at night to see Pereira. "I don't know what the Governor has against you", he said, "but I do know that he has posted twenty soldiers on my ship. Now I've been your man these twenty years. Just say the word, and I'll sweep the soldiers off my good ship and we sail, Governor or no Governor. And my crew thinks just as I do."

But Pereira shook his head. "I can't let you do that, Marquez. It's more than decent of you and your men—but Dom Alvaro would have you hanged for it—and perhaps me, too. Tomorrow Father Francis is sending a new deputation to the Governor—including the Vicar-General. They will show him the documents Father Francis brought from Goa. That should help, if anything helps at all against that madman."

"It's a pity though", said Marquez. "Now if you could come back with me and get Father Francis from wherever he is, we might steal away tonight. There isn't a ship in the harbor that will catch up with the *Santa Cruz,* take my word for it, Senhor Pereira."

Pereira thought it over. It appealed to his sense of adventure. But he had vast possessions in Malacca. If he disappeared, Dom Alvaro would seize them. And even if he came back from the Chinese venture with all the success in the world, the Governor would have him put in irons.

"Let's wait until tomorrow", he said, and Captain Marquez departed with a sigh.

*　　*　　*

The deputation consisted of the Vicar-General, João Soares, Father Perez and the royal judge, Francisco Alvarez. Francis had given them all the documents, including the decretal making Pereira Ambassador-Extraordinary of the King at the Chinese court.

At the last minute Francis wrote a letter to the Vicar-General, briefing him. "Beg him in the name of God and of the Bishop not to thwart my expedition nor hinder me from carrying it out in the manner arranged by the Senhor Viceroy, for if he does, he will be excommunicated, not by the Bishop, nor by Your Reverence, nor by me, but by the holy Pontiffs who made the canons. Tell the Governor that I beg him by the Passion and death of Our Lord Jesus Christ not to incur so grave an excommunication, entailing, let him have no doubt, the terrible chastisement of God. . . . Will Your Reverence let me have the reply as quickly as you can, as the monsoon is ending. . . . It is impossible that he should refuse me once he has seen the decretal. . . . "

It was impossible, but it happened. Dom Alvaro d'Ataide listened to what the Vicar-General said, without interrupting. In his pale, sallow face his large eyes burned like coals.

Then he jumped up from his chair. "Hypocrites", he shouted. "Drunkards! Seducers! I know them. I suffered enough from them, when *they* were in power. But I knew the day would come when I could pay them back and this is the day. Do you expect a da Gama to believe that the King of Portugal would ever agree to have this wretched upstart Pereira represent him? His Majesty will be grateful to me for preventing such an affront to his good name and to his majesty." He tore the documents from Soares' trembling hands, threw them on the floor and trampled on them.

"That is what I think of the Viceroy and his instructions."

He spat on them. "As for your wonderful Father Francis, the lickspittle of Martim de Sousa, he can go wherever he likes, he can go to the devil, for all I care. He an apostolic nuncio? You make me laugh. He's a forger, more likely than not. But he can't bluff me. No, I will hear no more, Senhores and Fathers. You may go."

The same evening a crowd of hooligans assembled before the rectory of Our Lady of the Mount yelling insults and throwing stones.

Captain Marquez came to see Pereira again. "It's too late now", he said sadly. "Dom Alvaro has had my crew evicted from the ship. What's more, he had the rudder and the tiller taken off. They are hanging over the door to his office in the palace."

* * *

"News from the battle front?" asked Dom Alvaro, grinning.

The agent nodded. "We had the priest hooted and booed wherever he went. Pereira too, of course. He doesn't dare leave his house. But the priest did. He with his Tamil and his Chinese went to the port and on board the *Santa Cruz*."

"What for?" asked Dom Alvaro, frowning. "Why didn't the soldiers stop him?"

"Your Excellency has given no such instructions", said the agent.

"Idiot. Must I think of every possibility myself? What is he doing on board?"

"Praying and writing. He sent a letter to Pereira and my men intercepted it. He writes that it is all due to his sins and asks Pereira to forgive him."

Dom Alvaro rose and began to pace up and down. "This will do no good", he said. "He is trying to play the martyr. If it goes on, he will get the people on his side again. It is difficult enough as it is to keep them in hand. And if he dies on board, it'll be worse."

He stopped abruptly. "We must get rid of him, Mateo. But how?" After a while he grinned again. "I know. We shall let him go. With the *Santa Cruz*. We are merciful. Have the rudder and tiller put back."

"Your Excellency will give the ship back to Senhor Pereira?" asked the agent, his voice high with surprise.

"Oh no, no, no. The *Santa Cruz* is now in the service of the government. Captain Fernam will take over, and a government crew. She will sail for China. For Sancian, that is. It is all we can do for the worthy Father. From there he must get on by himself. No one has been able to get on from there so far, but if he is such a great and holy man, surely there will be a miracle. . . . "

The agent's grin acknowledged the Governor's brilliant wit.

"Sancian has a rather unhealthy climate, I'm told", said Dom Alvaro lightly.

*   *   *

The new crew took over.

The Vicar-General came to say goodbye. He did not feel happy about his own role in the matter. Should he have resisted the Governor more strongly? But when Dom Alvaro screamed and raged—he was not accustomed to such treatment. There was his dignity, too. Nevertheless . . .

As he and Francis were standing on the quay he asked: "Should I try to bring about a—a reconciliation between you and Dom Alvaro?"

Francis stared past him. "I have no bitterness against him, but the only place where I shall see him again is in the Valley of Jehoshaphat."

A glum, silent crowd had assembled. There was no jeering. The Vicar-General mopped his forehead.

Francis made the sign of the Cross and prayed. Then he bent down, took off his shoes and shook them, as Christ had commanded his disciples to do at a place where they had been rejected.

The Vicar-General bit his lip. In a faltering voice he asked, "Is this parting forever?"

Francis put his shoes on again. He said, quietly, "That is as God wills."

Then he went back on board.

*　　*　　*

Sancian was exile.

No Portuguese ship dared go any nearer the Chinese coast, no more than six miles away. Only Chinese junks sometimes slipped through—Imperial police junks kept a constant watch—and made the little island the center of smuggling operations. A Chinese might land on Sancian. No Portuguese, no white man could land on Chinese territory.

Fifty miles to the northeast, the Chu Kiang, the Pearl River, led right up to the twenty-foot-thick, forty-foot-high walls of Canton.

Francis moved heaven and earth to get a Chinese junk to take him to the coast—anywhere on the coast.

A smiling, rubber-faced Chinese, master of a small junk, at last promised to take him, but only at the end of the trading season, in November. On November the nineteenth. It was fixed and settled. The price for the run of six miles was two hundred cruzados, to be paid beforehand.

The few Portuguese living on Sancian warned and warned

again. It was certain death, they said. If Francis was very lucky he would have two, perhaps three days in China before he was caught. Then he would vanish, into one of those unspeakable dungeons of Canton. Far more likely, the Chinese captain would simply have him pushed overboard, as soon as he had his cruzados.

The *Santa Cruz* was doing a bit of trading for Dom Alvaro, and Captain Fernam had pointed out to Francis that he would not let him leave for the coast, even if he managed to get a ship, before the *Santa Cruz* had left. He wanted no trouble with the Chinese authorities.

Francis knew that he was being watched day and night.

He knew that Anthony and the Tamil Christopher were deadly afraid, but did not dare show it.

He knew that what the Portuguese told him was quite true.

He was going to China.

From Singapore—*do estreito de Symquapura*—he had written a number of letters. To the King of Portugal; to Bishop Albuquerque of Goa; to poor Pereira who had put a fortune into the Chinese venture; to the new Rector of the college in Goa; to the Viceroy.

Now all he could do was wait for the junk. With the help of Anthony and Christopher he built a little chapel, where he said Mass every day, usually offering it up for the soul of Dom Alvaro d'Ataide da Gama.

The rains came. All Portuguese ships left Sancian, except the *Santa Cruz*. What was she waiting for?

* * *

On the nineteenth of November Francis stood all day on a little promontory overlooking the bay, waiting for a sail to appear. Christopher and Anthony exchanged uneasy glances.

There was no sail. The Chinese captain did not keep his promise.

The rain came down in a constant, monotonous drizzle.

"Heaven is crying", said Anthony sadly.

Next morning Francis awoke with heavy limbs and a

burning forehead. He washed, dressed, vested as if in a dream. He said Mass. His voice was clear and resonant.

When he left the chapel, he staggered.

Anthony had to lead him back to the hut.

*　　*　　*

The days and nights were dreamlike, interrupted by sharp, lucid moments of pain.

They took him on board the *Santa Cruz,* but the man who had braved a dozen typhoons could not stand the rocking of the ship anchored in the bay and in the morning they brought him back to his hut. There was no physician. Someone with some rudimentary knowledge of medicine bled him and he fainted.

A sailor on board the *Santa Cruz* had given him a little bag of almonds, but he could not swallow anything.

The Chinese captain had not kept his promise.

How could he get to the Son of Heaven, if they did not send him a ship? How could he descend into the hell of the dungeons of Canton, if they did not let him land? How could he talk to the King of China, if they held him back here with iron fetters? They were so heavy, he could scarcely move a limb, and the iron weight on his forehead was the worst of all.

The anxious yellow face of Anthony, the anxious brown face of Christopher. But Christopher would die soon, very soon. Poor Christopher.

Set all afire. Go and teach ye all the nations and set them afire with the love of Christ.

The fetters of the world must fall, all the fetters of the devil, of sin, of ignorance. The whole world was weighed down under them, and Christ alone could free them.

Burning out. He was burning out. How could he set all afire if there was no flame left in him? There was no flame left in him because of his sins. Jesus, Son of David, have mercy upon me. . . . I have loved the beauty of thy house. . . . I have loved much, so much will be forgiven me.

Was it he who said that? It was Magdalena. Magdalena

was in heaven. Sister Magdalena was in heaven. Sister Magdalena, pray for me. I have loved much. Virgin Mother of God, remember me.

*   *   *

For three days he did not speak at all.

On the fourth he spoke only to God, and thus it was on the fifth.

Night came. In the second hour of the morning Anthony saw that the end was near. He lit a candle and put it into the hand of the dying man.

Once more Francis spoke. It was a single word; but with it he presented his credentials at the threshold of the King of kings:

"Jesus . . ."

*   *   *

He was buried the next day, in the afternoon.

Anthony and Christopher could not understand why the captain and the crew of the *Santa Cruz* did not come to the funeral. A friendly Portuguese of Sancian and his servant helped them to bury the body. He suggested pouring lime into the coffin. It would quickly consume the flesh, but leave the bones untouched. They used four sacks of lime for the task.

There was no priest on Sancian. Not now.

*   *   *

"You're a damned fool, Captain Fernam", said Dom Alvaro d'Ataide angrily. "Why did you have to bring the man's body back here?"

The captain of the *Santa Cruz* looked crestfallen. "I'm sorry, Dom Alvaro, I didn't think you'd mind. After all, the man's dead."

"Mateo tells me there is a procession forming", said the Governor. "A large one. You've given that wretch a kind of triumph in the end, Fernam. It's against regulations, too. A rotting cadaver on board a government ship!"

Captain Fernam gulped. "That's just it, Dom Alvaro. . . . You see, the body is not rotting. They put quick lime into

276

the coffin, but I had it opened, and . . . the body is not rotting. The lime hasn't done anything to it at all."

For one brief moment Dom Alvaro's face showed fear. Then he threw back his head. "They embalmed it, of course."

Captain Fernam shook his head. "Impossible on Sancian."

"There they come, by God", snapped Dom Alvaro. "They'll pass here, right under my balcony. Expect me to show my respects, I suppose. I'll show them. Up with you, Fernam. Sit down on the balcony. Here, take the draught-board. We're going to play a game of draughts, you and I."

"Dom Alvaro . . . "

"Hell and damnation! I'm the Governor here, I think. You'll obey orders."

They sat down on the balcony, in full sight of the procession, the draught-board between them on a small table.

"My God," said Fernam, "it's the largest procession Malacca has ever seen. Look at those hundreds of burning candles. . . . "

"Don't look at them, you fool", ordered Dom Alvaro. "Play!"

Priests and acolytes and an endless stream of people. The coffin was carried by six men.

"They're going to the Church of Our Lady on the Mount", said Fernam.

"They can go to hell, all of them", raged Dom Alvaro. "What are you staring at now?"

Fernam was trembling. "Your hand, Dom Alvaro," he stammered. "You . . . you have hurt your hand, I think. Badly."

Dumbfounded, the Governor looked at his hand. There was a strange-looking spot on it, still small, whitish.

"If you'll excuse me," said Captain Fernam, rising. "I would like to go. I . . . I don't feel well."

Dom Alvaro did not hear, nor did he see Fernam depart, rather hurriedly. He sat very still, staring at the whitish spot on his hand, his right hand. He had seen that kind of spot many a time before—as most people had who lived in the tropics. He had seen it on hands, arms, shoulders, legs and faces. They started small, like this one on his own hand. But they grew and grew and nothing could stop them. It was leprosy.

He was rotting alive.

The body of the dead man they were carrying down there was not rotting. But Dom Alvaro d'Ataide da Gama was rotting alive.

He wanted to get up and run. He could not. His body seemed to be made of lead.

And still the procession passed by, singing.

*   *   *

On the Feast of the Assumption Father Beira arrived in Malacca and went straight to the house of Diogo Pereira. He found the merchant in the company of Dr. de Saraiva.

"I've come from Goa", he said. "There is a rumor there that Father Francis Xavier is dead."

"It is true", said Pereira sadly. "He was buried in the Church of Our Lady on the Mount five months ago."

Father Beira broke down. When he had recovered, he said in a trembling voice, "Goa and all India is claiming the body of the saint."

There was a pause.

"The Father is right", said Dr. de Saraiva gruffly. "Malacca doesn't deserve him."

"They'll never let you take the body away", warned Pereira. "They'll resist."

"The Governor is ill, I'm told", said de Saraiva dryly.

"I know", Pereira replied. "And there is a rumor about what he is suffering from, too. He may live for many more years, but I don't think he will remain at the palace for long. I didn't mean the Governor, though. I meant the people."

The Doctor nodded. "It certainly would be a tremendous blow to their pride."

"Father Beira is right though", said Pereira. "We might do it in secret, the three of us." His eyes gleamed.

"If that is the only way, that is how it must be done", said Father Beira energetically.

*   *   *

The body had been buried near the high altar of the church.

They exhumed it that night by the light of a lantern.

There was no coffin. The body had been in full contact with the earth for nearly five months, yet it was as fresh as on the day of its first burial on Sancian.

"I once saw him, rapt in prayer", said Dr. de Saraiva hoarsely. "He . . . he seemed to be suspended in mid-air. His feet did not touch the ground. I thought at the time, that I might have imagined it, although I'm not given to imaginings, as a rule. But now . . . "

"Blessed Francis", whispered Father Beira, "pray for us."

They filled up the tomb again and left. It was very dark outside. No one paid any attention to them, as they carried the body to Pereira's house.

There it was laid in a coffin lined with damask. Pereira covered it with brocade cloth, the most precious the others had ever seen. "He was supposed to take that as a present to the Chinese Emperor", said Pereira with a sad smile. "It is good enough for an emperor—not for him. But I have no better."

The body remained in Pereira's house for many months—till the end of the year. Only then was there a ship going to Goa.

*   *   *

Thursday night in Passion week whispers went through Goa.

People rose from their beds and dressed and went to the harbor, singly at first, then in groups, more and more of them.

No one knew who started the rumor. But at midnight, when the ship arrived, thousands of people were lined up on the beach.

Someone began to sing the Credo. Soon they were all singing.

By dawn the Viceroy arrived with the court.

Father Núñez Barreto had the body brought ashore.

As the sun rose, the bell of the college began to ring, then a second bell, a third, till all the church bells of Goa were ringing.

The crowd began to sing again.

"The Te Deum", whispered a young priest, shocked. "And the church bells—and today is Good Friday."

Father Núñez Barreto looked at the open coffin, where Francis' body rested in serene majesty. "It is Our Lord's welcome to his saint", he said. "In death—and in life eternal."